finding more

also by larissa c. moyer

in our hands

finding more

larissa c. moyer

BOOKLOGIX®
Alpharetta, Georgia

ISBN: 978-1-6653-0798-7 - Paperback
eISBN: 978-1-6653-0799-4 - eBook

Cover Designer: okaycreations

First printing edition 2023

⊗This paper meets the requirements of ANSI/NISO Z39.48-1992 (Permanence of Paper)

1 1 0 9 2 3

To anyone that's ever yearned for the uninhibited
freedom that Pocahontas felt swan-diving into the water.

Maybe the journey isn't about becoming anything. Maybe it's about un-becoming everything that isn't really you so you can be who you were meant to be in the first place.
—Paulo Coelho, Hippie

prologue

dean

I am down the fucking rabbit hole.

My eyes travel along the bottles lining the back wall of the bar, watching as the lights from above retract and refract through the variety of clear and amber liquids before I tilt my head back and take the final swig of my beer. It slides down my throat like water. Dropping it back on the bar, I immediately find the bartender, signaling that I need another one.

Hook me up to an IV and fucking pump it into me.

It's all I can do when my world feels inside-out. *I feel inside-out.*

There's no other way to describe it.

My brother has never looked at me the way he did just an hour ago.

Disgusted, disappointed—enraged.

I'll never replace the image. It's something that can't be unseen—like mayonnaise being made.

My stomach turns at the thought and I grunt, just as the bartender switches out my empty bottle with a full one. I lift it appreciatively.

At least I think I do. I don't know. I've been here for an hour or so, and I've already knocked back a few so I'm sure my motor skills are suffering.

"Can I take it outside?" I ask, my eyes lazily dipping to the bottle.

He shakes his head. "The drink's gotta stay. But if you wanna pop out real quick, I can keep it behind the bar."

Damn. It's like *Sophie's Choice* for the pathetically downtrodden.

Cigarette or beer?

I take another sip before I push the bottle back toward him. My nicotine fix wins, knowing the drink will be tucked behind the bar waiting for me. I unsteadily slide off the stool before staggering toward the door and pushing out onto the sidewalk.

Springtime in Chicago might as well be summer. It's after midnight and over fifty degrees, and the wind from the lake feels refreshing. Plus, the comfort of not having to basically jog-in-place to keep warm is almost something you forget about until it revisits once May hits.

Flicking my lighter, the end of the cigarette illuminates, letting the toxins fill my lungs before I push them out, feeling a momentary release.

The only thing missing is my beer.

Cigarettes go so well with other things that are bad for you. Beer, coffee—after a gluttonous meal. Still, I pull it to my lips and haul in another drag as a few people walk out from the bar.

They look about my age. They're laughing and it instantly scrapes along the walls of my brain as one of the girls in the group hops on one of the guy's shoulders. They mosey on down the block, carefree and tipsy.

Another reminder of my former life.

One where my girlfriend wasn't slipping into some murky, far-off abyss. One where I didn't just betray her and annihilate my brother's respect for me.

A night out with friends feels as far away as the group of kids becomes.

Smaller, smaller—*gone.*

I take another drag, flicking the ash down to the sidewalk as the last twenty-four hours replay through my mind ad nauseam.

I flinch as my girlfriend's face passes through my mind. The way she looked at me last night . . .

Like I was a monster.

It's another thing seeping into the crevices of my brain, burrowing and festering.

It lives there now.

I flick the butt of my smoke out into a puddle on the street when I become vaguely aware of the door to the bar pushing open again, hearing some light conversation drifting between my busy thoughts.

I decide to light another one—*why the fuck not?* But the indulgence is less satisfying this time. My face scrunches up from a wave of nausea, and I wince at the ache on the bridge of my nose where my brother punched me.

Everything *fucking hurts.*

Groaning, I shake my head and take another puff when I suddenly hear someone beside me.

"Hey, man. Can I bum a smoke?" he asks.

I blink, pushing myself upright, but wobble as I pull the pack out from my back pocket.

Jesus. I'm more fucked up than I realized.

I flip open the pack and offer one to the guy. He pulls one out, lifting it appreciatively at me, saying, "Thanks," before he lights up. "Looks like your night is about as good as mine." He nods at what I'm sure is a bruise on the side of my nose, though I can't be sure.

Right after my brother handed my ass to me and left, I threw on a hoodie and came here. Looking at myself in the mirror was the last thing I wanted to do. At this point, I wouldn't be surprised to see someone else entirely in the reflection and the thought coils in the constant roll of my stomach.

"Let me guess? Lady troubles?" the guy asks with a commiserating eyebrow hitch.

Holy fuck. I don't know how to be any more obvious that I'm not in the mood to talk. I mean, I'm standing alone, outside a bar, chain smoking with a fresh shiner. I don't know how it doesn't get more obvious than that.

My eyes flick up to the guy. He looks like he's in his thirties—maybe? He's a few inches shorter than me with a stocky frame and what appears to be a large wet spot on his shirt. I mindlessly wonder if he spilled his drink on himself. Or maybe this *lady* he's alluding to threw her drink at him.

Does that ever actually happen in real life?

When I notice he still seems to be waiting for me to respond, I shrug. "All sorts of troubles, I guess."

Damn. I think I'm slurring. And if I'm not, the words are definitely coming out unnaturally slow and they're harder to say.

The guy chuckles. "Aw, man . . . " He shakes his head and blows the smoke out of his mouth. "You're too young for *life* problems."

I grunt, leaning back against the building, trying to shrug off my irritation. I'm not looking for a Mr. Miyagi moment here—and the statement is condescending as fuck.

"Well, maybe I won't live long. In which case, my problems are right on time," I mumble.

The idea of a short life sounds good right about now. It's unsettling, but if *this* is the kind of shit that life is made of—I'd rather go out quickly. My stomach turns, again, and my body sways from the whirlwind of booze and smoke coating my insides—*I don't think I ate today.*

"Hey, kid. You all right? You don't look so good."

Jesus Christ—just leave me the fuck alone.

I manage to stand back up, straightening myself, and my eyes narrow on the guy. It's *that* moment that it becomes abundantly clear.

There's the briefest moment of clarity, but it quickly lights with flames and spreads like wildfire.

No. I'm not good. I'm fucking gone.

chapter one

dean

eight years later

I turn onto my old block in Wicker Park and pull my truck into a spot on the street. After I shoot Marnie a text, I linger in the car for a minute longer.

My ex-wife prefers to keep our exchanges brief and sitting here will give her some time to get Ava's stuff together.

Navigating divorce with a kid—*a baby, nonetheless*—is like carrying around a detonated bomb. I just try to not make any sudden movements and I'm constantly prepared for the blunt impact of when something inevitably sets it off.

Honestly, though, Marnie doesn't really explode—it's more like I feel *I'm* going to combust any time we have an "argument."

Because it's not really an *argument*. It's her, using her calm, reasonable tone and telling me to "calm down," in between her small jabs about all the ways I fuck up.

And I guess it's not without merit because I really did fuck up our marriage. So the fact that she allows me to have equal time with our daughter isn't something I take lightly and I'll take every dig she makes if it means seeing Ava every weekend.

After another minute has passed, I hop out of the truck and walk quickly to the door.

Jesus Christ, it's fucking cold.

Once I've trotted up the stairs, I ring the doorbell while I bob in place, trying to stay warm.

It's still weird—waiting outside of a place that you once came and went freely.

Our divorce finalized just under a year ago and strangely enough, the street that used to be my home even *looks* different. Maybe that's just what happens when you see a place less frequently; anything new stands out a bit more and therefore, *feels* different.

I huff out a breath and a small cloud plumes out in front of me as I hear the deadbolt unlatch. The door pulls open and my eyes immediately fall to Ava's short brown curls and sparkly blue eyes. She grins wide and crooked at me from under her puffy pink hood.

"Hi, baby," I coo, and she reaches her little arms out toward me as I pull her into my chest. "I missed you."

I finally look back at Marnie and see Windbreaker Shaun walk into the doorframe behind her.

He won the affectionate nickname when Marnie insisted we meet five months ago because she wanted him to be able to spend time with Ava. We all took Ava to Navy Pier—*which was just as dumb as it sounds*—and this dude showed up wearing a windbreaker—*in August.*

Dweeby attire aside, he seems like a nice enough guy. He lives in Michigan and I guess they're able to visit each other pretty frequently.

"Hey, Dean. How's it going?" he says, extending his arm.

I tuck Ava farther into my shoulder and shake his hand. "Hey, good to see ya."

Marnie clears her throat before she tells me, "You just missed the blow out," handing me the diaper bag. "So she's clean, but you'll have to feed her at your place. Just no zucchini," she reminds me.

I suppress an eye roll by puckering my lips down at Ava. "No zucchini," I say, scrunching my nose and she giggles.

Marnie glares at me. "I'm serious! I tried again on Monday and her farts were insane! No zucchini."

Smile and fucking nod, Dean.

The kid is a farter. I don't think it's the zucchini, but I'm not in the mood to start an "argument" over it.

"Got it," I say, hiking Ava up on my side, starting to back away. We're on the brink of February and it's frigid outside, so I want to get her back to the heat. "Anything else?"

"Did you get the link I sent you? For the soap?" she asks.

Smile and nod.

"Yep. It's waiting at home."

Marnie nods, her expression still skeptical.

"Do you want to see the delivery notice?" I ask, not doing much to hide the annoyance in my tone.

Her head tilts, like she's actually considering it and my irritation grows.

This is the shit I'm talking about.

Her hesitancy toward me isn't unwarranted—*it really isn't*—but I just can't help getting annoyed when it feels like she's micromanaging me when it comes to Ava. And the most infuriating thing about it is I don't have two legs to stand on.

I fucked up.

It's something they *love* to remind you about at sober meetings.

Since I'm not really a religious person, I opted out of the bigger organizations that emphasize a lot of the "God stuff," and found a counseling group that holds meetings for people in recovery at the community center nearby.

But they constantly remind you that no one is obligated to forgive you for the things you did during your addiction. And it's not about a few good deeds or positive steps forward. It's about making the choice every day to *not* do the thing that got you into this mess in the first place—*that's the reward, supposedly.*

A life sentence.

Marnie finally shakes her head, denying my offer of proof that the fancy, organic soap she insists we use is waiting at my apartment. She leans into us—managing to wiggle her face under Ava's hood and squishing a kiss to her cheek. "I love you, my sweet girl."

I swallow down my tension as I turn to walk back toward my truck. "Say bye to Mommy and Shaun."

Ava sticks her hand out, opening and closing her fingers, and I take hurried steps down the sidewalk.

Once we're back at the truck, I secure Ava in her car seat and smile down at her. Her baby blue eyes stare back up at me and I quickly pull her hood off of her head and tuck it safely behind her back.

There's this thing that you develop when you become a parent. It's an inexplicable ability to create an honest-to-God phobia out of thin fucking air.

When the weather finally turned back in October, I was driving her back from Marnie's and I'd left her hood on while we drove home. About halfway through the drive, she got really quiet and in a matter of seconds—I'd convinced myself that she had suffocated because her hood smothered her.

In a more dramatic fashion than I care to admit—I pulled off on the side of the road, jumped out of the car and ripped the back door open—only to find her mouth wide open, expelling tiny snores, while her hood laid safely over her eyes.

She was fine. But now, it's a phobia. And I don't keep her hood on when we're driving.

So that's fun.

"I love you," I say, while signing down at her and she trills her lips before latching onto my index and pinky fingers.

She's not talking yet, but the girl knows how to make some fucking noise. I read somewhere that sometimes babies can learn sign language before they feel like they can speak so I've been trying to teach her some basic signs. Plus, she has a deaf uncle so the earlier she learns it, the better.

As I close the door, I remember that my brother texted me earlier—something about Evelyn wanting to organize a get together this week to celebrate my year of sobriety. The idea immediately tightens the muscles in my shoulders.

Sliding into the driver's seat, I exhale hard and sink further into the seat, trying to trick my body into relaxing.

The three of us have come a long way since a year ago, but it's still far from easy, and the idea of spending a night with them where *I'm* the reason for the occasion has my anxiety rising.

Clearing my throat, I stick the key in the ignition and crank the heat, then twist the vent behind the center console to make sure it's aimed toward Ava. I always worry that she's cold since her car seat is facing away from the vent.

I take another steadying breath before putting the car in drive. As I turn the radio up, some Shania Twain song starts to filter through the speakers . . .

Evelyn got me to go to a karaoke night.

There was no way in hell that I'd be singing, but she got me in the door.

Even more surprising was she got my brother to come along and it was definitely not his thing.

It was a nice change of pace to have Otis genuinely like my girlfriend. He'd never admit it, but he hated the girl I dated in high school.

We had actually met Evelyn together at a party three years ago, up at Northwestern where Otis went to school. She won him over when she signed her name while introducing herself. He had been working on ASL with her ever since and it made me love her even more.

Otis had a hard time making friends. He was the best guy I knew, but it was just harder for him—everyone he knew was hearing. And not many people knew sign language. Plus, he wasn't a particularly outgoing person but . . . he really liked Evelyn.

I could tell it meant a lot to him that she took the time to learn ASL but they also just . . . got along. Personally, I thought it was impossible not to love either of them, but the fact that they thought so highly of one another made it easier for all of us to hang out together.

Evelyn came back from the bar with three shot glasses. She put them on the table and signed, "If the bartender asks you, my name is Tina."

I eyed Otis and he chuckled before I looked back at her, curiously. "Why would the bartender ask me your name?"

She huffed, signing, "I'm just saying, if she does—my name is Tina. It's what my fake ID says."

"You're twenty-two," I reminded her.

"Is it my fault that I lose things?!" she signed.

Otis chuckled. "Whose fault would it be?"

"Whose side are you on, Otis?" she signed, narrowing her eyes at my brother.

He tossed up surrendering hands. "Okay, I'm on your side, but just so I'm clear—you lost your actual ID, but still have your fake one?"

She suppressed a smile but a laugh pushed through her lips anyway as she signed, "I'm very talented."

I pulled her into my lap until her forehead was touching mine and said, "Yes you are, baby," as I pressed my lips to hers. "Do you think Tina would want to come home with me later?" I whispered against her ear before she nuzzled her nose with mine.

She bit her lip before our friend Reggie squealed, "Evie!" from a few feet away and we both jerked in surprise.

Suddenly, Reggie was chant-singing, "Dun dun dun nuh nuh—nuh nuh! Let's go girl!"

Evelyn laughed and stood up as the iconic beginning of "Man, I Feel Like A Woman" started to play and she grabbed one of the shot glasses while Otis and I did the same.

"To Shania Twain," she signed.

"Who?" Otis signed.

"The hot country singer that Mom always listened to," I signed back and he nodded before we raised our glasses with Evelyn. "To Shania."

Ava squeals from the backseat, bringing me back to now and my eyes dart up to the rearview mirror, seeing her small limbs kick and bounce, before my hand moves to twist the radio knob—quickly cycling through the other stations.

Something less nostalgic.

I stop when I hear "In My Life" by The Beatles, crooning through the speakers and my shoulders drop, loosening the tension as my foot eases on the break to stop at a red light.

My mind floats to the few embarrassing occasions I actually sang this song to Ava while I tried to get her to sleep. I guess it's *better* nostalgia, at least.

Our song.

It was during our first few nights together, but I still play it every once in a while.

My eyes drift to my rearview mirror again, watching her small hand tap and play with the assortment of dangling shapes attached to her car seat.

Another exhale escapes me as the light turns green and I push on the gas pedal.

It takes a few more seconds of practiced breathing before memories subside and future worries start to pass.

They're still there, but I'm able to quiet them for the moment.

Focus on now.

Right now, it's my baby girl and me.

chapter two

amelia

L uuuuke-y." I peek around the corner to the kitchen island, finding my pouty little pal on the floor with a mixing bowl huddled in his arms. "Sittin' on the job already?" I tease, leaning against the counter.

He huffs. "I'm tired, Miss Melia."

The corner of my mouth pulls up. "Come on, kid," I grunt, pulling him off the floor. "Not just anyone can make pancakes. It takes hard work."

He's barely tall enough for his head to clear the countertop, but he lifts the bowl and scoots it onto the island. "You're always telling me what to do," he whines.

Tilting my head, I snort a laugh as I slide the step-stool toward him. *Punk.*

I've known this kid for two years now. I was actually his preschool teacher, and he was my favorite student.

Anyone who has taught kids and tells you they don't have favorites is a liar.

But he wasn't my favorite because he was well-behaved or sweet. Quite the opposite, actually. Luke was a tiny terror in the classroom—always throwing shit or roughing up other kids or lying through his teeth when he got in trouble.

He's also incredibly smart, so . . . there's a chance he'll become an evil genius someday.

But he actually made me feel like a teacher and not someone simply in charge of keeping a sea of four-year-olds alive all day.

I quit the preschool shortly after he left. It's a tough fucking job—but now I nanny for him during holiday breaks, summers, and the occasional weekend.

Grabbing the milk out of the fridge, I turn around to see him stirring the batter with intense concentration—so hard that he flings some of the mixture across the counter.

"Dammit," he groans.

"Luke!" My tone is meant to be scolding, but a small laugh escapes.

I fucking *love it* when kids curse. But I know it's my responsibility to let them know that they shouldn't . . . still, hearing it come from such a small voice is always funny.

He sighs. "Sorry, Miss Melia, I thought maybe your ears were off."

I walk over to him, giving his head an affectionate rub.

My "ears" are my hearing aids. I don't particularly *like* wearing them, but I've made a habit of doing it when I'm out in public—and I always wore them when I was teaching.

But I also used to teach the kids sign language, and on particularly rowdy days when they were non stop tattling on each other or bugging me for every little thing, I'd sign, "Sorry, I turned my ears off."

Strangely enough, it not only gave me some peace but the kids didn't turn into savage beasts and start picking each other off like Tributes. I never *actually* took my hearing aids out, but it seemed to be an effective way to at least try and get them to problem-solve on their own. It also helped tether my sanity.

"I like when your ears are off. Then we can sign," he says.

I smile. "We can sign anytime, dude." I open the pantry, then turn to face him. "What do we need, Chef?" I sign.

His eyebrows scrunch, and I can tell he didn't understand, so I sign slower, fingerspelling the word *chef.*

His mouth wiggles, thinking, and then he slowly fingerspells, "P-U-M-P-K-I-N."

My eyebrows pinch with a nod, showing him the sign for pumpkin before turning back to the pantry to find his unique choice for pancake ingredients, then sign, "You like pumpkin, huh?"

He shrugs and the smallest blush spreads across his cheeks.

I nudge his shoulder, giving him a *"spill it"* glance. He knows he can't hide anything from me.

He groans. "It's nothing. This girl let me have some of her pumpkin bar at lunch the other day. It was okay."

Oh my God. Does my boy have a crush?!

I have to play it cool. If he catches even the smallest hint of "gooey-ness" as he calls it, he'll shut down . . . but this is seriously the cutest fucking thing.

"That was nice of her," I say, my inflection rising, like a nosy detective.

He shrugs again. "I guess. She probably just did it so I'd stop chasing her at recess."

"Why do you chase her?" I lean against the counter, ducking my head to meet his eyes.

His cheeks flush again, and that's enough for me.

"Hey, if you like her—that's okay. In fact, that's better than okay, it's great!"

His eyebrows pinch, taking his middle finger to the side of his right cheek and twisting it, signing, "Gross," and I laugh.

It's his favorite sign; he uses it liberally.

"It's not gross," I chuckle. "It's a sign that you're growing up."

His eyebrows hitch, and I know he likes the sound of that. Luke's one of those kids that longs to be treated like an adult. His brother, Malcolm, is ten years older than him, and I think he makes Luke feel lame for liking childish things.

"Instead of chasing her, you know what you should do?" I lean to my elbows on the counter. "You should share a snack with her."

He scoffs. "That's stupid!" He shakes his head, adding, "And dumb."

"*That's* redundant," I mumble.

"Huh?"

I sigh. "Dumb and stupid—*both are not nice words, by the way*—mean the same thing." I shrug. "But hey, you do what you want. I'm just . . . oh, I don't know, a *girl*. I might know what I'm talking about."

I don't, but he doesn't need to know that.

"Yeah, but you're old." He tilts his head saying, "Pass the pumpkin?"

Damn. Burned by a six-year-old, and it's not even noon.

My legs slug down the steps of the L platform, feeling completely worn out from my morning with Luke. He's an endless pit of energy.

My limbs are actually aching from chasing his crazy-ass around the house all day.

Hurrying down the sidewalk, I start toward the market to grab some supplies for this week.

I began what I've coined my "Chef's Kiss Challenge," when I started living on my own in an attempt to heighten my culinary skills.

I've been cooking since I was nine years old. But it wasn't until I was fifteen and went to live with Doris and Wally that I really got into it. As a kid in "the system" I really lucked out with them.

It's not uncommon for kids in foster care to experience placement changes two or three times a month, and I was averaging *five* by the time I went to live with them.

Wally was retired, but he was a chef back in his heyday and he's the one who taught me how to really cook. Up until then, I had learned what I could out of necessity, but watching Wally in the kitchen was what I imagine it was like watching Michaelangelo sculpt marble. And he *appreciated* food on a level I had never seen before.

He'd spend hours, sometimes days, preparing for a single meal and it drove Doris nuts.

I snort a laugh, thinking about all the times he'd sign, *"Don't shit on the journey, Doris!"* Wally was deaf and he and Doris were the first ones to start teaching me ASL.

God, I miss them.

I still don't know why they chose to let me stay with them until I was eighteen, but the only conclusion I can come to is some sort of cosmic intervention. It had to be *some* kind of higher power because I was . . . *a lot.* I still am, but I like to believe I'm a manageable kind of chaos now . . . like a fidget spinner.

As I finally reach the market, I push through the door and faintly hear Rhonda say, "Hey, honey," from behind the register. I give her a small wave and then move toward the refrigerated section, grabbing some eggs and cheese, then quickly pick up the filo pastry a few aisles down.

This week's challenge is Spanakopita.

The market is small. It only has a few aisles with two wall coolers and she only has produce on the weekends.

Maybe I can weasel some spinach from Tim . . .

What are fuck buddies for, right?

He lives in some co-op in Lincoln Park and runs a rooftop garden on top of the building. I met him a few months ago and he's been a very reliable playmate.

Plopping the items on the counter, Rhonda eyes them curiously. "We baking this week, honey?"

"No," I chuckle. "Baking is reserved for apocalyptic times, remember?"

It's true, baking is *not* my forte—so the only time I do it is when my life is in such a massive upheaval that I need to refocus the distress into something outside my comfort zone. It's almost a form of punishment; a reminder that I need to get my shit together.

Rhonda laughs. "So everything's good?"

I nod, handing her the cash. Rhonda is cool. She's had this market forever and I've lived across the street for thirteen years so we tend to check in on each other from time to time. Sometimes I'll bring her some of whatever dish I've made that week. The recipes usually make more than I can eat, anyway.

I shove my wallet in my backpack as Rhonda hands me my bag.

I thank her, starting back toward the door and then pushing it open before I pause to ask, "You like Greek?"

She nods. "Honey, you know me. If *you* make it, I'll eat it."

The praise fills my chest and my mouth timidly inches up my cheeks before I toss her a parting wave and continue out the door.

Jesus, fuck—it's cold!

After giving a quick glance in both directions of the street, I dart across it. But my eyebrows flinch—I forgot a hat today—and the whipping wind is causing some feedback in my hearing aids.

As I reach the top of my stoop, I quickly pull the door open and stand inside the small lobby. My head shakes from the discomfort of the feedback, but I turn the aids off and the relief is nearly instant.

After a heavy exhale, my body starts to feel heavy again. My aching muscles resurface from clenching them, and I trudge my way up the two flights of steps until I'm outside my door.

My hand jiggles the key in the lock before I lift up on the door-knob. I apply the practiced amount of pressure, and then shove my shoulder into the door, pushing it hard, before it jaggedly opens.

I'm not sure what's wrong with my door. It's been that way since I moved in. But I accept it for what it is. It's just . . . bad at being a door.

Or too good.

As I drop my keys on the small table just outside my entryway, my feet start to move toward the kitchen and I place the groceries on the small breakfast bar. I go to my bedroom, tucking my hearing aids away in my nightstand, and then change into sweats.

When I return to the kitchen to put the groceries away, I'm finally greeted by Beatrice—excuse me, *Queen B*—as she hops up on the counter and stares at me, her tail rippling up and down like a slow, steady wave.

Her expression reads, *"Human. You're here. Why are you not feeding me?"*

After putting the eggs and cheese in the fridge, I walk over to the counter and scoop her up. Her body immediately writhes and her front paws push against me before she flails out of my arms, shaking her coat before she trots away.

I breathe a laugh. *She's to be looked at but never held.*

"A cat?!" I signed.

Wally nodded. "Isn't she cute?"

I blinked down at the small tortoiseshell fluff ball and then back up at Wally. "I have no words."

He chuckled with a shrug before he signed, "Well, it'll be nice to have a friend."

I squinted back at him. I was used to not having friends. I liked being alone. But I could see a distant concern in his eyes—like maybe it would make him feel better, somehow.

It was such a warm feeling that my mouth quirked at the corner before I forced a skeptical eyebrow tilt. "I don't know . . . aren't cats like, mostly evil?"

He laughed and shook his head, signing, "No! They're a symbol of fortune and good luck. Egyptians loved the damn things so much, they shaved off their eyebrows to mourn when their cats would die."

It was too bizarre of a fact for him to have made up, and I was again lost for words, but a small laugh managed to puff through my lips.

He scooped the tiny cat back up and handed it to me.

Ahh. What the fuck?

I didn't know how to take care of an animal! I never doubted my ability to take care of myself—but another living, breathing thing?!

I slumped onto the big coral armchair I had bought at the thrift store earlier that week and glanced around the sparsely furnished apartment. I slowly imagined it filled with things that made it my space. Lots of string lights and pictures . . . an evil cat lazing on the windowsill.

The things that make a place a home.

Doris and Wally's house was the closest thing I'd ever felt to that in my life. But I couldn't keep staying with them. They'd already done so much for me and now Doris was sick . . .

Wally's eyes became cautious. "Did you end up stopping by your mom's?"

My limbs immediately tightened and a coldness flowed through my veins.

I had told him I might go see her on my way into the city. It had been eight years . . .

But I quickly shook my head, only then noticing that my hand was running over soft, cotton fur. It felt nice—soothing.

Wally's mouth tilted watching me pet the cat before his expression shifted to something a little more serious. "Dr. G's going to do virtual visits with you?"

He signed it like a question but I could tell it was more of a statement. Both he and Doris supported my decision to move out, but they insisted that I keep seeing the therapist they found for me almost immediately after I started staying with them.

I probably should have come with a shrink . . . like batteries included.

I nodded. "Yeah. We're going to do every other Thursday. And I start working tomorrow, so I'll pay you back as soon as I get my check."

I had saved a decent amount of money the past two years. It's not like I had a thriving social calendar and I liked working—really, I loved making money. But part of the reason I was able to save so much was because they paid for all of my necessities. And part of moving out was to make sure they didn't have to do that anymore.

Wally shook his head, signing, "Whenever, kiddo. No rush." Another moment passed before he smacked his palms on his thighs and then stood up. "Well, I'm going to head home. I'm making French Onion Brisket tonight and it's only been marinating for two hours . . ." His mouth pulled back tightly and the expression somehow shook me from my odd, sentimental state.

I laughed. "So you're going home to make Doris a snack? She's going to kill you for not feeding her till ten o'clock at night!"

He shrugged and I laughed again.

I scooped up the cat and held it out in front of me, signing, "Are you sure I need to keep it? What if I fuck it up?"

He chuckled, shaking his head, before making the A handshape with his right hand and then tapping his middle finger twice over his chest.

A. Heart.

My name sign. He'd given it to me three years ago and I still didn't understand why.

I was anything but a warm and fuzzy person, but that's the thing about name signs. They can only be given to you by someone that is deaf and you're kind of stuck with them.

I guess there were worse names out there.

He cautiously pulled me into him, giving me a light hug and I tentatively returned it, but not for long. I eased back, signing, "You're not going to bring an animal with you every time you come, right?" I smirked, but my hidden motive was to gauge whether or not I thought he would actually still visit me.

He had no obligation, but . . . I hoped he would. And I would go see them too, but I didn't want to intrude on their lives anymore than I already had.

Wally shrugged. "I guess it depends on what you classify as 'animal' and whether or not Doris is 'hangry' when I bring her over . . . " he laughed to himself.

He loved the word "hangry." After I'd introduced it to him, he honestly believed that the word somehow originated with his wife—more specifically—what he did to his wife.

He pulled on the door, scrunching his eyes as he struggled to open it before he yanked it back. He glanced back at me, signing, "Call management and get that fixed, okay?"

Suddenly, Beatrice's silky fur weaving between my ankles makes me jump and I glance down at her. The soft fluid motions are like watching a figure skater glide gracefully along the ice, but all the while singing, "Feed me, bitch."

The thought makes me chuckle and I open the cabinet above the sink, grabbing her kibble and then pouring it into her bowl.

She immediately shoves her face into the saucer and I'm quickly forgotten.

Seems about right.

chapter three

dean

I show Ava the sign, "more," and she stares at me blankly before she squeals and slaps her palms against the tray on her highchair.

I sigh, picking up her bowl of mashed sweet potatoes with a medley of soft veggies—*sans* zucchini.

"All right, all right," I concede, scooping some out and feeding it to her.

Every time I pick her up from Marnie's, I wonder if that will be the time she tells me that Ava said her first word. She's bound to start talking soon—*any day now*—and there's a chance I'll miss it.

It's inevitable that I'll miss things. I already have. She took her first steps at Marnie's. Luckily, my ex-wife was feeling generous that day and took a video of it and sent it to me.

But Marnie didn't learn much sign language while we were together. Not that she really had a real reason to—I wasn't seeing much of Otis while we were together. But I'm determined to teach Ava. And I *know* that it's a "first" I'll definitely get.

My eyes roll at my stupid, mental scoreboard, scooping out Ava's last bite and feeding it to her.

After cleaning her face and fingers, I plop her in her playpen and she immediately goes to town banging on her keyboard. It was a gift from Evelyn to Ava, and it's a loud, plastic torture device to me.

That checks out, actually.

When I catch myself humming to the pre-recorded song, I groan.

Goddammit. When did I become that guy?

Rinsing out the bowl, I stick it in the dishwasher and glance back over at Ava. A heavy sigh pushes past my lips while I watch her play . . .

At least *that* guy doesn't drink.

I'm two days away from my "Soberversary," an unfortunate term my buddy Reggie gave to the milestone.

A year of no drinking. Like most things in life, it doesn't feel as momentous as it's built up to be. And I'm still waiting for that profound shift that people talk about all the time at sober meetings—the divine clarity one supposedly gets from a life without booze—but it might all be bullshit.

One thing is for sure, when you stop drinking, you're highly aware of just how much other people *do* indulge. A few months ago, I learned that there's a "Mommy and Mimosa" gathering at the park on Saturday mornings, where the sole purpose of getting together is for the women to drink champagne while they watch their kids play.

At nine in the morning.

My phone buzzes on the counter and I see a message from Otis.

Otis: Pizza and 2016 World Series tomorrow?

My lips tilt at the offer. He knows how mopey I get after Ava leaves, and he usually tries to make some sort of plan with me on Sundays. But since the Cubs aren't in season yet, we have to settle for watching old games on DVD. I'd feel pathetic, if I didn't feel so grateful. Not just for the gesture but because . . . well, there was a time—*only a year ago*—that I thought my brother and I would never talk again.

But I suddenly wonder . . . *is Evelyn coming?*

Probably not. She hates baseball.

I hold the phone in my hand and try to think of a discreet way to ask him if it will just be him, but everything I type just sounds like I'm *asking* him about Evelyn.

Huffing, I type out a quick response.

> **Me:** Sounds good.
> I'll text you after Marnie picks her up.

It's not worth the awkward conversation. I'll just assume she's coming and if she doesn't, then it'll be a relief.

Thwack!

My heart jumps at the abrupt noise, and my chin jerks up toward Ava. I hurry out of the kitchen and see her pointing and giggling at a lone block in front of the playpen wall. After another second passes, she stops giggling and stares wide-eyed at me, still pointing toward the block.

"Go get it, baby," I tell her.

She immediately starts crying and I flinch from the unexpected outburst.

Jesus. I don't know if she's crying because she wants it, but doesn't want to get it—or maybe she's disappointed that throwing it didn't turn it into a unicorn—*who the hell knows.*

But I'm doomed, because the second I see her watery blue eyes, I'm a fucking goner. I scoop her up and over my head, making goofy faces and wiggling my fingers at her side.

She pouts out a residual sob but slowly, I see the two little stubs of teeth poke through her smile. After I tickle some giggles out of her, I lower her down to the floor. As soon as both of her knees and hands touch down—she takes off.

It's amazing, really. She still walks like she's been drinking at a Cubs game all day, but when she crawls, she's as quick and agile as a goddamn cheetah. She darts away from me and I crawl after her, chasing her. Every once in a while I tug her back toward me by her ankles and her bubbling laughter fills the room.

It's my favorite sound. And I spend my Saturday trying to get it as much as possible.

Later that night, after Ava is asleep, the quietness sets in. But instead of sinking into the couch cushions and relaxing, the dread of Sunday starts to creep in.

Tomorrow she leaves.

This has pretty much been the arrangement for the last nine months, but it doesn't make it any easier. It's *this* feeling that freaks me out.

I fucking hate the way I'm wired. It's like the present doesn't even matter most of the time. The few days with Ava are always the best, but I might as well not even have Sunday with her since I spend the majority of it feeling sorry for myself.

Maybe it's part of the reason the "accomplishment" of my sobriety year mark doesn't feel like a success. Because whether I want to admit it or not—*she's* the reason I don't drink. And since I only have her Thursday through Sunday, it's like my purpose for all of this is non-existent through the rest of the week.

But it's all or nothing with addiction. If I were to drink on the days I didn't have Ava, they would slowly—inevitably—creep into my time with her. And that's not an option.

Because that guy was the fucking worst . . .

I sat on the stoop of my townhouse, chain-smoking.

Otis had left an hour ago and I still couldn't seem to calm the fuck down.

"We're in love, Dean."

I shook my head, hauling in a heavy drag. Not many people have their worst fear play out in such spectacularly shitty fashion, but I guess I was just one of the lucky ones.

My brother was in love with my ex-girlfriend.

She was in love with him.

And he knew. *He knew about what happened during mine and Evelyn's last year at school and one thing was for sure—he didn't give a fuck about where my head was after what happened.*

Why should he?

It's the question at the center of my self-loathing. Why would anyone care that I was having some sort of breakdown?

Nothing happened to me.

But I felt like an entirely different person than I was back then, so I guess something happened—just nothing that anyone cared about.

I took another swig of my beer and stamped the cigarette out under my boot. I should have gone back inside. It was nearly midnight, but the cold November air was slowly numbing my face, my limbs—and I liked it.

Numb was good.

But it didn't last. It never did. I needed more.

More booze, more destruction . . . more numb.

Suddenly, Otis's face flashed through my mind. His angry, unforgiving eyes as he told me he hated me right before he left.

My eyes clamped shut at the fresh memory, feeling like it burned even more as I replayed it in my mind. I was already pretty toasted by the time we got into it and I said . . . awful things to him.

Another thing that played through my soundtrack in hell . . .

"She just feels bad for you, Otis—she always has."

I winced before taking another sip as my fist tightly squeezed the bottle. For as fucked up as I was, the booze wasn't working hard enough. Everything it usually suppressed somehow felt intensified.

I picked up my pack and went to light another when I heard the front door crack open. Tossing the unlit cigarette as quickly as I could, I slowly craned my neck around to see Marnie peeking her head through the door.

"Hey, babe," *I slurred.*

Her strawberry blond hair was rustled and her mouth was in a tight line. The crease between her brows deepened and her light blue eyes narrowed at me. "Dean, it's late. What are you doing out here?"

"J-Just getting some fresh air." *My speech was slow, it was taking extra concentration to focus on the words. And it was a ridiculous lie because the wind was whipping around us like the final scene in fucking Jumanji.*

Her eyebrows pinched before she eyed the pack of cigarettes. I guess they didn't make it back in my pocket.

Sighing my defeat, I wobbled to stand, grabbing the neck of my beer bottle on the way up. When I got in the house, Marnie shut and locked the door before she slowly looked over at me.

I could only imagine what she saw. The gaunt shadows of my ashen face, my bloodshot eyes from the wind and booze. She was looking at me so hard I almost wondered if she could see my insides too.

Her nostrils gave a slight flare as a disgusted sound scoffed from her throat. "You smell like a bowling alley." I stepped farther away from her, like maybe that would help, but her face stayed the same. "This is some real top notch behavior from a guy who's about to have a kid in five months."

My chest caved from the blow. I deserved it, but it still hit hard.

"I had a fight with Otis," I mumbled, tracing my thumb around the lip of my bottle. "I just needed to take the edge off."

She nodded, but it wasn't in understanding. It was the same nod I'd seen lawyers give in courtroom dramas when they were about to annihilate their opponent.

I was fucked.

"So . . . at three o'clock this afternoon, when you started drinking . . . was that a preemptive measure? For this fight you just had with Otis a couple of hours ago?"

An inward groan sat in my throat. I had actually started drinking at noon but I put it in a coffee tumbler so she wouldn't notice.

Top notch behavior, indeed.

When I didn't say anything, she rubbed the pads of fingers across her forehead with the frustration of dealing with a petulant child. "What did you guys fight about?"

Fuck.

Telling Marnie that we fought because he was with Evelyn now was sure to open up another argument. She wasn't insecure by any means—but my history with Evelyn was always a point of contention.

"Stupid stuff," I shrugged, placing the beer bottle on the table, avoiding eye contact.

A deep sigh pushed past her lips and I swear I felt the heaviness of it from a couple feet away.

She was tired. Tired of dealing with me, tired of me shutting her out. Tired from being fucking pregnant.

God, I was an asshole.

I'd spent the greater part of our relationship on autopilot. But the problem with that, is the plane still needs to fucking land, eventually.

And I was crashing.

"I'm sorry, babe. I'll do better," I offered lamely.

I had gotten good at lying. So good, that I was even able to convince myself more often than not. But I didn't this time. I didn't believe I'd do better—maybe I'd hide it better . . .

Marnie also looked unconvinced. "I'm going to bed. I suggest you shower and do the same."

My chin dipped with a tight nod before she walked back up the stairs. When I heard the door to our bedroom door close, I grabbed the back of the chair.

"Fuck," I hissed, squeezing the chair harder.

The white-knuckle grip was a consolation prize. I wanted to break it against the wall. I wanted to crack the table in half. I wanted to destroy everything.

But the alcohol subdued me enough that I didn't do any of that. I just stood and seethed.

My wife looked at me like I was pathetic. And I was.

My brother hated me. And he should.

I hated me.

I finally shoved the chair, and staggered toward the kitchen. Whipping the door to the fridge open, I glanced inside but closed it quickly and moved to the cabinet with the whiskey.

I just needed more.

My palm smacks my forehead before I rub it and then pull my hands through my hair, grabbing the wavy strands like I can somehow extract the memory and throw it against the wall.

I've been trying really hard to keep my mind present. Letting my past haunt me is part of the reason I ended up in this situation, but it's *fucking hard.* Just like it's hard to enjoy Sunday, knowing Ava will be leaving.

There's too much bullshit in life. It overcrowds the good parts of it like weeds.

A deep sigh pushes past my lips as I begrudgingly pick up the remote and click on the TV. I turn the volume down and the subtitles on but I'm not actually paying attention.

A year of no drinking. But I still don't feel different. I thought after a year . . . I just thought I'd feel *better.*

chapter four

amelia

*M*an. For someone that's been using ASL for fifteen years, my interpreter's program is *kicking my ass*.

And it doesn't help that my lecture videos keep stalling.

I shut the screen to my laptop and toss my pen onto the desk before pressing my thumbs to my temples.

Deep breaths.

School was never my forte—even less so when I was put into foster care and moved around so much—but interpreting feels like the closest thing I've ever had to a "calling."

I didn't lose my hearing until I was ten, and I was put in "the system" shortly after. But it wasn't until I went to live with Doris and Wally that anyone even *tried* to effectively communicate with me. As a kid, I didn't really think much about the lack of accessibility, but as an adult, it's fucking *baffling*.

My situation was *unique*. They *loved* to use that word with me. I could verbalize, so people assumed I could understand them—and to a certain degree, I could. More often than not, caseworkers were asking me the same questions over and over and they were the only people I was *obligated* to talk to.

But the problems came when foster parents or other kids in the house would try to talk to me. People assume lip reading is as easy as listening, but it's not. It's a skill. And quite honestly, it fucking sucks. Plus, something like only thirty percent of the English language is actually *able* to be lip read.

And God help you if they have any facial hair.

But I can't help but feel like my situation—*unique* as it is—can lend itself to this field.

If I survive the program, that is.

The alert light on my phone blinks and I pick it up.

Tim: Heading over.

Hell yeah.

Maybe he can fix my laptop. I learned recently that my hippie, gardener fuckboy is also surprisingly tech savvy.

Rolling my neck, I stand and stretch my limbs from the hunched position I've been in for the last hour. I walk to my bathroom to wash my face and swish around some mouthwash—not that I really need to make the effort for Tim—but it makes *me* feel a little better to get clean before we get dirty.

At least I hope it's dirty.

But, if he can fix my computer and give me an orgasm, it will have been well worth it.

Beatrice trots through the door and hops up on the counter, helping herself to the water running from the faucet. She has a water dish, but any time a sink turns on—there she is. I think it's her way of staking her claim. *"You may pay the bills, but I own this place."*

I let her finish her bougie fountain drink as I walk over to my nightstand and pull my aids out, attaching them to my ears one at a time. It takes a minute to adjust to the sudden sound and I hum mindlessly for a few seconds to reacquaint myself.

Ten minutes later, there's a knock at the door and I wrestle it open to find Tim standing in the hall with a burlap bag in his hand.

His gray-blue eyes crease at the corners, under the edges of his shaggy blond hair.

"Hey," he says.

"Hey, yourself," I toss back at him, stepping aside to let him in.

He smirks, and walks through the doorway, lifting the burlap bag. "I brought you that spinach."

My eyebrows hitch as the corner of my mouth quirks. "Thanks."

He hands me the bag, then shrugs out of his coat and hangs it on the hook by the door before he shakes his head. "Most girls want flowers but you . . . want roughage," he chuckles.

After tossing the bag onto the breakfast bar, I shrug, putting my practiced smirk in place. "Well . . . luckily I have a botanist that can service *all* my needs." I cock my eyebrow, leaving nothing to subtlety. "My laptop needs some attention, too."

He takes a step toward me, pinching my chin between his thumb and index finger. "Too much porn?"

Psh. I read my porn.

But I shrug, giving him a teasing grin. The truth is, I'm pretty sure I missed the past few software updates. It infuriates me that *I* need to do them—*just update, if you have to*—but letting him think it was the former might spice up whatever's about to happen.

"First things first," he whispers. "How do good girls say thank you?" His voice is raspy and wanting and it sends a small shiver down my spine.

He's still holding my chin, but I eventually break the eye contact to look down at my fingers as they start to unbutton his pants, then pull his zipper.

As my hand sinks into his boxers, he inhales sharply and his eyes flutter closed.

"Is that good?" I purr. My fist moving slowly at first, teasingly slow, and he plants his hands on the wall behind me, caging me in between his arms.

Heat fills the gray in his eyes, like clouds before a thunderstorm as his hips start to move with my hand. "Such a pretty girl, Cece. Even prettier when you're thanking me."

Excitement stirs at the use of my alias. I never give my real name to guys. I'm not sure why, it happened once, naturally, and now it's just become a habit but it spurs me on more. My hand moves a little faster until I release him—only so I can pull down his pants and boxers.

Sinking to my knees, I stare up at him, widening my eyes like I'm not really sure what to do from here and a small smirk tilts up his cheek.

"Did my pretty little slut forget how to do her job?"

I nod, playing along. I can suck a dick better than anyone and he knows it.

But it's fun to pretend.

Hours later, I'm in the back room of the kitchen at the women's shelter where I cook every Saturday, washing the dishes with Patty.

Well . . . *I'm* washing the dishes while she *"dishes."*

Despite my aversion to people, Patty and I hit it off pretty quickly. On her first night here a couple of years ago, I recognized a smutty romance novel tucked under her arm when I was plating her food and she noticed me eyeing it.

A wry smile inched up her cheek and she asked, "Do you think all men secretly like anal penetration?"

I laughed so fucking hard. I didn't know this woman *at all*—I was in the middle of scooping potatoes onto her plate—and she opened with *that.*

Needless to say, our shameless chats have become a thing, and I've come to actually enjoy her company. I think it's because I never have to worry that the conversation will take a turn. Like it's an unspoken agreement between us.

I don't even know how old she is. The only indication that leads me to believe that she's older than me is from the gray roots at her hairline. But her dark brown skin is flawless and she carries herself with such silly, youthful energy.

"So, did he return the favor?" she asks, her hazel eyes brightening.

I had just finished telling her about Tim's visit earlier and now she's practically salivating.

I breathe a laugh before dumping the silverware into the sanitizing solution, then I peek back up at her. "Of course."

"Sounds like I need to get myself a gardener," she sighs, wistfully.

I laugh again, before I drain the big sink. Once the water has swirled away, I take the faucet sprayer and wash away the leftover suds, then use it to rinse the middle compartment of the sink where some remnants of food have dropped.

As I turn back around, Patty's staring off toward the floor. The usual lightness of her expression has shifted to something far off—almost sad—and my feet shuffle nervously.

We may not *talk* about the real shit. But . . . this *is* a shelter. No one's here for a weekend girls' trip and Patty has left and come back five times in the years I've known her, the most recent time being last week . . .

But asking her about it would be rude and a direct violation to our silent agreement.

I clear my throat, walking toward my backpack. "I've got a book for you," I tell her, unzipping the bag and fishing out my latest read, but then my other book catches my eye and I grab that, too.

I hand them to Patty and her eyebrow cocks just a little bit as her lips tilt. "*Plucking Ever After* and . . . what the—?!"

I laugh. It's one of my many copies of J. K. Rowling's *Harry Potter and the Sorcerer's Stone*. I have so many different versions, even a Portuguese edition, and I always keep one on me. I use it as my shield on the L.

"I know. It's not our usual genre but . . . it's the best book I've ever read."

Even that feels like an understatement.

She pages through them both and looks back up to me. "I make no promises for the one with no spice, but I'll try," she says skeptically.

I zip my bag up and pull my coat on before I shrug back at her, saying "They'll both rock your world. In . . . very different ways," and we both laugh again.

Pushing through my door a half hour later feels like a victory. In the winter months, finding the will to leave your apartment at all is a feat, but today felt exceptionally long.

I toss my keys on the small table, mindlessly scanning my small apartment while I shrug out of my coat.

I love coming home. It still feels like a reward.

The place is small, but it's more than enough space for Beatrice and me.

An oversized coral chair and matching ottoman sit in the living room in front of my small TV in the corner. I hung a full length mirror on the wall just behind the chair and painted the frame with black chalk paint.

My eyes dance along all the things I've written on the frame through the years. I decided on a gold paint marker, giving the frame a starry night aesthetic. And the honey colored walls feel even more warm from the twinkly lights strung over my desk in the corner.

After taking a deep inhale, the tension from the cold air outside lessens and I finally start toward the bedroom.

A hot shower sounds good.

As I push through the bedroom door, I find Beatrice curled up on her pillow—which is really *my* pillow—not even raising her head as I walk into the bedroom.

I grumble, "This is why people say dogs are better," as I pass by her, but predictably, there is no reaction.

I chuckle as I take off my aids and then pull off my hat, tossing it on the dresser as I flick on the bathroom light. I crank the shower before pushing the small window above the showerhead open.

The bathroom is small and it fills up with steam pretty quickly, so this helps it feel less like I'm stepping out into a murky rainforest.

After peeling off the rest of my clothes, I step into the hot stream of water, feeling my limbs instantly loosen. Turning, I let the water run down my face and the muscles in my cheeks and jaw relax. My mouth drops open and the heat starts to clear my airwaves.

When I turn back around, the water falls on the back of my head and trickles down my spine.

My back was wet. The rain had been coming down in buckets and my coat wasn't water resistant.

My friend Alex quickly ran up his driveway, yelling, "See ya, Amelia!" over his shoulder as he made it to his front door. His mom was standing on their covered porch, smiling as she pulled him into her before she tossed a wave in my direction.

I waved back but walked quickly—just a little farther down the street to my house. It was a relatively short walk from the bus stop and I usually tried to prolong it as much as possible but I was freezing.

Not only was I not wearing a raincoat, but I had a hole in my shoe so my foot was soaked and that coupled with cold December air, had my teeth chattering already as I hurried toward my front porch.

I climbed the steps and shook off the excess water as best I could before I grabbed the knob and turned it.

Locked.

I was already shaking from the cold but my sudden unease only tightened my body more. I tapped on the door but heard nothing from the other side. Peeking through the window next to the door, I stared into the living room.

My mom sat upright on the couch with her neck bent back, her mouth wide open toward the ceiling.

Why did she lock the door?

I couldn't remember a time where she ever locked it so the fact that she did it that day, when I still wasn't home and she was . . . sleeping . . . seemed strange.

My body twitched. I swear the threat of being stuck out there actually made me colder and I moved back in front of the door. I knocked harder and louder. I didn't want to yell because I was worried the neighbors might hear.

No one could know.

I moved back to the window and banged on that, hoping maybe since it was slightly closer, it might wake her up. But she sat there, unmoving and a looming dread hung over my head. I knocked on the window again. "Mom," I said but my voice was pathetic—small.

I started to worry that something was wrong. Her head lulled to the side and the tiniest bit of hope bloomed in my chest, but it was quickly squashed again when she lowered to the cushions and curled up on the couch.

It was the start of Christmas break. Everyone was home and starting to celebrate the holiday. I had a second where I thought maybe I should go back to Alex's house, but there's a chance they'd see my mom's car in the driveway and know she was home.

She was just sleeping.

I shivered again, pulling my hood up and then sat on the porch next to the door. For a moment, I just sat, listening to the rain. If I closed my eyes I could pretend I was behind a waterfall.

That's it. I was behind a waterfall . . . in Iceland.

I was cold because I was on an adventure.

I sat in my imaginary world before a car zipped down the road and knocked me from my daydream, reminding me of my reality.

I grabbed my backpack and pulled out Harry Potter. My hands shook as I held the book but I tried to focus on the words. I tried to focus on the world inside the book.

I pretended to be a girl reading a book on her front porch.

"Shit!"

The water turns cold and I twist the knob on the shower to turn it off. My heart races from the abrupt temperature change and the lingering memory still passing through my mind.

I open the shower door and grab the towel nearby, quickly wrapping myself.

Breathe.

My hand fumbles to grab my necklace, fiddling with it.

It's a simple chain with a lightning bolt pendant. My fingers outline the edges of the bolt before my thumb presses into one of the pointy edges. I don't press hard enough to draw blood, but it redirects my racing mind. I focus on the small poke instead of my fluttering heart beat. My thumb taps a few more times, lighter and lighter on the point of the bolt until my heart rate eventually evens back out. I gulp, peeking my head out toward the bedroom to see my cat still curled up, but one menacing eye stares at me while the other one remains shut.

The sight loosens the remaining tension in my shoulders and a small chuckle finds a way to push past my lips. I wiggle my toes on the tile floor, letting them curl into the grout. The contrast of the rough feeling under my toes to the smooth, cold surface of the tiles under my heels is oddly soothing.

I catch a glimpse of myself in the mirror and see that my usual olive skin is pale, and my green eyes have taken on the color of a deep hunter. I finally drop my necklace and run my index finger over the indent in my thumb.

My lungs finally expand and I release a heavy exhale.

Jesus Christ.

chapter five
dean

My heart sinks as I hear the knock at the door. I finish putting the rest of Ava's things into her bag and zip it up.

Turning toward her, I plaster on my fake smile. "All right, baby. Mommy's here."

Her wide eyes stare back at me as she slowly shoves an oversized block in her mouth and I snort a laugh as I walk over to her, scooping her off the floor and then grabbing the bag.

We walk to the door and open it, finding Marnie on the other side.

"Hi," Marnie coos as she looks at Ava and my arms reluctantly move to hand her to Marnie. She takes Ava, squeezing her tight while she kisses her all over her face. Ava giggles and squeals and my mouth tilts on my cheek.

Marnie's a good mom—*a really good mom.* I always knew she would be. She always had a lot of patience and her temperament has always been calm, collected. Even when she's upset.

The exact opposite of me.

I move to hand her the bag and she peeks back at me. "Actually, do you mind if I come in for a second?"

Uh-oh.

This definitely can't be good. She's only been in here *once* and it was because it was our first "baby exchange" and I wasn't yet aware that I was supposed to have Ava completely ready to go.

"Sure," I draw the word out, making it sound like a question.

I move aside to let her in and glance at Ava over Marnie's shoulder, making a *yikes* face—silently begging her not to fart and start a fight between her mom and me.

Marnie plops her in the playpen before she straightens back up, not-so-subtly taking in the living room space. It's not decorated. Like, at all. It's blank white walls, and neutral furniture. Aside from Ava's toys and playpen, the place would give no indication as to who lives here.

I feel like I should offer her something, but I'm too anxious to hear what she needs to talk about.

"So . . . what's up?" I ask.

Her eyes finish scanning the walls before they float back to me and she releases a heavy exhale.

"Maybe we should sit," she says.

Oh, fuck me.

It's ironic how that suggestion immediately makes me want to run through the wall, but I try to stay calm.

This could be another zucchini situation, I remind myself. Her re-solved calmness also makes it incredibly difficult to gauge the severity of whatever she needs to discuss and it only heightens my unease.

Reluctantly, I take a seat in the armchair while Marnie sits on the couch across from me. She fidgets for a second and glances over at Ava who is babbling quietly to herself in her playpen before she meets my eyes again.

Her shoulders drop with another exhale and she finally starts to talk. "So . . . things have been going well with Shaun. Really well . . ." she explains jaggedly before swallowing hard.

Why is she so nervous?

She shifts her weight on the couch before she adds, "But it's been hard doing the distance thing, ya know?"

Okay . . .

My face must look as confused as I feel because she huffs out a breath and shakes her head, then says, "Anyway, we were talking the other night and . . . we want to move in together." She says the last part so fast that it takes my brain a second to catch up.

Oh . . .

I'm not really sure what to say. *This is awkward as fuck.* But I guess it's the first in a long line of uncomfortable conversations we'll inevitably have.

And it *is* soon. They've only been dating for five months. I'm honestly kind of surprised that Marnie's willing to take such a big step. Especially given the way everything went down with us.

I remind myself that it's *my* fault things happened the way they did with us and put on my most supportive expression. "That's great, Marn. Shaun seems like a good guy."

"He is," she agrees with a timid nod. "The thing is . . . his firm won't let him work remotely and since I work from home, the only way we can do that is if I uhh . . ." she trails off again, and tugs her bottom lip between her teeth.

My hand tightens on the arm of the chair as she clears her throat, straightening her spine before she says, "If we move to his place . . . in Michigan."

My heart drops, but my thoughts scatter like ants. I blink back at her and the only word I seem to latch onto is *"we."*

"You want to move my daughter to Michigan?!" The surge of adrenaline propels me to stand and Marnie quickly follows.

"Dean. Calm down. We're *talking*," she says. There's an edge to her voice—warning in her tone—but her demeanor remains calm.

Always fucking calm.

My eyebrows pinch. "So you're *not* moving to Michigan?"

Her head tilts and her eyes drift to the side. "Nothing has been decided. But . . . I'm considering it."

My insides feel like they're shriveling down to nothing *and* about to explode. I grab onto the back of the chair, and pull in some deep breaths, trying to ease the abrupt sense of panic.

I can't lose Ava.

Giving her back every Sunday already feels like torture. If she lived hours away, I . . .

"Dean . . ." I faintly hear Marnie's voice through the pounding in my temples. My chin pulls up to see her staring at me, cautiously.

I shake my head, trying to reel in my anger but I'm already teetering on the edge of the cliff.

I can feel it.

One wrong move and I'll plummet. I take a steadying inhale before I pry my hands from the chair. One of them moves to the back of my neck, trying to loosen the tension bunching at the base.

"So . . . you're *considering* moving my daughter to another state. How do we navigate that? You're going to spend eight hours round-trip to bring her back here once a week?" My voice is tight and I can't hide the facetious tone of the last question.

Calm down . . .

She scoffs, "No, weekly visits would be ridiculous. I don't know. I haven't figured out all of the details yet—"

"The details?" I cut her off. "You want to move out of the state with a guy you've only known for a few months, but you haven't thought about *'the details'* of how your daughter will continue to see her father?"

I am *not* calm. A switch has been flipped and fighting it is as useless as trying to stop a train with your fucking hand.

Marnie's eyes narrow before she shakes her head. "I should have known this would be a mistake. Trying to have a reasonable conversation with you is impossible."

She starts toward Ava but I move in front of her and she stops suddenly, her body becoming tense and I freeze.

Jesus Christ. Is she . . . scared?

The notion alone stunts my anger, allowing the looming feeling of doom to move in. It's been a long time since I've felt this amped up and I'm struggling to regain control. But I can't let her leave like this. I can't give her a reason to make a rash decision just because . . .

I'm losing control.

"I'm sorry," I say, my voice raspy and tight. "This is just . . . this is a lot."

Her mouth flattens as she inhales deep with a tight nod. She picks up Ava from in the playpen and rests her on her hip. "We really have to get going. We're going to Shelly's for dinner."

I suppress an eye roll. *God forbid you're late for dinner at your sister's when you just dropped a fucking bomb on me.*

"Can you say bye to Daddy?" Marnie says to Ava and the words seep into my veins as my hands tighten at my sides.

Saying goodbye to her always sucks, but right now . . . it feels like the walls of my chest are caving in and burying my heart under the wreckage.

I can't lose her.

Ava's head peeks up toward me and her bright blue eyes shine. She reaches her hand out, opening and closing her fingers and it tightens my throat.

"Nothing's been decided."

Yet . . .

I take her small hand in mine, kissing her fist, but my throat still feels swollen so all I do is sign, "I love you," to Ava.

She giggles as Marnie grabs the bag off the couch. I'm in such a haze that I barely register that they've walked over to the door. Marnie's eyes float back to me for a second as she straightens herself up before she opens the door and leaves.

An hour later, I'm still sitting in the chair I sank into right after they left.

I wish I was one of those people that somehow channeled anxious energy into something productive, but I'm not—it paralyzes me. *Well, physically, anyway.*

All I can focus on is how the fate of my whole world is in someone else's hands. And because it's me, my mind keeps cycling through the worst case scenario.

They'll move away, I'll see Ava whenever Marnie feels like coming to Chicago and she'll grow up calling Windbreaker Shaun "Dad."

My hands curl around the arms of the chair, again. Even if for some reason we *could* work out an arrangement for this, I still wouldn't be an easy car ride away. As she gets older, she'll make friends—maybe get into sports or music—and I'll miss it. I'll hear about it over the phone or . . .

I'm spiraling.

God, what I would do for a fucking cigarette.

Somehow, my brain and my body seem to agree with that idea. Without further thought, I quickly grab my coat and walk down the steps, then push outside the building and start toward the corner mart.

The only thought I have is how that first drag will feel when it hits my lungs. I might even get a nicotine buzz since I quit cold turkey last year.

The warning bell in my head starts to ring but if anything, it feels like it's making me walk faster. I pull open the door to the market, stalk to the counter, and it's the first moment that I falter.

I don't know the man behind the counter, and he doesn't know me, but I suddenly feel like a kid trying to buy booze with a fake ID.

This is a bad idea.

I blink the thought away, clearing my throat before I ask, "Can I get a pack of Marlow 27s?" as I grab one of the lighters off the stand by the register.

After paying, I push back through the door and the bell above it jingles, joining the warning alarm in my head. *But I don't care.*

All I can focus on is the relief as I unwrap the pack, tapping the box a few times before I open it up and pull one out.

This will help.

Out of habit, I pull out a second cigarette and flip it, so the end with the tobacco is facing up.

The motion is so distantly familiar that I find myself momentarily soothed by the muscle memory. I hold the cigarette between my teeth and huddle my hand around the end, blocking the wind as I light the tip. The immediate burn trails down my throat before the smoke hits my lungs, filling them with an aching relief.

I nearly groan on the exhale, blowing a billowy cloud out into the air. I immediately pull it to my lips again before I start to walk. It's freezing outside, and the wind is stinging my cheeks, but now that I'm moving, I'm afraid to stop. I even walk past my building and onto the next block in an equally dazed and anxious haze.

Two more cigarettes and ten minutes later, I'm starting to feel a little sick. I also feel like my nose and ears might break off from the bitter cold. My feet slow to a stop, wondering if I should keep walking or turn back around and go home when a door opens on the building next to me.

The rowdy sounds from the bar spill out onto the street—laughter, music, ease—it feels like a carpet being rolled out in front of me.

I bet it's warm in there.

It's a dumb idea. *So, so, so stupid.*

But my mind is frozen with the rest of my body and my feet carry me through the door anyway. The place is crowded for a Sunday night. Nearly every stool is taken, except for two right by the door and there's different clusters of people standing among what appears to be a dance floor. I walk to one of the empty stools and slump onto it.

This is the reason I stopped smoking.

The relief is never enough on its own. My ears catch on to the various conversations happening around me. I try to use them as a way to distract myself, but unfortunately, bar conversations are barely interesting even with the addition of booze.

There's a woman resting her cleavage on the bar top while she slurs at the guy next to her about how she *usually never* drinks on work nights.

Maybe she doesn't work on Mondays . . .

I grunt a chuckle at the thought but my weight shifts on my seat. There's a couple of guys huddled together watching some fight on the TV screen above the bar when the bartender notices me. He starts in my direction and just as he does, my peripherals pick up on someone sitting next to me.

A sweet, fruity scent finds my nose. But it's mixed with something more tenacious—musky, even.

Jasmine.

It's a unique scent. My mom grew it in her garden every spring and when a heavy breeze would come through, I could smell it from the treehouse in our backyard.

It's so intriguing that I glance over to my right to see where it's coming from.

chapter six
amelia

Okay. *Whoa.*

Is this what the bar scene has to offer?! The only time I've spent in bars is to pick up a take out order, but I hopped in here on a whim after returning a book to the library.

My mind has felt . . . *busy* all day and I didn't want to call on Tim two days in a row. But I may need to rethink my prowling grounds because . . . this guy could be the hottest man I've ever seen.

His wavy brown hair is thoroughly grabbable and the chiseled cut of his jaw is prominent from beneath his short, copper-colored scruff.

I have a strong urge to bite it.

When his eyes drift over to me, I do my best to pretend I wasn't just inches away from him, contemplating what it would be like to bite his face. Instead, my mouth pulls up at the corner and I tuck my hair behind my ear.

A timid smirk tilts on his lips as his eyes drift from my ear and then back to my eyes. "Hey," he signs.

A sharp inhale inflates my chest. *The hot, broody man signs?!*

My lips pull to smile and I almost let it happen. *Almost.* But instead, I simply lift the corner of my mouth as I sign, "Hi," back to him.

Our small exchange is interrupted by the bartender. He places two napkins down in front of us but then directs his attention to the Tall-Dark-And-Bend-Me-Over-The-Bar man next to me. "What can I get ya?" he asks, a flirtatious smile inching.

I'll fight you for him, tapster . . .

The guy next to me shifts in his seat and clears his throat. It takes him a solid ten seconds to finally answer, "Club soda with lime, please."

Oh fuck. The timbre of his voice is downright . . . *irresponsible.* It's low and husky and it sends a jolt of electricity through every one of my nerve endings.

You thirsty bitch. Calm down.

He looks over at me, signing, "Do you want something?"

Um . . . yes, sir, I do.

My lips tilt, taking a subtle glance at his ring finger. When I find it bare, I nod before glancing back at the bartender. "I'll take the same."

He nods, giving one more scan to the guy next to me before he turns to get our drinks.

"I think you've caught his attention," I sign, eyeing the bartender.

His eyebrows raise with a nod, signing, "Well, flattering as that is, he's not really my type." His eyes darken toward me, silently suggesting that *I* might be more his type and my heart nearly skips a beat.

His thumb absentmindedly taps on the lip of the bar while his knee lightly bounces below it. Turning back toward him, I sign, "So . . . you're not deaf?"

He shakes his head. "My brother is."

He tosses it out there so casually that the light flutter in my chest suddenly feels like a goddamn bat cave. I know for a fact that plenty of deaf kids grow up in homes where their *parents* don't even learn sign language.

The statistics are kind of insane, actually. At least ninety percent of deaf kids are born to hearing parents and only ten to fifteen percent of those people ever learn sign language.

So . . . he's not only gorgeous, but he's a fucking unicorn.

I clear my throat as the bartender sets our drinks down, breathing a laugh before I sign, "We might be the lamest bar flies in Chicago."

He tilts his chin up in a lazy nod, staring at his glass with an expression I can't quite place before he turns toward me. He raises the glass just slightly between us, signing, "To lame," with his other hand.

I pick mine up too, clinking it with his glass before we each take a sip. As I set my glass back down on the bar, his eyes catch mine again and the cool liquid seems to soothe my burning loins enough to notice that he seems . . . distressed.

His warm, coffee-colored eyes look a little worn and tired. I notice the slight tension he's holding in his jaw and forehead.

I wonder what's wrong . . .

I shake my head, quickly reminding myself that it doesn't matter. *Broody,* after all, is the male equivalent to *unhinged* in females. We're the most adventurous in the bedroom, but God help you if you have to deal with us outside of it.

Something about his demeanor tells me that he's looking for an escape, too. Which is odd, seeing as he ordered a drink with no booze.

But then again, so did I.

"What's your name?" he signs.

I'm about to give him the name I give to all men but . . . the fact that I'd be signing it stops me. I've never signed that name before and . . . I don't really want to.

I fingerspell my name and then show him my name sign, "A. Heart."

A soft smile pulls up his cheeks before he signs, "I'm Dean," but he only fingerspells his name.

My eyebrows pull together. "You don't have a name sign?"

He sighs, taking another sip of his drink before he looks back to me. "No, I do."

I sit waiting, staring at him in anticipation and he chuckles while he shakes his head. As I bring my glass back to my lips, another sigh escapes him before he signs, "D. Fart."

My hand moves to cover my mouth as I snort a laugh. Once I swallow, the laughter trickles out.

D. Fart?!

He nods, still chuckling himself. "Yeah, laugh it up. But my brother gave it to me when we were kids and he *refuses* to give me a new one."

Something in my chest swells. He might not *like* the name sign, but he respects it. And . . . it's cool. My shoulders relax and my head tilts, signing, "Hey, ya know, audibly—our name signs rhyme."

The ghost of a smile pulls on his lips as he nods. Another moment passes and we both take another sip of our drinks, letting a slightly awkward pause loom between us.

For someone that's as bold as I am in the bedroom, I don't actually have a lot of experience with picking up men. And I'm out of practice. My consistency with Tim has allowed me to be an exclusive slut for the last few months, but even when I met him, it wasn't in this kind of setting.

One where I saw him walk in and positioned myself next to him. One where he noticed me and struck up a conversation.

"So do you live in the neighborhood?" I sign, mostly to make conversation. It only occurs to me after I ask the question that it totally sounds like a pick up line—*and a bad one, at that.*

My eyes widen, but the unease passes quickly when his mouth tilts up. He takes another sip of his drink and then runs his tongue along his bottom lip.

Lord, have mercy . . .

He contemplates my question for a second before he looks back over at me, his eyes scanning my face for another moment before he signs, "Yeah, about ten minutes from here."

I nod. Unsure of how to play this. I don't think I actually expected to find someone at all when I came in here and now I'm realizing how slutty it would make me look to leave with him—a stranger.

I take another sip of my drink, closing my eyes for just a moment while I try to quiet those voices—*well, one voice in particular*—before I glance back at Dean.

His eyes are squinting in my direction, studying me, and I feel my cheeks heat.

Jesus. Why am I yucking my yum?

I am a slut—and I don't care. So why am I getting all up in my feels about letting this guy find that out?

I huff out another breath, strengthening my resolve. I'm here for one reason and one reason only, and if this guy isn't willing to facilitate that need then I might as well move along.

"Want to show me?" I sign.

We pummel through his door fifteen minutes later.

He pins me to the wall and kicks the door shut behind us and then devours my lips again.

Good God, this man can kiss.

Not even the cigarette smell on his breath deters me. Kissing has never really been my focal point but our lips just . . . get along. Mine fill where his leave and our tongues intermingle. A soft groan pushes through his lips and vibrates down my throat and I swear I feel it all the way to my toes.

His hands move to the buttons on my coat as he trails his soft, plush lips down my neck. My fingers sift and drag through the back of his hair while his breath tickles my skin.

"Goddamn, you are beautiful," he rasps against my neck.

Beautiful?

I don't have time to dive into it because Dean's mouth takes mine again and his fingers are trailing up my stomach. He makes this deep, masculine *"mmm"* sound when his hand reaches my breast and it sends a stirring pulse between my legs.

"No bra?" he muses against my lips as he gently pinches my nipple. I whimper out a response as his eyes lock with mine. "Do you ever wear one?" His hand moves down to the waistline of my leggings.

My throat is dry so I swallow. Maybe it's oxygen deprivation from kissing, but my mind is in a haze as I shake my head. My throat tightens before I tell him, "No underwear either," and my lips quirk, playfully.

His smile darkens and he removes his hand from my waist, pulling my coat all the way off and hanging it up.

I suppress a laugh. I'm not sure why. It's just . . . such a gentleman-like gesture for someone who was a second away from shoving that same hand down my pants.

After he hangs up his coat he turns toward me. "What's so funny?" I fight another smile and his eyebrows pinch. He stands a second more, just staring. "Why do you do that?"

My brows furrow. "What?"

It takes him a second longer before he shakes his head and the devious glint in his eye returns. It's the moment that everything else falls out of my head completely because he kisses me again. But this one is deeper, longer, harder.

His hands slide down my waist until they're grabbing my ass before he lifts me. He pulls his mouth from mine for a second, murmuring, "Wrap your legs around me."

Yes. Fucking. Sir.

I do as he says and he carries me—somewhere—I don't know. I'm like Christine in *Phantom of the* Fucking *Opera* right now. Just along for the little cavernous boat ride while some sexy stranger lures me to his lair.

He deposits me on the bed and hovers over me. His smile is soft, and a couple of loose waves fall across his forehead while he traces his thumb along my bottom lip.

"What do you like, Amelia?" he asks, low and husky.

Hearing my name come from his mouth sets something off in me. The sound of his voice is quiet but commanding. It's somehow smooth *and* rough—but hearing my name out loud is a little jarring. Especially like this. I've never given my real name to a guy before.

I grab his shirt and pull his mouth to mine in an effort to drown out the blip of unease. His mouth moves slowly, possessively, and I think I'm quite possibly addicted to his lips.

My need for control has me pushing him onto his back and straddling him. He looks a little surprised by the power play but his hands slide over the sides of my ass and rest at the small dip just above my hips. His fingers tighten around me and a small smirk pulls up my cheek.

I've got a good ass.

This I know. My boobs suck, but the girl downstairs is a ten. "What do you want?" I turn his question around on him and his eyebrows pinch.

"Uhh–I . . . sex—with you?"

Oh this poor man.

The dirty talk leaves something to behold, but there's this deep want in his eyes that's twisting the already tightened coil in my stomach.

"Take off your shirt," he says, his eyes hooded as his iron hands continue to grip my waist.

I pull my shirt up and over my head, tossing it to the floor. When I look back at him, his face is . . . well, I don't know *what* that expression is, but it makes me feel like I'm dancing naked in a field of dandelions.

Sitting up, he discards his shirt and I take a second to appreciate all the cut, lean muscles of his biceps and stomach.

A beautiful man.

His lips press to the valley between my breasts. Keeping one hand planted on my hip, the other one trails its way up my stomach while he slowly kisses from the base of my neck to my breasts where his hand and lips meet.

A small moan escapes me as his mouth closes around my peaked nipple while his hand roughly massages the other one. His tongue alternates between fast and slow, but he's fully suctioned to me and my eyes roll.

He stares up at me, still teasing my nipple. "You like that?"

I tug my lip between my teeth and dip my chin with a nod. Words seem impossible while he's paying this kind of attention to my unimpressive rack.

Suddenly, his grip tightens around my hips and my back meets the mattress before his lips are everywhere. He kisses, licks, and even nips a little as he gets closer to the hem of my leggings.

He stops and peeks back up at me. I'm panting and wild with need. *What is he waiting for?*

I grab his hands and hook them on my leggings, gently starting to wiggle my hips.

Dean chuckles, still looking into my eyes and I lift a shoulder, giving him a tiny smirk. "I thought you needed some help," I sign.

His eyes turn darkly amused, and he pulls my leggings off with the finesse of fucking Houdini before he hooks his arms under my thighs and pulls me to the edge of the mattress.

Instead of diving into me, he gently presses his lips to my inner thigh. "And I thought maybe I'd make you work for it."

Goddamn. Well. I take back what I said about the dirty talk.

But I'm so wound up, I'm already desperate. My hips buck toward his mouth. "Please," I beg.

Dean's fingers find the heat between my legs while his other hand lays flat along my stomach, anchoring me down to the mattress.

"Please what?" he asks, teasing my slit.

I am totally at his mercy. He slides one finger inside of me, but it's not enough. My hips move to create some friction and he withdraws his finger.

I whimper at the lost contact and he chuckles. "So needy."

"Just trying to help you out," I tease.

He rises and leans over me, his fingers meet the apex of my thighs again before he slides two fingers in and immediately finds my spot.

I gasp. He smiles. "Do you think I need assistance, Amelia?"

I'm too wrapped up in what he's doing between my legs to care *what* he calls me right now. My hips grind against his hand and a smug grin tilts his lips. His thumb starts to circle my core and an untamed moan falls from my mouth, quickening his pace.

But I need more.

"Please fuck me," I pant desperately.

Dean growls and covers my mouth with his, again. I hear his pants hit the floor before his fingers withdraw from me. Before I have time to protest, I see him moving to the nightstand and opening the drawer. I'm too enraptured by his impressive length and the muscular globes of his ass to pay attention to what he's doing.

I register him tossing a package to the side and gather that he was grabbing a condom, so I flip to my stomach, slowly raising my ass up.

He hesitates and I peek behind to see him squinting. My lips pinch up on my cheek as I wiggle my hips, taunting him.

He stays still a moment more. His eyes home in on my left ass cheek—the one with a small beauty mark on it—and I arch my back a bit more, silently begging him.

Do it.

His expression darkens before he moves toward me. He rubs my ass once before delivering a firm smack right over the beauty mark and my core tingles as I fall forward with a moan. I prepare myself for another, but instead he straightens me up so that my back is pressed to his chest.

I feel the tip of him settle between me as his thumb hooks my chin and he pulls my face to look at him. "We can do it this way, but eyes on me." His voice is rough and authoritative and I've never been so grateful for my hearing aids.

He slides into me from behind and we share unison moans before my head falls back against his shoulder.

He doesn't stop moving, in fact, he goes deeper but his hand pulls my face back to his. "Eyes on me," he reminds me. "I want to watch those pretty eyes lose their mind."

This is oddly intimate. I like the deep penetration of doggy-style but it's also the least personal position. But this feels *so good*, and watching his dark, handsome features sift between need and desperation isn't half bad either.

His thrusts become harder and faster. He inserts his thumb into my mouth and I nibble on it before sucking it between my lips.

"Fuck," he hisses. The pad of his thumb pushes on my bottom teeth, pulling my jaw down, never ceasing his movements behind me. Noises I didn't even know I was capable of start to spill out and I can feel my eyes turn desperate.

My arm hooks around the back of his neck as he groans, "Fucking beautiful," between his thrusts. "Come for me, baby."

I detonate. My stomach tightens and the deep tickles of my orgasm spiral. Dean's hips move a few more times, burrowing his face into my neck before he growls out his own release.

I can feel his heart beating against my back, and I can feel mine thrumming against his arm, still pressed against my chest, his thumb lazily still resting on my bottom teeth.

We stay still, frozen in our heat for a moment more, before I realize I'm still looking at him.

Jesus.

A few more beats pass before he removes his thumb from my mouth and shudders as he slowly pulls out of me. Now that we're not fucking, the eye contact feels a little weird so I break it, allowing my eyes to scan the room for my shirt.

I find it on the floor at the foot of the bed and move to pick it up. After I shove it over my head, I timidly sign, "Can I use the bathroom?"

He still looks like he's coming back to Earth but he nods. "Yeah, of course. It's right across the hall."

My knees wobble and there's a mighty-fine ache between my legs as I walk to the bathroom. When I come back, Dean is in sweatpants but still hasn't put on a shirt.

Oof!

I mentally pat myself on the back for my over-achievement tonight. I went on a manhunt and bagged me a fucking king. My leggings sit folded on the bed and my mouth quirks, signing, "You folded my leggings."

Dean eyes them, then me. "Are you not supposed to?"

I shrug, signing, "I mean, *I* don't but . . ." My thoughts trail off because I can't seem to concentrate. Not when he's standing there looking like he models men's loungewear.

I clear my throat and pick up the leggings, slipping them back up my legs. Now clothed, we both stand still, unsure what to do from here. In an attempt to fight the awkwardness, I sign, "Well, I'd better go."

"Oh—um," Dean stutters. "You don't have to leave."

It's a polite offer to someone you just wam-bammed, but . . . I've achieved my goal. I achieved it so hard, I'm certain it will be the center of my fantasies for the coming weeks.

Pun intended.

It's kind of bizarre honestly. In the grand scheme of my sexual experiences, what we did was fairly vanilla. There were no kinks or toys but . . . I guess he doesn't need any of that because it still managed to rock my goddamn world.

I almost think about asking for his number but decide I'd rather let the memory live on untainted. I'm starting to think that the "regular" fuck buddy is a mistake—it's the only conclusion I can reach as to why I sought someone out other than Tim tonight. Maybe the consistency I came to appreciate is a little too close to a relationship.

Finally, I shake my head. "I've got a hungry cat at home," I sign, lamely.

He snorts a laugh with a nod and leads me out of the bedroom.

This boy has some manners for being such a stud!

He hung up my coat, folded my leggings. He's walking me to the door.

Following through with the chivalry, he shrugs my coat over my shoulders and we stand in the small entryway. I button up, before I turn back toward him. "Well, uhh . . . thanks," I sign, breathing out a nervous laugh.

Dean laughs and I like *that* sound, too. He shakes his head, signing, "You're thanking me for sex?"

I shrug, awkwardly. "Sure, why not? It was fun and I needed to get out of my head."

What the fuck? Why did I say that?

He chuckles, dipping his chin with a small nod as he signs, "Me too. So . . . thanks."

Our eyes meet again, lingering for a few seconds and the playfulness subsides. His gaze becomes that of quiet intensity and it holds my eyes with his before I blink and break the contact.

"It was nice to meet you," I sign, moving closer to him. "D. Fart."

His grin widens and it's a beautiful sight. I take a mental picture to keep in my back pocket when I need to swoon over something.

"You too, A. Heart."

I almost cave and ask him for his number. I almost kiss his soft, full lips one more time. But instead, I twist the doorknob, and I leave.

chapter seven

dean

My alarm goes off Monday morning and I hit the snooze button before pulling the comforter over my head, breathing deep. As I turn on my pillow, the faint smell of jasmine fills my nose and my eyes open as memories from last night pass through me.

I see her shiny emerald eyes locked with mine. Her plump rosy lips and smooth olive skin. It was so random and abrupt that if the memory wasn't still so vivid and her smell wasn't still fresh on my sheets, I might have thought she was a dream.

Great. And now my dick is hard.

Well . . . harder.

I reluctantly push out of bed and shuffle to the bathroom, groaning a bit as I start the shower. As I brush my teeth, I remember I've got a meeting with the owner of the roastery first thing this morning.

Red Line Roastery was a small operation when I started there five years ago, but it's really grown in the last two years. It's now considered one of Chicago's elite coffee roasting plants and I'm one of four Senior Roasters, which essentially means I'm one of the longest standing employees. Come to think of it, it's just about the *only* consistency I've had in the last eight years.

After my DUI last year, I really thought I might get fired—or at the very least shunned—but the guys all kind of rallied around me, and I'm really fucking grateful that they did. If nothing else, I like that I'm one of the company's "veterans." I feel like it will help as Ava gets older. Maybe I can get a more flexible schedule.

I spit out the toothpaste and my heart drops, suddenly remembering the whole reason I ended up in that bar last night.

Groaning again, I wince at the tightness in my chest. Not just from the reminder of my current predicament, but the deep familiar ache from the cigarettes I smoked.

Fucking idiot.

My phone buzzes on the counter by the sink and I pick it up.

Otis: Congrats on one year!
See you tonight.

Goddammit. I swipe my palm down my face and then scratch the back of my jaw.

A year sober today and I almost blew it.

I drop the phone and then pull my sweats down before stepping into the shower. I turn the knob to make the water even hotter, hoping it will help wash away the smell of stale smoke. Not to mention, the thick coat of shame from walking into a *fucking bar* last night.

I didn't intend on actually drinking. The truth is, I don't really know why I went in there. But it was too close of a call. If I hadn't started talking to Amelia . . .

My stomach twists at the idea, but I lift my chin and let the scalding stream of water run down my face.

You didn't do it.

You're going to the meeting tonight.

You didn't completely fuck it up.

In the midst of my silent pep talk, the memory of the gorgeous stranger passes through me again.

Last night sucked for a multitude of reasons, but getting laid for the first time in a little over a year wasn't one of them.

Not at all.

She was every mind-blowing adjective under the sun. But still, I grab the soap and scrub myself clean. I scrub until my skin feels raw. I wash away my momentary lapse in judgment, which unfortunately includes her, and let it swirl down the drain.

"Dean! Hey man," Dan says, tapping away on his keyboard.

I slide the big wooden door shut and walk to the chair on the other side of his desk. His fingers continue to tap as I sit down, my eyes taking in the industrial aesthetic of his office. The exposed brick walls; the various pictures of Red Line's operation throughout the years.

I moved out to Colorado right after I graduated college. And after a few years out there, I had applied to a few different roasteries all over the country.

I've always loved Chicago but when I left, it felt like the city itself had been tainted. Red Line ended up offering me the most money, so I took it as a sign that it was the right move to come back.

But I never expected to love this place so much. Dan has a real passion for the coffee industry and it's infectious. He finally stops tapping and quickly closes his laptop before he looks back up at me. "Sorry, bean emergency."

I snort a laugh. "It's all good. What's going on?"

He nods, clearing his throat. "Well, it's no secret that we're developing quite the reputation around the city. We're experiencing a major influx of interest from all these restaurateurs—you know, with Chicago being a foodie haven, and all—and I wanted to see what you thought about . . . taking on a new role here?"

My eyebrows hitch. "What kind of role?"

I can't imagine doing anything else. When I first started in the industry, it was intriguing to find out the precise intricacies that go into roasting. It's essentially an art form when it's done properly and I'm finally at a place where it feels like second nature to me.

"I haven't come up with an official title for it yet. But I was thinking of something like a Brand Ambassador. You'd essentially go to all of these high-profile places to meet with the team and sell them on Red Line's product."

Ugh. Sales. I'm pretty sure that's the worst idea ever. I'm not exactly what you'd call a "people person," and I've grown comfortable with being able to zone out in the roasting room.

Dan must read my expression and quickly extends one of his hands out. "Let me rephrase—you wouldn't be blindly visiting these places. It'd be based on inquiries we receive through the website or one of their people directly contacting us for a meeting. I need someone that knows the ins and outs of our operation. Someone that knows coffee like I do."

My weight shifts in my seat, slightly taken aback. "I—uhh . . ." I stutter, before I continue, "I definitely don't know this shit like you do, Dan. You taught me everything I know."

It's true. I was still a punk-ass kid when I moved back here, but Dan took me under his wing. Not only with everything that went into roasting but the value of hard work—showing up—the perseverance it takes to build something from the ground up.

He smiles warmly. "You're the only guy for the job. I can't think of anyone better suited to represent Red Line than you."

I honestly don't know what to say. It feels like so much more than what he's asking.

Dan is fully aware of everything that happened last year. I had to come into *this* office with my tail between my legs and tell him that I'd be on probation for the following year. I had to explain what happened, the community service and random drug tests I'd be subjected to. I had to tell him *everything* and hope he didn't fire me.

And now he's offering me a promotion. Asking me to represent his legacy.

"You're the only guy for the job."

His smile widens. "It comes with a raise," he says, his eyebrows raising.

I snort a laugh and shake my head, unable to understand why he's offering this to me. But he is, and all I can do is extend my hand to shake his before I ask him, "When do I start?"

People are filtering into the community center and for some reason, I feel nervous.

"Is anyone else getting a chip tonight?" Otis signs as we sit.

I shrug, signing, "I don't know. They'll do all the 'accomplishments' at the end."

He nods. I can tell he seems a little jittery too, though I'm not sure why. He glances around the room and I wave my hand low in front of us before I sign, "I told the moderator I'd be interpreting for you," wondering if that's why he seems fidgety.

His mouth tilts. "Thanks, man. But don't worry about that. I just want to be here . . . it's a big night."

My unease thickens and the guilty feeling that's been lingering in the back of my brain all day intensifies.

I haven't mentioned anything about the bomb Marnie dropped on me yesterday or the precarious situation I found myself in last night.

One thing I've come to realize through the clarity of sobriety is how hard it is to rebuild trust once it's been broken. My family has of course been supportive through the whole ordeal, but I also feel like they're waiting on the sidelines for me to slip and fall.

And why wouldn't they? I've given them no reason to believe I can handle my shit.

But . . . I don't know. It just feels like I shouldn't worry them unnecessarily.

"Nothing's been decided yet."

"Let's get started," the moderator says, and I pull in a deep breath, trying to steady myself.

Some part of me feels unworthy of the reason my brother is here with me, but I also think it's because these meetings have been a solitary venture for me up until now.

But then I remember my first meeting a year ago. It's the only other one I didn't go to alone . . .

"Thanks for going with me tonight," I mumbled.

"Of course," Evelyn said, quiet for a few more slow steps before she cleared her throat. I was walking her to the L station. It was the least I could do after she came with me tonight.

But there was this other feeling that I couldn't make sense of . . . this urge to cling.

She had come over earlier that day and we'd laid everything out. Everything that I'd spent the last seven years trying to forget and . . . I don't know. I felt like once she left, I'd actually have to deal with it.

All of it. And I wasn't even sure what it was.

"D-Do you, uhh . . ." she stuttered and then pulled her lips into her mouth.

My eyebrows pinched, glancing over at her. "What?"

She exhaled hard and stopped walking, so I did too, but she kept staring ahead. "Do you think your drinking is—uh . . ." she trailed off, again, glancing down to the ground before peering back up at me. "Do you think it has anything to do with what happened? With us?"

Any relief I felt from our talk earlier solidified in my chest and sunk. It was a fair question to ask given everything that happened between us, but that didn't mean it was something I wanted to answer.

I glanced down the block, trying to stall, like maybe we'd see a natural phenomenon or a naked parade or something. Anything that might allow me to side step her question.

But there was nothing.

It felt like another silent sign from the universe. Another thing to remind me that my time with avoidance and denial was over. There was nothing left.

Just an empty sidewalk.

I breathed deep and then sighed. Finally murmuring a barely audible, "Yes," and turned to look at her.

Her big, hazel eyes were already glassy from the wind but I saw them fill a little more.

My hand instinctively moved to her shoulder, but I pulled it back just as quickly before my chin dropped and I shook my head.

Jesus Christ. It was like I'd forgotten how to be a fucking person.

I timidly looked back up at her. "It's not your fault, Evie. I meant what I said earlier. Nothing that happened between us—then or now—is your fault."

It was important to me that she knew that.

She hesitantly nodded and then started walking again. I followed her, silence hanging for a few steps before I mumbled, "It's my fault. I just . . . lost control. And I have no fucking clue how to get it back," partially to her, but mostly to myself.

I was completely lost.

And truthfully, though I would never say this to her, it was all intensified by the fact that I had a front row seat to watching her move on with my brother. But even that felt like it was just a symptom of something bigger. Like it was another way of life telling me I had to move the hell on.

Not that it didn't hurt.

It hurt a lot.

Otis helped her in a way that I was never able to. I could see it. She was closer to the girl I met almost a decade ago and I knew it was because of him.

As we approached the L station, Evelyn stopped, turning toward me. Her eyes pulled up to mine and the fine lines on her face slowly softened before a small smile tilted on her cheek.

"I know you can do this, Dean," she said. "So does Otis."

I huffed, skeptically, mostly to relieve some tension. Despite trying to accept it, hearing my brother's name from her mouth—the reminder that they were together—was still hard to swallow.

When I looked back up at her, she had this contemplative expression on her face.

Finally, she sighed. "You know what's crazy? The amount of times I've needed to remind myself to breathe when I'm having a panic attack."

My eyebrows pinched, confused. "Did you get high while I used the can after the meeting?"

She laughed, shaking her head. "No–I . . . I just mean . . . it's breathing. It's something humans are innately supposed to do, yet our bodies are capable of forgetting."

I nodded, still unclear of where she was going with this.

"I guess I'm just trying to say . . . you want your control back but, you already have it. You're capable. You just . . . forgot," she shrugged, timidly.

I tried to let her words sink in, but they were stuck somewhere between my ears and my brain, unable to fully immerse themselves into belief.

We stood a moment longer and the clinging feeling from a few minutes ago returned just in time for her to hesitantly close the distance between us and wrap her arms around me.

It took me a couple of seconds to return the embrace, but I did. We stood on the sidewalk hugging before she finally pulled away. The earthy color of her eyes gleamed and a small smile tilted up her cheek. "It's always in our hands, Dean."

"Dean?" My name filters through the memory and I blink at the moderator who is now staring at me. She waves me up toward her and immediately, I want to find the closest hole to crawl into, but Otis claps my shoulder and I peer over at him.

His eyes move toward the woman running the meeting and I slowly stand. As I walk to the woman whose name I don't know, I take the bronze colored chip she's holding and turn it around in my hand.

It's stupid. It's something I barely deserve. But my eyes peek back up to see my brother watching me.

Last night's slip suddenly falls away for the moment. Any future issues that arose yesterday fade into the distance because last year, on this exact day, he could barely look at me. And now he's here, staring back at me with pride.

And *that* actually does feel like an accomplishment.

chapter eight
amelia

D r. G squints at me through my laptop screen. "You *thanked him?*" she signs.

I still don't get why it's so weird. If someone does something nice for you—you thank them. And what's nicer than a mind-blowing orgasm?

Nothing.

Standing by my gratitude, I shrug. "It doesn't matter. It was a one-time thing."

"This is my shocked face," Dr. G signs, deadpanning.

I laugh, nodding. *What can I say? The woman knows me.*

I've become a little less diligent about my sessions with her in the past couple years, but it always feels good to talk to her. It helps that her demeanor is less formal than what I imagine other therapists to be.

Plus, her wife is deaf so she's fluent in ASL.

Sometimes I can't believe we made it past my first session . . .

I was sitting on her big, velvet green chair. I had just turned sixteen and had the personality of a rabid raccoon. She walked in wearing a Nightmare Before Christmas *T-shirt and ripped bell bottom jeans.*

I thought it was cool, but I refused to let her know that so I mumbled, "You don't look like a doctor."

She was on the younger side—maybe mid thirties. Her blond hair was short and choppy and she had a small hoop in her right nostril.

Not cool at all.

She simply smiled and handed me a cell phone. When I stared back at her, confused, she dropped her eyes down to the phone so my eyes followed hers to the screen.

There was a message in the text app, so I opened it.

Dr. Garrison: *Hi Amelia. It's nice to meet you. We're just going to use these until you get more comfortable with sign language. Is that cool?*

I peered back up at her and she wiggled her own phone back at me.

Wally and Doris were trying to teach me ASL, but it seemed like a waste—same with the "doctor" they wanted me to see. It would only be a matter of time before I got moved to another home and all of this shit would be for nothing.

But I'd never had a cell phone before . . . I slowly typed a message back to her.

Me: *This sucks.*

I snort a laugh at the memory.

A real gem, I was.

Dr. G sighs. "Well, we know that 'sex talk' is the easier part of our conversations, but I'm about to bring up the thing you hate."

I groan. There are *so many* things I hate. But there's one thing in particular, and something about her face tells me that's *exactly* what she's about to bring up.

"How long has it been since you've been out to see your mom?" she signs.

Ding, ding, ding.

Maybe *I* should be a therapist. Though, I can't think of a soul alive that should seek me out for life advice.

I squirm a bit in my seat, signing, "I don't know . . . a year, maybe?"

I'm lying. I know it's been exactly thirteen months because I foolishly went out there on Christmas last year, and then cursed myself for not upholding my tradition of watching all the *Harry Potter* movies and eating soup and pie until I passed out.

Dr. G nods, signing, "In your email, you mentioned you were having some flashback episodes again. You want to talk about those?"

Yep. She's right. I hate this.

A groan mixed with a sigh escapes me and I sign, "I don't know. It's just been a while since I had them so it kind of freaked me out."

She nods, quietly studying me. "Do you think it's because it's been so long since you've been there to see her?"

"Why would that matter?"

She shrugs. "It might not. But our subconscious has all sorts of ways of manifesting things. If you're feeling more scared or even guilty for staying away for so long, this could be your mind's way of coping with that."

I consider what she's saying. The whole reason I even started going to see my mother in the first place was in the name of self-preservation.

It helps to make her less of a "monster under the bed" in my mind. The visits are like shining a light under there and seeing that it's just your cat lurking underneath it or something.

I sigh. "So, you think I need to go see her?" The thought fills me with unease even as I mention it.

Dr. G shrugs. "It couldn't hurt."

Yeah, that's where she's wrong. It always fucking hurts.

But at the same time, if it works and the flashbacks ease up then I guess it will have been worth it. I look back up at her, signing, "Fine. I've got some time tomorrow."

It'll suck no matter what, but the less time I have to dread it, the better.

She nods. "Cool. Let's set up a time for early next week, just to check back in."

A couple hours later, I'm on the floor at Luke's house, losing miserably at some video game to my ruthless, six-year-old opponent.

Usually, we'd be working on homework but I'm pretty sure he's going to be in trouble when Annie gets home.

She had a last-minute appointment and texted me asking if I could go pick him up from school and I'll never turn down some extra cash—or the opportunity to hang with my favorite dude. But when I picked him up, the vice principal was with him . . .

Never a good sign.

Since I'm not his mom, she didn't share the details with me, but made sure to let me know they'd be contacting Annie immediately. All Luke would tell me was that he got in a fight, which is what I suspected.

The kid has a temper. I've seen it plenty of times. But I've also seen how bad he feels after. Not that it excuses the behavior, but I don't think the outbursts stem from truly violent urges. To be honest, I think he does a lot of it for attention.

I hear the door open and Luke glances over at me, nervously. I quickly turn off the TV because I definitely shouldn't have rewarded him with video games after whatever happened but . . . this is one of the many reasons why I gave up teacher life.

Annie walks in, quietly seething. All she does is tell Luke to go get his things packed to go to his grandparents' house and he runs up the stairs like the Roadrunner.

My legs wobble as I get up from the floor, while Annie stands at the kitchen island, grasping the counter.

"Did the school call?" I ask.

She nods and turns to the fridge, pulling out a bottle of water, then turns back toward me. "Would you like one?"

I shake my head. "I'm good, thanks."

She pulls off the bottle cap and takes a delicate gulp.

This is a little awkward.

I clear my throat. "Is everything okay?"

She nods, again, less convincingly and takes another sip of water. "I just . . ." she sighs, trailing off for a moment before she adds, "I don't know what to do."

I want to tell her that it's okay. That this is normal. That he's just acting out. I want to tell her all of that and the thing is, I genuinely believe it's all true. But I can also see it won't help her right now. Her eyes look slightly wider than usual. Her shoulder-length blond hair is still tidy, but her posture is sagging and her face looks completely defeated.

This woman is carrying some shit.

She pinches the bridge of her nose, tightly closing her eyes before she shakes her head.

"Look, it's been a while since this happened—" I start but she cuts me off.

"Yeah! I thought that's because we were past it all! I mean hitting, biting, those I guess I could understand, but *punching*?! He's six years old, for Christ's sake!" Her voice rises but she catches herself and lifts the water bottle to her mouth again.

Punching?

I swallow hard, feeling completely unprepared and nowhere near qualified to be giving advice in this situation.

Clearing my throat, I stutter, "Well—uh . . . I mean, his brother *is* ten years older than him. They probably play a little differently. Maybe it's something you can talk to Malcolm about?"

She nods, and I think I see the smallest bit of relief light her eyes. "That's true."

It's funny how the human brain works. And by funny, I mean fucking bizarre. It's like I saw her synapses latch on to the tiniest lifeline. One meager suggestion I tried to give her and she's holding on for dear life.

She nods, again. "Yeah, I'll talk to Malcolm," she reaffirms, and her spine straightens. Luke barrels down the stairs and drops his bag on the floor.

"Let's do this!" he yells.

"Hey!" Annie barks. "You're still in trouble, young man. And your dad is *not* going to be happy about what Mrs. Willer told me today."

Luke deflates and so does my heart a bit. He definitely needs to understand what he did was wrong but . . . *ugh,* I just want to give him a hug. And that's saying something. I'm *not* a hugger.

"Give Miss Amelia a hug goodbye," Annie tells him, like she was reading my mind.

I walk toward him and crouch down, pulling him into me. "You're the smartest boy I know," I tell him, quietly. "And smart boys fight with their brains, not their hands, okay?"

He nods and I pull away, standing back up. My eyebrows pinch when I notice a familiar book cover peeking out from his unzipped duffle bag.

Harry Potter?

He's still a couple years off from being able to actually read it . . .

But then I remember I told him that I always keep a copy with me. Just in case I need to feel better.

I crouch down, pulling him in for another hug.

I fucking love this kid.

My need to slip into a sweet, oblivious slumber will be contingent on two things: one, that I stay as exhausted as I am right now. And two, that if I *do* happen to get a second wind, that the carbo-load I called in at the bar around the corner is enough to push me over the edge.

I need to be well rested to make it through my day tomorrow.

I swear, a single day up there with her takes a year off my life.

Another reason not to go.

As I pull open the door to Barney's, I feel my phone vibrate. I pause just inside the door, and fish it out of my pocket.

Incoming call from Tim.

I consider answering, but I think I'd rather see if I'm up for some sweaty fun *after* I make it through the ring of fire tomorrow.

A *real* reward would be another round with the hot, broody stranger from a few nights ago. I huff, annoyed with myself again for not getting his number before I shove the phone back in my pocket.

When I look back up, my breath catches in my throat and then holds in my chest.

The coffee-colored eyes I was just imagining lock with mine from a table less than a hundred feet away.

Dean?

He's sitting at a table with two other guys and a woman with wavy brown hair sits across from him, her back to me.

Her neck slowly cranes around, looking toward me and my eyes squint.

Is that . . . is that the girl from my class?

chapter nine

dean

This is what it's like to be me.

I swear to God, things cannot just stay where they belong in my world.

Don't get me wrong. Amelia is fucking *mesmerizing*. She looks even more gorgeous now than she did a few nights ago.

At the bar. The one I should have never gone into.

But my gaze lingers on her long, raven hair spilling over her shoulders and her glittering green eyes keep catching the light from the sun pouring in through the window.

Suddenly, my eyes pick up on movement as Evelyn . . . *waves to her?!*

What the fuck?!

My body shifts quickly and Reggie eyes me, sipping from his straw. I've known the guy for nearly a decade—he's Evelyn's best friend— and he always looks like he's up to no good.

Amelia walks toward us and my heart rate increases. I honestly have no idea what the fuck is going on until she gets over to our table and signs, "Evelyn, right?"

Fuck.

Evelyn nods. "And you're Amelia? We have like . . . three classes together!"

Double fuck! Of course they're classmates.

Evelyn introduces her to Otis and I scratch the back of my jaw nervously as Otis squints in my direction.

Goddammit! Between him and *Sir-Slurps-a-Lot* next to me, I'm completely surrounded. My eyes meet Amelia's again and then catch the small glint on her collarbone. I remember that necklace. It's a gold lightning bolt. My mind floats to how it looked along her smooth, sweaty skin.

"Dean?" Evelyn signs.

I blink, and rub my hand down my jaw, thankful I don't feel any drool. "Sorry—what?"

"This is Amelia. She's in my interpreter's program," she signs.

Swallowing, my eyes drift back to Amelia and her lips tilt, a hint of mischief lighting her eyes.

I don't really care to discuss my one-night stand with this company—*or at all*—but my brother, my ex-girlfriend, and the nosy gopher, Reggie, are the last people I want to tell. And it's more complicated than not wanting to share my business. I can't tell them I know her without explaining where we met or why I ended up there in the first place.

I clear my throat, finally signing, "Nice to meet you."

"Likewise," she signs back with the tiniest, subtle lift of her eyebrows and I swear to God, my dick twitches like a puppet on a string.

I shift my weight again, as Evelyn signs something else to her, pulling her attention from me and I release a quiet, dissatisfying exhale.

This is just my fucking luck. I'm at a dinner I didn't want to go to, celebrating something that doesn't feel celebratory, and the gorgeous stranger I hooked up with a few days ago has made a guest appearance—*and she goes to school with Evelyn.*

A tension headache starts to throb across the back of my head and I tilt my chin up before I roll my neck, attempting to loosen the muscles. My eyes flick up to Amelia, again, but she's looking at Evelyn.

Evelyn twists toward Otis signing, "We could do game night!"

I missed something during my mental snafu and my eyebrows pinch as Otis chuckles. "Sure. But are you sure it's a good idea after the last one?"

Evelyn's eyes narrow in his direction before she turns back to Amelia. "See what I mean? I need some backup from these Neanderthals—pissed because they lost to a girl."

"Whoa," Reggie says, then signs. "Not a 'girl.' We lost to *you.* Three times! And you're notoriously terrible at games."

Evelyn's eyes widen, her mouth slacking but the corners tug up her cheeks just a bit. She looks over at Otis as his lips pull back, clenching his teeth, signing, "It did seem suspicious . . . " and she gasps.

She finally glances over at me but I'm still trying to process what's happening. It takes me a couple beats more to eventually cough out a nervous laugh, trying to relieve some tension building in my chest, before I sign, "I mean, none of us has a way to prove it, but we're pretty sure Evelyn cheated at Clue," to Amelia.

"What the fuck?!" Evelyn signs and Amelia laughs.

Looking back at Amelia, Evelyn signs, "They're liars. All of them. Let me grab your number and we'll set something up. Maybe without these assholes."

"Hey," Otis says, pulling Evelyn into him. His thumb brushes her jaw as he pulls her face toward him. "You're marrying this asshole. And he adores you."

Evelyn smiles, pressing her lips to his and my eyes instinctively dart away. Glancing up, I watch Amelia, watching them. There's this soft but intrigued expression on her face and I try to concentrate on *her* instead of my brother and Evelyn.

Watching them be affectionate with each other is still . . . difficult.

When they first got together, I was neck deep in my bullshit and I thought maybe the reason I was so torn up about it was because I wasn't over Evelyn. But after some time, I've come to realize that really, it's just hard to watch my brother love someone I used to love.

And they make it look so easy.

Reggie is saying something to Amelia about the boxing club and I see her smile lifting.

"Yeah, maybe," she signs, then slips her phone back in her pocket, presumably after getting Evelyn's number—though, I wouldn't actually know because it feels like my head is spinning off my shoulders.

"Well, I'm gonna go grab my food. It was nice to meet you guys," she signs. "And Evelyn, I'll see you Friday for Kane's class."

Evelyn rolls her eyes, groaning. "Unfortunately, yes. I swear that class is going to be the death of me."

Amelia's lips quirk at the corner with a small nod, but just as she turns to leave, her eyes meet mine again. Her mouth pulls up a little farther for just a second before she walks away.

My eyes follow her perfect ass, remembering the feeling of it in my hands, the beauty mark I . . .

I blink, realizing I'm staring. When I pull my eyes back to the table, all three of them are staring at me.

Fuck.

"Doin' okay, Helen?" Reggie asks between slurps.

The fucking slurps.

And the bizarre goddamn nickname he gave me back in college that seems to have stuck. I still can't quite remember how it started. Just that there was tequila involved and something about Helen of Troy.

I straighten my shoulders, unwilling to admit to anything. "Aren't you guys gonna be late?"

I only agreed to this "celebratory dinner" because Otis told me it would be quick. I had no idea so much would be packed into ten minutes but . . . at least it killed some time.

And my little indiscretion from the other night is still under wraps.

Reggie picks up his phone, checking the time. "Ugh. He's right. Come on, baby girl." He stands before he adds, "Congrats, Helen," giving me an emphatic kiss on the top of my head.

I chuckle as Evelyn rounds the table. Her eyes seem nervous as they meet mine before she surprises me and she pulls me in for a light hug. My breath catches in my throat and it takes a second for my arm to lightly wrap around her in return.

"We're proud of you, Dean," she says, before pulling back away.

The hug is awkward and the moment following feels the same. I haven't hugged her since . . . well, since about a year ago when she went to my first sober meeting with me.

And it was awkward then, too.

The two of them finish packing up and my eyes zone in on Amelia again as she shoves a slouchy purple beanie over her head before picking up her order off the bar counter and starting toward the door.

"Girl! Wait up!" Reggie squeals and Amelia stops to wait for him with Evelyn in tow. I suddenly feel nervous again, but . . . I don't think she'll say anything to them.

Why would she?

I'm just being paranoid, but it doesn't help when I catch Otis's curious stare from across the table. "You good?" he signs.

I nod on instinct, but there's too much running through my head at the moment for it to be convincing and I think he can tell. I just don't want him to worry. It felt surprisingly good to have him at the meeting on Monday, and I just want to keep *that* feeling.

His confidence.

Deciding to switch the subject, I sign, "I saw your book is killing it, man. Congrats."

He self-published his first book of short stories last spring and I check in on the reviews every once in a while.

"Thanks," he signs, smiling modestly. "I actually have a meeting with a publisher on Friday. If it works out, I'll probably get to release some paperbacks."

I nod, taking a sip of my coffee. "Hell yeah! That's awesome."

My brother is a great fucking writer. I'm not much of a reader myself, but I love his stuff. He always finds a way to make Chicago an honorary character.

My favorite thing he's ever written is about this disgraced architect who built a library and didn't account for the weight of the books, causing it to slowly sink. I think it's based on some old myth at Northwestern of the same nature. But Otis turned it into this compelling tale of a fallen man, lost in one mistake.

And the city of Chicago is ironically what brings him back to life. After he wallows in his self-pity, he still can't fight his passion to build. So he starts creating these small star sculptures just outside the city's most famous landmarks, painting them with different variations of the Chicago flag.

As his notoriety grows, the sculptures get bigger and eventually, they become something people seek out as much as the landmarks themselves.

I fucking love it.

I've read it a lot over the years, which checks out. Seeing as I've been some version of that guy for a long time.

Lost, downtrodden, hopeless.

Sad sack.

I rub a palm down my face, trying not to get too caught up in it and notice Otis's studying eyes on me just as the waitress comes over with the check.

He grabs it quickly, and I sign, "You don't have to do that."

Ignoring me, he sticks his card into the check presenter and hands it back to the waitress before he looks back at me, shrugging. "I want to."

I sigh. "Thanks, O."

His mouth pulls up at the corner, almost in a sympathetic manner. He clearly caught me lost in my thoughts just now, but he's also highly intuitive. I think he can tell that I'm overwhelmed by *something*, but he also knows I don't want to talk about it.

So he doesn't ask. He just sighs, glancing down at the table before he peeks back up at me again. "*This* is something to feel good about, Dean," he signs. "So . . . feel good about it."

chapter ten
amelia

It takes every bit of my self-control to not throw myself out of the car that picked me up from the train station, driving me to my mother's house. Car rides are tough for me as it is, but it feels like every pothole we roll over is sinking my stomach deeper and deeper.

She lives pretty close to the train. If I wasn't sure I'd just run back to the station, I would have walked. But it's also snowing.

I mindlessly run my finger along the line of my zipper on the collar of my coat. Pressing my thumb into the jagged grooves, I push until I feel the imprint of the zipper track on the pad of my thumb before I pull it away.

We quickly pass the line of houses on my old street and the cool, gray tone colors of the overcast day match my mood. Closing my eyes, I run through my prepared reminders.

This will help.

Chef's Kiss Challenge when you get home.

You're strong.

The last thought seems to stutter in my brain and as the car pulls into the driveway, a shaky exhale pushes past my lips.

God. The house looks as shitty as ever.

It's never been *nice,* by any means, but in more recent years it looks condemned. The white paint is chipped and worn, and the covered porch is riddled with dead leaves and dirt. There's also some rogue beer bottles decorating the banister and an ashtray overflowing so much, it might be considered a fire hazard.

That's actually a little surprising. For as much of a wrecking ball as my mom is, she usually keeps it contained *inside* the house.

I swallow, murmuring, "Thanks," as I timidly slide out of the backseat. As I step out of the car, my eyes glance along the street, checking for nosy neighbors out of instinct. My eyes roam to Alex's house at the end of the street. I only lived here until I was ten, but he was my only friend while I was here. And it didn't really count because he was my neighbor. But my breathing settles a bit as I take in the beige, ranch-style home with red shutters and matching door.

All of the homes on the street are pretty modest, but Alex had a cool backyard with a fire pit and a trampoline. Looking at it now, it seems like it belongs somewhere else. Not on this street. Not with *this* house. My eyes pull back to my mother's house and I take a deep breath.

Actually, I think it's this *house that belongs somewhere else.*

I release the breath and slowly walk up the wooden steps. I left my hearing aids at home, but I can feel the rotted wood from the staircase creaking beneath my feet. I never wear the aids when I come here. In the off chance she actually says anything to me, I'd rather not hear it.

As I reach the door, I pull in another deep inhale before I give a quick knock, but then immediately twist the knob.

Pushing the door open, I walk through and try to swallow my unease at the smell—stale and musky. My eyes scan the small foyer before quickly shifting to the living room. The ratty old curtains keep the small bit of daylight out, while one lone lamp provides just the smallest bit of light in the room. A second later, I feel my heart jump in my chest.

I finally see her. Cecilia James, hunched in her chair. Her eyes almost look black but they're glazed over, staring at the TV with a beer can clenched in her fist.

For fuck's sake, it's ten in the morning.

"Hey," I say, flatly.

Her eyes lift to me and I swallow. Her stare is hard—she also looks like she's completely out of it. But dead-eyed or not, a prickly feeling starts to pull up my spine.

I'm not sure which is more alarming: the possibility that she doesn't recognize me, or that she *does* and she's still looking at me like she wants to kill me.

Narrowing my gaze back at her, I peel off my coat.

You're not scared of her.

I sling my coat over the couch, and try to breathe out my unease before starting toward the kitchen. I silently wonder what she thinks when I come up here—*if she even remembers*. Usually I just clean up a bit or make her some food, but she seems so fucking gone, she might just think she went on a drunk cleaning spree when the buzz wears off.

Like I was never here.

As I reach the archway to the kitchen, I choke on a gasp. My eyes flinch and my hand quickly covers my mouth

Jesus Christ.

It's hard to pinpoint *where* the rancid smell is coming from—I'm surrounded! Is it the dried vomit on the floor or the sea of empty cans and bottles scattered across the counter? Maybe it's the trash overflowing and spilling out toward the back door?

Why the fuck do I do this?

This place may look condemned from the outside, but inside is the beating heart of hell.

I step back from the kitchen, still covering my mouth and nose—I'm actually worried I might puke—and I grab onto the edge of the dining room table, trying to steady myself.

I had spent an hour trying to work up the courage to talk to her.

She was in a bad mood—she always was.

She opened the fridge and slammed it shut as I finished up my math homework at the dining room table.

"H-Hey, Mom," I said, quietly.

She stared at me from the kitchen. "Amelia, it's been a long day. Spit out whatever you want to say so I can go relax."

My mom wasn't physically unattractive, but everything about her was ugly. Her eyes were actually a pretty blue-green color but they were lifeless, and the crease between her eyebrows was prominent, probably because she never smiled.

She had long, dark hair that would likely be the envy of lots of women if she took any care of it at all, and her complexion was mostly clear—but flakey, with a gray tinge to it.

I cleared my throat, closing my textbook. "Alex invited me over for dinner. Is it okay if I go?"

She snorted, taking a sip of beer. "The boy down the street?"

I nodded, trying to swallow down my nerves.

Mom never cooked. After a week straight of crackers and cheese, I had finally started to try and teach myself to make some basic things.

I'd have to plan it out and wait for a night where she drank earlier or the few occasions she went to the bar down the street. I'd sneak out to the market, keeping the nonperishables in my room, under the bed.

My eyes nervously looked up to her face again. "His mom is making spaghetti and—"

"We have food here," she cut me off.

We didn't.

"I know," I said quietly, "He's just—He's my friend, and he invited me."

Truth was, a warm, home-cooked meal sounded amazing. And Alex was always really nice to me. We both liked baseball and Harry Potter. `

A humorless laugh erupted from the back of her throat, her eyes narrowing at me. "You don't have to lie, Amelia." She tossed her empty can in the trash, then grabbed a big bottle of clear liquid, pouring it into a cup and taking a long sip. "Alex isn't your friend. He's your neighbor, and he feels sorry for you because you don't have any friends."

I felt the tears biting at the back of my eyes and my throat became tight. "Y-Yes he is. He said I'm the coolest girl he's ever met."

I straightened my spine, willing myself to be powerful. I was so scared of her, but I wanted to fight back. I wanted to prove her wrong. She didn't have any friends. I knew this. And she seemed to hate that I did.

Her eyes narrowed and she stalked toward me. "No. You're an ungrateful little bitch. You think you're better than everyone—including me, my food, my house—but you know what?"

She was so mean—so angry. I could actually feel the fury rolling off of her and I just didn't know where it came from—why I was the enemy.

When I didn't say anything, she grabbed me by the shoulder, hard, pulling me back toward my room. I tried to dip my shoulder to loosen her grip but she just held it tighter and shoved me into my bedroom.

"You don't need dinner. You're looking a little plump, anyway." She slammed the door behind her and I stood, stunned in my room.

Friendless. Fat. Selfish. Bitch.

She called me all of those things within five minutes and they seeped into my skin; they burrowed in my brain and I slumped to the floor. I felt my eyes well up, but I pushed back the tears before they trickled out.

My knees inched up to my chest and I hugged my arms around them, trying to calm myself down.

She was a nasty woman, and her own misery wasn't enough to fill her evil heart. She wanted mine too.

But I wouldn't give it to her.

I wouldn't cry and scream and beg her to let me go or love me.

I just wouldn't care.

"Miserable bitch," I mutter to myself, tossing can after can from the counter into a trash bag.

My heart starts to pound heavily in my chest and my limbs start to shake as I instinctually crush one of the cans in my hand.

Breathe.

My hand moves up to my necklace, pressing down on the end of the bolt so hard that it actually hurts. As soon as the pain registers, I stop, avoiding a puncture to my skin, but still shake out my hand, running my thumb over it, feeling the divot I made in my index finger.

This was a mistake. I stayed away long enough; I should have just pushed through the strange onslaught of memories that found their way back to me.

Coming back here isn't settling anything. *It's amplifying it.* The images, *the fear,* it all feels like it's in surround sound when it just felt like background noise before.

I drop everything, hurrying back to the living room to grab my coat when I suddenly notice the beer she was holding is on the floor, its contents spilled out over the dirty carpet.

Just go.

But I'm an idiot, so of course, I don't. Instead, I walk over to the can and pick it up, using more force than necessary to slam it on the small table by the chair where she's sitting.

"Hey," I bark. "Why don't you go to your room?"

She doesn't even flinch and I swallow hard. Getting a little closer, I tentatively grip her shoulder. "Cecelia." I shake her once and her head slumps forward.

Goddammit.

I crouch down in front of her, pushing back her shoulders so that her head rests against the chair when I suddenly realize . . .

There's no scowl.

She has a permanent furrowed brow, even when she sleeps.

But she actually looks . . . calm. Peaceful.

My eyes move and I see that there's no rise and fall to her chest, and despite her mouth being slacked open, she's . . . she's not breathing.

My throat tightens and I feel my voice creak, "Mom?"

I stand abruptly, my feet stumbling, taking a few steps back, wobbling as I choke on my breath.

Oh my God.

My eyes travel along the route of the train, feeling an odd combination of comfort and detachment as we get farther and farther away from her house. The events of the past couple of hours pass through my mind like the towns we're drifting through.

Her lifeless body, the ambulance, the coroner.

A prickly sensation crawls its way up my neck as I lean my head against the window of the train, the cool surface providing some ease.

I've thought about her death so many times. And never once in any of those imaginings, did I think I'd feel like *this*.

I always thought I'd feel *relieved*.

It's not a loss. A loss would imply that there was the potential for any sort of gain, and the only thing I *gained* from her is issues. *So what the fuck is this?!*

Maybe it's just the finality of it.

Now I'll never know why . . .

I rub the pads of my fingers across my forehead, shaking my head, trying to loosen the stupid thought from my brain.

It doesn't matter.

Even if the bitch had lived for another fifty years I'd probably never know why she hated me and . . . I don't care.

I don't care.

"Who fucking cares?!" I felt my throat rumble from yelling and my breath became heavy in my chest as I panted and glared at Doris.

All she had done was offer to take me to get my haircut for my birthday and I lost my goddamn mind. It was the craziest thing. Somewhere deep inside I knew I was overreacting, but the notion was too distant and it was suffocating below my sudden outburst.

It freaked me out. I didn't lose my temper easily. In fact, I went to such great lengths to avoid anger, I wasn't even sure I was capable of it. But apparently I was, and the realization slowly mutated the emotion into cold, hard panic.

I started to gasp for air. I couldn't fully take a breath and I fell to the armchair in the living room. My fingers dug into the upholstery as I fought back the tears pooling in the corners of my eyes, and Doris moved cautiously toward me.

My body felt like it was winding up and shutting down all at once and I jerked as she placed a gentle hand on my back, lightly rubbing between my shoulder blades.

Out of the corner of my eye, a blurry vision of her chest rising and falling caught my attention. I blinked over at her, meeting her warm, caramel eyes, as she took slow, exaggerated breaths. I watched her mouth make a small O shape any time she exhaled and slowly started to try and match her breathing pattern.

She nodded, encouraging me to keep going, and I began to find some comfort in the consistent circles she was rubbing on my back. It was odd that it soothed me, but I was too grateful for some relief that I couldn't even begin to wonder why.

The longer we sat there breathing together, the worse I felt about yelling at her. I had managed to stay with them for six months, which was a long time by my standards, and I was pretty sure I just blew it.

"I'm so sorry . . ." I choked out, dropping my chin in shame.

I was too much to deal with—I knew that. But this was the first place I lived that I really didn't want to leave. Wally had just started teaching me how to cook and Doris had introduced me to reality TV. They genuinely seemed to like me for some reason, and here I was, acting like an ungrateful brat.

I was an ungrateful brat.

"I-I didn't mean to . . . " I stuttered, pathetically. My breathing was better but it still wasn't totally normal, and Doris shook her head.

"Just breathe, Amelia," she signed.

I nodded and did as she said. I had only started learning sign language a couple of months ago, but I was catching on pretty quickly. It helped that it's all we did at their house, but I was still kind of surprised it was sticking in my stupid fucking brain.

My fingers started to trace the tightly woven zig-zag pattern of the chair and it finally felt like my heartbeat evened back out as I pushed a heavy exhale through my lips. Doris kept her palm against my back and I again found myself comforted by the feeling—the weight of her hand behind me—and I shook my head.

"Please, don't make me leave . . ." I signed, slowly, my heart jumping in my chest.

Her light gray eyebrows flinched, her expression saddening for a few beats, before her warm smile returned. "You think I scare easily or something?"

I could see the playful glint in her eyes but I couldn't match it. "I don't know what happened . . ." I signed honestly.

She stood up and went to the desk, grabbing the legal pad we used when they had something to say that they didn't think I'd understand with ASL.

She sat back down next to me and wrote for a few seconds before she passed me the notepad.

> That, honey, was your pain coming out. And it
> needed to . . . Keep the lesson, but let the rest of
> that shit go. Okay?

As the train pulls into Union Station my eyes stare down at the note, crinkled and worn from years of being shoved into my wallet.

I liked what she wrote. But mostly the tone of it was just so wonderfully Doris: sweet with a heavy dash of sass.

I miss her.

The train pulls to a slow stop in the terminal and I carefully fold the note up and put it back in my wallet, trying to let the memory and Doris's words sink into my current unease.

Blowing out a heavy breath, I stand up and start to walk off the train.

I'll keep Doris . . . but whatever this other shit is has to go.

chapter eleven
dean

I'm slumped on the ground and the rough surface of a brick wall scrapes against the back of my head.

I need to move. I need to get up. But I can't.

My limbs are heavy and my mind feels like it's sinking.

I'm in an alley. It looks kind of familiar, but it's dimly lit and hard to see. People are passing by, paying no mind to the useless lump on the ground.

I glance down at my hand and my eyes study the cuts and bruises on my knuckles. The skin is so torn and the bones are so mangled that it barely looks like a hand. I try to open and close my fingers but I can't.

Distantly, I realize it's my dominant hand. The one I use to draw.

My mind drowns further into the pool of doom as someone stumbles over my foot, extended out in front of me. I feel it twitch, trying to move it, but it doesn't budge.

My head lulls forward again. My vantage point only allows me to see *people from their torsos down as I watch them continue to pass when I sud-denly see her.*

Ava.

She's stumbling past me, toward the busy street and my body twitches.

No.

I need to stop her. I need to move, but it feels like every part of my body has anchors tied to it. Ava wobbles closer and closer to the street and a noise rumbles from me, but I can't seem to make words.

I feel the scratching sensation in my throat. I try to yell, "Help!" But nothing comes out. No one seems to be paying attention. I writhe, but still, I can't move by the time Ava is teetering on the curb.

Suddenly, a woman picks her up, pulling her away from the street. She holds Ava over her shoulder, rubbing her back.

My eyes squint. I still can't make out the woman's features, but she starts to walk toward me. When I see her feet on the ground next to me, my chin lifts and she lowers Ava down.

I finally see sparkly emerald eyes and long raven hair.

Amelia.

She urges Ava toward me, giving me a soft smile before she signs, "What are you doing on the ground?"

The obnoxious sound of my alarm blares and I groan. My eyes flutter rapidly, trying to blink myself into consciousness as I finally see the ceiling fan above my bed.

What the fuck was that?

Another tired groan rumbles in my throat as I sit up, planting my feet on the floor while rubbing my palms up and down my face.

That dream was . . . fucking bizarre. But oddly vivid.

My heart is pounding harder than usual. Shaking my head, it still kind of feels like I'm in the dream as I throw on some clothes for my run.

I'm a runner now.

Well . . . I've *been* running. It was a suggestion Otis gave me at dinner last week. Apparently, it helps "clear his mind."

I think I'd need to run to fucking Zimbabwe to clear my mind at this point.

But I grab my phone and ear buds from the coffee table and start to make my way downstairs.

By some miracle, I've managed to keep myself in decent shape throughout the years, but I never really bought into the "runner's high" my brother always talks about. The first couple days I think the "high" was from oxygen deprivation. But today, I actually find myself craving it—firing up my playlist, getting my heart rate up, the crisp, cold air filling my lungs.

I'm not dreading it.

I grunt. What a thing to strive for in life. *Not dreading it.*

I've been exploring different routes, trying to find one that allows me to zone out. This morning, I head south, keeping a steady pace as "Where Did the Party Go" by Fall Out Boy starts to blare through my ear buds.

Another startling development: I didn't even know I liked pop punk, but it seems to be my preferred workout music.

I'm probably just whiny . . .

About eight minutes into my run, I find myself passing by the bar I wandered into last week—the one where I met Amelia—and I'm reminded, again, of my weird-as-fuck dream.

My pace increases and my feet pound harder into the pavement.

I've found her sliding into my thoughts plenty since the night I met her. An embarrassing amount of times, actually.

I lost an hour or so last night trolling the internet, searching various social media outlets in an attempt to find her somewhere, but I came up completely empty.

Maybe this is just the universe's way of telling me I need to get laid more often.

As I round the corner of the block, a new song starts: "Chelsea Dagger" by The Fratelli's. The cadence of the song increases my pace again. I try to remind myself to slow down. That I need to last another ten minutes without collapsing on the pavement.

But still, I run faster. I run until I'm sprinting.

I think . . . I think I'm dying.

After slugging my way up to the second floor and shoving myself inside my apartment, I still can't catch my breath.

My not-so-ex-smoker lungs are burning as I fall against the door to close it, leaning my head back and gasping for air. Yanking the wire to my ear buds, they pop out and hang from my shirt collar as I drag my feet toward the kitchen and grab a bottle of water from the fridge.

I chug the whole thing, only taking breaks to gulp in some more heavy breaths, before I pull my phone out of my pocket and set it on the counter. After I toss the bottle in the recycling bin, I finally feel like my breathing is returning to normal and I hit the lock button on my phone to check the time.

This is the first week of fully transitioning into my new position and I've got a meeting with some celebrity chef opening a new restaurant in the Loop at noon.

As my eyes peer down at the screen they get distracted by a notification from one of the social media apps I was buzzing around on last night.

Notification: Evelyn Gray has posted a new photo.

Why, phone? I succumbed to the bullshit of trying to stalk someone online *one time* and now you think I need to know about this shit?

I really don't use it. I used to when I was in college, and now it's a fine way to see what everyone's been up to or if anyone's died, but the second they started adding features like "On this day ten years ago," shit, I was out.

Don't need more reminders.

Still, my curiosity piques. Evelyn doesn't seem super active on it either . . .

My fingers tap, already groaning to myself that I let the phone and evil internet win, when her page pops up. The most recent post was made ten minutes ago and it's a selfie of her and my brother outside the Harold Washington Library Center.

Her hazel eyes are barely open, but her smile is beaming as Otis's face nuzzles hers. His mouth is pressed to her cheek but pulled up at the corners as her hand rests against his jaw. My eyes slowly find the caption.

The date is set! June 6th at our favorite place.

The buzz of discomfort twists in my stomach and I quickly put the phone back down. I go to the fridge and grab another water bottle, gulping back some heavy sips.

Why am I letting this bother me? They obviously got engaged with the intention of getting married . . .

I take another sip of water and shake my head.

Of course they're doing it at the fucking library.

So much for a "runner's high." I peel my sweaty shirt off, and start toward the bathroom.

As I crank the knob, I run my hand under the cascade of water pouring out, keeping it there until the temperature becomes lukewarm.

Sometimes I wonder if the reminders of their relationship actually *do* still hurt me, or if—like so many other things in my life—I've allowed the initial shock and despair to somehow take root in my body. To become me.

A habit.

I groan, annoyed by my unexpected, existential meandering before dropping my sweats and stepping inside the shower.

Otis chewed on his lip. "Okay. We can tell them we're going to Mark's house for video games all day. He lives farther away so there's less of a chance they'll drive past his house."

My mouth quirked at the corner, already loving where this was going as I signed, "Why would they drive past his house?"

He rolled his eyes. "I don't know. But they might. And then they won't see our car, so Mark's is good." He nodded, still thinking before he signed, "But maybe we should tell them ahead of time that we might go to that shitty arcade off of State. That way if they do drive past the house and our car isn't there, we have a contingency plan."

A contingency plan . . .

I chuckled, shaking my head as I glanced back up at him.

He was a terrible liar. Like, so bad it was almost impressive. And watching him try to devise a plan to lie to our parents so we could sneak out to Chicago for the day was like watching someone plan a car crash.

After a few rounds of Mario Kart, he had put down the controller and basically called an unofficial meeting about "the plan" and now he was pacing the width of his bedroom while I stayed seated on the edge of the bed, highly amused.

"Dude. If Mom and Dad are doing a drive by—" I snorted a laugh, unable to wrap my head around how ridiculous the idea was, but Otis's eyes widened, waiting for me to continue, so I signed, "Why would we tell them that ahead of time? It's a good excuse to have in our back pocket if they . . . drive by Mark's house." I again suppressed the urge to laugh. "Plus, if we tell them, what's to stop them from driving over to the arcade and checking for our car there?"

He sighed with a nod.

"Look, we're not even really doing anything wrong. Yes, we're lying about where we're going but that's just because Mom would insist that one of them go with us, and we wouldn't blend in with her clutching our arms and pointing at everything."

Otis nodded again before he signed, "Yeah, but what if they find out? They might actually kill us." He still had this guilty look on his face, so I stood up and clapped his shoulder with my palm.

"You worry too much. It'll be fine."

He needed this. He'd had a shitty year and after summer was over, I'd be leaving him to go to college. But it would only be a year until he was out in Chicago with me, and I just wanted him to remember that. I thought sneaking him out there—having the memory—would keep him going in case things got rough next year and I wasn't around.

He released a heavy exhale, not completely rid of his nerves but slightly calmer.

He knew I had his back. He knew I wouldn't let him down.

I huff as I turn off the shower and grab the towel just outside it. Still, my mouth instinctively pulls up at the memory as I dry off.

Our parents *did* manage to find out—*how, I have no fucking clue*—but they did.

I sigh through a chuckle. It was totally worth getting caught. It was an awesome day. I took him to UIC, but we also explored the city, got hot dogs at Portillo's . . . and then I took him to that library.

The one he's marrying Evelyn at.

As I step out of the shower, my hand tightens around the towel at my waist. I walk to the sink and rub the excess water from my hair before I run my hand through the damp stands and then place my palms on the counter.

My fingers curl on the counter top as I try to fight off the low simmering feeling in the pit of my stomach, puffing out a heavy exhale.

It's fine. It's only been a year, and it's getting better.

The small reminders are something I've tried to repeat whenever I start to feel guilty for feeling weird when it comes to the two of them. Because it's not them.

It's me.

I know my feelings for Evelyn aren't there anymore. I know that *this* feeling is just because our history was so tumultuous and open-ended for so long that it's bound to stir up some unease.

I stare back at myself in the mirror. I take in the light, reddish-brown scruff on my face and the fine lines on my forehead under my wavy dark hair.

You've got this, I silently remind myself.

But it doesn't feel affirming. It feels more like I'm *trying* to convince myself.

I think *that's* the thing that's hardest about this is feeling. Like everyone I know is moving forward.

And somehow, I still feel stuck.

chapter twelve
amelia

"Carrots." The word comes out as a statement, but I'm confused as to why Tim brought me a bag of . . . carrots. "Is this a thing now? Any time you come over you bring a vegetable offering?"

Ironically, he's also wearing a hat with a carrot on it. I'm pretty sure it's for some charity his garden contributes to, but it makes me chuckle. His mouth tilts and his gray-blue eyes light deviously from under the hat before he shrugs. "You seemed to . . . *appreciate* the spinach."

Fucking fiend.

Still, I breathe a laugh before I shake my head and toss the bag on the counter.

He pulls off his coat and hat, hanging them by the door, and my stomach tightens as some jitters resurface.

It's been a week of grappling with the aftermath of my mother's death. Not with *grief* per se, but it also hasn't been anything resembling relief, either.

As next-of-kin, I've been bombarded with information I didn't care to know. The autopsy report sites takostubo cardiomyopathy as the cause of death—*whatever the fuck that is*—but it's clear that it was heart-related. I haven't found the will to search for what it is, but I've marveled at the irony of her dying from an organ I could have sworn she didn't have more times than I care to admit.

Either way, I'm in need of some escape.

I can't ignore the small itch in the back of my brain that would have rather hit up Dean but . . . I don't have his number.

Pulling a hand through my hair, I cradle the nape of my neck with my palms, pushing out an exhale. I glance back up at Tim and his eyes scan down my body with dark promise, sending a shiver down my spine.

This is better.

My hook up with Dean was intense. He essentially demanded that I be present. But I need to get lost tonight. I need to be someone else.

Tim closes the distance between us as his eyes pull up to my face and then float down to my chest. He invades my space further until my back meets the wall just beside the breakfast bar and he peeks back up at me, smirking. "Let's play a game," he whispers, planting one of his hands on the wall right beside my head while he runs his fingers over my collar bone, dancing across my necklace.

I swallow. "What kind of game?" My eyes float up to see his burning down at me from a foot above.

His shaggy blond hair falls right above his eyebrows. He cocks one of them before he says, "Cat and mouse." His fingers continue to explore my chest lightly as my eyes ironically drift to my cat curled up on the ottoman, her head buried somewhere beneath her body.

That can't be comfortable.

Tim's fingers hook my chin, pulling my attention back to him.

Right. Focus.

"How do you play?" I finally ask.

He smirks. "You're going to hide. And I'm going to find you. And once I do . . . you'll struggle. Fight me off." He leans into me and I can feel his hardness pressing against my hip. Dipping his chin, he feathers his lips to my quickening pulse before he adds, "But I *will* find you, Cece. And then I'll punish you for trying to get away."

Yes. This is the kind of crooked shit I need right now. I knew I could count on him.

As he pulls away from my neck, his stare becomes hungry, and I feel myself sink into my role.

"Close your eyes," I say, quietly.

He's still slow to move, but eventually he steps back, closing his eyes, and I pad away from him as quietly as I can. My heart starts to race as I slowly push through my bedroom door and tiptoe my way into the closet, keeping the door cracked as I swipe through the clothes and move back against the wall behind them.

The apartment is small, so it won't be hard for him to find me in here. I shift a little farther back, suddenly feeling my ankle brush against the door to the small crawl space in the corner.

My mouth pinches and I tilt my head from behind the clothes to see the sliver of light from the closet door and out into my bedroom. When there's still no sight of him, I crouch down and inch myself into the crawl space, leaving the small door open to keep an eye out.

It's hard to hear anything, so my eyes stare unblinking at the sliver of light—but even that's kind of hard to see through the hanging clothes.

I wait.

And wait.

Crouched, breathing, waiting.

I'm not sure how much time has passed, but it's long enough that my muscles start to ache from trying to stay completely still. My chest is heavy, aching for a deeper breath, but I'm trying to keep them shallow, quiet.

The longer I sit and stare at the door, the faster my heart starts to beat.

Thump. Thump. Thump.

Suddenly, the air starts to feel thick and my heart is crashing against my ribcage like it's trying to bust through my chest. The back of my neck prickles and I finally blink in an attempt to relieve my dry eyes.

Thump. Thump. Thump.

Dark, small, hidden . . .

A whooshing sensation starts in my ears and that's when I realize the excitement has shifted. The pounding in my chest no longer feels anticipatory. It's uneven and shaky and my fingers dig into the dusty floor of the crawl space, feeling the dirt sink beneath my nails.

Why didn't I just hide behind the clothes?

It's a game, I remind myself. He's *meant* to find me. But the longer I stare at that sliver of light, the more it feels like the room is closing in.

The more it feels like . . .

My lungs tighten and my eyes slam shut, but I still don't move.

Just stay quiet. Stay still.

I slowly open my eyes and peek around at the small, dusty space. *Hiding* here *was stupid.* Sure, it's out of sight, but it's also difficult to move in. *I can't see anything,* and it gives me very little chance to defend myself.

"Stupid, stupid, girl."

My breathing becomes frantic at the sound of *her* voice. It's so real that I swear I almost feel her breath on the back of my neck.

The adrenaline has taken over every one of my senses and that's when I see his boots through the crack in the closet door.

A small squeak escapes me and I suck my lips into my mouth, holding my palm over my nose as I try to cover the sound of my ragged breath. My heart pounds so loud and fast that I hold my other palm over my chest, like somehow that will slow it down.

Thump. Thump. Thump. Thump.

All I can see are his boots getting closer . . . closer.

And then there's this moment of dissonant silence. Like your ears ringing after an explosion.

Like the one you get after you've been hit.

My vision tunnels and in an instant, hands are grabbing my arms—hard—and I scream. Even from his crouched position, he yanks me out of the space and we tumble to the closet floor. I scurry away but my muscles are cramped from hiding. I only make it just outside the closet before he's hauling me off the floor.

I yelp, but my throat feels swollen as my eyes meet his, only an inch from his face. A dark, predatory glint heightens in his gaze as he murmurs, "Nice try, Cece," before he backs me up and throws me on the bed.

It's a game. It's a ga—

My reminders cut off as his weight sinks on top of me, suffocating me further, and I writhe beneath him as he slaps his hand over my mouth.

Oh my God!

I breathe deep through my nose, trying to let the small bit of oxygen feed my brain.

He just needs to know that I'm actually scared. He thinks this is part of the game.

But even if I could find the air or the words to say something, his hand is still tightly pressed over my mouth and the realization latches onto my fear. *It feeds it.*

Why did he cover my mouth?

I find enough oxygen to push out some sound, but it's not enough to scream while his other hand yanks down my leggings.

No! No, no, no!

His hand on my mouth slips just a bit and I start to bite down but he quickly jerks it away before securing it harder over my lips. His forearm is pressed over my chest and his weight is so heavy that I can't move my arms.

I can't breathe.

"Such a bad girl, Cece" he rasps, as his fingers move between my legs and I struggle harder against him, trying to clamp my thighs together.

Fuck. Fuck, fuck, fuck.

"And do you know what I do to bad little sluts like you?" His voice is rough as he pries my legs back open and slides a finger into me. An agonized squeal pushes past my lips from behind his hand but he adds another finger, ignoring my protest. "I fuck them till they're good again."

My eyes widen, trying desperately to show him the only way that I can that I'm freaking the fuck out, but he keeps going.

I'm completely pinned beneath him, unable to move as his fingers move harder and faster into me. I use every bit of air I can find to scream from behind his hand but it sounds more like a garbled whimper.

"That's good. Just take it," he rasps.

A roll of nausea turns in my stomach but he gets lost in what he's doing between my legs just enough that his weight shifts. It's *just* enough that I'm able to wiggle my arm out from beneath him and grab a handful of his hair, nearly tearing it from his head, before I bite down on his hand.

He snarls through his teeth but I use all of the adrenaline to kick him off of me completely, propelling him into my dresser.

He coughs from the impact, and my arms shake as I try to push myself up and scoot back against the headboard, putting as much distance as I can between us.

"What the—" he growls, but stops abruptly when he looks at me.

I can feel my teeth chattering, my lips shaking, but I can't do anything to stop it. I even feel tears pooling, but luckily, I somehow swallow them down.

Do not fucking cry.

Tim's eyes widen. "Are you *actually* scared?" He walks toward me, but I flinch and he stops before he slowly sits down at the foot of the bed.

My shoulders are visibly twitching. My abdominal muscles are contracting and releasing so violently that it feels like I might puke, but I manage a frantic nod, swallowing hard.

He stares back at me for a moment longer before he opens his mouth to say something, but then he closes it again. His shoulders shrug and he nervously rubs the back of his head.

I still can't speak, either.

Shock, embarrassment, panic. They've stunned me into silence. My muscles are tight but I pull a shaky hand to my lightning bolt pendant and I fidget it between my fingers before jabbing my thumb into the pointy end over and over again.

The small pinching sensation finally forces a deep breath to drop into my chest and I release the necklace, flicking my index finger over my thumb to soothe it.

I can't look at Tim, but I feel his eyes studying me. My throat feels raw, but after another breath I finally croak, "S-Sorry. I-It's my fault," stuttering, as I continue to try to breathe.

It *is* my fault. I shouldn't have agreed to something like that.

Hiding—*protecting myself* . . . it isn't exciting. Obviously, it's *triggering.*

And of course, *he* has no way of knowing that. We've explored plenty of kinks before, but this was . . . I can't believe I let that happen.

Why have we never come up with a safe word?

Not that it would have done much good with his hand covering my mouth . . .

A cold current runs down my spine, adding to the twitchy nerves still coursing through my body.

"Stupid, stupid girl."

My eyes snap shut as *her* voice filters through my mind again, taunting me while I'm already spiraling.

I feel Tim shift his weight at the edge of the bed, clearing his throat, and my eyes creep back open. He's still watching me cautiously, curiously, and for some reason the stare alone keeps my unease simmering.

I need him to leave.

I don't think I'll be able to fully calm myself back down until he's out of my apartment.

"Sorry . . ." I say again, but my voice cracks, hoarse from screaming and the emotion tightening my throat. "It's . . . been a weird week."

Traumatizing, weird—same difference, right?

His eyebrows pinch, nodding. "Do you wanna talk about it?"

Fuck no. I shake my head immediately. I've never been one for heart-to-hearts, and I'm not about to start now. He sits and stares a moment longer before he stands and I flinch again.

Jesus Christ, Amelia. Shake it off.

He picks up my leggings and hesitantly hands them back to me.

Right. I'm not wearing pants.

Oh my God, this is mortifying.

I just need him to leave. Actually, if demands are a thing, maybe he can just leave Chicago. Forget I ever existed.

After I wiggle back into my leggings, my heart rate slowly starts to even and I finally swallow. "I'll walk you out."

I walk to my bedroom door but he hesitates for a second before he comes to meet me. He shoves his hands in pockets before he says, "Look. I can't leave like this . . . you're upset."

Pretend, Amelia.

"It's nothing," I lie. "I just . . ."

Know your audience, Amelia.

I take another steadying breath and my shoulders drop, once again sinking into my role. "I just . . . want to be the cat next time." I force a smirk, feeling a nervous twitch in my lip, before adding, "Can we try again, some other time?"

The suggestion leaves a bitter taste on my tongue. He stares down at me a second longer before he brushes my hair off my shoulder. I wince, but manage to mask it by making it seem like a shiver as he lifts his thumb to my jaw.

"You can hunt me any day, Cece," he says quietly.

The notion rolls through my stomach but I put every bit of energy I have into pulling my lips up my cheek. "I'll call you."

He bends down and kisses me. *It feels weird.* I've never kissed any-one I didn't want to before and my lips feel tight, closed-off. I'm not enjoying it at all, but I move my lips against his until he hums against my mouth. The vibration makes me pull away, but he runs his thumb along my chin. "Till then," he whispers.

Just get him out of here.

My chest rises, but I keep my mouth closed, pushing as steady of a breath as I can manage through my nose before forcing another smirk.

Something has definitely snapped.

Why else would I be standing outside the community center? Lurking outside a meeting I have no business being at . . .

I'm not in recovery, I don't know anyone here . . . so the only con-clusion I can come to is that something tethering me to the land of sanity has finally been severed.

None of my usual distractions worked after Tim left a little over an hour ago. When I went to the kitchen to try and cook something, I just stood there while Beatrice stared at me from the countertop. Then I tried to get ahead on some schoolwork, but I couldn't concen-trate. Any time I started to try and work on something I kept hearing *her* voice creep into my mind.

I ended up blasting some music to try and drown it out while mindlessly surfing the internet until I found this meeting.

It's an "open meeting." It's something where non-addicts are allowed to attend as long as they don't speak—just listen—which is totally fine with me. Honestly, I kind of wish I had an invisibility cloak right now.

It feels intrusive and maybe it is, but something about coming here felt like it might help.

I'm convinced that the reason that hellish experience with Tim even happened was because *she's* set up camp in my brain.

She's fucking haunting me.

I huff out a breath and finally push through the doors, relieved when I see that there's a decent amount of people in attendance. It'll make it easier to not draw any attention to myself.

My eyes scan the big room, finding a wide variety of men and women, teenagers to elderly, and I'm struck with the thought of how they're all someone's *something.*

Someone's favorite uncle, someone's older brother or younger sister. *Someone's troubled mother.*

They're all *here*, trying to be better for whatever *"someones"* love them.

I didn't think it was possible to feel more out of place, but the reminder somehow makes me feel even more self-conscious.

I'm no one's someone.

My chin drops and my fingers fiddle with my necklace when I suddenly feel eyes on me.

I feel them before I see them, but even the *feeling* is charged, and I slowly lift my chin to turn toward them.

chapter thirteen

dean

No. Fucking. Way.

What is she doing here?

It's not like I've taken the time to really get to know any-one here, but I *know* I would have remembered her . . .

She looks a little different than the two other times I've seen her. She's still the prettiest thing in the goddamn room, but just . . . different. She almost seems . . . *muted* under her vintage Cubs cap and black bomber jacket.

We're staring across the room at each other but neither one of us are moving. For all the time I've spent thinking about her, I still honestly can't believe I'm running into this woman again.

Here, *of all places.*

Eventually, my lips tilt up and I manage to give her a small wave.

Smooth, dipshit.

Her mouth pinches at the corner like she tried to smile back, but it didn't quite reach her eyes. My feet slowly start toward her at a casual pace. As I get closer, I notice the sparkle in her green eyes is missing. They almost resemble a cloudy forest as she peeks up at me from under the bill of her hat.

"Hey," she signs.

My eyebrows draw slightly together, still unable to hide my surprise at seeing her. "Hey–uhh," I sign and then shake my head, trying to gain some composure.

But it's hard. I feel completely blindsided. And even in her understated, casual clothes she's fucking gorgeous. Her face is free of any makeup, but her plump rosy lips have the smallest shine and the apples of her cheeks are just a little pink.

We're again, standing and staring for a few more beats before her eyes drift around the room, nervously, from under her thick lashes. She flicks her gaze back to me and signs, "I should go," then turns on her heel, walking quickly toward the door.

What the—

My feet are moving before I even realize. Just as she pushes out the door, I catch up to her and lightly tap her shoulder.

She yelps, her body jumping as she quickly moves her hand to her mouth. I pull my hand away and step back, trying to give her some space, but the reaction is jarring. It's a pretty common thing to tap someone deaf or hard of hearing to get their attention, and I haven't seen if she's wearing her hearing aids yet.

She stands with her back to me for another moment before I notice her shoulders drop and she turns to face me. There's tension in her jaw and the fine lines between her eyes grow a little deeper.

I'm not sure what brought her here tonight but she seems . . . nervous—*upset*, even. People don't exactly come here for the ambiance so if she's here, it must be for *something.*

And then she saw me.

I push out a heavy exhale, signing, "Don't leave because of me," breathing out a nervous chuckle.

"Oh," she says, a hint of remorse to her tone, before she signs, "No, that's . . . not it." Her eyes float down to the sidewalk and scan it while her feet shuffle. "I'm not . . . I'm not an addict."

I nod, trying to meet her eyes but they seem glued to the ground. Another beat passes before her eyes pull back up to me and I sign, "Do you know someone here?"

She shakes her head through a heavy sigh. "No."

God, she looks so fucking sad that my chest actually aches.

"I don't know anyone and I don't belong in there," she signs. There's a light glassy film over her eyes as they glance back toward the community center. It could be from the wind, but there's a distant sadness to them that suggests otherwise.

"You know *me,*" I offer.

I *need* to be here tonight, but something brought her here too. If she wants to be here, she should stay.

I want her to stay.

Her shoulders ease, only slightly, before her mouth quirks at the corner, signing, "I *do* know you," and the smallest glimmer of amusement dances through her expression.

The night I met her, I noticed a few times where she'd start to smile but then push it down. It makes me think she doesn't give them away easily. So getting even the hint of one now, when she's clearly out-of-sorts, feels like a small victory.

I pull my shoulder back toward the building, silently suggesting we both go inside—ride out our respective storms.

Shoulder to shoulder.

Her eyes drift toward the building, then back to me. "Can I sit with you?"

Good God, her expression is so sweet—asking for something so innocent—I swear, my knees buckle, but I cover it by bouncing in place like I'm trying to stay warm.

Her jasmine scent wafts through the air and infiltrates my senses, making me stare back at her with what I can only imagine is a dopey-looking smile and I nod. It's all I can do before I start to turn, urging her to follow me.

Timidly, she does, and we walk back through the door.

As the meeting comes to a close, people pinch off into small huddles around the room, sipping the complimentary coffee that tastes like plastic. I keep meaning to bring some coffee from Red Line, but it's rare that I *plan* on attending a meeting. I tend to just . . . end up here.

Amelia and I are still in our seats. She's quiet and still, seemingly absorbing the experience.

It's not often as dramatic as it's made to be on TV, but there were some tough stories tonight.

I lightly wave my hand in an attempt to get her attention. I've noticed that she *is* wearing her aids but she's *chosen* to sign all night, so I gather it's how she would prefer to communicate.

"What'd ya think?" I sign.

Her cheeks puff a bit as a small stream of air pushes past her lips and she shrugs. "I don't know."

My brow furrows but I recognize her expression.

Despondent, dazed.

"Do you live nearby?" I sign.

She snorts a laugh and it takes me by surprise, but then I realize it's what she asked *me* the night we met, just before we left together.

"I–uhh—" I shake my head. "Sorry. That's not what I meant. I just meant I can give you a ride home. If you want."

Jesus Christ. It's like I'm trying *to be bad at this.*

I can't help it. She makes me so fucking nervous—but I'm also wildly intrigued. Her demeanor tonight is such a stark contrast to the woman I met just over a week ago at that bar. And I honestly have no idea what would bring someone here who isn't an addict, or here supporting someone else.

Her lips pinch at the corner as her eyes squint before she signs, "You have a *car?* You know we live in Chicago, right?"

A chuckle escapes and I nod. It's a fair judgment.

She sighs a residual laugh before her expression becomes contemplative. "I was just going to walk. It's only about fifteen minutes."

I mask the sting of disappointment with another nod. If a woman would rather walk in the bitter cold for fifteen minutes than take a warm, five-minute car ride, she's not interested.

But she tugs her bottom lip between her teeth and peeks back over at me, signing, "Would you want to walk with me?"

My eyebrows pinch, even more confused.

So it wasn't the me *part of the ride that she didn't want . . .*

My intrigue swells, and now I *know* I'm interested. Because instead of hopping in my warm car and driving home, I sign, "Yes," to a freezing-cold walk with her.

One thing I hate about living here is how much people stress about the wind chill. At a certain point, can't meteorologists just say, *"It's fucking cold. Stay inside if you don't want to feel like the wind is stabbing your face"?*

We've gone an entire block without saying anything, but our stride is slower than I would typically walk with the violent wind pulling around us. As we get farther from the lake, it slows, but it's still steady.

Rounding the street corner, we head south and Amelia finally signs, "Is it rude to ask you why you stopped drinking?"

The question causes me to pause mid-step. Given where we just were, I guess it's a fair thing to ask. And it's not rude, just . . . personal. And it's an answer I don't quite know how to articulate. But as I stare at her, I see the nervous tension that was there earlier, return.

"No . . ." I shake my head, but pause again. My brain tries to muscle up a response as Amelia turns toward me. She stares down at her feet for a second and then tilts her chin back up, releasing a heavy exhale.

"My mom drank," she signs, before her eyes drift back down to the ground.

Oh . . .

My stomach tightens. She seems too somber to assume that this is a resolved issue, but I also notice the past tense of the statement. She fiddles with her necklace, and for some reason her nerves seem to settle something in me. She's not asking to be nosy or intrusive.

She's searching for something.

The wind blows again and we start walking. In the interest of being able to continue the conversation while moving, I clear my throat and tell her, "I stopped drinking because I had to." Her eyebrows thread together, confused, but her eyes are imploring so I continue, "I got a DUI last year. Three months before my daughter was born."

She stops suddenly, like she's hit a wall, her eyes widening. "You're a dad?!"

For some reason, it surprises me she doesn't know that, but then again, how would she?

Despite how many times I've thought about her or replayed our night together, we don't *actually* know each other.

The shock on her face comes back into focus and I quickly nod, starting to walk again. "Yeah. Her name is Ava." An instinctive smile pulls at my lips before I glance over at Amelia, who is matching my slow stride.

"Ava," she muses. "Pretty name."

My smile widens. "Thanks."

A few more steps, a few more quiet seconds. Oddly, the silence doesn't feel awkward this time. It feels like I'm giving my confessions some space—some room to breathe.

"So you quit for your daughter?" she asks.

Something between a sigh and a humorless chuckle pushes past my lips. "Not exactly. I mean, yes. I want to be better for her, but addiction is . . . more complicated than that."

She's quiet for another few steps, her eyebrows furrowing, almost like she's trying to solve a complicated word problem.

I run my teeth over my bottom lip, signing, "It's hard to explain if you've never been in it, but it's just . . . chaos. And you *can't* quit for one single person or circumstance because that would mean you had any sort of control over it. But the nature of addiction is just that. It's a complete *loss* of control."

Jesus Christ. What a thing to tell a woman you're walking home.

I don't know what compelled me to tell her all of that. I haven't even really talked about this with my brother and here I am, word vomiting on the sidewalk next to a beautiful stranger.

My eyes peek over at her, catching her looking over at me. But she doesn't look disgusted or like she's ready to bolt. She just looks . . .

Sad.

It's a heavy sadness, too. The kind that you feel just by seeing it.

I stop walking and so does she, but her eyes are slower to meet mine. When they finally peer up at me, I get momentarily lost in the deep hunter color before I sign, "Are you okay?"

She nods through a swallow. Her eyes float down to the sidewalk again before they pull back up to me, curiously squinting. "What's your last name?"

My neck pulls back a bit, slightly thrown by the subject change and the reminder of again how little we know about each other but I answer her, signing, "Roberts."

Her lips quirk at the corner, pushing the ghost of a smile down. "Ava Roberts," she signs. "Sounds like a classic movie star or something."

I snort a laugh. I love that she asked for *my* last name with a secret motive to learn *Ava's* last name.

"What's yours?" I sign.

Her mouth twists, dropping her gaze from mine again. A few seconds pass while she shuffles her feet. When she finally looks back up at me, her eyes study me a moment longer before she sighs. "James."

chapter fourteen
amelia

This has been a supremely fucked up day.

I won't go as far as to say it's my worst, but *fucked*, nonetheless.

And somehow, I'm back in the presence of Dean.

I can't believe he's a dad.

And an alcoholic . . .

So many red flags, and I didn't see any of them.

Must be a side effect of thinking with your lady bits.

An involuntary laugh pushes past my lips. Because while he may *have* red flags, I *am* the red flag, which isn't so much funny as it is pathetically ironic.

"What's so funny?" Dean signs as we near the steps to my building.

"Nothing," I sign before stopping at the foot of the steps. "This is me."

He glances up for a second, taking in my modest four-story building.

The brick is light, almost a beige color, with bay windows on the street-facing wall and a small patch of grass just beside the steps. It's not impressive by any means, but it's home, and *I'm* proud of it.

Slowly, his chin pulls back to me and his warm, coffee-colored eyes hold mine.

Goddamn, he is fine.

His wavy, windblown hair, his perfectly stubbled jawline. They're just . . . *dreamy as fuck.*

Wave one of those flags over the lady bits, Amelia.

I blink, finally signing, "Thanks for walking me home," still gawking, but if he notices he doesn't make it known.

God. This is so unlike me.

I swear I've been buck-naked and felt less exposed than when he's looking at me like that. It's not even particularly devious or sexual, it's just . . . *charged.*

"Thank you for *letting* me walk you home," he signs, tilting his lips in this sexy way that makes my brain leak out my ears.

Jesus Christ. Get it together, woman.

I'm just fucked up right now. It's been a crazy ass day, on the heels of a bizarre week, and my brain is too exhausted to keep its composure.

But I'm lingering. There's something anchoring me across from him. My instinct is to invite him upstairs, but the memory of what happened just a few hours ago pummels through me, making me wince.

I rub the pads of my fingers over my forehead, breathing deep.

"Hey," he says, quietly. "Are you sure you're okay?"

Fuck.

"Headache," I lie.

"I can—" He stops himself, running his thumb over his lip nervously before he signs, "I can walk you upstairs if you want?"

I shake my head, but there's this sudden blip of intrigue about what it would be like to have some gorgeous man drop me off at my door. Like we were on a date instead of . . .

Whatever this is.

I've never *been* on an actual date, but he seems like the kind of guy that would take a girl somewhere nice. He'd probably pull her chair out for her but also let his hand find the small of her back as she sat down.

He'd tell her how pretty she looked, but spend the night undressing her with his eyes.

Dean shifts his weight, suddenly, knocking me from my reverie.

Go upstairs, Amelia.

As my eyes find his again, my cheeks heat, despite the chill in the air. "Well, goodnight," I sign quickly and move for the door, but he holds out his hand. He doesn't touch me, but it still gets my attention and I stop and turn back to him.

He closes the small bit of distance between us, clearing his throat. "Would—uhh," he stutters, low and gravelly. "Can I ask for your number?"

Oof. His voice. It's as if chocolate had a sound. It's rich and smooth—sweet.

I can almost taste it.

It soothes me just enough to bring back some playfulness. Cocking an eyebrow, I sign, "Didn't your mom ever tell you to not give your number to strangers?"

He chuckles. "I'm pretty sure my mom would smack me over the head for not getting your number the night we met," he signs, then shrugs. "But you're *not* a stranger. You're Amelia James."

I huff, my chin dipping in a slight nod.

Right. Another casualty of my fragile mental state. He knows my full name.

My real name.

I tug my lip between my teeth, unsure if I should cut this strange stream of uncharacteristic honesty off, or let it ride out.

And then his dreamy-ass smile pinches up his cheek.

Damn him.

I groan, rolling my eyes at myself. And maybe him, too.

Seriously, his looks are just obnoxious.

But I fight a smile as I say, "Give me your phone."

I've been staring blankly at the wall behind the professor's head for the whole class. Actually, I've been watching his *shadow* on the wall behind his head for the whole class.

My brain hyper-focused on whether or not I'd be able to follow the lecture by watching his shadow and it has gone about as well as one would think.

Just call me Jon Snow. *I've learned nothing.*

I'm fucking *exhausted.*

Strange, eerie dreams have woken me up every night for the past week or so. And then once I'm awake, I toss and turn from the itchy, unsettling memory of my night with Tim a few nights ago.

I groan involuntarily just as my eyes pick up on the fact that everyone else is packing up their stuff.

Shit. Maybe he'll post the slides . . .

I pull a hand through my hair, huffing a frustrated breath. My attention span is even worse than usual, and it's pretty inconvenient with midterms right around the corner.

I begrudgingly start to pack up my things when I suddenly notice someone standing in front of me.

"Hey," Evelyn signs.

I finish slipping my laptop into my bag and sign, "Hey," back before my eyes pull up to her.

I'm not sure if it's my delirious state, or the fact that this is the first conversation we're having without other distractions but for some reason, I register how pretty she is.

She has big, sparkly, hazel eyes and her long, brown hair is billowy with soft, natural waves over her gray peacoat. But her smile is . . . *luminous.* Something about it is so warm that I actually find my own lips pulling up.

Jesus Christ, she's going to think you're checking her out.

"Got time for that coffee we talked about?" she signs.

My eyebrows pinch. I *don't* remember what she's talking about. A second passes before I remember that she suggested it the night I ran into her at Barney's.

With Dean.

It occurs to me now that I don't actually know *how* they know each other. And she doesn't know that I know *him* outside of our little run in.

I think I've managed to fuck up meeting people . . .

I'm still sitting while she stands in front of my desk, waiting, and I shake my head, trying to refocus. Clearly, I could use some caffeine. Plus, maybe she'll let me borrow her notes since I decided to watch the shadow puppet version of class today.

"Sounds great." I swing my backpack over my shoulder and stand, walking with Evelyn out the door.

It's a short walk to the coffee shop, but it only takes about a minute to kick up my nerves.

This is weird.

I don't know how to act in social situations, period. But one where I've secretly hooked up with her friend is making me feel . . . twitchy.

We stop at the end of the sidewalk, waiting for the crosswalk to change, and I search for some small talk. When my eyes peek across the street to the café, I suddenly remember . . . "Didn't you used to own a coffee shop?"

She bobs in place, her eyebrows pinching. "How did you know that?"

A breath stutters in my chest, immediately feeling awkward as I quickly sign, "You mentioned it in your presentation at the beginning of the semester."

Jesus. She really *is* going to think I'm hitting on her.

But she doesn't look freaked out or anything, she just signs, "Good memory," as a small smile inches up her cheek. "Yeah. Bohemia. I had to close it about a year ago."

Her eyes float down to the sidewalk and there's a small, fleeting expression that passes through her features, but I can't quite place it.

Honestly, it's pretty impressive that she's owned her own business.

By the looks of it, we seem to be the same age and the only thing *I've* ever owned is Beatrice. And I'm pretty sure she would argue that.

"Do you miss it?" I sign, feeling my phone buzz in my pocket.

She nods. "It was a lot of work, though. It's been nice to slow down a bit. And Otis and I set a date for our wedding, so I'm sure that'll keep me busy. *That* and this fucking program."

Right. Her fiancé. He was pretty swoon worthy himself. Come to think of it, Dean and him look incredibly similar. They both have that Disney prince hair and sweet, chestnut eyes.

He said he had a deaf brother . . .

My thoughts are interrupted as the crosswalk changes and we hurry across the street. I take the opportunity to check my phone, my steps slowing when I see two messages from the man himself.

Dean: I don't approve of the name.

An involuntary laugh pushes through my nose. I had saved my name as "Bar Slut" in his phone and he is clearly not amused.

It seemed appropriate to me.

But his second message is what catches my breath in my throat.

Dean: Can I see you again?

We reach the entrance of the coffee shop and my feet come to a stop.

This is the obvious progression of giving someone your number, so I'm not sure why I'm so surprised. Actually, I think *surprised* is the wrong word. But whatever the feeling is, it's similar to it. The idea of seeing him again is making my heart rate pick back up, sending a strange, buzzing sensation through my veins.

Evelyn pulls the door, holding it open for me, and I peer back up at her, suddenly feeling like she somehow knows her friend—*or potentially*—soon-to-be brother-in-law is texting me.

God, I feel like I'm living in a teen drama.

"Will Evelyn find out that her new friend is a slut? Find out next week on Amelia the Slut."

I huff a laugh. *I'd probably watch it.*

Still, I shove my phone back in my pocket without a response and walk through the door.

Later that night, I wrap the last piece of Salmon Wellington and put it in the fridge before I close the door and lean against the cool surface.

My coffee with Evelyn gave me a bit of a second wind, so I got ambitious and did a last minute Chef's Kiss challenge. My eyes scan the countertops and sink, slightly marveling that I finally got everything cleaned up. I usually clean as I go, but it was a fairly technical dish.

Beatrice chooses *that* moment to hop up on the counter and sit, staring at me.

Of course she plops her butt up there right after *I've wiped down the counter.*

She looks pissed, but then again she always does. This time, her face says, *"I know you had fish, bitch."*

I snort a small laugh and reopen the fridge. Unwrapping one of the pieces, I dig inside the puff pastry, pulling out some unseasoned salmon and tossing it in her bowl. She hops off the counter immediately and I chuckle again before my body slumps.

I am wiped.

I slug my way to my bathroom and get ready for bed. By the time I get back into my room, Beatrice is curled up like a croissant on her pillow, already deep in sleep.

It's not the first time I've been jealous of a cat, and I'm certain it will not be the last.

Pulling the duvet up, I slide under and sink into the mattress. After I flick the light off, the heaviness in my eyelids immediately hits me. In a matter of seconds, I release a long exhale, quickly drifting off to sleep.

She seethed from the driver's seat. The anger was so thick, it felt like it was suffocating me, squeezing so tight, I couldn't breathe deep enough.

"I-I'm sorry," I squeaked.

She barked an incredulous laugh as she shook her head. "You are some-thin' else, kid," she grit through her teeth. "Really got everyone feeling sorry for poor little Amelia. I should have just left you there."

I cringed at the harsh tone of her voice—her words. I had run away and tried to wait out the night under the bridge by the old boat casino.

But some lady caught me and told me she had to call the police or my parents. I didn't want to give her my mom's number, but I thought I'd get in even more trouble with the police.

According to Mom, cops don't help.

"Villains in hero's clothing," she always said.

Truthfully, I was kind of surprised that she answered the call at all. Given the state she was in just before I left, I figured she'd be . . . sleeping, already.

"Stupid, stupid, girl," she muttered under her breath.

My eyes clamped shut and I sunk farther into my seat, but her rage—her words—somehow seeped into me and my fists tightened at my side.

"Why didn't you just leave me there?" I mumbled.

"What?" she snapped.

It startled me enough that my eyes reopened, but I didn't repeat myself.

I didn't have to. Her grip clenched on the steering wheel, slightly swerv-ing, making me grab the side of the car door as she scoffed. "Because if I had, the cops would have gotten involved. You would have batted those big eyes and told them some sob story. Getting me in trouble because you're a selfish brat."

She swerved the car again and my hands tightened on the door.

"Can you—slow down?" I stuttered.

She shook her head as another humorless laugh spilled out. "Now she has a problem with the way I'm driving! News flash—you're the reason we're in the car right now."

I'm the reason we're in the car right now.

chapter fifteen

dean

Ava's giggles fill the room as my mom blows raspberries on her belly from the floor in my living room.

"You're so cute, I just need to—" Mom cuts herself off, pressing her mouth to Ava's stomach before the fart sound erupts, spurring Ava's laughter to continue and my dad, Otis, and I chuckle from various seats around the room.

My parents insisted on coming over today to spend some time with Ava, and I invited Otis for backup. Not that I don't love them, because I do. But it's nice to have someone to share the parental in-quisition with. Especially when my life has been . . . *precarious* at best lately.

Otis has taken the brunt of it so far with questions about his book before Dad shifts to me and signs, "How's the new job?"

I shrug, signing, "It's more money and less work. So, good," I chuckle.

He nods as Ava finally wiggles away from Mom, standing on wobbly feet and walking to me. I scoop her up, peppering some kisses on her cheek and neck before bouncing her on my knee.

"I can't believe she'll be a whole year old in a couple of months," Mom signs.

I push her brown curls out of her eyes and my lips pull up.

I can't either.

It's such a strange combination of feeling like yesterday *and* another lifetime ago all wrapped into one overwhelming emotion.

Luckily, the feeling is given almost no time to linger before Ava is climbing up my body. I lean forward as she folds over my shoulder and then I tickle her sides, making her laugh again.

Otis signs, "She's really living up to her namesake, huh?" chuckling, himself.

My lips quirk at the corner at the reference to her name sign.

A. Laugh.

She's always been a happy baby, but Otis only gave her the name sign a few months ago. Name signs can be anything—a physical feature, a personality trait—but Otis always prefers the latter. He gave it to her because when he was reading one of her books to her, he was signing through the storytelling and she giggled so hard that she farted.

He said since I was *D. Fart,* it seemed appropriate.

Asshole.

Still, I breathe a laugh just as Mom signs, "How's Marnie doing?"

Luckily, Ava's spider monkey movement on me is able to hide my unease at the mention of my ex-wife. She still hasn't mentioned anything about her potential move since a couple of weeks ago, but something tells me that has more to do with *my* reaction than it does with her reconsidering it.

"Fine," I answer, simply.

"Is she still dating that guy . . . what was his name?" she signs toward my dad, who shrugs.

Jesus. Leave it to my mom to get right into it. She claims it's not "nosy" when *she* asks this kind of shit—apparently since she birthed us, she owns the rights to all information, indefinitely.

"His name is Shaun, and yes, they're still together," I sign.

I pry Ava off of me, putting her back down on the floor, and she promptly finds the next lap to climb into as Mom signs, "When are you going to get back out there, huh?"

"Jesus, Gloria, give the kid a minute," Dad signs, slightly scolding.

Her furrowed brow only lasts a second before she shrugs. "I'm just saying! Hot single dads are an entire trope in romance books. Better get on it before you're old and fat. Though, I don't think either of you boys need to worry about losing your hair."

Otis scoffs, signing, "Mom, don't say 'hot,'" then helps Ava onto his lap.

Mom laughs but then quickly turns to Otis, emphatically signing, "Oh! Did Evelyn show you the tux I found for you?!"

It's small, but I notice his eyes flick to me before he looks back at Mom. His hands are occupied, holding back Ava's grabby fingers, so he says, "Yeah, she showed me. But I don't think it's gonna be super formal."

Mom gasps. "Otis Eugene Roberts! It's a wedding! It's formal by definition!"

"Eugene?" he asks, breathing a laugh.

We don't actually have middle names, for no other reason other than Mom didn't feel like giving them to us, but she always inserts a random one when she deems it appropriate.

She shrugs. "It's better than Eleanor."

We all laugh. "Eleanor" was my most recent middle name. And luckily, her small outburst was enough to kill the slight tension that came with the mention of the wedding.

It's the only bit of awkwardness that happens before we spend the next hour or so leisurely catching up. Dad tells us about the storm that almost took out our treehouse, but luckily, it's still standing.

Stupid as it is, I'm relieved to hear it. That treehouse was Otis and my fortress growing up. We'd spend hours up there—even when we were teenagers. He'd write, I'd draw—there were even a few times that I got him to drink up there with me.

It was our safe haven, and I really hope that when Ava gets older she gets to use it too.

My nose presses down into her hair. She fell asleep on me about ten minutes ago, just as Mom and Dad started packing up to leave, but of course they're lingering a bit. Mom brought some food that she's just finished putting away before they finally make their way to the door.

I give them a quick wave as I stand to go put Ava in her room. I love holding her while she sleeps, but she'll get a better nap if she's in the crib and it'd be great if I didn't hand off a cranky baby to Marnie.

After she's down, I walk back into the living room and see Otis sitting on the couch with a Nintendo controller in his hand. My eyes drift to the TV to see he's got Mario Kart cued up before I look back at him.

An involuntary *"uhh"* sound escapes, as my mouth tilts, signing, "Marnie's going to be here soon."

Otis blinks back at me before he shrugs. "Oh, okay. So you forfeit?" His eyes catch a glint of challenge and he smiles, smugly.

Damn him.

I scoot next to him on the couch, grabbing a controller, then sign, "No crying when I beat your ass. There's a baby sleeping in the other room."

He snorts a laugh, satisfied with himself. "Right. Who's the one who broke a controller?"

My eyes roll, but it's true, unfortunately.

Still, we play a few races. And just like when we were kids, we waste no opportunity to try and annihilate each other with items. I swear, we barely pay attention to the race. It's all about hitting each other with shell bombs or placing bananas directly into each other's path—knocking each other off the road.

But it's fucking fun.

By the end of the fourth race, we're both cracking up before we put the controllers down.

"Okay, we're definitely going to wake her up," I sign, still laughing.

Otis nods, coughing out a residual laugh of his own. As the moment settles, his eyes nervously meet mine and then pull away. He does it a few more times before I finally sign, "Spit it out."

My brother's poker face is nonexistent. When he has something he wants to talk about, there's absolutely no hiding it, and I have a feeling I already know what it is.

"So you heard about the wedding?" he signs.

Not from you, is my initial thought.

But honestly, I know why he didn't tell me. He doesn't know how to navigate this weird-ass situation any better than I do but . . . I don't know. Something about him *not* telling me just reinforces how tangled this whole thing is.

In an attempt to avoid the awkwardness, I sign, "Yeah, man. That's usually what happens when people get engaged."

He rolls his eyes but the corner of his mouth pinches up. "Dick."

I shrug through a small laugh and he meets my eyes again. He runs his teeth along his bottom lip before he signs, "Well, like I was telling Mom and Dad, it's going to be a small thing. We're doing it at the library."

I know. But again, I don't draw attention to it as he shifts his weight nervously.

"It's just going to be family and a few friends. Mary's going to officiate," he signs.

I'm pretty sure Mary hates me. She used to work at Evelyn's coffee shop and Red Line was her coffee bean provider. Any time I'd come in to drop off the order, I'd usually find Mary scowling at me from behind the register. There were even a few occasions where I'd go to the bathroom and when I'd come back, a coffee that Evelyn made me would be mysteriously gone.

But I'm trying to be supportive. Maybe part of the weirdness surrounding all of this isn't just from the fact that he's marrying my ex, but because we tiptoe around the subject so much. Maybe talking about it—*normalizing it*—will help.

I don't really know what to say, though, so I sign, "That's great," and then pick up my phone to check the baby monitor app. I don't hear anything that would make me think Ava's waking up, but it's as good of a distraction as any to give myself a breather.

After seeing Ava still sound asleep in her crib, my eyes pull back up to Otis.

He clears his throat, then signs, "Anyway, we're not doing the wedding party thing, but Evelyn was going to ask Reggie to stand up there with her and I was thinking . . . you know, if you're okay with it . . . that maybe you and Ava could stand with me."

Oh . . .

I wasn't sure where this conversation was going—mostly I thought it was just to acknowledge the elephant in the room—but I can't hide my surprise that he's actually asking me to stand by his side at the wedding. Not just because of my history with Evelyn, but because at this time last year, we were barely speaking.

Emotion itches my throat but I swallow it down. Otis stares back at me expectantly before I clap my hand over his shoulder and give it a firm shake. "Of course, man. We'd love to."

It's only been a couple hours since Marnie picked up Ava but I've been buzzing with nervous energy ever since. She again made no mention of the move, and part of me is afraid to bring it up—like maybe somehow she forgot, and my mentioning it will remind her. But I know that's fucking stupid and now I'm stewing in another anxiety pool.

Pulling my phone out of my pocket, I shoot her a text, asking if we can talk next time I pick up Ava and then I slump onto the couch. My head leans back, tilting my chin up toward the ceiling and I release a heavy exhale.

This is good. If I make a plan to talk to her, then I can't chicken out next time.

I swallow and lean forward, resting my elbows on my knees. This is the exact kind of thing I would have fought endlessly to keep hidden away in the dark back when I was drinking. I would have denied,

denied, denied and then drank till I couldn't see straight when the denial weakened.

My phone buzzes and I quickly pick it up, but my eyebrows pinch when I look at the screen.

Amelia: Hey.

My eyes stare at the phone like I'm trying to dissect a secret code or something. But I'm surprised to see a message from her. She never answered me back a few days ago.

Me: Hey. How's it going?

Amelia: Okay. Wanna hang?

I snort a laugh. It's hard to decipher the tone of a text message but her messages seem so clipped that it's kind of amusing.

Me: What'd you have in mind?

Three little dots appear and then disappear before a message comes through.

Amelia: I'm making dinner.

Good Christ. Trying to get a read on this woman is impossible. Is she *telling* me that she's making dinner or is she *inviting* me over for dinner?

I'm about to call her but then realize she might not have her hearing aids in. My thumb hovers over the video chat button and I must have a slight brain aneurysm because for some reason, I click it.

Oh shit.

Immediate regret drops the phone from my hands and it slips between the cushions. I dig my hand in between them and when I finally fish the phone out, I see Amelia's gorgeous green eyes squinting back at me.

"Hey, sorry," I sign, awkwardly. "My phone fell between the cushions—must have accidentally called."

Fucking idiot. You just told her your couch butt-dialed her.

Her eyebrows pinch deeper but a curious smirk inches up her cheek.

I clear my throat, signing, "What are you making?" while simultaneously trying to swallow my nerves.

Her long dark hair is pulled up in a full, messy ponytail and she's wearing a dark purple tank top while her lightning necklace lies delicately across her collar bone.

I wonder if she always wears it . . .

"Chili," she signs. "And cornbread pudding."

Well, that sounds great.

I nod, my eyes falling to her apron and goddamn. *It's so fucking cute.* It's a mustard yellow color with two pockets—a small, embroidered brown heart on each of them.

And the way it hugs her waist . . .

Huh. Never thought that'd be a turn on but, we learn new things about ourselves every day, I guess. Plus, I'm pretty sure this woman could wear a garbage bag and still look like a knock-out.

Another moment passes before she signs, "Well? Are you coming over for dinner?"

The same swell from the other night comes back—the one that

happened when she asked if she could sit with me. I'm not sure why she ignored me a few days ago but . . . I definitely want to go over there.

"Give me twenty minutes," I sign.

I pull up to her block seventeen minutes later and take a quick scan of the street. It's surprisingly calm for how close she is to Wrigley Field. I push out a breath before hopping out of my truck and walking toward her building.

As I make my way up to the entrance, I notice the building doesn't require a security code or granted access, so I open the door.

Jesus—anyone can walk in here.

I roll my eyes as I start up the steps, irritated that even *internally* I sound like an old man. She texted me before I left, letting me know she's in apartment 209, so I step onto the landing of the second floor and walk to the end of the hall before I see her door.

But suddenly, my nerves start to surface. The promise of a distraction from my neurosis over Marnie and the excitement over seeing Amelia again had me moving over here without a second thought.

But now . . .

I shake my head, taking a deep breath. My hand lifts to knock, but then I realize she might not be wearing her aids, so I send her a text to let her know I'm here. Then I shove my hands in my coat pockets and rock on my feet while I wait.

A moment later, the door unlatches. A wriggling sound of wood-against-wood screeches from the top corner of the door and my eyes peek up, widening, just as it's unevenly yanked back.

My face twists, mildly horrified at the sound and state of her door, before my eyes drift back down to see Amelia standing in front of me. She looks beautiful as ever, completely unfazed that she just had to man-handle her door open, signing a casual, "Hey."

Her bright green eyes hypnotize me for a moment before I blink and shake my head, letting a small laugh push past my lips. "That might be a fire hazard." I shift my eyes toward the door and she laughs.

Shrugging, she signs, "We have an understanding," before she moves aside to let me in.

I walk through the doorway and into a small space with two closets before turning into the living room.

There's multiple strings of twinkly lights hanging over her desk in the corner and a series of pictures capturing lightning that hang behind it. She has a big arm chair in front of her TV with a purple crocheted blanket draped over it.

Cozy.

When I turn back to her, she holds her hand out, signing, "I can take your coat."

I shrug it off and hand it to her, my lips tilting as she takes it from me and I again get lost in watching her.

She's just . . . so pretty.

Jesus Christ. I feel like a fucking teenager.

I inhale deep and my nostrils flare at the sudden, divine invasion of my nose. "Whoa. It smells amazing in here."

Her mouth pinches at the corner, signing, "It's all done. Just sitting in the slow cooker."

I follow her over to the small breakfast bar and she rounds the half wall, walking into the kitchen. She scoops some chili into two bowls before taking a spoonful from one. Lifting it to her lips, she tastes it, then pulls a spice off the rack and puts a dash in each serving.

When she pulls a small jar out, as soon as she pops the top off, I instantly recognize the smell.

My brows furrow. "Coffee?"

Amelia smirks, sprinkling a bit into each of the bowls before she plops a scoop of corn pudding on some small plates and slides them toward me on the other side of the breakfast bar.

"It's the special ingredient," she signs, and then walks back around the small wall. "It's an ongoing challenge I have with myself. If I'm making something I've cooked before, I have to add something new—something that makes it unique. Slow-cooking it with finely ground coffee is supposed to enhance the flavors of the vegetables. I think it adds some richness to it, too."

And my dick just got hard watching her describe soup.

I shift in my seat, trying to be discreet, as she moves next to me. Once she's in her chair, she looks over at me and then eyes the food. "Try it!"

I chuckle, but *damn*—it really does smell incredible.

Scooping some into my spoon, I give it a quick blow before tasting it. *God. Damn.*

I'm far from a food critic, but it's fucking amazing. It's smoky and rich—the mix of flavors actually sends a chill down my spine. I take another bite, not bothering to blow on it this time and groan, signing, "So good," as I take a bite of the corn pudding.

Amelia's smile visibly brightens and it's the first time she doesn't seem to try and suppress it.

She wiggles in her seat before she picks up her spoon and tries it for herself. Her eyes close for just a second and she breathes a little deeper before she gives a small nod. "Not bad."

My eyes widen. *"Not bad?!* It might be the best thing I've ever had."

She picks up her glass of water, breathing a laugh as she takes a sip. "It's just soup," she signs. "You're an easy audience."

I shrug, taking another bite, suppressing another groan. "How'd you learn to cook?"

She twists the rotating chair from side to side. Her eyes fill with a distant emotion for just a second before she signs, "My friend taught me."

We settle into a charged, but comfortable silence. Honestly, watching her eat is an experience.

She takes small sniffs every few bites and her head tilts with a soft appreciation every once in a while. Her shoulders sink with her last bite as she slumps into her seat before she rubs her stomach. The purple tank top she's wearing has wiggled its way above her belly button and something about watching her hand move across her skin makes me want to replace it with my hand.

Oh my God. Focus on something else.

"Are you a chef?" I sign, realizing I don't actually know what she does for a living.

She snorts a laugh and shakes her head. "No. I mean, I cook on Saturdays over at the women's shelter off Sheridan, but to call me a 'chef' would be a gross embellishment.

"No. I used to be a preschool teacher and now I nanny a few times a week—but I'm mostly focusing on school right now." I nod as she shifts in her seat before she signs, "What do you do?"

"I work at Red Line Roasters," I sign. "I was one of the head roasters until a couple of weeks ago. Now I'm scouting retailers and restaurants that may want to carry our coffee."

Her eyebrows perk up through a small nod. She stares at her empty bowl for a few seconds before her mouth tilts up her cheek. "So . . . you're a coffee guy . . . what'd you think of the special ingredient?"

I smile and drop my chin before glancing back up at her. Her eyes look curious, darkly playful, and my stomach stirs again.

Her eyes fall to my mouth and I run my teeth along my bottom lip, signing, "It was fucking amazing. Thank you."

Her eyes stay locked with mine as she stands up and takes a step toward me. She glances down between us before she meets my eyes again. Her jasmine smell mixes with the smoky scent still lingering from the chili, surrounding me as I swallow, and she timidly takes my hand. Slowly, she rubs it along the gap between her shirt and jeans, right over her belly button.

I remember my urge to do exactly this just a few minutes ago and my lips quirk at the corner.

I didn't necessarily come over with the intention of doing this with her again, but the look in her eyes says it's the *exact* reason she invited me over and I am more than happy to oblige.

Her hand continues to move mine along her stomach as she signs, "I mean, if you want to thank me," before her eyes flick down to my hand. She slides it just a little farther down so my fingertips dip into the hemline of her pants.

Game on.

chapter sixteen
amelia

Oh my God. The way he's looking at me . . .

He stands suddenly, keeping his hand in place but now I'm forced to look up at him.

He really is such a beautiful man. A rogue wave from his dark hair falls to his forehead and I'm already aching to feel his stubbled jaw run across my skin as he leans down and brushes his lips against my neck.

"Dinner," he murmurs against my skin, "was delicious." He nibbles on my ear, making my eyes roll before he slowly works his way to my mouth.

I didn't *have* to wear my hearing aids since I can sign with him—but *this* is the exact reason I put them on.

I want to hear him.

I've also never cooked for a guy before, so I've never been in a position where he's complimenting my food while simultaneously working me up—*but I am fucking here for it.*

When his lips take mine, he groans. It's almost pained, like he's been holding it in for years, and it sends a jolt of excitement straight to my core.

Our mouths move slowly, but desperately against each other. I tug his bottom lip between my teeth and he holds the nape of my neck as his tongue moves possessively against mine, making my knees shake as his fingers move to unbutton my pants. His eyes peer down at me as he pulls down the zipper and steps back just a little.

His smile darkens. "Strip."

I somehow straighten up, attempting to resculpt myself from the putty he turned me into with his mouth and I match his expression, signing, "Make me," with a challenging grin.

It was an impulsive statement, but my breath suddenly catches as I remember Tim's heavy weight on top of me, forcing me down on my bed. The unease thickens when Dean's eyes lose their amusement and his mouth flattens into a tight line. My heart stutters in my chest, but his strong hands grip my ass over my jeans, making me gasp.

"I like my women willing," he rasps, reigniting the buzz of arousal that was coursing through me. His dark, brown eyes burn as his nose grazes mine and he whispers, "So if you want me to thank you, I suggest you take your fucking clothes off."

The quiet command sends a pulse between my thighs and it chases away all reservation. His ability to dominate while still giving me the control is . . .

Fucking hot.

"Yes, sir," I tease and his expression darkens.

The excitement stirs through me as I push down my smile, hooking my thumbs into the waistline of my jeans and wiggling them slowly down over my ass.

Dean watches me with lustful awe, his eyes never leaving mine as he mutters, "Shirt too," and I fight another smile.

Someone's getting bossy.

Once I'm completely naked, his eyes rake over my body like he's memorizing every dip and curve, sending a shiver through me as he sinks to his knees.

Fuck yes.

Suddenly, I catch the sight of us in my full-length mirror directly across from the breakfast bar and my eyebrows thread together. I step to the side before Dean's eyebrows pinch, craning his neck around and noticing the mirror. He's facing away from me, but I see his reflection as his lips tilt deviously and he turns back toward me.

He grabs the meatiest part of my thigh and pulls me back in front of him—back in front of the mirror. When I look down, his primal expression is still in place and the coil in my stomach tightens.

"Watch me worship you," he says through a hoarse whisper.

Holy fuck.

It's the last thing he says before he dives between my legs.

"Oh, shit!" I gasp, clutching onto the small sliver of counter to my sides.

Dean doesn't miss a beat. He guides my leg over his shoulder while his mouth works me deeper and harder, driving me toward insanity with his tongue.

It takes him no time to work into a rhythm—*licking, sucking, nibbling*—completely devouring me. My eyes clamp shut, overwhelmed with how good it feels, before they slowly flutter open again to find the mirror, and a loud, unbridled moan pushes past my lips at the sight.

It's untamed. A fully clothed, gorgeous man is kneeling at my feet and eating me out like an animal on the fucking floor.

"So, good." His muffled groan fuels me just as he adds his fingers to the delicious torture and I start to grind against him.

More. I need more.

"Please," I whisper, breathlessly.

His tongue slows, but it swirls my core, just once, before he pulls his mouth away. "Please what?" His fingering is torturously slow. He's still got my leg hooked over his shoulder, fully exposing me. I feel his breath on my heat, watching in fascination as I lose my goddamn mind. "I'll give you whatever you want, baby. But you've gotta ask for it."

I moan and my eyes roll back, my hips rocking into his hand like a proper slut. I can't remember my own name right now, let alone conjure up a response.

Suddenly, he stands, moving behind me. Before I have time to protest, he plants one, calloused hand on my hip, while his other hand resumes its place between my legs, his fingers teasing my slit.

"Look," he whispers, roughly in my ear.

My eyes pull up, seeing us again in the mirror and my body slumps against his chest, my gaze meeting his in the reflection. His lips trail down my neck, sending a wave of goosebumps in their wake and I get lost in watching us.

I feel like a voyeur. *Me, watching him, watching me.*

His stare is intense but somehow soft—kind of like his voice—and I whimper, "Please, give me more. Please."

God. I can't even mask the breathy desperation in my voice. I've played the part of "needy girl" before, but I *feel* it right now.

Enthralled, wanting, lost.

He groans into the crook of my neck. "So sweet," he mumbles between kisses to my shoulder blade. His fingers pump me a couple more times before he pulls them away. I whine at the loss, but he cuts it off by shoving them in my mouth.

Jesus fuck.

Still, my lips respond. I suck on his fingers and he watches. I moan around them at the sight of the desire pouring from every bit of his stare and he rasps, "Keep touching yourself."

It's like I'm fucking hypnotized. My hand moves on its own accord, replacing his between my legs. I start to rub myself and he pulls his fingers from my mouth, undressing behind me, but his eyes stay locked with mine while he unbuttons his shirt.

This is so . . . erotic. It's so different from what I'm used to—and my hand slows the more naked he becomes. My eyes trace all of the firm, cut lines of his biceps, his abs, but my ogling is halted when I catch his smug grin in the mirror.

"Why'd you stop?" he asks.

It's then that I realize I'm no longer touching myself. I'm just staring at his reflection in the mirror—taking in his rugged, masculine beauty.

I gasp when the heat of his chest meets my back, feeling his hardness press into me. "On your knees, please." The rough edge to his voice tickles down my spine as he kisses my neck again. I start to turn around and lower myself, but he stops me.

He twists me back so that I'm facing the mirror again and gently pushes on my shoulder so that I sink to my knees. He follows behind me, tearing a condom open with his teeth and *fuck* if that doesn't turn me on.

He situates himself between my legs from behind. "I think you like watching . . . " His voice remains breathy, but low, swirling the heat between my legs and I nod.

Because I *do* like this. It's a different kind of escape. One I've never had before.

Dean smirks again and pulls my waist back to him. My hands use his thighs to hoist myself up before I lower myself back down, feeling him slowly fill me.

"Ohh—" I moan, my eyes closing as I hook my arm around to the back of his neck, rocking my body with his as he thrusts into me, slowly.

He groans, burying his face in my hair before he rasps, "Open your eyes." And because I'm under his spell, lost in an oblivion I never want to leave, I do. My eyes open again and meet his through the mirror while his hips keep their slow and steady motion. "You take it so good, baby."

Fucking hell. His praise talk is unraveling me. I start to bounce up and down on him.

He chomps on his lip, watching where our bodies are connected before he wraps his arm around me, pressing his thumb to my core. "Fuck, yes, Amelia," he growls. "Ride me."

Desperate whimpers punch out of me as I work myself on him hard and fast—chasing this escape—desperate to hold onto this feeling. The sound of our bodies slapping together consumes the room as his length fills me deeper, hitting the spot inside me that edges me into madness.

I ride him to the motherfucking stars..

After multiple trips to the moon, we both lay on the floor, sweaty and sated. It's at this moment that Beatrice skulks out of my bedroom and sits next to Dean, still laying flat on his back on the floor.

He lifts his head. "You actually do have a cat," he signs.

I breathe a laugh, still slightly dizzy, signing, "Why would I lie about that?"

He shrugs. "I don't know."

I guess it did seem like an excuse—and a bad one at that. I'm usually quicker on my feet. But I do in fact have a cat, and she's currently sitting beside Dean, judging us and our nakedness.

"That's Queen Beatrice," I sign. "Though if you ask her, she'd probably say *she* has a *human*," I laugh.

Beatrice rubs her body up against Dean's torso. He chuckles, giving her cheek a small scratch and my mouth gapes.

Of course she's nice to the hot guy. The little slut is definitely *my* cat. Another small laugh escapes me as my head rolls back and I stare at the ceiling.

My fingers start to trace the patterns of the wood floor at my side. As the high from multiple orgasms dissipates, my unease from earlier slowly creeps back in. I start to scratch against the floor with my nails, letting the rough vibration bring me back to now before I puff out an exhale.

If I have a breakdown, naked on the floor next to him, I'll need a new fucking identity.

After a few more breaths, I sit up and paw around for my clothes, shoving my tank top over my head and then sliding on my pants while Dean gets dressed too.

I'm not exactly *eager* for him to leave. This whole thing started with trying to put a distraction in place, something to keep my busy mind occupied. But now that I've fucked and fed him, I don't really have anything else to offer.

"Slut."

My eyes snap shut. *Jesus Christ.*

I swear, when she was alive, I hadn't exactly *forgotten* everything, but it was contained, controlled. Now it's like her death blew it all back into the air for me to inhale every day.

The sight of Beatrice slinking around Dean's ankles pulls me back to now and my eyes squint in her direction.

Unbelievable.

When I look back up at Dean, his eyes are studying me and I'm instantly worried he caught my silent, mini-spiral, but his eyes drift down to Beatrice and then back to me.

This is the part where he's supposed to leave. *He should leave.* And if I wasn't feeling so pathetically desperate to try and fight off my mother's invasion, that's exactly what would happen.

I quickly sign, "Want to watch *Harry Potter*?"

What the fuck?!

My eyes flinch as Dean's eyes squint back at me, almost like he's unsure if he misunderstood before he chuckles. "Uhh—"

"Nevermind," I sign quickly.

Dammit, why didn't I let him just leave? I could have been the woman he fucked in front of the mirror three times but now . . . *now* I'm a loser asking to watch a kid's movie.

"No—uhh—that sounds good," he signs with a shrug. "I haven't seen it in years. My brother loved the books. I'm pretty sure he had a thing for Hermoine."

"Didn't we all," I muse, letting out a small breath of relief. "The books are amazing." I move to the TV and start to get it synced up. "Is your brother the guy I met at Barney's? Evelyn's fiancé?"

He shoves his hands in his pockets, swallowing through a nod and my eyebrows pinch. The question seems to have shifted his mood a bit, but I'm not sure why.

"Do you not like her or something?"

"No. I like her," he signs, but doesn't elaborate.

Interesting . . .

I can't say I'm not intrigued by his demeanor, but I'm also not one to pry, so I turn on the TV just as another thought occurs to me.

"Wait—does this mean you don't know what house you're in?" I sign.

Dean's eyes squint toward me before the corners of his mouth pull up and he shrugs.

Oh my God!

"Well we need to get to the bottom of *that* before we start," I sign, then grab my laptop.

You'd think I was devising a plan for a bank heist with the intensity I bring to setting up the quiz. Once the page is loaded, I scoot over so Dean can sit next to me on the oversized armchair. It's close quarters but to be fair, he was just inside me, so from that perspective this is nothing.

I hand him the laptop and try to temper my excitement. *I actually really want to know this.*

A few minutes pass and Dean's intermittent clicks and swipes to the mousepad only fuel my impatience before he finally hands the laptop back to me.

Glancing down at the screen, I see . . .

Slytherin.

Resourceful. Clever. *Misunderstood.*

My heart flutters as my eyes float back up to him. There's slight amusement shining in his deep, brown eyes but his eyebrows flinch. "That's the bad one, right?"

I shrug. "Slytherin gets a bad rap for being deceitful. And their long line of dark witches doesn't do them any favors."

I close the laptop and put it on the side table and then look back at Dean, signing, "But . . . I've always thought of them as survivors. By whatever means necessary, they figure their way out."

Dean's mouth twitches with a half-nod, turning to face me. "What house are you?"

My heart does its weird flutter thing again before my lips instinctively pull up. "Slytherin."

chapter seventeen

amelia

twenty-one years ago

T*here is no good and evil, there is only power, and those too weak to seek it . . ."*

I was rereading *Harry Potter and the Sorcerer's Stone.* It was my favorite book and I found myself picking it up whenever I needed an escape.

Which was always.

Mom had shut me in my room again. But I liked my room. It was a safe space for the most part. I could *pretend* in my room. I could make believe that I was just a girl reading while her mom cooked dinner in the kitchen.

That wasn't the reality . . . but in my room—*by myself*—I could make up my own reality.

Suddenly, I startled, catching movement by my window, but calmed slightly when I noticed it was my neighbor, Alex.

My eyes bulged and I quickly scurried to the window, opening it.

"What are you doing here?" I whispered, "Why didn't you knock on the door?"

Truthfully, I was grateful he didn't. My mom usually *pretended* herself in front of people, but she had already been . . . out-of-sorts . . . when she put me in here an hour or so ago.

I peeked over my shoulder to make sure my door was still closed then looked back at Alex.

He smiled. "I did, but no one answered and I knew you were home 'cause of the light," he said, nodding toward the small lamp on my bedside table.

Despite my fear that she could come in at any minute, my own smile inched up my cheeks.

He knew I was home and he wanted to see me.

"Wait—no one answered?" I asked.

He shook his head. "Car's gone too."

She left? Where did she go?

His eyebrows pinched. He looked worried and I had to shut it down. I fixed my expression and shrugged. "We're out of popcorn. She must have gone out to get some. It's our favorite snack."

I had started what I coined as a "Truth-Lie" last year when my teacher asked about some bruises on my arm. It was where I'd weave a piece of truth into a lie. It helped me feel less guilty about my frequent dishonesty.

In this case, the truth: I loved popcorn. The lie: that my mom and I had a favorite *anything* together.

"Well, my parents made a fire in the backyard. Do you want to come?"

Crap.

I was getting good at lying but it was hard with Alex. He was always inviting me to stuff that I really wanted to do and I worried about the day that he'd give up and stop asking completely because I always said no.

But . . . she was gone. I had no idea where she went and I didn't know when she would be back. If she could leave, so could I . . . right?

It really did sound fun.

"Sure, I'll meet you over there."

"I can wait, if you want?"

I shook my head. "I just need to get a jacket and leave a note for my mom."

Truth: jacket. Lie: note.

He left and I started to close the window but then I suddenly wondered if I should keep it open in case I needed a way back in.

It wouldn't be the first time she locked me out of the house, but if she caught me *sneaking* back in . . .

A chill ran up my back but I huffed out my nerves.

She left. I could too.

Still, I left the window cracked. *Just in case.*

It was like freaking Disneyland in Alex's backyard—or what I imagined was like Disneyland—I had never been.

The fire provided a soft light to all the faces smiling and laughing. His mom made us all hot chocolate and we roasted marshmallows, then smooshed them between chocolate and graham crackers.

My cheeks actually ached from smiling, probably because I didn't do it very much.

Alex's dad took his guitar out and played while his mom sang along. She had such a pretty voice and the way they looked at each other made me feel as warm as the fire blazing in front of us.

I never knew my dad, but I truly couldn't even imagine someone looking at my mom the way Alex's parents looked at each other—like they were in a world of their own making and the rest of us were just observers to the magic.

From the corner of my eye, I noticed Alex looking over at me, as he mumbled, "They're gross, huh?"

A quiet laugh escaped as I shook my head. "I think it's sweet. Your family's . . . really cool."

I tried to keep the longing out of my voice, but I felt out of my element. I didn't know how to interact with people who loved each other and it was hard to mask that. I felt like an intruder and it made my stomach tighten.

I wondered why some people ended up happy and in love. How some kids had loving parents who would do anything for them and some kids . . . just didn't.

It seemed unfair.

No. It seemed cruel.

The world was full of husbands and wives, sons and daughters, and only the lucky few got *this?*

The only conclusion I could come to was that it was me. *Maybe I was cursed.* It would make sense. I tried so hard to do everything right, but it never worked. Darkness always found me.

I began to feel even more uneasy. Like somehow my darkness would consume the light from this moment. My mind wandered with all the ways I could screw this up without even trying—just by being here.

I could say something stupid that would ruin everyone's fun, or maybe someone would want a second cup of hot chocolate and there wouldn't be enough because I had one. But the worst thing that could happen is if my mom came home and saw I wasn't there—*if she came here to get me.*

That would definitely ruin this.

A shiver chased down my spine and I immediately stood up. It wasn't likely that it would happen. Usually, when she put me in my room, she didn't bother to stop back for the rest of the night. But once the fear was there, I couldn't shake it off.

I thanked Alex and his parents, and as I went to leave his mom did something.

She hugged me.

My body stiffened but quickly melted. On instinct, my arms wrapped around her too and she squeezed me a little tighter. It was . . . nice. But it also felt foreign, like I didn't quite fit inside the hug.

"Come over anytime, Amelia. We'd love to have you," she said.

Tears bit the back of my eyes at the warmth and comfort of her arms, her invitation, her kindness.

"Thank you, Mrs. Wade," I spoke just above a whisper as my throat tightened.

I wished I could stay forever. Actually, if wishes were a thing, I wished that *this* was my family and *this* was my home.

After a reluctant, parting wave to Alex, I scurried along the street. My eyes darted around on high alert as I hurried back toward my house.

As I got closer, I saw that the car was in the driveway.

Crap.

I swallowed hard, but I tried not to panic. I left the window open, so I could sneak back in that way and there was still a good chance she didn't even know I was gone.

After pushing the window up, I used a pipe just above the base of the house to climb in.

As soon as I was inside, my eyes scanned the room, making sure she wasn't in there. I stayed still for a second longer, listening for any sign of movement, but when I heard nothing I finally pushed out a heavy exhale and closed the window as quietly as I could.

I shrugged out of my coat and put my sweatpants back on, then crawled under the sheets and picked up my book from the nightstand, opening it to the dog-eared page.

My shoulders sank with a relieved exhale, a small, victorious smile inching up my cheek but then . . .

I heard uneven footsteps from the hall. I peeked at the window again to make sure I'd closed it completely. I had, but my heart continued to speed up the closer the steps got. I thought about hiding, but my mind flashed to the only time I *had* hidden from her.

Under my bed.

Footsteps. Darkness. Stillness. Pain.

It made it worse. And I ended up telling the biggest truth-lie I'd ever told. I had to explain to my teacher that during a game of hide and seek, a curtain rod had fallen and hit my cheek.

Luckily, she bought it. And I actually found myself feeling proud of my ability to conceal.

Suddenly, I heard the steps stop right outside my door and my spine straightened.

I was in bed, reading. She had no idea. I just had to stay calm.

But the problem was, I never knew *what* would set her off. I seemed to make her angry by simply existing.

As she pushed the door open, I swallowed hard as her chin slowly turned to lock eyes with me. She looked . . . awful. I could always tell how much she'd been drinking just by looking at her. On the good nights, she would just fall asleep. But then there were nights where she seemed like she was *looking* to get angry. Her blue-ish green eyes would become nearly black, the color would drain from her face . . .

She *looked* evil on those nights.

And I was staring at it right now.

"H-Hey," I said, working to even my expression.

She always said I was stuck up and I didn't want her to notice what I'm sure was a disgusted look on my face. She simply stared at me and it twisted the unease in my stomach.

"Sneaking around with the neighbor boy?"

I felt myself shrink, knowing she caught me. But she said it in such a way that made me feel defensive, like it was dirty or something.

My muscles tightened. "You weren't home and he invited me over for hot chocolate."

Her unfocused gaze narrowed on me, her eyes searing.

This was the problem. I made things worse by talking back—standing my ground.

Stupid.

In an instant, she charged toward my bed. Stumbling a bit before her fingers locked around my jaw, squeezing so tight that I had to suck my lips into my mouth to keep from crying out.

I wouldn't give her the satisfaction.

"You want to be a slut, that's fine. But don't think for one second I don't know what you're up to." Her hand shook, tightening her hold on my face and I couldn't help the whimper that escaped. "Pretty ain't permanent, kid. And then all you'll be is a stupid girl." She jerked my chin and then finally released it.

Her eyes remained lifeless but her chapped lips tilted into a satisfied grin when she saw my hands shaking as I held my book.

I think she liked the power in scaring me and I hated giving it to her. I breathed deep and tried to let the air erase her words. I could feel them beating against my brain, but I glanced down at my book, trying my best to ignore her presence still looming over me.

I don't care.

In a second, she grabbed the book and the small bit of strength I managed to find deflated.

I took a steadying breath. *It's okay. I'd get another one.*

Maybe I could save some money so I could buy a few copies— *backups.*

She staggered toward the door. "Just don't get pregnant. You'd be a terrible mother," she slurred, over her shoulder as she left the room.

A gasped sob released the second the door closed. *I was horrified.* I was only nine years old and it was a disgusting thing to say. But my final thought before I turned over on my side and rested my head on the pillow was . . .

Well, you would know, bitch.

chapter eighteen
dean

Sitting in my old dining room is bringing on a strange swell of emotions.

The wedding pictures that used to decorate the walls have been replaced with various pictures of Ava, a few of Marnie's family and even one with Shaun. I stare down at the table, tapping my thumb nervously on the surface as Marnie comes back in with "Windbreaker Boy" in tow.

Two against one. This is gonna go well.

But seriously, why is Shaun even part of this conversation? He wants Marnie to move in with him, *fine.* But he's lost his fucking mind if he thinks he gets *any* say in what happens with our daughter.

They each settle into the seats across from me and I can't shake the sterile, cold feeling of the room. It feels like a doctor is about to tell me my results are terminal.

We sit, staring, blinking back and forth for a few seconds before Shaun clears his throat.

"Okay, well . . . this is a bit uncomfortable . . . but why doesn't Marnie start with what she and I have discussed and then Dean, you can, uhh—have the floor?"

Good Christ. Do not punch Shaun.

At least he's actually talking. Marnie is just sitting across from me, worrying her bottom lip between her teeth while intermittently glaring at me. I lean back in my chair, feeling anything but calm—but I sweep my hand out in front of me, inviting her to "take the floor."

She takes a deep breath before her eyes finally float up to mine. "Well . . . we were thinking that I'd move this summer. It will give me some time to tie things up with work and sell the house. After that, the plan is that I'd be making monthly trips back to Chicago to meet with any clients. I can stay with Shelly and I'd bring Ava with me so she can stay with you while I'm here."

My head shakes. *Once a month?*

Clearing my throat, I ask, "How long would these monthly visits be?" unable to mask the tightness in my tone.

She shrugs, her mouth staying flat. "Five days or so? It would depend on the workload."

I shake my head. "See, I don't think my time with our daughter should *depend* on what you have going on with work. *That's* the first issue—"

"Let me finish, Dean." She lets out an exasperated sigh, rolling her eyes as Shaun takes her hand, lightly running his thumb over the back it. Another wave of irritation flows through me at the display of support, but I roll my shoulders in an attempt to shake it off.

It doesn't matter. I just need to get to the bottom of this for Ava.

"I was thinking that Ava could spend her summers here—in Chicago, with you. Maybe we could reverse the schedule that I have for nine months out of the year and June through August you could bring her out to Michigan once a month?"

My fists curl as my adrenaline rises. "And what the fuck am I going to do in Michigan for a week while you spend time with Ava? Count the ceiling tiles in the hotel room?"

Marnie crosses her arms. "Look. I'm trying to be as fair as possible. This isn't an ideal situation, but at least this way we both get to see her all year. I think I'm being completely reasonable."

I want to flip the fucking table. She acts like she's doing me a favor by even considering my role in all of this and it's fraying the already thin thread inside of me from snapping completely.

A deep inhale does nothing to calm me, and I can't hide my disdain as I say, "I think if you really wanted to be *fair,* you'd explore options that kept Ava's parents in the same place. Somewhere we can actually raise her together."

Marnie's nostrils flare before she stands and roars, "But we're not *raising her together!*" then promptly storms out of the room, leaving me speechless.

The outburst takes me aback. Marnie rarely loses her temper, so *that* was surprising in and of itself, but mostly, it's the hidden implication behind her words that are seeping into me.

"We're not raising her together . . ." because of you.

She didn't have to say the last part. It's been evident in every bit of our lives post-divorce and her bitterness just now solidified it. The guilt sinks its teeth into my anger—slumping my body in the chair as I rub my palms up and down my face.

Another few beats pass, my hands still pressing against my face, when I hear Shaun clear his throat.

Jesus Christ, why is he still here?

"Dean," he says and I apprehensively meet his eyes. Not because I have any interest in hearing what he has to say, but because I desperately need to focus on something else before I ransack the dining room in a fit of rage.

He shifts his weight in his seat before he peeks back toward the kitchen and then back to me. "I know this is . . ." he trails off before he shrugs. "I imagine there's nothing that will put you at ease but, I really love Marnie—and Ava. I'm no expert, and I won't insult you by pretending to know how hard the idea of all of this is but . . . I think there's a way for this to work. We just need to find the best option."

My fist tightens on my thigh below the table. Being therapized by my ex-wife's boyfriend makes me want to smother him with his sweater vest, but I somehow swallow the urge.

Killing Shaun accomplishes nothing, and it's a sure-fire way to only see Ava through a glass window.

I shake my head and run my hand through my hair before I rub the back of my neck. I need to let the situation breathe. At least I've confirmed that this is still an option that they're exploring and it gives me some time to process and figure out what I need to do to *stop* it from happening.

"Will you go get Ava, please?" I ask, tightly.

Shaun sits a second longer before he nods, tapping the table twice with his knuckle before he gets up and leaves the dining room.

Weenie.

My eyes mindlessly drift around the room again. This hasn't been my home for a year, but it's like the ghosts of my life here still linger in corners of the space—like they watch every change Marnie makes and nod their head in approval.

"Get rid of him. All he did was fuck up your life."

But she can't get rid of me entirely. We have a kid, and therefore, my presence can never be wiped completely and I've never felt the animosity from that fact more than I do right now. She's acting like I'm trying to yet again, fuck up her life. But I'm not.

I want her to be happy, I really do. But should her happiness come at the expense of mine and Ava's relationship?

Later, back at my apartment, I sit across from Ava, but I can't stay present. Intrusive thoughts are sitting on the outskirts of my mind. Not just about my current predicament with Marnie's move, but about how we ended up here at all.

It took me longer than it should have to step up—with our marriage, impending fatherhood. My mind processes things in mind-numbing, painstakingly slow ways, and it always ends up biting me in the ass.

I didn't get where I needed to be fast enough. I didn't immediately react appropriately.

I fuck up.

I've talked through everything with Ava, but . . . she's a fucking *baby.* Plus, she slept through the ride home so I was really just muttering aggressive nonsense to myself.

I've picked up my phone, and put it back down no fewer than five times to call Otis, but I haven't actually gone through with it.

Because telling Otis makes this a *real* problem. And problems with *me* are cause for very *real* concern among my family.

Ava's hands bang on the tray to her high chair and I jerk at the noise. My lips tilt as I look over at her, looking hungry and impatient, before she squishes her tiny hands into loose fists, tapping her finger-tips together and my eyes widen.

Did she just sign?

I scoop some mashed sweet potato onto the spoon and give it to her but pause before giving her another bite.

A few seconds pass before she again bangs her tray and then squishes her fists, tapping her fingertips together.

"More."

I taught her that.

My chest swells and my eyes mist as I feed her another bite. My body sinks back in the chair and for a brief, euphoric moment all the other bullshit falls away.

I meet Ava's big, sparkly blue eyes and keep feeding her.

I'll always give her more.

A few hours after I've put Ava to bed, I'm nowhere near sleep. I've been laying in bed, feeling like the wheels in my mind are hydroplaning through the same murky puddle and it's starting to fuck with me.

I don't want to drink. *I don't.* But the idea of a temporary shut off from everything sounds so enticing right now and the idea itself just won't leave me alone.

Rolling on my side, I see my phone on the nightstand, suddenly remembering my most recent night of distraction.

I still can't look in a mirror without wishing I had Amelia's gorgeous, naked body in front of me.

I grab my phone and open my messages. After finding her name, I quickly tap out a text.

Me: Hey. Are you awake?

A few seconds pass and I lean my head back on the pillow. I haven't seen or talked to her in a few days—*since that night*—but I've thought about it every goddamn day.

My phone buzzes and I immediately check the message.

Amelia: Depends . . . is this a booty call?

I huff a laugh. I guess it's a fair assumption to make.

Me: Unfortunately, no. I've got Ava till Sunday.

Three dots appear, then disappear. It happens a couple more times before a message comes through.

Amelia: Wanna make a bet?

I'm already smiling. I swear I can almost see the devious gleam in her green eyes as I read the text, again.

Me: You have my attention . . .

The dots appear and ripple for a few seconds before I get the next message.

Amelia: I bet I can get you off
from all the way over here in Wrigleyville.

I pull in a sharp inhale and my dick immediately twitches, but my brain might be short-circuiting. The bet seems too good to be true, because I have no fucking doubt that she can do what she's suggesting.

Me: What do I get if I win?

A few seconds pass, but unlike last time, there aren't any dots.
Shit.
Why didn't I just say yes? If a gorgeous woman wants to give you an orgasm in any *way—you always say fucking yes!*
Another moment goes by as I try to think of a non-dweeby way of saying, "Just kidding! Yes, please?" before another message comes through.

Amelia: Prize is TBD.

She emphasizes her point by sending a purple devil emoji and my smile widens.
She's fucking fun. And that's what I need right now.

Me: Your move, A. Heart.

I'm waiting on pins and needles for her response. I have no idea what she's got planned but the anticipation has already got me buzzing and I lightly rub myself over my pants.
Suddenly, a picture message comes through.
Her face isn't in it, but her chest and collar bone are, with just the base of her neck. Her delicate hand is splayed just below her lightning bolt necklace as her fingers lie knuckle deep in her shirt.

I rub my dick a little harder, squeezing it just a bit over my sweats.

Amelia: Your hands feel so good on me . . .
Strong, rough.

My eyes close for a few seconds, imagining the feeling of her smooth skin as I tease her nipples with my fingers. My hand slowly sinks into my pants before I get another message.

Amelia: No touching, yet.
Bad boy . . .

How she knows this, I'm not sure, but my dick twitches again—like he's saying "I'm the bad boy! Pick me!"
Had no idea that would turn me on, but here we are.
I reluctantly pull my hand out of my pants and type back.

Me: Such a tease.
You sure you're not the bad one?

Another picture comes through and this time she's topless in front of a mirror. She's leaning against the sink in a way that I can only see from her mouth down, with the counter cutting off just above her hips. Her forearm is draped tastefully over one of her breasts while her fingers rest over her nipple on the other one.
Goddamn.
I groan as my hand instinctively moves to my dick, again, before I stop. I'm rock-fucking-solid, already aching for relief, but she said no touching yet.

I kind of can't believe she's sending me pictures. Don't get me wrong, I fucking love it and I'll delete them all if she wants me to but . . . part of me is really hoping she doesn't want me to.

My eyes are still tracing all the soft curves of her body when the video chat screen appears on the phone.

Oh fuck.

My breath is heavy already, but I swallow hard and try to compose myself as I click the accept button.

Her smirk meets me through the camera as she signs, "How am I doing so far?"

God, I wish she was right in front of me. She's naked, sitting on her bed and the soft lighting of the room makes her long, dark hair look even more billowy. There's a challenging sparkle in her fiery green eyes, and that's when I remember she asked me a question.

I swallow again. "You're doing so good, baby." My voice is low and hoarse, strained from arousal.

A devious glint catches in her eyes as she quietly says, "Give me some dirty words, Roberts," tucking her hair behind her ear and tilting her chin just a bit to show me she's got her aids on.

Roberts.

Hearing her call me that *does* something to me.

Or maybe it's just her. I'm already wound the fuck up, but just like last time, it's almost like she's tapped a well somewhere deep inside of me—somewhere so deep, I thought it was gone. A primal instinct takes over and I sit up against the headboard.

"You wanna make me come?" I rasp.

She nods as her fingers crawl from her stomach to down between her legs.

I keep my voice low as I ask, "Do your fingers feel as good as mine?"

She tugs her bottom lip between her teeth before she shakes her head, but a small whimper manages to escape as she reaches the apex of her thighs.

"Show me how wet you are, Amelia."

Her mouth is slightly open, her expression lost in lust but still, the corner of her mouth pulls up as she slowly removes her fingers from below, lifting them to show me the very evident arousal coating her fingertips.

I suck my bottom lip into my mouth at the sight. "Rub it over your nipples, pretend it's my tongue."

She does as I say, and her head lulls back as her eyes close.

"Eyes on me," I growl.

She lowers her chin back to me, begging for something with her gaze, but she keeps her eyes on mine as her hand moves back between her legs.

I smirk. "Good girl."

She moans and my dick hits a hard twelve o'clock. I could tell the other night that she was into the praise thing—and I'm more than fucking happy to give it to her.

Her hips start to rock against her hand and a low groan rumbles in my throat.

I'm almost afraid to start jerking myself. I know the second I do, I'll fucking explode. She's already got me completely wound up just from watching her—letting my words work her into oblivion as she plays with herself.

Still, the need to get some relief is too strong and my hand finally sinks down into my pants. My eyes shut as my fist tightens, stroking myself slowly.

"Eyes on me," she teases, breathlessly.

My eyes reopen and I have to stop moving for just a second, watching her watch me with such a thick desire that it's almost hard to breathe. My hand picks up speed and I become nearly feral.

"Lean back, baby. I'm about to blow my load all over that gorgeous body."

She leans against the headboard while her other hand keeps moving between her legs. "Please, give it to me," she begs, her voice just above a whisper but panting and desperate.

"You want it?" I growl, pushing up on my knees, jerking myself so hard it almost hurts but the pain is good. It feels like a fucking dream.

This whole thing does.

"I want it, please. Give it to me," she almost looks like she's about to say something else but she doesn't, instead she sucks her lips into her mouth, suppressing a desperate whine. "Can I come?"

I'm wild—untamed with need—and I mindlessly mumble out, "Not yet. Not until I do."

"Please, please, please," she chants as quietly as she can—and I fucking *come.*

It's so intense and it lasts so long that I nearly black out. I faintly hear Amelia on the other end of the phone, but the blood rushing through my ears makes it sound even quieter.

Jesus Christ.

I didn't doubt her ability to get me off but that was . . . *crazy.*

I didn't even feel like myself.

As the high starts to settle, I try to run through everything I said. I almost felt drunk—but instead of feeling dumb and shitty after, I just feel . . . *fucking rocked.*

Looking back at her, her cheeks look slightly flushed, but the corner of her mouth is tilting up as she signs, "I won the bet."

I breathe a laugh before pulling in a deep inhale. "Uhh—I think I won too."

She shrugs, signing, "Too bad *you* didn't state your terms before we started. No dice, Roberts. I won."

I think both parties *won* tonight, but I let her take it.

"Call to collect your prize—whatever that is."

She smiles deviously before signing, "Oh, I intend to." She runs her hand through her hair before she adds, "I've got an early class tomorrow, so . . . I should go. Can't spend all night trying to satisfy a fiend."

I chuckle again. "Hey, you made the bet!"

"I was referring to myself," she signs with a wink and it somehow sends another wave of arousal through me. But she quickly signs, "Goodnight," hanging up before I even sign it back to her.

I nearly have whiplash from how quickly she got off the phone. It reminds me of the first night we hooked up and she immediately scurried out of my apartment . . . to feed her cat.

At least I know the cat is real.

I sigh a heavy exhale, leaving the phone on the bed as I walk quietly into the bathroom. I clean myself up and splash some cold water on my face.

My body is overcome with heaviness as exhaustion starts to set in. When I get back to my room, I open the baby monitor and see Ava still sound asleep, pushing a relieved exhale past my lips.

Her room is right across from mine so I would have heard her if she had woken up, but I was so lost in the moment. I'm kind of surprised I let it happen.

I sink back on the bed, turning the light off before my head falls on the pillow and, thankfully, any guilt or worry gets completely swallowed as I immediately fall asleep.

chapter nineteen
amelia

This level of exhaustion is dangerous.

My chin is propped up only by my hand as my head bobs in front of my laptop screen for the umpteenth time and I finally groan, slamming the screen shut.

Beatrice perks up from her lounging spot on the ottoman in a small stream of sunlight, glaring at me for the disturbance.

"Excuse me, I'm cat napping."

I groan again, slumping into the chair and tilting my head back.

It's a Saturday afternoon, so the logical thing to do would be to take a nap myself, but I know the second I lay down, my mind will wander or if I actually *do* fall asleep, I'll have another fucking night-mare.

I don't think I've slept a full night since . . . well, since about a month ago when my mom died and unleashed the seventh circle of hell on me.

The alert light on my phone blinks from the desk and my eyes stare down at it longer than necessary before I finally pick it up.

Tim: Hey kitty cat. Wanna play?

Good God—and the punches don't stop coming. *Can't he take a fucking hint?*

I haven't contacted him since our mishap last month, but like most things in my life . . . shit always finds a way of resurfacing.

I'm not one of those cynics who doesn't believe in God. I *know* the bitch exists because she fucking hates me. Maybe humanity has had it all wrong and God is the bad one, while the Devil is actually good— just getting a bad rap because she wears dark lipstick and combat boots.

Sounds like something the villain would say.

I shake my head, tossing my phone back on the desk before I pull my fingers through my hair and tug at the roots.

I am losing my goddamn mind.

Last night—when I woke up for the third time—I emailed Dr. G and asked if she would be willing to do a session today.

I'm sure she's irritated that I canceled the one I was supposed to have with her when I got back from my mom's but . . . I wasn't expecting my mom to die. I just didn't want to talk about it.

I still don't.

But I'm desperate. It's been years since I've had episodes like this. And even then, somehow I had gotten used to them and they didn't feel so overwhelming. Maybe it's like a muscle you need to exercise and I've been metaphorically sitting on the couch eating chips for a decade, wondering why it's so hard to stand up now.

I got comfortable, lazy . . . and now I'm paying for it.

The alert light on my phone blinks again and I whine. I consider ignoring it, but I don't want Tim to just show up here. It's unlikely, but not unheard of—and the idea immediately tightens in my stomach.

Picking up the phone, I release a breath I didn't realize I was holding when I see that it's not him.

Evelyn: Hey! We're doing game night tomorrow.
Please come!! I need back up!

Game night?

It takes my tired mind a second to remember she mentioned it that night at Barney's and again when we had coffee last week.

I wonder if Dean will be there . . .

I squirm in my seat as the memory of our little phone rendezvous a couple of nights ago passes through me. It's been the gorgeous, sexy chandelier in the haunted mansion of my fucking brain for the past two days.

I actually slept a whopping four hours that night.

But I'm not sure hanging out with them all together is such a good idea right now. I'm already pretty antisocial, and adding my delirium to the mix might be a recipe for disaster.

Still, it was really nice of her to ask . . .

Me: Thanks for the invite!
I'm out right now, but let me check
my schedule and I'll let you know.

Truth: I appreciate the invitation. Lie: That my schedule consists of anything but sitting on my couch with my cat while trying to fight off a haunting from my recently deceased mother.

Totally fucking normal.

"She died?" Dr. G signs, her eyes widening at me through the laptop screen.

I nod. "Yep."

Her chin tilts down, shaking her head before she peeks back up at me with a concerned expression. "Jesus, Amelia. You should have called me!"

I shrug. "It's not a big deal."

That's part of the problem. This *isn't* a big deal. *It's a nuisance.* But it won't leave me alone.

Dr. G leans back, farther away from the screen. It almost seems like she's waiting for me to answer a question, but she hasn't asked me anything, so I raise my eyebrows, inviting her to elaborate.

"Well . . . here we are," she finally signs. "It feels like a big deal, don't you think?"

I loathe when people do this—when they ask a question they think they already know the answer to. I can literally feel the notch in my blood pressure.

"No," I sign.

Her mouth flattens into a tight line, rubbing the pads of her fingers across her forehead before she closes her eyes but reopens them a moment later.

"Well then, why are we talking today? You blew off our last session—so what changed?" she signs.

I can feel my defenses rise, but . . . she has a point. She's never hesitated to call me out and I've actually grown to appreciate her no nonsense demeanor, but it feels overwhelming at the moment—so much so that I start to feel the distant slow simmering in my chest.

I instinctively grab my necklace but then quickly let it go, dropping my hand below the screen. My thumbnail pushes into the corner of my palm, just under the base of my pinky until I feel the sharp pinch.

"Why are you angry?" she signs.

I don't know if it's sleep deprivation or anxiety—*maybe both*—but it feels like she's provoking me right now.

"I'm not," I sign, tightly.

"Let me see your hand," she challenges, her eyes drifting to the arm down by my side.

I retract my thumbnail to clench my fist, sitting and staring at her. She doesn't approve of my self-soothing tactic—she never has—but she also knows I avoid anger at all costs, so her question irritates me.

I start to count how many times I blink back at her, just to give myself something to focus on, and just as I reach sixteen, she sighs. "This is tough, Amelia."

The statement takes me aback. I'm not sure what I was expecting her to say but something . . . *commiserative* was definitely not it.

"Have the flashbacks gotten worse?" she signs.

My instinct is to lie, even though the onslaught of memories are the whole fucking reason I set up this emergency session. Well, *that* and the fact that her voice is creeping into my mind more and more.

God, it's exhausting to be me.

After another few seconds pass, I nod, but decide to keep the fact that I'm hearing her to myself.

She nods too, signing, "I figured as much," as she scoots forward in her chair, writing something down, and I feel my heart stutter in my chest.

The pad of my index finger starts mindlessly rubbing along the nail bed of my thumb as she leans a little closer to the camera, signing, "I think you really need to pay attention to your feelings right now, Amelia. I know you avoid them because there's a lot of pain mixed up in there but . . . this shit has a way of finding us and there's a chance yours is coming to collect."

"You think I haven't felt my pain?!" It strikes a nerve. Heat crawls up my neck and over my cheeks just as she puts a steadying hand out in front of her.

"I think you felt it when you were *in* it. And it's normal to try and stuff it down. All I'm suggesting is that you give it some space—allow it the room to breathe."

Jesus Christ. She's really playing the role of doctor tonight and I am not fucking into it. I look at her with an unamused expression and she leans back in her chair.

In an attempt to calm down, I study her features. I take in the familiarity of her choppy blond hair, her casual Red Hot Chili Peppers T-shirt and the timid concern in her light blue eyes. I remember that it's Saturday and she had no obligation to do this today.

She's not the enemy. She's just trying to help.

"Sorry," I mumble, fidgeting again with my necklace before I meet her admonishing stare through the screen. I drop it, blowing out a heavy exhale just as she clears her throat.

"You'll never know unless you try, Amelia. And I'm not just talking about feeling the pain—I'm talking about feeling everything. The good stuff, too."

I blink back at her a couple of times before I snort a humorless laugh. "So, you think I need to 'feel my feelings?' Damn, Dr. G, what a *shrink* thing to say."

She huffs a small laugh through her nose with a shrug. "I mean . . . it's what they pay me for. But, I'm serious. Remember that time you told me about freaking out at Doris?"

I swallow, nodding.

"I know the *moment* was overwhelming . . . but do you remember what happened after?"

"They made me start seeing your annoying ass."

She ignores my comment as she shifts in her seat. "You started to actually enjoy your time with them. You learned sign language, started cooking more—*actually* participating in life. It was a catalyst for change. Maybe it's time to change again. Let her death set something in motion instead of . . . whatever it's doing to you . . ." Her eyes point at me, inviting me to elaborate, but I don't.

I don't really buy into her whimsical idea, but . . . it's worth a shot, I guess.

It's a place to start.

My desperation to make this all stop has me signing, "I'll try," but even as I promise it, I'm not sure I believe it.

Dr. G studies me a second more before she nods. "Good. And I think we should keep up with weekly sessions for a bit. Just until the dust settles on this. You've been slacking, anyway, and I'm sure that's not helping." She grabs her planner, before peeking back up at me. "Thursdays?"

I run my hands through my hair, pulling a little harder than necessary as I nod and push an exhale out through puffed cheeks.

We end the session a minute later, but I linger in front of my laptop. I'm not sure what I was expecting. There was this irrational hope that she'd just wave her pen at me like a magic wand and somehow erase it all.

I snort a laugh, knowing it's ridiculous. *Woulda been nice, though.*

But that's never the way it works. Therapy isn't even really about feeling better.

It's inventory.

My eyes float down to the desk, noticing my phone.

"Let this be a catalyst for change."

I sigh, picking the phone up. I can admit that it sounds nice—in theory—but it also feels impossible.

Still, I unlock my phone. I contemplate texting Dean, but that seems like a bad idea right now. Instead, my eyes fall on my thread with Evelyn and I click it. My thumb moves slowly, tapping out a text, but it shakes a bit as I hover it over the send button.

Before I can think about it too much, I click it.

Me: Hey. Count me in for game night.

chapter twenty

dean

R eggie!" Evelyn yells, then signs, "Can you take a break from twerking and help?"

Reggie is in rare form and it's kind of hilarious. He spent the afternoon at some work party where it was all you could eat and drink and . . . well, he did.

He straightens up and prances to the kitchen, grabbing Evelyn, and promptly waltzes her around the apartment. She squeals and then giggles before quickly falling into step with him.

I snort a laugh, signing, "They really are just grown theater kids," to Otis.

He chuckles, but his eyes stay glued to Evelyn.

Game night wouldn't have been my first choice, but I'm glad I had *something* set up for tonight. Marnie was cryptically quiet while picking up Ava—*not angry, per se*—but not pleasant either, so I'm grateful to get out of the apartment at least.

But my real motivation for coming is that Otis told me Amelia would be here too.

My eyes peek over to my brother, who is still watching Evelyn, and strangely enough, the usual discomfort of watching them isn't there. Instead, I actually find myself chuckling at his dopey face.

He's the best guy I've ever known, but he's always had some trouble with girls. Actually, with meeting people in general.

"Who did this?!" I roared, slamming Dipshit Derek into the wall next to the lockers.

Someone thought it was funny to leave pictures of pigs fucking on my brother's locker and I was about to fuck them up.

Derek played some sport. I didn't know what, because I didn't give a shit. He was also a complete dumbass but I knew he had answers.

Otis always had a tough time at school. People just . . . didn't know how to talk to him. No one tried. But this was different. There was a nasty rumor going around that Jen "Saggy Tits" Bernard took his virginity and was now running her mouth all around school about how awful it was—something about fucking a farm animal.

She was a cunt.

My fingers curled around Derek's shirt, shoving him harder into the wall.

"Dude, you're fucking crazy! It wasn't me," he laughed, but there was the smallest shake to his voice.

He may have been a jock, but that didn't mean he knew how to fight.

I pulled him away from the wall, just to shove him harder back into it. "No, dickwad. Crazy is what you're about to see if you don't tell me. Who. The fuck. Did this?"

A humorless laugh escaped him and I saw my brother's face flash in front of my eyes. The one he was wearing when I first heard the rumor a couple of weeks ago.

The one full of defeat and shame . . .

My jaw clenched. A few other kids started to crowd around us but I didn't care. Derek tried again to shove me away, but I had the upper hand. He was positioned in a way where he couldn't use his full weight. I, however, might as well have been a fucking semi on his chest.

I pulled my lighter out of my pocket. "How're those reflexes, Derek?"

His eyes widened, but he seemed determined to play it cool. Still, I could feel his breath get heavier under the weight of my forearm.

"You're a goddamn psychopath, Roberts," he heaved, still fighting to take a deep breath.

I shrugged, flicking the lighter before staring back at him.

"You wouldn't," he spit back at me.

I could feel the heat from the flame on my cheek. My eyes narrowed at him and I brought my hand closer to the collar of his coat . . .

"Jesus fuck! It was Weaver."

I didn't let on how relieved I was that he didn't call my bluff. I was mildly unhinged when I got mad, but I wasn't a complete psychopath. I just flicked the lighter again before shoving off of him and stalking away.

The crowd in the hallway had gotten a little bigger. Kids were staring and speculating—but I didn't give a shit. I had to knock an asshole's teeth out.

Evelyn and Reggie's laughter knocks me back to now and I rub my palm down my face.

I *did* find Brandon Weaver that day. He was outside some convenient store and I knocked him out clean with one punch.

So maybe I was a little bit *of a psycho.*

But honestly, I'm glad I did it. Because it was fucking rough. Otis stopped talking—he detached completely. He was so down, I wasn't sure there'd ever be a time where I saw him like *this.*

He only started using his voice again last year—after he and Evelyn got together. And I don't think that's a coincidence.

A sudden knock jerks my chin toward the door.

"Ah, that's probably Amelia!" Evelyn sing-songs, scurrying toward the door and my spine straightens.

The last time I saw Amelia was a few nights ago through the camera phone. And like a real pig, I've looked through the photos she sent no fewer than thirty times since then.

Aaand . . . there's my half-chub.

Fuck.

God. My dick is like a soldier, ready to salute at the mere thought of her.

Evelyn opens the door and Amelia stands on the other side with a casserole dish.

Her plump, pink lips quirk from under her vintage Cubs cap. My eyes drag along her black bomber jacket, down to her tight, dark skinny jeans. I force my chin to drop in an attempt to *not* look like I'm actively checking her out.

But of course I am. She's a fucking goddess and I've been gifted the sight of her naked three times. *Thirty-three if you count my pervy ass checking out the pictures.*

My shoulders twitch, suddenly feeling a little antsy. No one knows we've hooked up, so unless we want to admit it right now, I've got to keep my ogling discreet.

Otis walks over to them, taking the casserole dish from Amelia as Evelyn signs, "Oh my God, you didn't have to bring food!" moving aside to let Amelia through the doorway

"It was no trouble," Amelia signs, as she shrugs out of her coat. "I love cooking."

"You remember Reggie and Dean?" Evelyn signs.

She gives Reggie a timid smile before her eyes lock with mine. It's cut off quickly by Reggie pulling her into a dance and Amelia flinches, laughing, nervously. "Oh, if you value your toes you won't make me dance with you."

Reggie pouts, signing, "Girl, haven't you seen *Bridgerton?* How're we gonna find you a man if you can't dance?"

My jaw ticks at Reggie's suggestion, but I subtly bend my neck back and forth to release the tension.

Great start. Hungry eyes and irrational possessiveness are definitely *a way to send a message that you're* not *sleeping with someone.*

"Luckily we've evolved past the Regency era," Amelia signs, breathing another laugh. "I would have been fucked."

"Me too," Evelyn signs with a nod.

Otis puts the casserole dish on the table and then moves to Evelyn, circling her waist and kissing her temple. "I would have picked you in any era," he says against her hair.

She presses a small kiss to his chest before nuzzling in while Amelia watches them with a soft expression before her eyes peek over to me, still over by the couch.

"Hey," I mouth.

Her lips tilt—almost bashfully—but there's also this hint of something else I can't quite place.

Nervous? Tired?

Otis signs, "So . . . not to be *that* guy but . . . what'd you make?" to Amelia, and then eyes the dish on the table.

"It's just spinach and artichoke dip." Otis's eyes widen and she chuckles, signing, "Help yourself."

All three of them descend on the dip like seagulls at the beach, and I take the distracted moment to wander a bit closer to her, unable to keep myself from taking her in.

Her green eyes have a touch of the sparkle they had the night we met, albeit, heavier than usual. And her pearly white teeth keep peeking through the smile she keeps trying to fight.

My own mouth pulls up, watching her. "You should do it," I sign.

Her eyebrows furrow, but the corner of her mouth lifts, amusedly. "Do what?"

"You should smile. It's pretty."

She huffs a breath before she puckers her lips, but still showing her teeth—almost like she's wearing an invisible mouthguard. It's the goofiest-looking face and I can't help but laugh, shaking my head. "Still pretty," I sign.

She rolls her eyes but the corners of her mouth quirk back up as the faintest rosy color dusts her cheeks. I'm close enough now that her jasmine scent fills my nose, sending a direct message to my groin.

Jesus Christ. Maybe she was *right the other night. Maybe I am a fiend.*

I mean, she *is* the hottest woman I've ever seen, but it's also the way we seem to . . . lose ourselves when we're together—like we're shedding our skin.

My sex drive didn't disappear completely, but it faded to the background with the rest of me when I was drinking. And I don't know if it's just the excitement of having that back and then some with her, or . . . if it's just her.

"You're staring, Roberts," she signs, smirking, still watching everyone inhale her dip.

"Your fault," I sign, moving a little closer. I keep my eyes on the group for a second more, but then turn my face and glance down at her, noticing her hearing aids are in before I whisper, "The tastiest thing is standing right next to me."

She lifts her chin toward me, a devious glint catching her eyes and I have to suppress the rumble in my chest.

"Can I drive you home later?" I sign, still leaning into her.

Her eyes look slightly dazed as she looks up at me. It feels like our eyes are magnets, charged and pulling us toward each other before Reggie's squeal makes us jerk and lean away quickly, simultaneously looking back over at them.

Luckily, they're still lost in the dip and whatever argument has Reggie clapping back at Evelyn right now.

I release a heavy exhale. *I need to relax.* She hasn't even been here five minutes and my control is already slipping. "I'm going to get some water. You want some?"

She nods, but then follows me into the kitchen. Evelyn and Otis's place is small. The kitchen is basically the size of a walk-in closet, which Reggie appropriately named "the clitchet," and it's forcing a proximity to Amelia that is doing nothing to calm me down.

I grab two glasses from the cabinet before pulling out their water pitcher from the fridge. I pour some in each of the glasses and hand her one just as Reggie walks in. He grins, like he actually caught us doing something when we're literally just standing side by side, sipping from our water cups.

Always up to no good.

He turns back to the fridge and pulls out a bottle of wine before turning back around. He already looks a little toasted, but he says, "Will it bother you?" swishing the bottle.

I shake my head through a grunt. "No, man. Have at it. But I'm not carrying you home later."

He shrugs and wiggles between us to get to the cabinet. "That's fine. You're not my type anyway, Helen," he stretches, grabbing a wine glass. "Plus, you've bumped uglies with my best friend so you're off limits."

At first, I'm taken aback because my history with Evelyn isn't something that gets casually thrown out there—*like ever*—but then my eyes widen when I see Amelia's face crease with confusion.

Shit. She doesn't know *about Evelyn and me.*

Reggie tilts a wine glass toward Amelia. "Want some?" he signs.

She blinks a couple times before shaking her head. "No. Thank you, though," she signs and then glances back at me.

Evelyn quickly comes into the kitchen—where the party is, I guess—signing, "Okay, well, there's been a significant dent made in the dip."

"That's mostly my fault," Otis signs. "It was fucking amazing. I'll be over for dinner every night."

Amelia adjusts her face quickly, wiping it clean of any unease and breathes a laugh, signing to Otis, "You're welcome any time."

A strange, territorial wave ripples through me and I fight to swallow it back.

I know it's ridiculous. Amelia isn't even *my* anything and here I am ready to puff my chest up at my brother—*my engaged brother.*

Engaged to your ex-girlfriend.

I scratch the back of my jaw, claustrophobic from the intrusive thoughts and the six, grown bodies shoved into a fucking closet-kitchen.

For a brief moment, Amelia's eyes find mine. I'm trying to get a read on her but she looks away too quickly.

Goddammit.

Everyone finally starts to move to the living room, settling around the coffee table and I follow. But as I lower to the floor, my eyes float up to the ceiling.

I can't believe I have to sit with this feeling while Evelyn cheats and annihilates us all at Clue.

Evelyn pulls the board out just as her narrowing eyes sweep along all of us. "I get to be Mrs. White."

Fucking game night.

After three rounds of Clue and one sad excuse for a round of Pictionary, I think I've endured as much as I can of game night.

Reggie is practically asleep on the couch as Amelia pops up. "Well, I'd better head out. I've got some shit to do tomorrow," she signs, avoiding eye contact with me. "Thanks for inviting me. This was fun."

Evelyn stands too, signing, "It was! And thanks for bringing food," then pulls Amelia in for a hug. And . . . well, it's awkward.

For some reason I think the fact that Evelyn is very much a hugger makes it even more evident that Amelia is *not*. I actually have to suppress a small laugh as they pull away.

I stand up, signing, "I'm going to head out too."

Smooth, jackass.

Evelyn's eyebrows perk before she looks back at Amelia. "Why don't you let Dean drive you home?" she signs. "It's late."

Oh. Well . . . that worked out.

"Oh, no, that's okay. It's just a quick L ride," Amelia signs.

My eyebrows pinch but I realize now that she didn't actually answer me earlier. I'm trying to gauge whether or not she actually wants me to drive her home, but I suddenly remember her rejecting a ride after she came to the meeting last month, too.

Evelyn tilts her head, signing, "Humor me. Please. I don't like the idea of you being by yourself this late."

Amelia lets out a slow sigh and her eyebrows pinch just a little bit before she tentatively glances over at me. "You don't mind?"

I clear my throat, quickly nodding. "Not at all."

Evelyn's eyes squint at me for just a second before she looks back at Amelia. "Boxing? Wednesday?"

Amelia breathes a laugh, signing, "Yeah, okay," and Evelyn smiles again.

I say quick goodbyes to her and Otis before Amelia and I are heading down the stairs and out the door.

Street parking is even easier the farther north you go, so luckily, I snagged a spot right outside their building. The wind is whipping as I open the passenger door to my truck. Amelia does a quick peek at me before she grabs onto the bar above the door and hoists herself in.

After I close the door, I round the front of the truck and hop into the driver's seat, immediately starting the car and cranking up the heat.

Goddamn, I hate winter.

Amelia's shivering too, holding her hands out in front of the vents. "Every year I think I'm used to it, and every year I'm wrong," she signs.

A small laugh rumbles in my throat but my muscles are tight from the cold.

"It's the wind," I sign. "Denver gets just as cold but the wind is brutal here."

She chuckles but then squints back at me. "Is that where you're from?"

Shaking my head, I sign, "No. I just moved out there for a few years right after college. I grew up in Rockford. It's about an hour and a half west of the city."

She nods. "I know where Rockford is. I lived there too for a few months."

My eyebrows hitch but my mind latches onto the last part of the sentence.

"Just a few months?" I sign.

She rubs her hands together again, holding them in front of the vent for another second before she signs, "Yeah. I was a foster kid, so . . . I moved around a lot." She shrugs awkwardly and her eyes float back down to her lap.

Foster care?

I run my teeth along my bottom lip. I'm not really sure how to respond to that new bit of information, but it doesn't seem like she wants to elaborate, so I simply shrug. "A few months is all you need in Rockford," I chuckle, but her expression seems less playful, almost lost in thought.

Deciding to change the subject, I stutter, "I'm—uhh . . ."

Good start.

I clear my throat, trying to figure out what to say before I slowly sign, "I'm sorry if that was weird for you. To find out about me and Evelyn like that."

She's quiet for a few, long seconds before her eyes peek back up to me. "Why would it be weird?"

"Uhh—I don't know," I sign, awkwardly. "Because you and Evelyn are friends and you and I are—" I stop, having the good sense to realize how stupid it will sound to say "hooking up."

I see her chest rise but her expression stays even before she tilts her lips and her eyebrows crease. "Oh, don't worry about it," she signs, seemingly unfazed. "When were you guys together?"

I swallow, signing, "Back in college. We broke up after graduation."

She nods but doesn't say anything else for a second. Eventually, I flip the windshield wiper and the sheen of ice clears, but I see Amelia's hands move in my peripherals.

"Is that why you moved to Denver?"

A long sigh pushes past my lips. I'm not sure if she's just wildly intuitive or if I'm more transparent than I realize, but *this* is one of the many reasons why my situation sucks. Because nothing about my history with Evelyn is simple. It's convoluted and uncomfortable— and I don't want to talk about any of it—especially with someone I hope to continue to sleep with.

But I don't want to lie to her either, so I simply nod.

"Does she know about what we've been doing?" she signs.

"No," I say quickly, then shake my head and sign, "No. Definitely not." But I can't help but ask, "Why?"

Amelia's eyes pull back down before she shrugs. "She just seemed so adamant about you driving me home. I wasn't sure if she had ulterior motives."

I snort a laugh. I don't know why exactly, but it happens instinctively. The truth is, it *does* actually sound like something Evelyn might do for one of her friends. But I know that's not the reason.

I shake my head. "No. She's just . . . cautious." I shift my weight, not wanting to sit in the thought of all of it for too long, before I reach for my seatbelt. When I look back over at Amelia I can see her throat tighten through a swallow as she grabs hers too, timidly clicking the seatbelt in place.

I remember again, her hesitancy to accept a ride. I'm just about to ask if she's okay when she signs, "I really don't want to go home yet."

My eyebrows thread. It's not what I was expecting her to say. Though, I'm not sure *what* I was expecting . . .

"You can come to my place?" I offer.

Her shoulders lower just slightly and she pulls her lips into her mouth before she exhales with a nod. "Okay."

chapter twenty-one
amelia

My anxiety feels like a fucking relay race lately. Where one spell ends, another one taps in, ready to continue to the finish line.

My knee is bouncing wildly against the floor of the truck and my heart is pounding so hard I can feel it in my throat.

We're driving.

I haven't been in the passenger's seat of a car in . . .

Jesus—nearly twenty years.

And there's a reason for it.

Do not have a panic attack in this man's car.

He isn't driving particularly fast but the vibrations from the poorly paved streets are jittering me further and the passing of each building out the window feels like it's adding momentum to my racing pulse.

The more I concentrate on trying to not panic, the more the feeling builds. My heart rate accelerates and my nose struggles to inhale while my lungs fail to fill completely.

Everything I need in order to breathe is working against me.

I yelp involuntarily as the passenger's side wheel dips into a pot-hole, dropping the truck and rattling the cab.

As we return to the flat road again, I notice I'm also clutching the grab handle above the door. I try again to pull in a deep enough breath but I don't need to look over to Dean to know he's staring at me.

Maybe it's the panicked, baby goat noise you just made, dumbass.

My one hand continues to hold onto the grab handle while my other palm starts to rub against the rough, coarse denim of my jeans.

Jesus Christ. He's going to have me committed . . .

I'm sure I must look bizarre right now—a white knuckle fist, grab-bing at a handle made for distress and rubbing my thigh like I'm try-ing to start a fucking fire with my hand.

"S-Sorry. I . . ." My throat feels dry and my voice sounds squeaky so I swallow and then finish, "I don't like cars."

My nails work their way into the mix and start scratching at the grooves on my pants. My thumb nail is a little longer than the rest so I dig that one in as hard as I can and twist it, feeling a small pinch on my thigh.

When we come to a red light on Lake Shore Drive, the car slows to a stop. I'm too embarrassed to look over at him. If I felt like I could say anything, I'd tell him that he can just take me home, but my throat feels too tight to speak and my hands are . . . busy.

Movement in my peripherals startles me but then I feel Dean's hand cover mine on my thigh. I instinctively flinch. I'm still struggling to breathe but I distantly register that he still hasn't said anything.

He hasn't responded to my admission about not liking cars or asked me what's wrong, but he's . . . holding my hand?

Well . . . he's resting his hand . . . on mine.

The heaviness of his palm on top of mine feels oddly comforting, like a weighted blanket, and I stare down at it, losing myself in the way it completely covers my hand . . .

"Just humor me," Wally signed. "Doris says some girls 'bling them out.'"

I rolled my eyes, but breathed a laugh. They had insisted I get hearing aids if I was going to live on my own in a city, so they had me fitted for them a few weeks ago.

Another thing they didn't have to do but did for some reason.

I'll never know why they chose to let me stay with them or insisted on doing such nice things for me since I wasn't even their actual kid, but I'm not sure I'd ever appreciate anything more than the bone life threw me when they came into my life.

"You spent years teaching me sign language just to make me listen to people again?" I signed, my usual sarcasm poking through.

He chuckled, but then his soft blue eyes tilted as he signed, "It's a hearing world, Amelia. You use your voice, so that's helpful for them, *but communication works both ways. What if you can't read someone's lips or . . ." he trailed off and scratched at the patchy white scruff on his cheek and sighed. "I'm not worried about you surviving. I know you can do that. But being part of the world is harder. Just take them. Just in case."*

I really didn't foresee wanting to use them much, if at all. It was already hard enough trying to have an identity as a kid in foster care, and adding "selectively deaf" or "selectively hearing" somehow muddled that more.

Plus, the one thing I actually appreciated about my hearing loss was that it kept me isolated by default. But I took the case, thanking him anyway.

Maybe I was buttering him up. I wanted to get something off my chest— something I'd been thinking about for the last year when I made this plan to move. But now that it was happening, my nerves were getting the better of me.

"I was thinking I'd go see her on my way in . . ." I signed.

Wally casually leaned back, studying me, but then dipped his chin ever so slightly with a small nod. "If that's what you want to do, you should do it."

My eyes widened. I didn't necessarily expect him to fight me on it, but he also didn't seem as worried as I imagined he would be.

I still kept all the specific shitty details of my life with my mother to myself, but as my guardians, Wally and Doris knew whatever Dr. G was obligated to tell them. And they were intuitive people; I think they had put enough together to know at least the gist of what happened.

"I don't want to. You and Doris are . . ." I lost the words. I didn't want him to think I had just been waiting until I turned eighteen so I could go back and see her, because that definitely wasn't the case. I couldn't explain it, but something about seeing her—going back there by choice—before I left it all for a life I was going to make for myself, felt like the ultimate challenge.

A pass through the ring of fire before I victoriously walked away for good.

He sighed. "You're a brave kid, Amelia. You remind me a lot of Doris, actually. You're tough and . . . I know you're not actually related to her, but I think you've acquired her sass as well," he chuckled.

A small laugh trickled out of me too but the humor was overtaken by warmth. To be compared to Doris was such a compliment to me. I didn't see it, but it made me feel good that he did.

He shifted so that he was facing me head on. He placed one of his hands over mine and it was the first time I didn't wince at the contact. I glanced back up at him and he offered me a small, tilted smile.

"You've got this, Amelia."

I've got this . . .

It's not until we're pulling into a parking garage that I notice I've turned Dean's hand over my lap and I'm tracing the lines of his palm with my fingers.

Oh my God, you're such a freak!

I stop what I'm doing immediately but I can't help but notice that the panic has calmed. Between the memory and the soothing nature of tracing Dean's hand—it's almost like the two exorcized the adrenaline out. It also helps that he's parking the truck.

I finally feel my lungs expand as he cranks the gear and shuts off the car.

"Thanks," I sign, finally braving a small peek at him.

His lips tilt timidly, signing, "I've had panic attacks before. They're the fucking worst."

The admission surprises me for some reason but I'm not sure why. I think there's something about the nature of your body feeling like it's shutting down that makes you believe no one, except a person on the brink of death, has felt that way. And therefore, after, maybe it's just surprising to know that someone else *has* passed through that hell, too, and lived to tell the tale.

"Well . . . thanks for letting me borrow your hand," I sign awkwardly before I glance back up at him.

His coffee-colored eyes catch the smallest twinkle from the overhead light in the parking garage before his mouth inches up and he signs, "Anytime," with a slightly devious expression.

A relieved laugh pushes past my lips. He's not acting any differently; he's still looking at me with every bit of attraction I saw earlier.

He's had panic attacks too.

Our eyes lock for another second before he breaks the contact and opens his door. I do the same, but I'm a little slower to move after the adrenaline surge, and by the time I'm climbing out, he's at the passenger door, helping me step down the sizable distance between the floor to the truck and the ground.

When our eyes yet again catch on each other's, I can't help but wonder what's brought on *his* panic attacks.

He just seems so . . . steady. But then again, I don't know him very well. And I find it odd I have to keep reminding myself of that. I also remind myself that he seems steady *now*.

But he's a young, single dad, he's struggled with addiction—his brother is marrying his ex-girlfriend.

God. I could panic for *him if I think about it all.*

I shake my head and follow him toward the stairwell.

We make our way up the steps before the distant familiarity of his building starts to find me. I haven't been here since that night we met at the bar, but I remember the smell in particular. In general, Lincoln Park's neighborhood has this strong, earthy smell to it. I don't know if it's the zoo nearby or Lakefront Trails, but the neighborhood has this almost mossy scent.

Dean slides the key into the lock of his door and opens it, stepping in and then moving aside so I can enter. When I walk through the doorway, my eyes curiously move along the expanse of the space.

Last time I was here there wasn't much time for noticing his apartment, but this time, I take it in before I've even started to slip out of my coat.

It's a simple space, tidy but not decorated—which doesn't surprise me. I wouldn't exactly expect to see him at HomeGoods or anything. I do notice a playpen in the living room with a bunch of toys piled in one corner. A couple of rogue binkies are strewn about on the couch and side table. But my eyes zone in on a small picture frame next to the binky on the table.

Folding my coat over my arm, I take a couple steps closer to get a better look and see Dean, wearing a dreamy-ass smile as he stares adoringly down at a baby girl with sparkly blue eyes and a crooked grin, and my mouth inches up my cheek.

My ovaries feel like they're doing a fucking hula dance so I look away from the picture before it somehow impregnates me, but when I turn I'm met with the man in the photo.

Feeling caught *and* nosy—maybe a little intrusive—I smile up at him sheepishly. "She's beautiful," I sign, angling my eyes toward the frame.

His smile is soft as his eyes pull down to it for a second too and then back up to me. "Thanks," he signs before extending his hand out toward me.

I hand him my coat and try to avoid poking around his apartment any more. I'm not really sure what's appropriate in these situations and it was nice enough that he brought me here after my little episode in the car.

"Are you hungry?" he signs. "I don't really have much but you didn't even get to eat any of your dip."

I shake my head but then my eyes lift to his, signing, "Neither did you."

He nods, chuckling. "I know. I'm pretty sure my brother blacks out when he's eating something good and I know you're an amazing cook so . . . I prepared myself."

A laugh trickles out before an idea blooms. "I could make *you* something?"

He shakes his head. "Thanks, but I really don't have anything. I *do* have a stack of microwave dinners in the freezer?"

My mouth gapes as my eyes widen.

Oh no.

My appall quickly subsides when I see the potential for an interesting challenge—one I think we can both have some fun with—and my lips tilt on my cheek.

I peek over toward the kitchen with lighter energy before I glance back to him. "What will you give me if I can whip something up that isn't riddled with chemicals?"

Dean's eyes squint and a smile pokes at his cheek before he runs his teeth along his bottom lip. "Don't I still owe you for the last bet?"

I'm pretty sure his comfort in the car and the fact that he didn't make a big deal of it are repayment enough, but I don't want to bring attention to it again so I simply sign, "You afraid of racking up debt, Roberts?" as I cock an eyebrow.

He snorts a laugh but then gives me a sexy grin before he strides over to me and my eyes slowly float from his chest and up to his eyes.

He leans down toward my cheek and whispers, "I think you're severely overestimating the supplies in my kitchen."

Jesus Christ, his voice. It has the rough edge of sandpaper and the smoothness of silk at the same fucking time.

It takes some effort, but I pull in a deep inhale, lifting my chest as I pull away from his face and glance back up at him.

"I think you're *underestimating* my abilities," I sign back up at him, playfully.

His head tilts with amusement before his expression darkens just a bit. "Fine," he signs, and then pulls his phone out of his back pocket. "Can you whip it up in . . ." he glances down at the phone and finishes, "Twenty minutes?"

My eyebrows hitch. I wasn't expecting him to up the ante but . . .

I glance at the kitchen one more time like a runner scanning their route before I look back at him. I close the small distance I put between us and hover my lips over his like I'm about to kiss him, but instead I say, "Start the timer."

chapter twenty-two
dean

Amelia has pulled her hair up into a ponytail, rolled up her sleeves, and been hard at work for ten minutes already. I've taken up residency on the couch but I haven't been able to take my eyes off of her from the cut out in the kitchen wall.

Her emerald eyes hold a determined excitement as she peeks around the expanse of the counter, seemingly taking inventory of the things she's already gathered while bacon crackles on the stove.

Forgot I had bacon.

But she's a fucking vision. I'm not even sure I'm blinking. Luckily, she's too busy to catch me gawking, but I see her lean over toward the coffee maker, moving it aside as she apparently discovers something.

She pulls a sweet potato out—like a bunny out of a fucking hat—and holds it up at me. "Rogue vegetation!" she signs victoriously and a laugh bursts out of me.

Guess I missed that one when I bought them for Ava. But leave it to the lioness hunting and gathering in my kitchen to find it.

She smells it, then mutters, "Still good," to herself as she nods and continues to work. As much as I would love to keep watching her, I need to stop. It's bordering on creepy. And I think the challenge is helping her shake off whatever happened in the car, so I want her to enjoy it without leering eyes.

I felt terrible when I saw her fighting the panic off. I had gathered that she avoided car rides, but . . .

Wherever *that* fear comes from, it seems . . . deeply rooted. She's clearly someone that keeps things close to her chest, and . . . I kind of like that about her. It certainly makes getting to know her a little more challenging, but it also makes me feel that much more worthy when she actually *does* share something with me.

She makes you work for it.

But it's interesting. It's a strong contrast to how she is with her sexuality. She's so brazen and adventurous—seemingly up for anything.

A low hum rumbles in my chest at the thought, but I clear my throat and pull my phone out of my pocket to try and distract myself.

I kill some time by responding to some emails and checking my meetings scheduled for the week. I also check a social media account where I have an inbox full of messages from Reggie—well, not messages, grumpy old man memes—reminding me again of why I don't check this shit.

Suddenly, Amelia emerges from the kitchen with two bowls. I blink at her and then look back at my phone, then back up at her again.

She smiles. "Four minutes to spare," she signs. "Sweet potato hash with like . . . four sauteed spinach leaves and bacon. You have rosemary and parsley so I sprinkled some of that in there, too." She points to a dollop of sauce on the side and signs, "Oh, and a garlic aioli."

Disbelief floods my face.

She made this *in* my *kitchen?*

It looks fucking amazing and smells even better. I knew she'd win the bet, but *damn.*

She sits on the floor across from me and my eyebrows pinch. I want to invite her to sit next to me, but I think if she'd wanted to, she would have, so I sign, "We can sit at the table, if you want?"

She shakes her head, signing, "I like sitting on the floor. It's good for your posture."

I have to stop myself from hopping down to the floor and sitting next to her but I manage to stay put and sign, "Thanks for making this."

She wiggles where she sits, signing, "Another victory!" as she smirks and stirs her bowl.

I tilt my head, feeling the need to tease her with, "Well, we have to try it first . . . it's not a victory if it's bad," but even I don't believe it.

Her eyes squint with faux-offense as she fights a smile. "Leave room for your words, Roberts. You're going to have to eat them too when this is the best thing you've ever tasted." She gives me a "take that" look, but my eyes involuntarily drift down her body, and a smirk pulls up my cheek.

I don't say the dirty thought about how *she* is the best thing I've ever tasted but something about her returning grin tells me she knows exactly where my head went.

I stir what's in my bowl, knowing it's going to be delicious. I make sure to get a little bit of everything on the spoon, before taking a big bite. My body immediately slumps back on the couch and I actually laugh.

It's so fucking good.

I lose my playfulness, immediately starting to shovel more into my mouth before I catch Amelia watching me. When I look back up at her, she glances down—like she was caught—but her smile is wide.

And I was right. Her smile is achingly beautiful. But it's gone as quickly as it appeared as she pulls her bottom lip between her teeth and then takes a bite herself.

Her eyes close with the first bite, just like they did with the chili, and I'm currently trying to decide if watching her cook or eat is better. It's truly a toss up.

When her eyes reopen, she gives a small, approving nod before she takes another bite. "I totally won."

I nod. She definitely did. I'm again, unsure of what we were betting, but I also don't really care. I take another bite, enjoying the sweet and salty combination from the potato and bacon. Challenge or not . . . her ability to make something out of nothing is impressive.

"The friend who taught you how to cook—are they a chef?" I sign.

She nods, a bit timidly. "He *was.* He had retired by the time I met him."

My eyebrows pinch, confused. "Retired?"

She swallows her bite and nods. Her eyes scan the table for a second before she sheepishly peeks back up at me. "His name was Wally. I started living with him and his wife Doris when I was fifteen."

"So, they were your foster parents?" I sign.

She snorts a laugh. "I never referred to them as that. I mean, I was already a teenager when I met them and . . . I wasn't exactly the well, put together woman you see here today," she signs, chuckling nervously before she shrugs. "They were just . . . Wally and Doris." Her eyes become a bit distant and she continues to push her food around in her bowl, her mood becoming a little more solemn.

My eyebrows pinch, signing, "I'm sorry . . . I didn't mean to—"

I'm cut off by her shaking her head. "No, it's really fine," she signs. "I just . . . miss them sometimes."

"You don't see them anymore?"

She shakes her head. "Doris passed away just a little bit after I moved out here, and Wally followed a year or so later." Her eyes squint and she tilts her head, still mostly looking at her food. "It sounds weird . . . but I knew he wouldn't be here long after she went."

"What do you mean?"

She shrugs, pulling in a heavy breath before she pushes it back out and chuckles. "Wally used to tell me that the two of them were like gibbons." She stares at me, but I have no fucking clue what a gibbon is so I stare blankly back at her and she breathes another small laugh. "They look like monkeys but they're actually, 'lesser apes,' or so Wally said." She shakes her head, with a soft smile before she signs, "I guess they're known for their lifelong partnerships and when one of them dies, their mate can ultimately die from heartbreak."

Wow, that's . . . really sad.

I feel bad having brought it up, but she doesn't look upset. She actually looks a little more relaxed, but I take another bite in order to keep myself from saying something else stupid.

We settle into a comfortable silence for a few moments. I keep catching her peek over at me to watch me eat and it's fucking adorable. Her eyes float over to the side table, staring at the picture of Ava and me again, and then they drift back to me. "How old is your daughter?"

I put my bowl back on the table. "She'll be one next month," I sign.

Her eyes widen as she nods, signing, "So she spends half the week with her mom and the other half with you?"

I nod, but the mention of Marnie dominos into the reminder of her "to-be-determined move," turning my stomach. My face must give me away because Amelia quickly signs, "I'm sorry. That was probably rude . . . I might as well be a troll in conversations."

I snort a laugh. "A *troll?*"

She laughs, too, signing, "No manners," lifting her arms with a shrug and my eyebrows pinch.

On the contrary, I think she's incredibly polite. Hell, she's the only one who was thoughtful enough to even bring food to game night and she didn't even eat any of it.

"No, it wasn't rude," I sign, in an attempt to reassure her, but then I realize my obvious discomfort must seem weird.

This shit with Marnie is eating me alive. I get small blips of relief when I'm distracted or busy—but the unease, the unknown—it always seems to creep its way back in.

Talking about it with my family seems too risky but . . . telling *someone*—someone that won't worry about me—isn't something I'd considered.

I clear my throat. "Marnie, Ava's mom . . . she wants to move them to Michigan with her boyfriend."

Amelia's eyes widen as her brow furrows. She sits for a second longer before her eyes squint back at me. "Can she *do* that?"

I shrug. "I don't know. But with my . . . background, it wouldn't surprise me if a judge sided with her—if it came to that."

She shakes her head, again, quiet for a few beats. "That's . . . not right. Taking a kid away from their dad to move away with some guy," she signs, looking down, saying the last part of the sentence almost to herself.

I have the briefest moment where I feel the need to defend Marnie, but it just as quickly passes because . . . Amelia's right. The situation might not be as black and white as she's suggesting, but the sentiment is all the same. Marnie's *choosing* a life for our daughter that doesn't regularly involve both of her parents and it's *not* fucking right.

I breathe deep, feeling at the very least *validated* from Amelia's response. It does the smallest bit to give me some ease and my shoulders slowly loosen.

My bowl was empty a long time ago and I can see that Amelia's finished hers too. I use the opportunity to give myself a second and hopefully leave the conversation behind while I carry the bowls to the sink and rinse them out, then load them into the dishwasher.

I notice the dishes she used are already clean and the counters have been wiped down, giving the room a faint lemon scent.

I swear, I *feel* her eyes on me before I turn around and see her, smirking devilishly as she leans against the archway to the kitchen.

"Four minutes to spare *and* I cleaned up after myself," she signs.

"Impressive," I sign, moving slowly. My hands are itching to touch her, but I keep them to myself for the moment.

Her eyes flutter, staring up at me from under her thick, dark lashes as she signs, "I'm good at other things too, ya know," while her lips quirk at the corner.

Oh, I fucking know. But she seems to want to . . . *play* . . . and I am more than down for that too. My eyes fall to her collar bone, staring at her necklace again. She seems to always wear it and it just looks . . . *right* on her neckline, like it'd be weird to see her without it.

I peek back into her green eyes, signing, "Our word is lightning."

I can't be certain what compels me to say it. I'm not actually worried about needing a safe word, but . . . I kind of like the idea of having *something* with her. Something I can see, or a word I can hear that makes me think of her, and this seems as good of an excuse as any. I'm not sure what it means, only that I like it.

She seems to like it too, since she nods. Her eyes pull down as she whispers, "Lightning," almost to herself, through a reluctant smile. I suddenly have my own challenge turning over in my mind . . . I don't tell her what, I just gently pin her to the archway by holding my palm over her chest, right over the bolt, my fingers lightly curling at the base of her throat.

My mouth travels to her jaw and my lips just barely press to her skin. "What makes Amelia smile?" I muse, as her head tilts back, giving me more access to her neck. But I'm more interested in her face right now, so I pinch her chin, pulling it down until her eyes are back on mine.

The hand I have splayed on her chest travels down to the waste line of her jeans, hooking two fingers inside and running them along the hem line as I rasp, "After she comes, maybe?"

Her breath hitches and something sparks in her eyes. Without any warning, I hoist her up, guiding her legs around me as my lips crash against hers. It's teeth and tongues, swallowing each other's desperate sounds as her thighs tighten around me and my dick starts to strain against my jeans.

God, I've wanted to do this all night.

Actually, I've wanted to do it since our night in front of the mirror, but admitting that—*even internally*—sounds pretty desperate.

It's true, but desperate nonetheless. I carry her toward the bedroom and her mouth moves to my ear, nibbling on it as I kick the door shut behind us. I lower her to the bed and hover over her, kissing her again with even more hunger than before.

So fucking good.

She bites at my lip, balling the fabric of my shirt in her hands and yanking it up. I tentatively pull away to let her get it over my head and she sits up, forcing me back. Her eyes rake over my chest, then down to my torso while her fingers trace the curves and divots of my abs.

"So beautiful," she breathes. Her eyes finally find their way back to mine and her expression becomes mischievous as she moves to stand.

I stand too as she slides herself off the bed. As soon as she's in front of me, her fingers start to unbutton my pants and slowly pull down the zipper as she says, "I believe I have a debt to collect." Her eyes peek back up and my mouth tilts.

"Whatever you want, baby," I mumble hoarsely, tucking some fallen pieces of hair behind her ear and her eyes light deviously.

"Anything?" she signs.

I nod because it's true. She's awakened something in me I thought was dead and now that it's risen—pun fucking intended—I'm pretty sure I'll do anything she asks.

She smiles, and I hold the victory in the bank of my silent challenge as she lowers herself, pulling my pants and boxers down at the same time, making me fully naked while she remains clothed.

"On the bed," she orders.

I listen, but the urge to pull her down with me is strong. She rewards me by undressing herself. As she steps out of her jeans, she glances over at me. "Do you have any ties?"

My eyebrows pinch but I nod, signing, "Top drawer."

She walks to the dresser, giving me a view of the beauty mark on her left ass cheek that drives me mad for some reason, before she finds my ties. Grabbing three, she places two on the bed before she ties a dark green one around her neck, making a perfect knot and straightening it out like she's got a job interview or something.

A breathy chuckle escapes me as she turns toward me and *god-fucking-damn*. I can't even believe how sexy she looks—completely naked with my tie fit loosely around her neck.

My dick jumps at the sight and she smirks before she signs, "Lie back."

She's in charge.

I do as she says, lying back against the mattress as she crawls over me, the tie dangling between us as she kisses me again. When she pulls away, she asks, "Condoms?"

I glance toward the nightstand and she leans over to grab one, then settles back over me. "I'm going to tie you up now," she says softly.

My heart jumps. I've never been restrained before—I've never tied someone up myself—but she looks down at me, signing, "What's the word?"

I swallow hard. "Lightning," I rasp, my voice low and gravelly, filled with desire so deep I'm fucking drowning in it.

"Good boy," she says and my dick yet again twitches and, yet again, it surprises me. But there's this fire in her eyes, like maybe this is the first time she's doing this to someone too, and the notion stirs low in my stomach.

She uses the neck ties to secure my wrists around the headboard and then moves her body down mine, kissing and licking her way to my dick.

She slowly lowers her warm, wet mouth down on me and my eyes slam shut as my arms pull against the ties.

Jesus Christ. Was she a fucking boy scout or something?

Realizing how tightly bound I really am has me pulling again, but my eyes roll back as she bobs on me from below, sucking and licking her way up and down me like it's a goddamn ice cream cone. My hips start to move into her, and she groans around me, sending a shockwave to my balls and a groan rumbles out.

Holy fuck. So good.

She pops off and urges me to sit up, so I do, but it's difficult with my hands tied.

"Wouldn't want you to miss the show," she signs, and then lowers herself onto me again.

"Eyes on me," I growl, and her eyes flick up, her mouth still tightly wrapped around me and the sight is enough to make me bust. She continues, watching me as she works me with her mouth.

I'm holding on by a fucking thread. Taking away my ability to touch her is somehow making what she's doing even more intense and her green eyes are watching, gleaming with excitement over what she's doing to me.

She releases me, but then lightly traces her tongue up my long, hard length. "Give me some dirty words," she whispers between her torture just before she teases the tip and a deep moan vibrates in my chest.

My brain feels like a live, fucking power line right now, but I breathe deep and watch her take me back in her mouth. I push my hips up, just a bit, groaning again at the sensation. "You look so good like this, baby."

She moans around me again, taking me deeper, mumbling, "So, good," around my cock.

Good fucking God.

I pull against the restraints again and she slowly pulls her mouth off of me, replacing it with the condom before settling me at her entrance. She peeks back up, her eyes unabashedly scanning me. "You look so hot, Roberts. Tied up and at the mercy of your needy little slut."

I blink as the word stutters in my brain. But I don't have much time to stew in it, because she slowly sinks herself down on me, inch by inch, burying me deep inside her.

"Fuck," I hiss.

Her hips grind on me and I start to meet her thrusts—slow and deep.

She smiles darkly as she leans down and takes my lips again. I vaguely count the point toward my original challenge, but I've lost count. I've lost everything—my name, where I am, *who* I am. I lose it all as she rocks my fucking world.

chapter twenty-three
amelia

*N*ewsflash! You're the reason we're in the car right now!"

I wake with a jolt and my eyes dart around the room, quickly noticing Dean on the other end of the couch. My neck is slick with sweat and I feel a sheen of it along my hairline, too. *Shit.*

I must have dozed off after we put on the movie. I blink rapidly and glance at the TV.

THE CHAMBER OF SECRETS HAS BEEN OPENED,

ENEMIES OF THEIR HEIR . . . BEWARE.

Ain't that the fucking truth.

My eyes brave a peek over at Dean, who is watching me cautiously and I shake my head. "Sorry . . ." I sign.

His eyebrows pinch. "Why are you apologizing?"

I shrug. *I don't know.* My mind is still partially caught in my dream—*well, memory*—and I'm still trying to adjust to waking up somewhere that's not my apartment. I've never fallen asleep at a guy's place before.

I've never let that happen.

My eyes squint at Dean while he continues to watch me, a worried expression deepening the fine lines of his face and I break the contact from his warm, brown eyes. An irrational fear starts to claw its way through me, like maybe he somehow *saw* the dream or something.

I try to control my shaky hand as I grab the water he got me before the movie started, gulping it down. I need to regain some control. Our sexy time earlier *cannot* be the intermission between panic attacks

Be the badass woman who tied him up. Not the scared, pathetic girl.

After the water, and some practiced breathing, my heart rate finally starts to settle.

"How long was I out?" I sign, my muscles still a little tight.

"About an hour," he signs.

I nod, glancing back at the TV. From the looks of it, we're about halfway through the movie.

I'm at Dean's. We're watching a movie. She's dead.

I continue to repeat the thoughts in my head as I feel Dean's hand slide onto my leg, just below my knee. I jerk at the contact but when I peek back up at him, he gives me a soft smile. For reasons completely unknown to me, the rest of the tension falls from my body at the sight.

Maybe he's actually a wizard . . .

He certainly works some sorcery in the bedroom and he's found a way to comfort me through two spirals in the span of three hours. My eyes fall to the square cut of his jaw, tracing his stubble like I'm trying to connect the dots with my eyes.

He's definitely a fucking wizard.

The thought makes me sigh out a laugh, and Dean's eyes squint, confused. Deciding I already look crazy enough, I keep my new discovery to myself and pick my phone up from the coffee table.

Shit. It's after midnight. L trains are going to be few and far between at this hour and I have class in the morning. I know Dean would give me a ride, but then I'd have to survive the screaming metal death trap again. And I'm pretty sure after three panic attacks—I'd be out.

And I don't want that.

"I should get home," I sign, moving to stand.

"It's late," he signs. "You can just . . ." he stops himself, scratching the back of his jaw.

He does that a lot. And I don't know if it's just from the rollercoaster of emotions I've felt all night, but it does something for me to see a nervous tick of *his*.

But why is he nervous?

"I'll take you home," he signs. I start to say no but he shakes his head. "It's not up for discussion, Amelia. I'll ride the L with you if you don't want me to drive you, but you're not going alone."

I ignore the little tingle downstairs from his bossy-protective pants coming out and instead, straighten my spine, signing, "I'm perfectly capable of getting home on my own, Roberts." Except, after I finger-spell the name, I make the R handshape and couple it with the sign for lightning.

His eyebrows hitch as his lips slowly inch up his cheek and mine do too. It's the first name sign I've given out, and a small swell of warmth flows through my chest when I can tell that he likes it.

Plus, it's what I call him most of the time. And it will be nice to not have to fingerspell it.

His lazy smile stays put as he closes the distance between us. He pinches my chin and pulls my face up to meet his eyes. "Be a good girl, and go get your coat."

Majority of the venture back to my apartment was spent waiting for a train. The ride itself only took about six minutes.

Dean insisted on walking me to my door but . . . I just don't think it's a good idea. I clearly have no control where he's concerned and I can't be held responsible for pulling him into my apartment and keeping him captive till morning.

But I've told myself—*promised* myself—I won't let it happen. Tonight has been . . . a lot. And I really do need some time to myself to decompress. But as we get closer to my apartment, our steps simultaneously slow, prolonging the last few steps.

When we finally reach the door, I turn to him, signing, "Should I escort you home now?"

He chuckles and dips his chin as one of his wavy, chestnut locks falls to his forehead.

Oof. Dreamboat.

I inhale deep, trying to feed my nonsense some oxygen. He's creeping into some dangerous territory for me—another reason why I need some time to myself. I'm trying to follow Dr. G's advice and just lean into whatever I'm feeling but . . . I don't know. It's too intense with him. *Too unknown*—and I just need to tread lightly.

Which is hard to do when he's looking at me like he is right now.

I swallow and pull my keys from my bag, moving them to the lock as I lift the handle and pop the door with my hip, but it's not quite enough. I give it a small kick and it finally pushes open while Dean breathes a laugh.

"I can probably fix that," he mumbles, glancing up at the uneven edge toward the top of the door.

I shrug. "I'm used to it. Plus I like that it's kind of hard to get in and out."

His smirk returns with a nod. "That actually . . . makes sense," he signs.

My eyes squint back at him. Something about his statement seems deeper than a casual commentary on my door but it's not something I'm willing to dive into right now.

"Thanks for the protection. And thanks for . . ." I again, stop myself from reminding him of my embarrassing displays tonight, but I really am grateful. Not just for the way he handled them, but he also didn't press me for explanations.

I might appreciate that even more.

"The sex?" he smirks, playfully.

I snort a laugh. *I'll never live it down, I guess.*

"Assume I'm always grateful for that," I sign and he laughs again.

He takes me by surprise when he leans down and presses his lips to mine. I actually feel him flinch a bit too, like maybe he surprised himself as well—but I don't pull away.

No, my delirious ass actually grabs his chin, holding him to me, enjoying the feeling of his coarse scruff against my fingertips, soaking in the warmth of his mouth. Eventually, he pulls away, his eyes slightly dazed before he blinks and glances down at his feet—*almost shyly*—making my goddamn knees wobble.

Amelia. What the fuck?!

When he looks back up at me, he signs, "There's another open meeting on Thursday. In case you're interested."

I tilt my head to the side, pulling in a deep inhale. The truth is, I do kind of want to go. I have no idea why . . . it's not like going there gave me any sort of clarity, but there was something about seeing other people—hearing their struggles—that made me feel . . . I don't know. Less alone than I thought?

I huff out a breath, shaking my head. There's a lot of "new" happening around me and it's messing with my instincts, my carefully laid out rules and guidelines for life.

"I have a study group that day. But I'll let you know."

Good. I left the door open for possibility, but didn't commit to anything. That's closer to the careful bitch I know.

He nods before signing, "Goodnight," as he backs away from the door.

It's the strangest thing. It really is. My urge to keep him here is combating my strong need to give myself some space. It runs through me so hard that I nearly call after him, but instead I suck my lips into my mouth and watch him reach the end of the hallway before he descends down the steps.

Definitely a wizard. And I'm under his sexy fucking spell.

Another beat passes and I finally realize I'm a weirdo staring wistfully into her hallway in the middle of the night, so I maneuver the door shut, then lock the deadbolt. When I walk out of the entryway, Beatrice darts out of nowhere, screeching at me like a howler monkey.

"I gave you extra food before I left," I mutter, but make my way to the kitchen and top off her bowl.

She is *queen of the manor, after all.*

Once I make my way to my bedroom, I remove my hearing aids, then go into the bathroom. As I wash my face, I suddenly notice the small window by the shower in the reflection of the mirror.

My eyebrows pinch and I turn around to face it.

It's open.

It's just barely open, so maybe I just didn't close it all the way after my shower. I step into the shower and shut it tight, flipping the lock on the top of the sill before my eyes instinctively scan the bathroom.

Nothing out of place.

I open the door but keep the towel in my hand, running it through my fingers as my paranoia pulls me to every room in my apartment, looking for . . . what? *An intruder?* Wouldn't they have made themselves known by now?

I glance around the living room and everything seems in order. Even my papers I fanned out along the desk look exactly as they did before I left. My purple blanket is laying in the exact same spot.

I roll my eyes, flicking off the light and walking back to my bedroom.

Get a grip, Amelia.

There's only one haunting happening here, and she didn't come in through the fucking window.

God. I've never felt soreness happening *as* I'm working out. But I can feel the chords of my neck tighten as I roll my shoulders and slug my way toward the bench at the perimeter of the room with Evelyn and Reggie.

They do this for fun?!

I drop to the hard seat as a symphony of huffs and puffs fill the room but my own breathing is the goddamn tuba line.

"Wasn't that great?" Evelyn signs, plopping down next to me as Reggie stands, stretching his arms.

I don't even try to fix my face. I stare at her like she's the deranged woman who just suggested anything about *that* was fun.

Punching shit hurts. And not just your hands. My shoulders, my abs—my fucking arm hair hurts.

"You're one of those people who thinks a woman's vag and her asshole becoming one during childbirth is beautiful, aren't you?"

Evelyn giggles before she signs, "It takes some getting used to," her lips tilting apologetically.

I shake my head, whining as my body folds over on my lap.

Reggie makes a *"Psh"* sound before signing, "Girl, you did great! I'd hate to be on the receiving end of your uppercut."

I don't really remember the names of the punches but there was one that swipes up in a vertical line at the opponent's chin. It seemed like such a specific move—super intentional—and it made me wonder about how often it's used in an actual fight. And then I was determined to get it down.

I shake my head. "Don't count on me if some weirdos try to shank us in the alley," I sign, breathing a laugh. After I toss the gloves in the sanitation basket, I see that both of their faces have dropped and the energy has abruptly dampened.

Shit.

I just want to switch the subject, but I don't know what I said to shift the mood to begin with . . .

This is one of many reasons why I shouldn't talk to people.

Reggie's eyes stay muted for just a second longer before he glances around the room, his eyebrows hitching. "Is it just me or are the asses in Wrigleyville just better?"

I snort a laugh and Evelyn's shoulders lift with a small chuckle as the air around us resets.

I'm pretty sure the best ass is over in Lincoln Park.

Reggie's hand grabs mine, tilting his chin toward the juice bar. "Let me buy you a smoothie."

I tug my lip between my teeth, feeling some apprehension creep in.

This is fucking weird, right?

Attempting to carry on a friendship with my classmate while having secret sex with her ex-boyfriend *slash* soon-to-be brother-in-law?

This week on Amelia the Slut . . .

Still, I find myself pushing myself off the bench, my eyebrows flinching as I drag my legs along behind us.

Reggie hisses when he looks down at my hands. My eyes follow, noticing that my index and middle knuckles are raw and cracked. I wince, opening and closing my fists a couple times to get used to the burn.

"Initiation knuckles," Reggie signs. "Evie's looked like she put them through a meat grinder her first time."

Evelyn plants her hand against Reggie's chest. "Excuse me, I'm pretty much a badass," she scoffs and Reggie falls forward with laughter. Evelyn's forced scowl flips and she laughs too, making my own lips pull up my cheeks.

My mind latches onto the phrase "initiation knuckles."

He meant initiation into boxing of course, but the weird little tired cloud I've taken residency on has weird little cloud ideas of its own.

They make friendship look easy—fun. I like that they tease each other, but don't get offended; they seem to know each other intrinsically. I don't have a lot of experience, but their friendship feels like an exclusive club. And they don't *need* another friend, yet they keep inviting me in.

And I think I want in.

chapter twenty-four

dean

I'm looking at my phone, again.

Staring at the message Marnie sent ten minutes ago, again.

Marnie: We're running late.
Probably won't get to you till 8ish.

I can't pinpoint *exactly* what is pissing me off, but my clenched jaw and tightening fists are a pretty good indication that I'm not calm.

Obviously, part of me is irritated that she'll be late, but I can just keep Ava a little later on Sunday, so I'm not really worried about "getting my time" with her.

Maybe it's just that Marnie takes every opportunity to remind me that *I'm* the reason we're in this mess, so for the past year, I've been trying to be as accommodating as possible—going with the flow. But now it feels like she's taunting me with it for some reason.

It's your fault, so just deal with it.

I take a deep breath and click the lock button before shoving the phone back in my pocket. I can respond after the meeting. Hopefully it'll calm me down a bit.

I've gone to the community center for the past three days. The "tabled" conversation regarding Marnie's move has been fucking with me and I need to be proactive.

Keep control.

I scratch the back of my jaw and release a heavy exhale. Getting up from the couch, I go to the kitchen and grab the bag of coffee I finally remembered to take from Red Line.

I'm just going to leave for the meeting a little early, I decide. *Maybe I'll walk. Clear my head.*

My phone buzzes in my pocket and I pull it back out, tensing up at the possibility of another message from my ex-wife.

Amelia: Can I still crash the meeting with you?

My mouth tilts and my shoulders sink with some relief. I've been wanting to text her since I left her a few days ago, but after not-so-subtly mentioning the meeting tonight, I thought it would be less pathetic to wait for her to contact me first.

She seems to like keeping me on my toes. I can almost see her teasing grin while she signs, *"Look alive, Roberts."*

The sudden memory of the name sign she gave me for "Roberts" stretches my smile.

Me: I've checked with the committee.
They'll allow it. But they said you had
to let me buy you a coffee after. Weird, right?

Stupid. So stupid.

But I won't actually get to spend any time with her at the meeting. And once Ava is here, I won't be able to see her again until Sunday so, I had to think of something.

Something stupid, apparently. Three dots have appeared and disappeared twice already and I'm watching my phone like it will somehow *make* a response come through.

Just as I put the phone down on the counter, it buzzes, and I can't help but smirk.

Look alive, Roberts.

Amelia: Throw in a muffin and you've got yourself a deal.

Amelia's muted green eyes glance up at me from under her slouchy, purple beanie as I push open the door from the community center, and we step out onto the windy sidewalk.

We aren't far from one of my favorite coffee spots, so I tilt my head toward the east block and Amelia falls into step beside me.

I noticed she left her hearing aids out today, and I think it's the first time I've seen her without them. Not that it matters since we typically sign anyway, but it must have been difficult to rely on lip reading through the meeting.

I intermittently glance over at her through the walk, noticing the dark circles under her eyes and wonder if she's been having trouble sleeping. The memory of her nightmare on the couch last weekend finds its way to me and a prickly sensation crawls up the back of my neck.

I roll my shoulders just as we're about to reach the cut out between two buildings, my hand reflexively takes Amelia's arm so she doesn't pass it. She jumps at the contact and I pull my hand away, but she settles quickly.

Her lips tilt apologetically as she signs, "Sorry. I slept like shit." She shrugs. "I guess I'm just a little jumpy."

Well, that answers my earlier thought about her not sleeping well. I have this overwhelming urge to pull her into my chest—hold her. But her eyes drift to the alley, noticing the sign for the coffee shop.

"Villains?" she signs, curiously.

I nod, leading her through the cutout between the buildings and into the alley. Her eyes pull up to the lights they've strung between the brick buildings, over the small seating area, while the cart with the espresso machine sits back against the far wall.

I sign, "The guys who own it are comic book fans. They thought it'd be cool to have a place where the villains could have coffee while they wait to terrorize the city," I chuckle, shrugging.

Amelia breathes a laugh too. "I guess that explains the graffiti."

I nod. They commissioned a street artist to come in and tag different parts of the surrounding buildings. It's a cool concept. We're technically outside, but the two surrounding walls and the back of another building block the wind. They also have a couple of heat lamps between the bistro tables and chairs.

As we get in line, she signs, "How do you know them? Clients of Red Line?"

I nod. "I've been working with them for years. They started with a coffee truck and about a year ago, they finally made enough money to start this place."

Ethan, one of the owners, looks up from the cup he's pouring milk into, just before handing it to a woman waiting at the small counter. "Dean, man! What's good?" His eyes move to Amelia, hitching his eyebrows before he looks back at me with a not-so-subtle nod. My teeth grind at the blatant perusal he just did, but I swallow it back.

She *is* gorgeous and I have no business trying to mark my territory like a barbarian.

But still . . . it's annoying.

"Amelia, this is Ethan. He's one of the owners," I say tightly, while signing.

Amelia nods before clearing her throat. "Nice to meet you, Ethan. Cool place."

Her voice is a little raspy, quieter than usual. It makes me wonder if it's from fatigue or maybe she's a little self-conscious about her voice without her hearing aids in. I know Otis told me he prefers not to talk, but he's profoundly deaf. I don't know the story of Amelia's hearing loss—like most things, she hasn't offered up the information and I'm sure as fuck not going to come out and ask her about it.

But it doesn't mean I'm not curious.

"Thanks," Ethan says to Amelia. "What are we havin'?"

We order two black coffees that Ethan insists on giving to us for free, so I put some money in the tip jar and we head to an open table, conveniently by one of the heat lamps.

Once we settle in our seats, her tired green eyes pull up to the light bulbs strung loosely above us, and a soft smile quirks on her cheeks, instinctually pulling my own mouth up too. I think about the lights over her desk . . . along her headboard.

She likes twinkly lights.

And I kind of think she should always have them over her, because they catch her eyes like sea glass in the sun, and they brighten the rosy tint to the apples of her cheeks.

She takes a sip of coffee, humming, "Mmm," then signs, "So good." She glances around the alley, adding, "This really is a cool place. I had no idea it was even here."

I nod through my sip. "Yeah, I mean from a marketing standpoint, a place that's hard to find probably isn't the best but . . . they committed to the concept."

She peeks around again before taking a big gulp of her coffee, then another, almost like she's trying to flood her exhaustion with it. I'm just about to ask if she's okay when she swiftly straightens her shoulders and signs, "Tell me about what we're drinking." Her eyes drift down to the cup.

My neck pulls back a bit, a little thrown by the abrupt question. "The coffee?" I sign, lamely.

She nods. "I want the full experience." A small glint catches in her eyes and she smirks back at me.

I chuckle, shaking my head. "It's a medium roast from Antigua."

When I don't say anything else, her eyebrows furrow. "That's it? You're in charge of promoting the brand!" she admonishes. "Come on, Roberts! Charm me! Sell me on Red Line."

I snort another laugh and look back at her. Our eyes linger for a few seconds before she takes another sip. It's then that I notice her other hand. She's pushing her finger into the clasp of one of the buttons on her coat, twisting it subtly into the groove. I avert my eyes in an attempt to not bring attention to the fact that I saw it, but I noticed it the other night in the car, too.

She has a thing with touch—a grounding method, it seems—but it makes me wonder why she's so nervous right now.

Whatever it is, I see the silent plea behind her eyes. She wants a distraction, and she's silently asking me to give it to her.

I scoot my chair around the table so that I'm not sitting across from her, but next to her, pulling my coffee along with me. I notice the round, reddish-purple indent on her finger as she drops her hand from her coat, seemingly taken aback by my new spot.

I again, don't bring attention to it, but instead settle my elbows on the table, signing, "What do *you* taste?" as my eyes glance down toward her cup.

She peeks back at me before she tentatively picks the coffee up. Her hands cradle it as she takes a small inhale, then takes a sip and her eyes close.

It's how she tastes food, too—like she can't possibly have any other senses distracting her. My mouth tilts just as her eyes reopen. They pinch for a second as she swallows, then signs, "I taste coffee."

I snort a laugh, shaking my head before I look back over at her. "This is a unique blend, actually. Medium roasts are usually a little brighter, more floral. But Antiguan coffee is smoky, kind of . . . spicy. It almost has a . . . charred finish."

A slow smirk pulls up her cheek before she signs, "All right. You sold me with spicy."

I lean back, taking another sip as I watch her eyes glaze over, seemingly lost in thought. The dark, forest color of her irises become just a shade lighter before she . . . laughs.

Like really laughs.

My confusion is thwarted by the infectious sound, and my own laughter starts to bubble in my throat.

She composes herself for a second signing, "Sorry . . . " pausing as a residual laugh trickles past her lips. "I'm just imagining you and a bunch of other full-grown men, out in some forest foraging for flowers and twigs . . . munching on burnt leaves like potato chips to get your tasting notes."

A laugh bursts out of me, which refuels her laughter and we lose ourselves to it for a few long seconds before it slowly settles.

"That's cool, though," she signs, coughing out one more chuckle. "I don't know anything about coffee. Other than I need it to live."

I lean into her, just a bit, signing, "Well lucky for you, you know a coffee guy now."

She swallows and a mischievous smile pulls at her lips. She shifts in her seat and her necklace catches the light.

"Where'd you get your necklace?" I sign.

Her eyes dip down and the corner of her mouth pulls back tightly before she looks back up at me, her eyes flinching. "Originally, I stole it."

My eyebrows pull up as a small chuckle escapes.

A little thief.

She shuts her eyes hard, breathing a nervous laugh. When she re-opens her eyes, she signs, "My friend gave me one like it for my birthday when I was younger, but I lost it. I ended up going back and paying for this one later that day. I had the money   I was just . . . an idiot. It was my sixteenth birthday and I was feeling rebellious."

"Why?" I sign.

She shrugs. "I had freaked out at Doris for offering to get my hair cut." Her eyes widen a bit, like maybe she didn't mean to say that, but I'm confused. I'm not really sure what one has to do with the other. My eyes absentmindedly fall to her long, dark hair before they pull back up to her face.

Our eyes meet and linger. Mine have questions that hers seem to be begging me not to ask and I don't, but *something* is passing through our gazes just as she breaks the contact, signing, "Does this place have a bathroom?"

It's becoming easier to notice when her defenses are rising—when she's deflecting. She's really good at it, but I've found myself catching the subtle way her posture changes, how the muscles in her face tighten into what appears to be a practiced expression.

"If you take your coffee sleeve into the restaurant next door, they'll let you use the bathroom."

Amelia glances at her coffee, then quickly back at me before she slides the sleeve off the cup, mumbling, "It's like the Marlborough House."

I want to say that was a *Great Gatsby* reference, but I can't be sure. She's already walking toward the building when my eyes finally leave her and return back to the table.

I space off, still caught up in whatever happened before she left. My mind is still turning the new information around, examining it from any possible angle, when suddenly a large figure stands beside my table.

"Hey, man, do you know where the closest L station is?" the guy asks.

My eyebrows pinch, annoyed, and I mumble, "Yeah, Belmont is two blocks west."

I pull my shield out—also known as my phone—but the guy lingers for just a second longer—long enough for me to notice his weird-ass hat with a carrot on it before he finally nods his head and mutters a quick "Thanks," as he leaves.

I need to start wearing sunglasses.

I text Marnie back, realizing I never responded to her earlier, just as Amelia comes back to the table . . . with a muffin.

I whistle, signing, "Fancy. The nicest thing I ever got in a bathroom was a free mint."

And a condom, but I leave that part out.

She laughs, shaking her head. "The restaurant has a bakery!" she signs, her eyes lighting with excitement. "It's a miracle I only walked out with a muffin. Plus . . . I was promised one."

She's right . . . "But you bought it," I sign.

Her lips tilt up and she shrugs. "Guess you'll just have to owe me, Roberts."

chapter twenty-five
amelia

Miss Melia, can we do karate when we get there?"

I huff a laugh as I hold Luke's hand and we walk to the park. It's the first day where the sun is out and it's over fifty degrees, so it might as well be summer. We usually get a couple days like this at the end of March—plus it's a Sunday—so the whole city is out and about. But I couldn't turn down a chance to get Crazy-Pants Magoo out of the house. I swear, his energy levels are that of a puppy with a caffeine addiction.

"Can we?" he asks, again.

"Sure, kid," I chuckle.

Annie put him in karate to hopefully help his "outbursts." I stand by my own thoughts on the outbursts, but I'm not his mom—and at least he seems to be enjoying karate.

We stand by the crosswalk, waiting for the light to change when I feel my phone vibrate in my pocket and pull it out.

Dean: Marnie will be here at 4.
How quickly do you think I can get to your place?

An involuntary smile pulls up my cheeks so quickly, I don't even have time to fight it.

A challenge . . .

The light turns, so I get Luke and me across the street and onto the playground. As soon as I step onto the wood chips, I pull my phone back out of my pocket, but I am immediately cut off by a hard chop to the hip.

"Hi-yah!" Luke yells as I keel forward.

"Dude! What the hell?!" I gasp, holding my stomach. But mostly, I just lose my breath all together. Something about the unexpected hit surges a small panic through me. I hold my weight by my hands on my thighs and squeeze them while I haul in some deep breaths.

It's okay. It was Luke. It was an accident.

"Sorry, Miss Melia," he frowns and walks right into me, hugging me. "I'm really sorry."

I hold him back, giving his head a quick rub before I move them around the back of his shoulders, hugging him a little tighter. My fingers start to pluck at the plushy material from his jacket. Between his small, but firm hold around my waist and my fingers squishing the smooth, puffy material, the feeling passes. I hold him a second more before I crouch down on his level.

My throat feels dry, so I swallow and tell him, "It's okay, buddy. You just scared me. I *did* tell you we could play karate, but both people need to be ready. If you hit someone out of nowhere, it's not a game anymore."

"Then it's just fighting," he says.

I huff a breath, nodding. "Exactly."

"And smart boys fight with their brains not with their hands," he chirps.

I hold my hand up and he rolls his eyes but still gives me a high five. I stand back up and tell him, "Go play. I'll be there in a few."

He literally bolts toward the wooden playground and I chuckle.

Border collie sipping a venti.

I pull my phone back out and sit on the bench to send a message back to Dean.

What's a fair amount of time but still not enough time to win . . .

> **Me:** How about a tier system?
> I'll get naked at 4 and I'll put an article of clothing
> back on every . . . 3 minutes?

Dean: No need to ruin your clothes, baby.
I'll just rip them back off.

My lips pull up.
Naughty boy.

> **Me:** It'll just add to your debt, Roberts.
> Soon enough, you'll just be my slave.

You are at a children's play park right now.

Dean: You already know I'll get on
my knees for you.

I have started something I can't stop.

"Miss Melia!"

My body jerks in surprise and I slip the phone back in my pocket, like I've just been caught with my hand in my pants.

Haven't you, though?

I shake my head, releasing a breath. "What's up, bud?"

"Look what I got!" He waves a little plastic cat at me and my eyebrows pinch, examining it.

It's a pretty lame toy, but he seems excited about it. "Wow. Cool, dude. Where'd you get it?"

Mostly, I'm making sure we're not stealing another kid's toy, but Luke shrugs. "I don't know, some guy gave it to me."

My eyebrows furrow. "Some guy? Like . . . like a grown up?"

Luke runs back off, but my paranoia is not equipped for this right now. My eyes immediately scan the playground, but there are a *ton* of people here. It could have been *anyone.*

It's not like they gave him a knife or a lighter or something . . .

Still, I get up off the bench and walk over to stand where Luke is playing and watch him from there. I lean against one of the wooden towers on the playground as he runs over to a group of kids before I pull my phone back out.

Dean: I'll be there by 4:17.
Nothing but the apron on, please.

I giggle. *I fucking giggle.* I don't know why the use of the word *please* makes me laugh, but it does. Plus, I just think it's cute that he likes the apron.

That apron's about to be traumatized.

Me: See you then.

And then I send an eggplant and a water splash emoji because . . . why the hell not?

After I drop Luke off, I stop by the market and catch up with Rhonda while picking up a few things for my little visitor later.

I've decided to make coffee-flavored Belgian waffles. Breakfast for dinner always seems to be a hit when I make it at the shelter, and I want to experiment with more dishes that have coffee in them.

Since I know a coffee guy now.

"Do I need to be worried, honey?" Rhonda asks, eyeing the ingredients I've put on the counter.

A small laugh sighs through my lips. I *did* tell her that baking was for apocalyptic times and she's ringing me up for flour, eggs, baking powder and buttermilk.

I shake my head. "Waffles."

She nods, scanning the items, curiously peeking up at me as she bags them, and a surreptitious smile inches up her cheek.

"Everything good?" I ask, my eyes squinting slightly back at her.

She shrugs, still smiling. "Seems so."

My eyebrows pinch, not exactly understanding her energy but I'm in too good of a mood to dissect it.

After paying her and a quick parting wave, I head across the street to my building.

As I make my way inside, I grab my mail—which looks fucking insane. I am not one to check my mailbox regularly—or even weekly—so I'm able to see through the thick stack that a couple of envelopes are from nearly a month ago.

Whoops . . .

Luckily, I pay all my bills online. But no matter how many times I sign up for paperless billing—somehow I still end up with this shit.

I start up the stairs and maneuver my way through the door before giving it a hard shove closed with my ass, but it's not quite hard enough to close it all the way. My attempt to toss the mail on my table completely fails, and I watch as it scatters across the floor.

"Dammit."

Beatrice prances out in front of me, purposefully trying to trip me as I trudge toward the breakfast bar. She nearly succeeds just before I drop the bags of food on the counter and glare down at her.

"I don't care what Wally said, I'm keeping my eyebrows when your time comes, B."

She yawns back at me in response and I huff a laugh before going back for the mail fanned along the floor. I start to gather the envelopes, my annoyance growing at collecting the bills I've already paid when suddenly, a letter from Kane County Court catches my attention and my heart drops.

Fuck.

I've been sitting on my chair for an unknown amount of time—reading and rereading the letter from the court. Basically, all I can gather is that I'm in charge of whatever's done with my mom's estate, but there's too much legal jargon for me to fully understand.

There's one thing that's undeniable, though. And it's been simmering just below my skin since I opened the letter.

You *have to deal with it* . . .

The longer I stare at the piece of paper, the more it begins to feel like it's burning in my hand. The words start to blur and shake.

Actually, I think it's me *that's shaking.*

"Fucking bitch . . ." I hiss. My harsh whisper echoes—*bounces*—off the walls in the living room and I distantly register that I can hear myself. I never took my hearing aids off. *This* stopped me dead in my tracks.

I fucking knew it . . .

I *knew* this wasn't over. The flashbacks, the memories—*her voice.* It was all a way to weaken me. It's what she did in life, so why would death be any different? She found a way to whittle me down to nothing—grind me into dust—just to blow me out into the air and leave me to settle like dirt on the floors of her nasty fucking house.

I'd have to go back there . . .

My knees start to bounce as I crush the letter in my fist. My other hand grabs my necklace, jabbing the pointy bolt into my thumb. The small pinch centralizes the adrenaline running rampant through me, but it's not enough right now.

It will never be enough.

My fists curl as tight as they can, and I shove every fingernail into my palms all at once. My fists shake from the pressure as my pinky nail breaks, making me yelp before I feel wetness on my palms.

What is happening? This is . . .

Whatever this feeling is—it's *blinding.* It's so bright that it's fucking dark.

Something *snaps.*

"What the *fuck?!*" I scream.

Beatrice darts out of the room like a bullet, but I can't be stopped. Something inside me is no longer anchored and words are just exploding out of me at their own volition.

"Didn't you do enough?!" I start ripping the letter violently, choking on my breath. "Just leave me alone! Leave. Me. The fuck. Alone!" My voice is guttural—*desperate*—louder than I've been in my entire life.

I catch my weight on my thighs, trying to steady my breath as my ears ring. I'm panting wildly, huffing through the surge, when suddenly, I feel a presence in the room.

My heart drops.

For a soul-shattering beat, I'm terrified to turn around.

Terrified.

Because after the split-second where I actually believe I'll turn around and see *her*—in an instant—I know it isn't her.

It's Dean.

Of course it is.

Of course he's seeing me like this. I guess the other breakdowns weren't enough. *Somehow,* she made sure he'd see *this,* too.

I slowly turn, locking eyes with him as he stands, horrified, by the door. I don't know how much he saw, but I'm sure it was *enough* by the look on his face.

My insides harden and my blood runs cold, like everything coursing through me just turned me to stone.

"Looking to add breaking and entering to the record?" I sneer, like a real bitch, my chest still heaving.

His eyebrows furrow as his eyes squint. "I called *and* texted you three times. And when I heard you screaming? You're damn right I opened the door—which was *unlocked,* by the way," he tosses the last part out there and all I hear is the cadence of three words over and over again. They pulse in my brain, syncing with the heavy thumps of my heart.

Stupid.

My posture straightens.

Stupid.

My glare deepens.

Girl.

"Get out, Dean."

His eyes narrow. They darken before he inhales deeply. "No."

My resolve shakes, just a touch, at the sound of his tight, hoarse voice before I steel my spine, again. "It wasn't a question. From what you've told me, you know how to leave. So fucking do it."

I storm toward my bedroom, putting some distance between me and my ugly words. Because for as much relief as I might feel spewing pure venom—it feels like poison to sit in it.

I pop the bedroom door open, but Dean is right behind me. He takes hold of my arm and I yank it back with too much force, making me lose my footing. He catches me before I fall completely, keeping me pinned against the wall for support.

My chest rises and falls heavily. My stare is so hard it feels heavy, but all the warmth has fallen from his eyes, too, as he seethes down at me. He straightens and places each of his palms on the wall beside my head, caging me in. "You've got a nasty fucking mouth when you're angry, baby."

"Fuck you." I shove against him but he holds my hands back, securing them at my side as I continue to writhe.

"Stop," he growls.

Still, I fight. I push against him as hard as I can. Freeing one of my hands, I beat on his chest with everything I have, but our proximity and his weight against me doesn't allow much leverage. He's like a fucking wall.

A wall I can't break. I can't hold back. I can't ignore.

I release a pathetic sound of defeat before suddenly, my eyes meet his again. They're dark and hollow, slowly filling with something I can't even begin to unravel, but it seeps into *my* eyes—burning them—and a pitiful squeak pushes past my lips.

I'm fighting . . . I . . .

"Do you like hurting me, Amelia?"

His voice scrapes like sandpaper through my chest. I feel some tears pricking the back of my eyes but I swallow them back, shaking my head frantically.

I'm fucking . . . breaking.

"Then why are you?" he asks, quietly.

Oh my God.

I hit him. *I actually hit him.* It wasn't hard, but not because I didn't try. He was just strong enough to stop me. But there's something about his expression that makes me think the physical blows aren't even what he's talking about.

I took the honesty he gave me and threw it back in his face. I took mistakes he shared and used them as a weapon.

"I don't—" My voice cuts off as my throat tightens, unable to catch my breath.

The dark edges of my mind start to fill into the cracks of my brain, seeping and festering and wobbling my weight.

You're just like her.

The notion heightens my distress. My heart starts to beat rapidly in my chest and my muscles tighten. I cough as my lungs seize and my eyes widen.

"Breathe, Amelia." I feel Dean's breath on my cheek and the sound of his voice filters through me like a small breeze.

It does the smallest bit to calm me, but a roll of nausea turns in my stomach.

What the fuck was that?

My fingers start to tighten at my sides, shaking in Dean's grasp.

"That was your pain coming out. And it needed to."

I shut my eyes tight at the thought of Doris's note—trying to reel myself in—trying to hold onto *this* part of me, instead of whatever she-devil just took over.

"I'm sorry," I squeak out. "I'm—" I shake my head, trying to rattle everything threatening to crash through the surface, but I can't even look at him.

How can he *look at* me?

I'm working so hard to keep the tears in my eyes—fighting so desperately to not let them fall.

I flinch at the feeling of his big, calloused hand cradling my jaw, the rough pad of his thumb brushing against my cheek.

"What happened?" he asks, gently.

My free hand immediately curls and twists the fabric of his shirt in front of me, grabbing it so hard I'm worried I might rip it.

"I can't—" I choke, tightening my fist.

God. Two words seem to be my maximum. I can't find the air.

I can't tell him.

He pulls me into his chest and his rich, coffee scent finds a way through my nose, opening my airwaves.

"I'm here, baby," he says, quietly. "You can tell me."

A sob breaks free, but my tears rattle on the edge of my eyelids.

Here.

It's one word. One small word that breaks me.

My tears finally fall. The hard feeling of his chest against my cheek reminds me again of a wall. But unlike before, I have zero urge to knock it down. Right now, it feels like it's the only thing keeping me upright.

Here.

I'm falling. Plummeting. Crashing.

But I'm not alone.

chapter twenty-six
amelia

twenty-one years ago

I woke up to a soft knock on my window.

Opening my eyes wide, I looked at my door before I even glanced at the window. I listened for footsteps or clashing noises coming from the kitchen but I didn't hear anything.

I finally looked over at the window and saw Alex standing outside. Quickly shoving myself off the bed, I walked to the window, pulling it up as a nervous smile inched up my cheeks.

"Happy Birthday!" he chirped.

My smile stretched, but I tried not to look *too* excited.

Trying to gauge a normal response was getting easier. Mostly, I just watched other kids—how happy or upset *they* got about things—and I tried to copy it.

In service of that, I giggled. "Thank you."

I was confused as to why he skipped the door again, but my eyes pulled over to the driveway, noticing my mom's car was gone.

Was she at work? She didn't usually work on Saturdays unless she needed the overtime.

The smallest bit of worry slid through me, but I looked back at Alex when he extended his hand—holding a small, red box with a black bow tied around it.

"Is th—Is that for me?" I asked.

He nodded, dropping his chin as he shuffled his feet. I felt tears pooling at the corners of my eyes, but I blinked them away as he peered back up and timidly handed the box to me. I couldn't remember ever being given a present for my birthday, but I knew that wasn't normal and I didn't want to look like a freak.

Still, my voice cracked as I said, "You didn't have to get me anything."

He shrugged. "I saw it at the magic shop my mom took me to last weekend."

He saw something and thought of me.

That alone felt special. A feeling so foreign it made me squirm a bit as I held the small box in my hand. His eyes widened, looking down at the present, urging me to open it and I bit on my bottom lip to keep from smiling wider.

Pulling on the ribbon, I opened the box, gasping when I saw what was inside.

It was a necklace with a delicate chain—so thin you could barely see it—and in the middle, it was connected by a small lightning bolt.

"Wow!" I squeaked. "Thank you . . . this is . . . really cool."

It was *better* than cool. It was the nicest thing anyone had ever done for me. I carefully took the necklace out of the box and found the clasp. It was so small that my fingers could barely pinch it open.

"Here, I'll help," Alex said.

Before I could protest, he climbed up and . . . well, *tumbled* through the window, making me laugh. It was a ranch-style house, but the window was just high enough that it didn't give you a lot of stability when you entered through it.

It was like they weren't meant for that, or something.

When he stood back up, I took in the redness of cheeks, feeling bad that I left him outside in the cold while he gave me a present.

I looked back down at the necklace, again. "Just like *Harry Potter.*"

Alex's lips quirked at the corner as he got closer to me. "Turn around. I'll help you put it on."

I did as he said and held the ends of the chain to the necklace around my neck before his fingers brushed mine and took it. I gathered my long hair and twisted it to the side while Alex worked on clasping the necklace.

It took him a while, but when he was done he let out a victorious, "Got it!"

I laughed, bending over to look at it on the small mirror that sat on my dresser.

I loved it.

The chain was so light you could barely see it, so it looked like the lighting bolt was just floating on my collar bone. I turned back to face him, my smile so big it actually made my mouth hurt.

"Do you like it?" Alex asked, his eyes drifting to the floor before looking back up to me.

I nodded, emphatically. "It's the best present I've ever gotten."

The only one. But still, my favorite.

His shoulders dropped and his lips tilted on his cheek. "I'm sure you're doing stuff today, but my mom is making brownies later. She said you're welcome to come."

A present and a birthday brownie?

"Sounds awesome," I said through a nod. The feeling of the chain on my collar bone was so light, but I could still tell something was there. And I loved *that* almost as much as the necklace itself. I liked the idea that I could forget that I was wearing it and then suddenly be reminded again.

Remind me of this moment.

My fingers ran along the chain and toyed with the lightning bolt. Alex shuffled his feet and I gave my head a quick shake.

I was supposed to not *be acting like a freak.*

I felt like I should give him a hug so I did, awkwardly. And I was met with him ineptly patting my back in return.

Good. We learned that was weird and we'd never do it again.

He started toward the window again and I told him, "You can use the door . . . if you want."

I knew it was weird that he came to my window instead of the door. I didn't want him to suspect anything.

But a blip of panic passed through me when I realized that I had no idea what the state of the house was in.

Luckily, he shook his head. "That's okay, the window's kind of fun."

I giggled, partially from relief and partially because this was such a nice way to wake up on my birthday.

Ten years old. Maybe double digits would be different. Maybe it was a good omen. Maybe my curse was lifted.

He crouched through the window, slipping on the pipe and stumbling to the ground, but he caught himself before he actually fell.

I went to the window, ducking below the sill. "Are you okay?" I asked, stifling a small chuckle.

He nodded. "Yeah, I meant to do that," he said, suppressing his own laugh.

I smiled, again. A real one. *Maybe this was the year I did that more too.* "Thank you again for my necklace."

Alex smiled. "I had to get something for the coolest girl I've ever met."

He only thought that because I let him see what I wanted him to see. But it thickened the good feeling already buzzing through me.

"Happy birthday, Amelia. I'll see you later?"

I nodded, watching him walk down the street and back to his house before I closed the window.

It had been a pretty great birthday so far.

My mom still hadn't come home, so I took a chance and ran to the corner market to buy some supplies to make myself a BLT.

After lunch, I heard the car pull into the driveway and my heart dropped.

Crap.

I had cleaned everything but the pan I used to make the bacon with, and I knew there wasn't enough time to do it before she got in the house.

I wiped it with a paper towel and opened the cabinet to put it back. I stuck a couple of clean pans on top of it, hoping it could at least stay hidden until the next time she left.

My back straightened as I heard the door open, then I shuffled to the archway of the kitchen, hearing keys drop on the table. I could still smell the bacon, but if I could make it to my room, I could just play dumb.

I listened to her drop something near the door and my heart rate sped up as I heard her steps getting closer.

Realizing it was too late to make it back to my room, I quickly grabbed a glass and turned on the sink. A shaky breath pulled through my nose and I tried to steady my voice as I said, "Hi, Mom," over my shoulder, trying to look inconspicuous. Somewhere, distantly, I knew this wasn't normal. I knew I shouldn't have to pretend I wasn't doing anything wrong—all I had done was make myself something to eat—but she had a way of making me feel like I was in the way just by being here at all.

She walked into the kitchen, wearing her usual scowl.

Her hair was tied up in a knot on top of her head and she had heavy bags under her eyes. I turned off the sink and took a sip of my water. She pulled in a deep breath, glancing around the kitchen and I worried she smelled the bacon.

I cleared my throat. "Are you hungry? I can make you a sandwich?"

I thought maybe if I offered to make her something and she *did* find any evidence of my little birthday treat, she might not be so mad. Plus, maybe it'd be just enough of a peace offering that she'd let me go to Alex's later.

She simply huffed, like the very idea offended her, before she walked to the fridge and grabbed a bottle of wine, pouring it into a glass and taking a few sips.

I couldn't understand why she loved drinking so much. It smelled awful and on one terrible night where she actually made me drink some with her, it tasted so rancid that I puked immediately.

My body fidgeted at the memory and a chill swept through me as I noticed her studying eyes. I saw them drift down to my chest and her eyebrow cocked.

"Where'd you get that?" she asked, walking closer to me.

I gulped. She only ever seemed to notice things about me when they made her angry. Her green-blue eyes glowered down. She raised her hand in front of me and I flinched. A sneer curled her mouth as her fingers ran along the chain.

I hated that she was touching it. Her touch was toxic. There was no affection—it only ever brought pain and I hated that she was tainting something special.

My contempt straightened my spine. "Alex gave it to me for my birthday," I said, then cleared my throat. "He invited me over later . . . is it okay if I go?"

"Your birthday," she mused through a sigh, taking another sip.

My throat worked to swallow as I waited. Waited for an answer to my question, waited to see a lift of recognition at the mention of my birthday. I stupidly waited—*hoped*—that maybe her toxic touch would magically become something safe and warm.

Maybe ten would be different.

She stared down at the necklace for another beat before lifting her glare to me. Tension tightened my muscles but I fought against the fear and met her eyes. Without another word, she simply turned around and grabbed the wine bottle as she walked away.

And I released a breath I didn't realize I was holding.

My mom had never answered me earlier, but I got ready just in case she decided to let me go to Alex's house. I also wouldn't have been shocked if she had fallen asleep already, so I opened the door to my room carefully, trying to make as little noise as possible.

The house was quiet, but it usually was—which unfortunately made it harder to plan for a good time to sneak out of my room. As soon as I stepped out, I heard her call from her room. "Amelia?"

My eyes clamped shut and I pulled in a deep breath. Even though her room was right across the hall from mine, I never went in there. Gulping, I slowly opened the door and saw her sitting on her bed, her glass now full of an amber-colored liquor.

"You want to go to the neighbor boy's house?" she slurred.

I nodded, my muscles tense. Her pupils were so big, her eyes almost looked black. They were glazed but still somehow pointed and I felt the hair on the back up my neck stand up.

She sighed. "Let me help you get ready."

My eyebrows furrowed, confused. Not only was I already dressed but . . . she never helped me . . . with *anything.*

Maybe ten would be different, I thought again. It had already been my favorite birthday to date.

She wobbled to stand, waving her hand toward the chair in front of her vanity, which was covered with an assortment of bottles.

"Sit," she said.

Just be good, Amelia.

I walked over to the chair and sat down, curling my feet around the front legs of the chair as I tried to keep my knees from bouncing.

She came to the vanity and pulled a small compact off the table. "Smile," she said.

I did, and strangely wondered if this was the first time I was smiling in her presence.

"Mouth closed."

My lips pulled into my mouth at the command and she opened the compact before she swirled a brush on top of it and brushed my cheeks.

I'd never worn it before but I'd seen enough movies to know that it was blush. I jerked when she snapped the compact closed before she smiled down at me.

It wasn't what I would call a *nice* smile. It didn't reach her eyes, but I tried to enjoy the fact this was something that felt like a mother and her daughter *should* do together.

Maybe the curse was breaking.

"Close your eyes," she said.

I thought maybe eyeshadow was next. I remembered in a movie I watched it was something that made girls' eye color pop. Girls wore makeup to impress boys.

She was helping me impress Alex.

A warm feeling passed through me as I closed my eyes and waited for the soft brush on my eyelids. I felt her move behind me before I heard an unexpected sound. It almost sounded like . . .

Snip.

My eyebrows pinched, and my eyes instinctively clamped tighter as my mind tried to rework what was happening.

She was cutting a tag off my shirt. But it wasn't new.

She was trimming a loose thread on my sweater. But it wasn't woven.

Snip, snip, snip.

My mind rejected the idea until soft tufts of hair fell on my arms and my eyelids screwed tighter. I felt air on the back of my neck—the part that my hair usually covered—and reality crashed over me. I bit onto my lip, digging my nails into the side of my thigh, but I stayed quiet.

I kept one hand digging into my leg while the other one curled around the wooden seat of the chair, my fingernails scratching against the grain, fighting the tears I could feel behind my eyes.

My drunk mother was cutting my hair and the sound of each snip was tantalizing.

Snip.

This year won't be different.

Snip.

Nothing's changed.

Snip.

She hates you now more than ever.

There was no denying it. I had tried to convince myself for as long as I could remember that maybe we just didn't understand each other. Like everything she said, I took the wrong way and vice versa.

But this wasn't something she could hide behind closed doors. This wasn't a bruise I could cover with clothing. There was no truth-lie I could tell. This was a blatant display of power. *Of hate.*

And just like everything else she ever did to me, I had no idea why.

"There we go," she said, brushing my shoulders.

The weight on my head felt lighter, but I kept my eyes tightly shut. My lips stayed in my mouth—holding back the emotion—preparing myself for whatever I might see in the mirror.

Don't cry.

Finally, my eyes creeped open, keeping the tears in them as I swallowed hard. A sharp inhale inflated my chest when I saw the mess she made on my head. My hair was no longer hitting the middle of my back. Now it fell just a little bit lower than my chin—the sides uneven and jagged.

I kind of looked like a boy.

I stared back at her with pure hatred through the reflection in the mirror as she placed the scissors on the vanity and her cold, black eyes met mine.

"You'll thank me one day, kid," she said, taking the final sip from her drink.

The ice clinked in her glass, rattling my chest as she walked back toward her bed. She grabbed the bottle of amber liquor and I stared at it through the mirror.

Was it that? *Was* that *what made her evil?*

It didn't matter. I stood up in an attempt to relieve my rising anger and looked her straight in the eye. My throat was tight, but I held the hard expression on my face as I said, "Thank you," hoarsely, keeping my eyes locked with hers.

It could have been my imagination, but I swear I saw her eyebrows hitch, the ghost of an impressed expression passing through her features before her mouth lifted with a smug grin.

"Have fun at your boyfriend's house," she mumbled, raising her glass.

My teeth clenched. I wanted to smash the glass. I wanted to take the shards and drag them along the walls of this stupid house and destroy it.

But I didn't. My fear still trumped my anger as I quickly moved across the hall and back into my bedroom.

As soon as I heard the door click, I leaned back against it. My fingers pulled through the jagged strands of my hair, yanking at the roots, and the tears I'd held in finally fell. I tugged harder at my hair as my knees gave out and I fell to the floor, catching myself on my palms.

I gasped for air, choking between sobs, unable to take a full breath.

Was I dying?!

It felt like it. The notion increased my panic, but even if I could find the air to call for help, there was no one here *to* help. My only "help" was the one who brought me to the floor.

My fingers curled into the carpet; they dug in so deep and so hard that I felt a sharp pinch at my fingers, but the pain somehow centralized the panic—like an electric shock. The rattle of my nails against the stale fabric of the rug expanded my lungs but my heart was still racing.

Slowly, my eyes pulled up and dragged along the perimeter of my small room.

My safe place.

Four walls. Four walls that were still in *her* house.

Seeing my backpack sitting by my dresser, I slowly unlatched my fingers from the floor.

She said I could go to Alex's house . . . so she was expecting me to leave.

Without a second thought, I grabbed the backpack and took out my purple beanie, shoving it over my head and then emptied my school books out on the floor. I put my new copy of *Harry Potter* back in the bag and then shuffled toward my bed, grabbing the jar of peanut butter and crackers from underneath.

After shoving as many clothes as possible into my backpack, my mind quickly devised a plan. If I could make it to the old boat casino, I could spend the night under the bridge. Past that, I didn't know— but anything was better than here.

I would leave the house, just like she said I could.

And I'd never come back.

chapter twenty-seven
dean

My eyes blink slowly. Almost like they can't decide whether or not they want to just stay closed. Like maybe clamping them shut will somehow keep everything Amelia's just told me from sinking deeper into my mind.

I test the theory, but when my eyes close—all I see are horrifying images of her as a little girl—waiting the night out under some bridge—hiding from her own goddamn mother.

"Baby . . ." My voice breaks as I move to hold her, but she wiggles away from me on the bed and stands.

"No," she grinds out. "Do not feel fucking sorry for me, Dean. I'm—" she chokes on her breath but manages to recover, clenching her fists at her sides and concentrating on her breath. She takes a steadying inhale, locking her gaze with mine. "I'm not some—sad, pathetic girl." The words stutter out, her voice cracking at the end.

My eyes squint back at her.

Pathetic?

Of all the things I'm feeling as I look at her right now, pathetic is *not* one of them. It's closer to *awe.*

Awe that she's standing in front of me at all. That she's survived such horrendous things and somehow still managed to become the most captivating woman I've ever met.

Since the night we met, there's been *something* about her that has stuck with me. I've been able to pass it off as intense attraction until this moment, but now it's clear what's pulling me to her.

It's her strength.

Talking to her is a balancing act, though. I can see her defenses are already rising again and regret is shadowing her features as she struggles to meet my eyes. I slowly get up and walk toward her, gently pinching her chin to pull her eyes up to mine and a small gasp inflates her chest.

Movement from her hand catches my eye and I peer down, noticing she's using her thumbnails to scratch against the sides of her fingers. It's not hard, like most of the times I've seen her do something like this, but I still move my hands down to hers to stop it.

It's then that I see a row of angry, purplish-red punctures across the top of her palms. A few even look like they're bleeding.

Jesus.

I can tell by the shape that they're fingernail marks and a pang hits my chest. She pulls her hands away quickly when she sees me notice them. Clearing my throat, I look back up at her. "Let's get those cleaned up. Do you have stuff in your bathroom?"

"I-I can do it," she stutters. When she blinks, a couple of rogue tears fall, but she swipes them away so swiftly that it makes me pause.

After another beat, I shake my head. "I'd like to do it. If that's okay?"

Her eyes squint at me before they drift off. "You want to . . . clean my hands," she says, kind of like a question, but mostly just echoing my words. After another long moment passes, her eyes find their way back to mine before she mutters, "Weird."

I breathe a small laugh and point my eyes toward the foot of the bed. She releases a heavy sigh, like she's too exhausted to fight me on it, and then sits.

I make quick work in the bathroom, my hands shaking a bit as I grab a washcloth and some hydrogen peroxide before going back into her dimly lit bedroom.

I walk over to the foot of the bed and kneel down in front of her. "Palms up." My voice is low, but I can't help it. There's so much filling the room right now that it feels nearly suffocating.

The ghost of a small smile pulls at her cheek and she turns her hands over. "Bossy," she rasps.

My lips lift. "I think you like when I'm bossy," I chuckle, keeping my eyes on hers for a second longer before I break the contact to pour peroxide over the washcloth, and then tend to the small punctures on her palm. They're not deep, but there's two that broke skin, so I pay extra attention to one of them and she hisses.

I smirk, softly. "My mom used to call this tickle water."

Amelia's eyebrows pinch and she winces when I move to the other one. "Uhh—I hate to be the one to tell you this but . . . your mom lied," she says quietly, her voice hoarse.

I huff, nodding. "I know. It's weird, though. She, like, tricked my brain. Not just me—Otis too." I mumble, "Maybe she's a witch."

She releases a slow breath. "That's sweet, Roberts. I think I'd like your mom. *Especially* if she's a witch."

I smile. *My mom would like her too.*

Clearing her throat, she says, "It was probably a smart move on her part. I'm sure two little boys made good use of 'tickle water.'" She huffs a small laugh, but there's the smallest glint of something longing that holds in her eyes. It only lasts a second before I see the hand I'm not cleaning pinch the side of her thigh and she blinks it away.

It's amazing how learning *one* thing about someone can shift the lens just enough that all the other elements make sense. *One horrible thing*—and suddenly I can see that the suppressed smiles are a shield. The touch mechanism is a way of warding something off.

I toss the washcloth in the hamper next to her dresser and then move to sit next to her on the bed. My arm slowly wraps around her shoulders, pulling her into my chest and her muscles tense.

She starts to push herself off of me. "Dean, don't—"

"Please let me hold you," I say, hoarsely.

Her green eyes meet mine, uncertain and exhausted, her neck tightening through a swallow.

"Please?" I ask, again.

I know she thinks this is pity, but it's not. *I'm* the one holding on by the skin of my fucking teeth right now. She mostly just seems . . . drained. Which is probably why she slowly slumps into me.

I pull her back so that I can lean against the headboard. Her jasmine scent infiltrates my senses and I close my eyes, attempting to let the smell and weight of her body sedate me.

We're quiet for a minute—just breathing—and her arms slowly circle my torso. My lips quirk and I hold her a little tighter, continuing to breathe her in before she releases a heavy sigh.

"She died last month."

My eyes snap back open.

"It was right after the night we met," she confirms, quietly.

My fingertips start to move along her back. I have no idea what to say. Given what she just told me, I'm actually fucking glad to hear that woman is gone. But obviously, I would never say that to her.

It's also not lost on me that her admission is happening *now*—now that we're not facing each other—now that we're touching. I run my fingers through her hair, swallowing the lump in my throat.

"Did . . ." My question is cut off by the roll of my stomach. I'm pretty sure I already know the answer to this, but I ask, "Did she hurt you?"

Fingertips tighten on the fabric of my shirt as her body curls against me, her arms tightening. For a silent response, it's as loud and clear as a goddamn siren and a heavy air fills my chest. I tilt my head back, eyes to the ceiling, as an intense burst of rage tightens my arm around her.

It's fucking vile.

My teeth clench as my mind immediately wanders . . .

A young Amelia. Hiding. Terrified. Alone.

I swallow my horror, and try to feed it some oxygen with a sharp inhale.

"She hated me," she whispers, cutting through my thoughts.

Her pained tone aches in my chest. My mind is still caught in the eerie vision, but the resolve of her statement hits me hard.

"No," I say, a bit louder than I mean to. I straighten up and pull her chin to me, but she keeps her eyes downcast. "Amelia, look at me."

She doesn't, but I take the few seconds to try and organize my thoughts.

I may not know all of the specific details of what happened with her mom. And while I could never understand how fucking *gone* someone would need to be to do things she *has* told me about—one thing I *do* know is that addiction is a beast. It has the potential to rob you of your humanity entirely. And it has absolutely nothing to do with her.

She was a fucking kid.

When her eyes finally pull up to mine, I can tell my face is anything but calm and her expression becomes nervous.

Keep control.

I release a heavy exhale, scratching the back of my jaw.

After one more breath, I brush some fallen hair out of her eyes. "She didn't hate you, baby. She hated herself." Her eyebrows pinch and I shift beneath her, moving my fingers to her jaw. "One thing all addicts share is misery. And when we see someone strong, all it does is remind us of how weak we are."

She shakes her head and her eyes fall again, unconvinced, and my mind searches for a way to get through to her.

Touch. She responds to touch.

I timidly pull her hand up to the stubble on my jaw. I've noticed that she seems to prefer textures that are more coarse—rough—and I gently take her wrist, using it to run her hand along my face.

Her tired, green eyes squint before they widen with recognition. Another second passes before she uses her nails to lightly scratch through the bristles on my jaw, flattening her fingers to rub along behind them.

I lean my cheek into her hand. It's the only thing I can offer her right now, but she seems responsive. She continues for a few seconds, gently scratching and rubbing as something shifts in her eyes. They lighten, just a bit, as she quietly says, "You're not like her," her eyes seemingly lost in mine.

Mine are lost in hers too, wandering in her words.

She slowly pulls my lips to hers, pressing them softly against mine.

It's different from our other kisses. This isn't hungry or rough. It's not a prelude. It's tender and slow—a five course meal filling me up.

It only lasts a few seconds before we pull apart, and it takes me a moment to catch my breath. Pressing my forehead to hers, I whisper, "You're perfect, Amelia."

And I mean it. She is fucking perfect.

Strong, beautiful . . . so *good.*

Still, she sighs, her expression skeptical as she lies back against my chest and I pull her into me, holding her with new resolve.

She *is* perfect. And I'm going to do everything I can to show her it's true.

Well . . . things have gone better.

My eyes scan the giant fucking mess I've made of Amelia's kitchen just as Beatrice hops on the counter with a judgmental stare.

"Think she'll notice?" I ask her.

She simply blinks back at me, seemingly bored and I release a deep sigh.

After falling asleep here last night, I decided to take the day off from work. I wanted to make sure Amelia was okay and then I decided to try and make her some breakfast. She had all of the ingredients to make blueberry pancakes, so I figured I'd give that a try.

But the pancakes look . . . *not* like pancakes. And the kitchen has the appearance of a diner after an explosion.

Beatrice still sits, eyeing the container of blueberries and I scrunch my brows. "Can you eat blueberries?" I wonder out loud, pulling out my phone and searching online to see if blueberries are safe for cats. When I see that they are, I open the container and put a few in my palm, feeding them to her.

It's then that I hear the bedroom door creak open. My eyes pull up to the cut-out in the kitchen wall to see Amelia walking out of her bedroom, rubbing the sleep from her eyes. Her long, dark hair is pulled up in a wild ponytail while she wears an oversized T-shirt—putting her smooth, olive-toned legs on display.

Goddamn. What a beauty.

She startles when she sees me in the kitchen. Her emerald eyes quickly filling with some unease before they squint at Beatrice, still eating some blueberries out of the palm of my hand.

Amelia slowly walks toward us, an amused smirk peeking up her cheek as she rounds the small wall to the kitchen. Her eyes float down to Beatrice, and then back up to me, again.

My unoccupied hand raises up defensively as I sign, "I looked it up. Blueberries are safe."

She snorts a laugh, her shoulders dropping the tension they were holding as they gently shake with soft laughter. Her chin lifts, looking back up at me, signing, "Are you seriously shirtless and hand-feeding fruit to my cat right now?"

I shrug, signing, "She's persuasive."

An amused huff escapes her as her eyes finally scan along the kitchen, widening with her smile as she takes in the mess along the counter. A slow, bubbling laughter starts in her chest.

"What the hell did you do in here?" She laughs harder, then notices the plate of my failed breakfast attempt and her laughter settles, melting to a soft smile. "You made pancakes?"

"Uhh—" I stutter, closing up the container of blueberries before glancing back at her. "I made . . . pan-blobs. And full disclaimer, they probably taste like shit."

She doesn't laugh, but her smile is . . . *God.* It's so sweet, it nearly brings me to my knees.

"You made me breakfast . . ." she says, quietly, almost to herself.

My heart clenches. She seems so genuinely appreciative that it makes me want to quit my job just so I can make her breakfast every day.

Still, there's no doubt in my mind that they're awful.

"You don't have to eat them," I sign. "I can run out and get some bagels or something."

Her eyebrows pinch before her gaze drifts back to the plate. She makes a small click sound from the corner of her mouth. "And miss the chance to try my first pan-blob?" She smirks playfully before walking to the fridge, pulling out some syrup and butter. She turns around, back toward me and signs, "Let's do this, Roberts."

chapter twenty-eight

dean

My eyes dance along the glow-in-the-dark stars Amelia has sprinkled along the ceiling in her bedroom. They're not the same alien-green color I remember from the '90s though. It's not dark enough that they're actually glowing yet—but when they are, they have a soft, blue hue to them and I've actually found myself missing them when I stay at my place.

It's been two weeks since the first night I stayed over here, and we've found excuses to see each other pretty much every night since. Well, every night I don't have Ava, anyway. Truthfully, I can't get enough of her.

She couldn't be convinced to let me join her in the shower after she got back from the boxing club—something about smelling like a foot—and I've been mindlessly staring at her ceiling for the last fifteen minutes.

Feeling myself start to drift off, I sit up and rub my palm down my face before my eyes wander around her room. Her honey-colored walls have a couple of black and white photos of Chicago landmarks—Wrigley Field, the Riverwalk. My mouth quirks as my eyes drift to her dresser, noticing the assortment of items on top.

Curiosity pushes me to stand. When I get closer, I see a picture of what I assume is Wally and Doris, with Amelia sandwiched between them. She looks a little younger, wearing a baggy sweatshirt and torn up jeans. Her hair is pulled back in a ponytail, while her evergreen eyes peek up from under her dark lashes, giving the tiniest smile. I notice that Wally's wearing a vintage Cubs hat—the same one I've seen Amelia wear a couple times—and my mouth lifts. Doris isn't looking at the camera. She's looking at Amelia. Her expression is full of adoration—her smile beaming—and a warm feeling swells in my chest.

My eyes fall on a lipstick tube next to the picture frame and I pick it up. Popping the top off, I twist the bottom just as Amelia walks out of the bathroom and catches me.

She's changed into some gray sweats and a tight purple tank top that's inching up just above her belly button while her wavy, damp hair cascades over her shoulder. Her eyes move from me to the lipstick and a smirk pinches.

"Not really your shade, Roberts," she signs, eyeing the lipstick.

I chuckle, my eyes hesitantly leaving hers to look back over at it, noticing it's a deep, red color. My eyes find the picture again, signing, "This is cute."

She smiles. "It's from right before I moved here. It's the only picture I have of the three of us." Her eyes stay on the picture for a second longer before she uses the small towel she's holding to shake out the excess water from her hair.

I realize I'm still holding the tube of lipstick. I'm just about to put it back when I sign, "I don't think I've ever seen you wear make-up."

Her shoulders lift. "I don't, really."

She doesn't need it. She's naturally gorgeous, but . . . I'm curious. "So why'd you get this?"

She breathes a laugh, signing, "I don't know. It was years ago. Why—you want to borrow it?" Her eyebrows wiggle, and I breathe another laugh.

But I see the shift. It's been easier to decipher in the weeks following the night she told me about her mom. Her ability to deflect almost reminds me of a wild animal trying to blend in with their habitat.

A spotted leopard in a forest; a rattlesnake between some rocks.

I close some distance between us and pinch her chin between my thumb and index finger. "You've never used it?"

She squints her eyes as a confused laugh pushes past her lips, signing, "No, weirdo. I've never used it. Never had an occasion that called for red lips."

But she bought it because she wanted *an occasion to wear it.*

"And what kind of occasion *would* warrant red lips?" I sign.

Her green eyes shift back and forth between mine, like she's looking for the answer in them before I see the camouflage start to ignite and she shrugs. "I don't know. A funeral."

I snort another laugh. *Jesus Christ.*

"I was thinking a date," I sign.

The smallest hitch to her eyebrows wavers her for just a second before she tightens her expression and rolls her eyes. "Sure, Roberts. If you want to wear it on a date—have at it."

God. I don't know what it says about me—but when she gets bratty, my dick immediately snaps to attention. My eyes lock with hers as I nudge her back toward the bed. Her knees bend just before her back meets the mattress and I hover over her. She gasps just before I kiss her slowly. My tongue parts her lips and she opens her mouth, stroking her tongue against mine.

A low hum rumbles in my chest as she nibbles on my bottom lip and I have to force myself to pull away. I'm still holding the lipstick and now that I have her pinned beneath me on the bed, an idea stirs.

I move my other hand to her jaw, holding it firmly as I bring the lipstick to her mouth. Her eyes widen and she starts to squirm, but I press my weight into her, tightening my fingers around her jaw. "Stay still, baby."

She wiggles once more before her gaze lifts curiously. A breathy squeak escapes her as I pull gently on her chin, opening her mouth, and I start to paint her lips. I take my time—I've never done this before—but I manage to stay in the lines of her mouth, dabbing at the corners to make sure they're fully covered.

Plush, velvety red lips.

She looks fucking delicious and my dick starts to strain against my pants as she rubs her lips together. My thumb brushes under her bottom lip, wiping away a small smudge before my own mouth pinches at the corner.

So fucking beautiful. The ruby lips against her dark hair and green eyes—the rosy tint to her cheeks.

She must feel the solid outline of my erection between us because she wiggles, pushing her hips playfully into mine.

God, I want nothing more than to get her naked but . . .

I reluctantly push myself off of her, and then pull her up to stand. Her eyebrows pinch, confused, before she signs, "Was that fun for you, perv?" smirking, playfully.

She is not *making this fucking easy.*

Still, I match her energy, pulling her into me. "Keep it up, brat," I sign. "It'll only make what I do to you later *that* much more torturous."

Her eyes darken but her eyebrows furrow. "Later?"

I nod. "First I've got to take those lips out on a proper date," I sign.

Some of her amusement is replaced by sudden discomfort. She swallows, glancing down at the floor before timidly looking back up at me. "You . . . really want to do the date thing?"

My eyebrows pinch, studying her for a moment.

Our relationship shifted after that night a couple of weeks ago, but I still need to tread lightly. I know that a relationship in general is new territory for her—she told me as much herself last week when she confessed she had never had a boyfriend before.

I close some of the distance between us, signing, "How about a bet?"

Her eyes pull up to mine as a slow smile inches up her cheeks. "I'm listening."

I smirk. "How about I buy you a hot dog and we take a walk? If you have fun, I get to do anything I want when we get back."

Her smile grows and she barely tries to fight it. "And if I don't have fun?"

I shrug. "You will."

She huffs a laugh. "That's some big-dick energy you got there, Roberts," she signs, pausing a moment before she adds, "Luckily, the equipment matches."

God. I want to kiss her. But if I do that again, we'll never leave. Plus, it'll also ruin my handiwork on her lips so I sign, "Do we have a deal?"

She sighs, shaking her head once before she signs, "Deal."

We end up downtown. I make good on my promise, buying us some hot dogs and fries from Portillo's before Amelia suggests we take it to a park nearby.

I get bold and take her hand as we walk. Her eyes drift down to our entwined fingers and her pearly, white teeth peek out from behind her red-stained lips.

God, her smile. I literally can't stop looking at her.

It's like there's a magnetizing current running from my eyes to her face and her lips tilt, but she keeps her eyes ahead, signing, "You're staring, Roberts," before she peeks over at me.

"You're pretty, James," I sign back.

Her eyes narrow at my use of her last name, almost like she's silently saying, *"Hey, that's my thing"* before a soft smile pulls up on her cheek.

We walk another block, and it's not until I see the botanical garden that I realize I've been here before. It's been years, but . . . it's actually not far from where I used to live with Evelyn.

As we reach one of the picnic tables, the memory hits me like a concrete wall.

The lapping sound of the river hitting the bridge, the smell of the flowers from the garden . . .

I actually feel the color drain from my face as Amelia's hands catch my attention. I blink, glancing over to her as she sits across from me at the picnic table and she signs, "You okay?"

I swallow, nodding, trying to shake it off, but it lingers.

"Are you sure?" she signs. "You kind of look like you're going to puke."

I huff a small laugh, scratching the back of my jaw.

"Ah, see. Now I *know* something's bothering you," she signs.

My eyebrows pinch, confused.

After she pulls the food out of the bag she signs, "You scratch your stubble when you're nervous."

My eyes squint as my lips quirk. I guess it shouldn't surprise me that she's noticed it, but it does for some reason. In all the ways I feel like I've started to recognize her ticks, it never really occurred to me that she might pick up on mine.

She slides one of the hot dogs in front of me, eyes expectant, and I release a long, drawn-out sigh.

Leave it to me to kill the mood immediately.

And it's even worse because I know telling her about *this* has the potential to fuck up whatever is happening between us, but . . . she's already trusted me with so much—things I'm not sure she's ever told to anyone.

I push out another exhale and my eyes nervously meet hers. I get lost in the vibrant, emerald color for a second, silently begging them to not hate me after I tell her this.

After another beat, I drop my gaze from hers and hesitantly ball my fist, extending it toward her, pointing to the fairly prominent scar between the knuckles of my index and middle finger.

She peeks down, her lips pulling back with a small hiss. "Ouch," she signs.

I nod, glancing back down at the scar, giving myself a second before I sign, "I got that the night Otis caught me cheating on Evelyn."

Her eyes widen. "You cheated on Evelyn?! And then *punched* Otis?!"

"No," I sign. "I mean, *yes*. I did cheat on Evelyn but I didn't punch Otis. He punched me, actually."

She scoffs. "Sweet, cinnamon roll Otis? Never."

I huff, humorlessly, shrugging. "Well, he did. But I deserved it."

She shakes her head and a potent silence overtakes us. A few seconds pass before her eyes drift back up at me, wildly confused. "You really cheated on Evelyn?"

I nod, swallowing.

Her eyes squint. "Why?"

And here we are again.

It's the natural train of thought with a confession like this, but I still don't know how to answer it. There's no way *to* answer it without falling down the rabbit hole of my whole sordid history with Evelyn, so I sign, "Does it really matter? Is there ever a *good* reason to do something like that?"

Her lips slope down as her chin dips with a timid nod. I start to scratch the back of my jaw again before I catch myself. My eyes tentatively pull back to hers—*waiting, processing*—and I finally shrug. "I was just . . . fucked up, Amelia. I was hurting and lost and I just . . . fucked up."

It's a vague response, but it's all I can give her. Something I can't quite place passes through her expression before she nods slowly, clearing her throat. "So how'd you get the scar?"

Right. That's how this whole thing started.

I shift my weight in my seat, signing, "After Otis caught me, I went to a bar, got wasted. I don't really remember much, but I was outside having a cigarette, and some guy asked to bum one. He was just . . . making small talk but I was so drunk—*so fucking miserable*—all I could think about was . . . " I stop, suddenly, realizing that *this* is actually the worst thing I could admit to her.

I rub the pads of my fingers along my forehead, feeling a headache come on and she surprises me by taking my other hand in hers and holding it.

She doesn't say anything. She just waits, patiently, keeping me anchored with her hand before I continue, "I can't explain it, but . . . I just . . . I had this insane urge to hit him."

Her quiet gasp pulls my eyes up as her hand tightens in mine, but she doesn't let go.

Honestly, *hit* was the delicate way of putting it. Really, I wanted to beat him into the ground.

He was just . . . adding to the noise—something to take it all out on.

I push an overwhelmed exhale out. "Thankfully, he left before I actually *did,* but then I walked around the side of the building and hit the wall . . . the *brick* wall."

My heart picks up speed as the memory finds its way to the surface. *Thwap. Thwap. Thwap.*

I cringe. I can still hear it—*feel it.* The sound—the feeling of the rough, hard brick against my fist—the unrelenting fury that was pounding through me—it's all still *so* visceral. I hit it so hard and *so many fucking times.*

Amelia's thumb brushes against the back of my hand, making me realize that I'm squeezing hers—*hard*—and I immediately loosen my grip.

"Sorry," I sign, quickly—taking a breath, trying to steady myself. I fight off the roll of nausea before I finally sign, "Anyway, I ended up here that night. I couldn't go back to the apartment and face Evelyn, I couldn't go to Otis, so I just . . . sat here."

And it's strange being back. *Almost surreal.*

The last time I was here was the night I lost myself completely. What I'd done to Evelyn was awful, but . . . I was already gone by the time it came to that. It was everything that led up to the betrayal that still haunts me.

A chill runs through me at the thought before my eyes slowly drift back up to Amelia.

She pulls in a long inhale, her eyes regarding me thoughtfully for a few, long moments. "Seems like you were really going through it, Roberts."

I huff through a lazy nod, but there's this questioning gleam to her expression. I'm not sure if it's my own paranoia, but it's almost like she can tell there's a missing piece to the story.

Still, she doesn't press it. Her eyes float back down to the table, staring at her palm. The fingernail marks from a couple of weeks ago are mostly gone, but the two that were bleeding are still faintly visible. Another second passes as her eyes drift from her palm to my hand, still holding hers.

"We match," she signs. "Kind of."

Something between a sigh and a nervous laugh escapes me. I think I'm relieved, but . . . it's also . . . kind of fucked. We *do* match.

Kind of.

But where my scar is from a desperate attempt to get the pain out, hers seem to be a way of keeping it all in.

Still, a wave of comfort rolls through me. There's no trace of judgment or disgust coming from her. Instead, something about this moment feels . . . *binding.* Like we're no longer just seeing the *idea* of one another, but all the cracks and bumps we've each collected.

I told her the truth and it didn't ruin everything.

She listened, she reacted, and then she held my hand.

She brought me back.

A relieved breath pushes past my lips as a small smirk pinches my cheek. "I really like you, James."

Her red lips tilt just as she finally takes a bite of her hot dog, immediately groaning while signing, "So good," as she wiggles in her seat and then pops a fry in her mouth.

I smile again. There are few things better than watching this woman eat.

It *is* good. *So, so good.*

chapter twenty-nine
amelia

I'm a weirdo. *I know this.*

But it's extra apparent as the plate of brownies I made to bring over to Dean's ex-wife's house stare back at me on the dining room table.

Who the fuck brings a baked good to a meeting like this?

"Hi, you're fucking my ex-husband?"

"Yes, but I brought brownies."

I lift my eyes toward the ceiling in an effort to not groan at my own awkwardness.

Since Dean and I have been spending more time together, he wanted me to meet Marnie so there wouldn't be any friction about me being around while he has Ava—but I underestimated how uncomfortable this would be. I feel like a rubber band wound around barbed wire.

My fingers run under the lip of the table. The unfinished wood scrapes softly against the pads of my fingertips and I concentrate on running them back and forth while my body tries to relax.

"So, Amelia, you're in class with Evelyn?" Marnie asks, sipping her drink.

I'm not sure if it's my imagination or not, but it seems like she won't even look at my awkward brownies and I wonder if it's a silent protest to meeting me. I'm pretty sure I'm just being paranoid. From what Dean tells me, she's happy with her new boyfriend.

"Yeah," I say tightly. "We're both on an accelerated learning plan because we're already fluent in the language, so we have a few classes together."

She nods. "That's great," she says, her tone equally strained. "Dean and Evelyn go back aways so I'm sure it's . . . *nice* that you get along."

Dean shifts in his seat, mumbling, "Nice, Marn," before he clears his throat.

I wonder if she thinks I don't know about his history with Evelyn . . . Truthfully, I wonder what *she* knows about their relationship.

It was clear last night at the park that he's still harboring a lot of guilt from it and it makes me wonder how much he's ever really talked about it.

Noting the palpable tension arising, I quickly say, "Evelyn's great. We've become good friends." Glancing over at Dean, he looks equal parts annoyed as he does uncomfortable. My fingers are still running underneath the lip of the table, but I move one hand to hold his knee, trying to anchor him and myself. He places his hand over mine and it feels like we're hunkering down for hurricane winds, if we have to.

It's what he did for me—*and then some*—a couple weeks ago during what I've decided to refer to as the *Mommy Issue Meltdown*, and I want him to know that I'm here for him too.

Plus, he warned me that things have been tense with Marnie since she brought up this idea of moving.

Marnie takes the slightest notice of our closening and pulls her shoulders back with another small nod. "When are Evelyn and Otis getting married?" she asks Dean.

The tension in my spine stiffens. Evidently, my anxiety is not equipped for casual talk with ex-spouses. Every question feels like it has an ulterior motive.

I grab a brownie in an attempt to eat my feelings as Dean shrugs, saying, "Early June. They're doing it over at Harold Washington Library."

She nods, taking another sip of her drink. "And I guess Ava will be there too?"

Dean's body *does* tighten at that. "Yes. It'll be over a weekend. And even if it wasn't, we can work something out. We've switched days before when your parents were in town."

This is the worst.

Her eyebrows hitch and she raises her hand with slight defense. "I was just asking."

Was she, though?

I need to calm down. Dean seems a little on edge but he's a fucking zen garden compared to my twitchy ass. I just need to take his lead.

Still, the tension in the room has heightened. Dean finally clears his throat, asking, "Are we good? Can you go get Ava, please?" to Marnie and his voice has the exact rasp that makes my toes curl, which helps loosen some of the stiffness in my neck.

Marnie's mouth flattens and she sits a moment longer before she pushes back out of her chair and leaves the dining room.

Dean exhales hard and my hand instinctively tightens on his leg. He looks over at me, slightly apologetic, but mostly just uneasy.

I wish there was something I could do to make him feel better but . . . mounting him here—mere moments before I meet his daughter—in his ex-wife's dining room—seems highly inappropriate. My eyes drift to my awkward brownies. I decided to add peanut butter and they turned out pretty damn good if I do say so myself.

Keeping my eyes on the plate, I sign, "She didn't eat any," before I turn back to him, sticking my bottom lip out dramatically. He chuckles, and the sound trickles through me like a gentle wave.

He runs his thumb over my bottom lip, then signs, "More for me," with his signature, sexy smirk. Suddenly, his eyes light up, looking just past me. I turn around to see Marnie carrying Ava and . . . she is *so stinkin' cute.* Her round blue eyes sparkle and she grins at Dean immediately, giving my uterus a fucking heart beat.

Ugh. I hate that I'm that girl. But I can't help it. I mean, seeing her giggle and reach for him, watching him pull her into his chest and cover her in tiny kisses . . .

Lord, have mercy.

I keep my hand on the back of the chair as I stand, my knees shaking with wily, feminine swoonery as I smile at the wide, blue eyes peeking over at me.

"Ava, this is Amelia," Dean says and my head tilts, raising my hand to give her a small wave. She lifts her hand out to the side, opening and closing her fist in a little baby wave, pulling my smile wider.

"Hi, Ava. It's nice to meet you." I stick my finger out, and, as babies tend to do, she grabs it while I lightly shake it up and down. It's stupid, but it's something I used to do when I was in the infant room at the preschool. When one of the teachers needed a bathroom break, I'd walk around to all of the babies and give them a "baby handshake."

Ava giggles and then snuggles her face into her dad as I straighten back up. Marnie is shuffling her feet across from us, nervously watching and a strange pang hits in my chest.

Our interaction tonight hasn't exactly been smooth, but something about the visual of her right now pulls at me.

Right now she doesn't feel like a bitter ex-wife. Right now, she seems like a good mom—worried about letting a stranger spend time with her daughter.

I have no way to reassure her, and neither does Dean, but I want her to know that I come in peace.

"Let me grab her bag," Marnie says, disappearing into the kitchen.

Dean hikes Ava up higher and looks over at me. "Don't forget the brownies," he whispers through a grin.

Breathing a laugh, I move to put the lid back on the tupperware, but before I do, I take a few out and put them on a plate.

I come in peace. With snacks.

I'm pretty sure my first suggested activity with Ava has now traumatized her.

The aquarium.

It seemed safe, but of course we caught the belugas fucking each other. *Hard.* It was all blubber and thrashing. Even as an adult—it was pretty horrific.

Luckily, she went to sleep easily, and Dean and I have been lounging on the couch, watching *Order of the Phoenix* since she went down about an hour ago. We've been slowly working our way through all the *Harry Potter* movies. It's fun watching them with someone who's basically seeing them for the first time. But we often get . . . distracted.

Even now, our hands are roaming. There is a sleeping baby down the hall, and yet we just can't seem to keep our hands to ourselves. What started as his hand on my hip is now cupping my breast. His thumb keeps feathering over my hardened nipple, while my hand that started out on his knee, has now inched closer to the bulge in his pants.

His rich coffee smell cocoons me, and my eyes float up to the square cut of his stubbled jaw, following it until his full lips come into sight.

Ugh.

And watching him be Daddy Dean today—I'm ready to fucking pounce.

So I do.

Dr. G would be proud. I'm feeling my feelings.

Though, *these* feelings aren't the difficult ones. This man turns me on by merely breathing.

I slowly slink to the floor in front of him. His eyes widen before darting to the baby monitor on his phone, and then glancing back at me.

"You're going to have to be quiet, Daddy," I whisper.

"Fuck," he hisses, giving me a rush that shoots straight to my core. My fingers move to unbutton his jeans and he pets my face as he lifts his hips, allowing me to pull his pants down. His length bobs up before I take it in my hand, fisting it slowly as I watch him sink his lip between his teeth, stifling a moan.

"Shh," I tease.

His head rolls back on the couch as a breathless chuckle escapes while I continue to stroke him up and down. My tongue runs along his length while my hand still pumps. I swirl the tip of him in my mouth, hearing a low rumble in his chest as his fingers rake through my hair, gripping the strands tightly.

His chin drops back to me, watching while I work him between my lips. There's deep desire in his coffee-colored eyes—it's not as untamed as usual—it's softer, more awe-struck, but it fuels me just the same. Our eyes stay connected and his thumb traces my stretched lips while I lower myself deeper, moaning quietly around him and feel him shudder—making my mouth pull up at the corner.

"Oh, fuck," he chokes out on a whisper. "Fuck, baby—you smiling—with my dick in your mouth . . . *fuck.*" He's babbling hushed nonsense and the praise pulses between my legs as I pop off of him.

He's being too loud.

I pull my pants down and Dean's eyes darken, dragging along my legs and up to my thighs before they drift back to my face. Slowly, I straddle him, settling a leg on each side of his lap as I nestle him at my entrance.

A sharp gasp inflates his chest and that's when I realize . . .

No condom.

He's just barely inside me, but my eyes search his and all I see is want. I've never done this bare before, but the heat swirls low in my stomach thinking about feeling only him.

"I'm on the pill. And . . . I'm clean," I sign.

His fingertips lightly run up my back as he nods. "I'm clean, too," he rasps.

My lips quirk before I slowly sink down on him. He starts a deep, low groan, but I quickly put my hand over his mouth, his eyes widening as his hands grip onto my waist.

I lean over to his ear, whispering, "What's the word, baby?"

I'm teasing him. His mouth is covered—but after another beat, he reluctantly pulls his hands from my waist and signs, "Lightning," before he latches back onto me.

My lips tilt. *Always full of surprises.*

The coil in my stomach tightens and I use my other hand, the one not holding his mouth, to push some of his hair off his forehead. He breathes heavily through his nose, whining a bit and thrusting his hips into me, silently begging me to move, and a small smile pulls up my cheeks.

I start to rock into him slowly, at first, savoring every inch of him—*just him*—while my hand keeps him quiet so he can enjoy.

And we do. Like a couple of belugas.

My eyes flutter open to see Beatrice glaring at me from her pillow.

"The food dish ain't gonna fill itself," her face says, and my eyebrows flinch before I roll over to my other side, toward the nightstand. I grab my phone to check the time and see I have a message from Dean and a missed call from an unknown number.

I barely answer the phone for people I *do* know, so I ignore the missed call but click away to get to my message from Dean. It's sad— *no, it's pathetic*—but it was actually really hard to force myself to come home last night. He insisted that I could stay, but . . . I just felt like I should give him his time with Ava. And give myself some time.

I can't deny that I've really been enjoying our time together. And I sleep better next to him, but . . . it's been a lot to adjust to—being with someone in a real way like this. On one hand, it feels like the most natural thing in the world with him, but I have to actively suppress the intrusive thoughts. It's like fighting through an allergic reaction to a meal I desperately want to devour.

I finally look at the message.

Dean: Should have stayed over.
Made chocolate chip pan-blobs.

Smiling, I see the follow up picture he sent. It *is* the ugliest pancake I have ever seen—but warmth still spreads through me thinking about him ineptly flipping pancakes with Ava playing on the floor nearby. *Wishing I was there.*

My fingers tap out a message back.

Me: I'll teach you how
to make them at our next sleepover.

I push out of bed and tiredly shuffle toward the kitchen, pouring some kibble for Beatrice, and starting some coffee for myself. As the coffee brews, the smell immediately reminds me of a certain bossy lumberjack and I groan, annoyed with myself that my mind keeps finding ways to wander back to him.

Something like this wasn't even in the equation for me, but here I am—daydreaming. All that's missing is the bluebird on my goddamn shoulder.

"Want to be my bluebird, Beatrice?" I sign, sleepily waiting for caffeine.

The cat is shoving her face into her dish, not paying attention to me at all, but even if she were I bet she'd say, "Bitch, I'd eat the bluebird."

I wonder if everyone has hypothetical chats with their cat . . .

The alert light on my phone blinks, saving me from pre-coffee ponderings and I pick it up, seeing another message.

Dean: Tomorrow night, baby.

My smile pulls. I kind of love that Sundays have inadvertently become our thing. It started because that's when Ava goes back to Marnie's, but now it feels like *our* day. Like a reward for powering through the rest of them.

I send him a series of emojis— some peppers, doughnuts, a banana—before I prepare my coffee and sit down at my desk, firing up my laptop. As I wait for it to boot up, I take a sip, trying to taste it the way Dean taught me—*smell, sip, slurp, sip*—but chuckle when I still just taste coffee.

Jesus Christ. I really can't stop thinking about him.

I click through my student portal with purposeful taps, determined to be productive with the energy I woke up with today.

I'm feeling better—more alert. I'm not sure if it's because of the proper sleep I've actually been getting lately or if it's . . . *something else . . .* but I need to take advantage of it. I'm watching Luke tomorrow and between that and my standing Sunday nights with Dean, it won't leave a lot of time for school work.

My mind slips once more to ideas of what our Sunday will entail but then I shake my head and open the study guide for one of my impending finals.

Focus.

Saturday dinner at the shelter is a hit!

I made Chicken Divan and nearly everyone has come up for seconds and it does my heart good to know they're enjoying it. I start to stack the empty pans and toss in the extra utensils. A woman I recognize, but can't remember her name, timidly walks up to me at the serving station and asks, "Is there any more?"

I smile. "Yep, I think you're getting the last scoop." I use the spoon to plop a generous helping onto her plate and then glance back up at her. "Hey, do you know where Patty is?"

She's usually moseying her way up here when she sees me starting to get ready for dish duty, but I haven't seen her all night. The woman's mouth pulls back tightly, glancing down at her plate. She nervously looks around before she leans a little closer to me. "I heard she left earlier this week."

A heavy sigh escapes me. *Damn.*

I nod, muttering, "Thanks," as I mindlessly busy myself with collecting more dishes.

There's only two reasons the women here leave. One is that they've found some stability, set themselves up safely to continue on with their lives, and the other is because . . . well, because their *former* life found a way to steal them back.

Just as I stack the last pan, I see someone from the corner of my eye walking up to the station.

Jesus. She can't be more than eighteen—*if that.*

She's petite—I'd guess only about five feet tall—and she has long, blond hair with baby blue eyes.

"Hi," I say, glancing around at the empty dishes. "Did you get any food?"

Usually I'm pretty good about making sure everyone has eaten before I dole out seconds, but I don't even remember seeing her.

She shakes her head. "I just got here."

Well, shit.

"It's okay," she quickly says, turning on her heel.

"No—wait," I stutter. "Let me—uh. Let me just see what's in the pantry." She lingers just outside the serving station, nervously glancing around at all the tables.

She just got here.

"Do you want to come?" I ask her.

She contemplates me for a moment and I just can't get over how young she looks. *Young and pretty.* She looks like she could be modeling some overpriced, surfer brand but . . . she's *here*.

Looks can be deceiving that way, I remind myself.

I tilt my head and she slowly walks around the counter to the station, following me back.

I open the pantry, seeing a box of rice, some noodles . . . but it's mostly snacks. I move over to the fridge, seeing one chicken cutlet and three packages of cheese.

Jeez. Slim pickins'.

I think I remember them telling me that their food delivery was usually on Sundays, so after Saturday dinner, it must be bottom of the barrel.

A challenge.

The girl is hovering by the archway to the kitchen when I turn back around. "Any allergies?" I ask her.

She shakes her head, glancing around the kitchen aimlessly before her eyes pull back to me. I start to boil the water, and grab some spices from the cabinet above the stove. I usually leave some here, just so I always have a variety. It's amazing how much the right combination of seasoning can give life to an otherwise bland meal.

I concoct a rub with smoked paprika, rosemary, garlic powder, and a dash of some dried thyme, then start to coat the chicken cutlet.

"Y-You really don't need to do all that," the girl says quietly.

"It's no trouble," I tell her. "It's fun for me." After I finish the rub on the chicken, I add a little jasmine to the rice and give it a stir before I look back over at her. "What's your name?"

She sits on the counter across from the fridge, watching her feet dangle below before she mumbles, "Darlene."

Huh. She doesn't strike me as a *Darlene.* It seems too old for her.

"Well, it's nice to meet you. I'm Amelia. I cook here every Saturday."

She nods. "Do you—Do you live here?"

I shake my head, plopping the chicken cutlet on the pan, just to give it some crisp before I put it in the oven and bake it. "No, I live over in Wrigleyville with my cat."

"Sounds nice," she says, almost to herself.

I flip the chicken in the pan, letting it sear, and then turn and lean against the counter. I want to ask her how old she is, but that seems insensitive for some reason, so I stir the rice again and then move the chicken to the oven.

Once it's cooking, I lower the pot for the rice to a simmer and cover it before turning around and leaning against the counter, again.

Darlene's wide blue eyes stare at me blankly and I see them drift to my hearing aids. "Do you know sign language?" she asks.

My mouth quirks as I nod. "I do. I'm actually in school to become an interpreter."

"That's cool," she says. "My gram taught me some when I was little, but I barely remember it." Her hands move to pull her hair up and her long, baggy sleeves fall, revealing some heavy-duty bandaging up her forearm before she quickly shakes the sleeve back down.

She peeks over at me and a few unpleasantries pass through her expression before she sighs. "I guess you'd know I was lying if I told you I fell . . ."

I work to keep my expression as passive as possible, shrugging. "Depends. How'd you fall?"

Her eyebrows pinch but she tugs her bottom lip between her teeth as the ghost of a smirk pinches her cheek. "Saving a litter of kittens."

I nod, suppressing a small laugh. "What'd you save them from?"

Her eyes stare off for a few beats before they fall back to her legs, gently swaying as they hang off the counter. She's quiet for a few seconds more before she says, "A snake."

The look in her eyes is enough for me to realize that this analogy, farfetched as it may be, might hold some truth.

A truth-lie.

"Sounds brave," I say, giving the rice another stir when I hear her snort, incredulously.

"I'm definitely not brave," she mumbles. Her heels knock a little harder into the cabinets behind her dangling feet and her defeatedness aches in my chest.

Pulling in a deep inhale through my nose, I release it back out before walking a little closer to her. I lean against the fridge across from where she is on the counter, and her eyes nervously float up to mine.

"How old are you, Darlene?" I finally ask.

She shifts her weight before she says, "Nineteen."

Maybe it's just her tiny frame, but she looks even younger than that.

Still. Nineteen, and here . . .

I take another deep breath before I point to my ear. "I wear these because I lost my hearing when I was ten."

Her eyebrows pinch, probably with some confusion from my subject change but then she asks, "How?"

I clear my throat. "Car accident."

"That sucks," she says, under her breath.

I shrug. "I don't know. I mean, it *did.* I missed hearing certain things but . . . I also didn't . . ." She looks over at me, her eyes becoming curious, so I continue, "I had run away from home. The crash happened on the way back—after my mom had to come get me."

"Was she mad?" she asks.

"Uh—yeah," I breathe out. "Yeah. She was mad. She was *always* mad."

Her expression lifts, an understanding passing over it as she nods. "So, what happened?"

My fingers start to twist the hem of my shirt, the itchiness under my fingertips starting to twitch as I tell her, "The cops found me a few hours after the accident, a few hundred feet away from the car. I guess even half conscious with a severe head injury, I was still trying to get away from her."

Her eyes widen. *"Jesus . . ."*

My shoulders shrug, involuntarily. I'm not exactly sure why I'm telling her all of this. Until recently when I spilled my guts to Dean, these memories were something I kept tightly locked down in the darkest part of my soul. But I guess I just want to offer her some perspective. Not that I'm a poster child for life after abuse, because I'm definitely not, but . . .

I *do* have an apartment in Wrigleyville. I have a cat. I'm in school, and I even have a couple of friends.

I have a Dean . . .

I guess I just want to feed her hope. I can see that she still has some, and I want her to lean into *that* instead of letting it blow away from the gusts life hurls at you.

"It sounds like *you're* the brave one," she finally says. "I can't believe you ran away when you were ten. I never even tried."

I swallow. "It takes a lot of courage to stay too. And hey, you made it here," I offer. "This building is full of the most badass women I've ever met."

She tugs her lip between her teeth, keeping her eyes with mine before she asks, "What'd you say your name was?"

"Amelia," I tell her, and that's when I take notice of her necklace.

In a cursive font it says, *Paige.*

The timer to the oven goes off and I smile. *I like Paige.*

chapter thirty

dean

"Ma-ma!" Ava yells and then crashes her open mouth to my cheek. It's the way she kisses, and it's equally as adorable as it is gross.

"I'm Da-da," I enunciate through a chuckle. "But good job."

She's learned one word, and of course it's *Mama.* It wouldn't surprise me at all if Marnie was playing it as white noise while she sleeps, but I don't care—as long as she's talking.

And I still got her first sign.

"More."

I smile at the memory as Ava tackles me to the floor again. I lift her above my head and tickle her sides, making her laugh wildly before I put her back on the floor. She wobbles over to her blocks and starts clacking them together, squealing, like she's calling a meeting to order.

Peeking over at the clock on the microwave, I notice that it's almost four.

I'm surprised I haven't gotten a warning text from Marnie yet. She's regressed back to the way we did things in the first few months after Ava was born—when she wanted to limit our interactions to a simple hand off—so she'd text me a play-by-play of her arrival.

I pull out my phone to make sure I haven't missed any texts from her, but the only notification I have is from Amelia.

Amelia: Start stretching, Roberts.
And grab an energy drink.
You're gonna need it.

It's followed by the purple devil emoji and my lips tilt.

I won't even let my mind wander to what she could possibly have planned—*I mean, my daughter is right here*—so, I go the teasing route.

Me: Why? Is Half-Blood Prince
really that intense?

I send her a wink, just to rub in my snark. We both know that we'll only make it through about twenty minutes of the movie at most.

Not that I'm complaining.

Literally ever.

I suddenly hear a knock at the door and my eyebrows pinch, checking my phone, again.

Still nothing.

My limbs tighten as I start toward the door, peeking out the peephole to see . . . *Shaun* standing outside.

What the—?

I unlock the deadbolt and pull the door open, my eyebrows furrow as Shaun and his trusty windbreaker stare back at me.

"Hey, Dean. I'm here to pick up Ava. Marnie got caught up with something and asked me to come get her."

Several alarms sound in my head, and I try to prioritize them. *"Caught up with something,"* is an ominous statement. Too vague for someone that has "tabled" any conversations regarding a potential move out of state with my daughter. And why didn't she text me to tell me that Shaun would be picking Ava up?

I move aside to let him in before closing the door behind him. I move toward the hallway, asking, "Do you mind watching her for a second? I've just gotta pack a few things from her room."

He nods as he crouches to the floor. "No problem," he says and then looks at Ava. "Hey, sweet pea."

Ugh. Sweet pea.

I move toward Ava's room, fishing my phone back out of my pocket as I push open the door. Immediately, I get to Marnie's contact and hit call, listening to the ring back twice before it sends me to voicemail.

She buttoned me.

My heart races and I take a steadying breath before my thumb moves to call her again, but just as I do, a text comes through.

Marnie: Busy. Sent Shaun to
pick her up.

No shit!

Anger surges through me. What is she busy with?! It's Sunday, for Christ's sake!

I pull in a deep breath and force it back out. I have *got* to calm down. All in all, I'm probably overreacting, but it doesn't provide me any peace at the moment. I mentally make a plan to talk about it with Marnie next time I see her. It's honestly probably better that we don't talk about it right now—I'm too amped up, and I'd probably say something that would earn me one of her classic "Calm downs," which would sufficiently make me lose my shit.

I take another moment to steady myself before I grab a binky and Ava's plush little marshmallow stuffy, mostly to seem like I was in here gathering her things—not seething in a fit of anger—before I push back through the door.

Still, the death grip I have on the two wholesome items feels ridiculous as I push back through the door to see Shaun sitting on the floor with Ava in his lap, reading her a book while she slumps against his chest. He peers up at me, his expression a little uneasy as he says, "All good?"

Good, isn't exactly the word that comes to mind, but seeing Ava comfortable does the smallest bit to soothe me—*and annoy me.*

I nod tightly, shoving the binky and stuffed marshmallow into her diaper bag before zipping it back up. Shaun lifts Ava and puts her on her feet before standing himself, grabbing the diaper bag as I pick Ava up.

I hold her tight, peppering kisses on her neck. "I love you, baby girl."

"Ma-ma!" she says, through her bubbling laughter.

I keep the choice words I have for "Mama" at the moment to myself as I hesitantly hand her over to Shaun.

It's harder than ever right now.

"Drive safe," I tell him.

I think I've snapped.

It's the only explanation.

Why else would I have shoved a hat on my head and discreetly followed Shaun back to my old townhouse, keeping myself two cars behind the entire route and then sneaking onto the street and crouching below the dashboard?

What was I expecting?

That Shaun would take off and kidnap Ava? That I'd show up at Marnie's and see her car packed up and ready to move away without telling me?

The answer from a man who has snapped is, *yes.* I one hundred percent believed either one of those things was possible. Which makes me feel like an even bigger dipshit when I see Marnie's car completely empty as Shaun passes by it to carry Ava up the few steps to the house and walk her safely inside.

Marnie got busy with work and asked her boyfriend to come pick up Ava. *That's it.*

I stay a few minutes more, sitting in the pathetic pool of my paranoia and, honestly, to avoid any suspicion. I roll my eyes again, groaning as I put my seatbelt on, and then I shift the truck into gear.

I pull out of my stalker spot and start to drive away from the house. I start to drive toward Wrigleyville.

But something still feels off.

Twenty minutes later, I'm at Amelia's door. I send her a text to let her know I'm outside and a minute later, the door jaggedly opens.

This fucking door.

Her eyebrows pinch, taking in my appearance and probably confused by my scowl as she moves out of the way to let me in before maneuvering the door shut behind me.

"Are you incognito?" she signs, stifling a small laugh as she eyes my baseball cap.

I pull it off my head and bend it in my hands, squishing the bill until it makes a perfect triangle. Her small, soft hands cover mine and she holds them there for a second, before my eyes find hers and she signs, "What's wrong?"

I shake my head. *I don't want to talk.* It's not like I have anything concrete to tell her, and the only thing I'll end up admitting is that I followed my ex-wife's boyfriend because of a hunch that was neither confirmed, nor denied.

No. I need escape *right now.*

And I'm looking at it. It has dark, raven hair and bright green eyes with smooth olive skin and plump rosy lips.

"You said you had plans for tonight?" I mumble, my voice low and tight.

She looks at me cautiously. "Yeah, but it can wait—"

I stop her by pinching her chin with my fingers. My thumb runs along her bottom lip as I rasp, "Tell me," continuing to pull along her chin so that her mouth is slightly open. I resist the urge to cover her mouth with mine. Instead, I admire the plush curves of her lips—the dip in the middle of the bottom one that cushions mine like a pillow.

She pulls my hand from her chin and kisses my palm and then holds it to her cheek.

"This is what you need right now?" she asks.

God, yes.

I can feel my eyes burning into her as she keeps her contact with me, kissing the pad of my thumb and then giving it a gentle nibble as I nod.

"Well . . ." She smiles, pulling me toward the bedroom. "Your *need* could work in perfect tandem with my plans," she signs, not skipping a beat.

I follow along behind her. Beatrice perches herself on the back of the oversized, coral chair in the living room and I give her head a quick pat on our way toward the bedroom.

Have to at least acknowledge *the queen.*

Amelia turns back toward me and signs, "I thought we'd make ourselves something to get us through our time apart . . ." before she sets her phone on the nightstand, leaning it against the small lamp to prop it up.

She wants to record us?

The idea zaps through me, straight to my groin, and I pull in a deep breath through my nose. "I kept the pictures you sent . . ."

She stops adjusting the phone for a second, peeking back at me. "Did you?"

I nod. I can already tell she likes that I kept them—*that I look at them.* Her finger taps the screen of the phone and I hear the faint beep sound indicating that it's started recording.

I'm feral right now. I'm so outside of myself, I don't even know who I am, and that's *exactly* where I want to be. I want to be someone else. *I want to be . . .*

"Strip," I order. I don't even recognize my voice, but Amelia doesn't hesitate. She pulls her leggings down, and then tosses her shirt away before she slinks back on the mattress.

"Did I tell you to get on the bed?" I ask, my voice low and gravelly.

She gives me a defiant glare before she smirks and stands back up, giving me a glorious, full-length view of her naked body. I close the small distance between us with two, slow steps, my fingers toying with her nipples as I watch her eyes roll back.

"Look at you," I muse, quietly. "So perfect." My mouth meets my fingers, swirling and teasing the pebbled flesh with my tongue and teeth. She whimpers before scraping her fingers through my hair and holding me tightly to her.

My mouth travels to her other breast, giving it the same attention and her breathing picks up, swelling my dick against my jeans.

I finally work my way up her neck and then I devour her mouth. I groan, loud and hard at the sweet, hot feeling of her tongue against mine, ebbing and flowing in a greedy way that mirrors my own. We lose ourselves to it for a few seconds—kissing and sucking, nipping and licking—and when we finally pull away, my weight wobbles.

I push some fallen hair from her eyes and bend to nibble on her bottom lip again. "Be a good girl and bend over the bed."

Heavy panting hits my cheek but she swallows and slowly turns, draping herself over the mattress. I yank my shirt over my head as I'm gifted the sight of her beauty mark and my hand itches to smack it, like a perfect bullseye, but I don't. Instead, I adjust the phone, so that it's aimed at us.

Her face isn't in the frame right now—just mine—but I'll change that at some point.

I tug her so that her knees are underneath her and her ass is up in the air, making her squeal.

My dark chuckle sounds foreign as I sink to my knees behind her. "Grab a pillow baby, we don't wanna piss off the neighbors." I trail my lips up the inside of her thigh and she whimpers desperately.

"What are you gonna do to me?" she asks, between breaths.

The corners of my vision blur. I'm chasing a need, a release—an out-of-body fucking experience, right now. My mouth moves her slit, groaning when I find her hot and slick, sucking the bundle of nerves into my mouth and toying it with my tongue before I mutter, "Whatever the fuck I want."

"Oh, God—" is all she gets out before I bury my face between her legs—eating her from behind—and she cries out. Her noises are only partially muffled as she rides my face, backing up into me, and I tightly grip her around her thighs, steadying the movement.

"Easy," I mumble, the noise muffled by my invasion of her heat.

"Ohh . . ." she moans. "Holy sh—" the rest is lost to the pillow and my smile widens. I fucking *love* watching her lose her mind. I love being the one to teeter that line and it fuels me. I lick and suck her harder, my nose even creeps it's way between her ass cheeks but I don't fucking care.

I want it all.

I pull away and flip her on her back, dropping my pants and boxers quickly before I pick up the phone and hold it over her. I move the camera along her body, lifting her just a bit to get a quick glimpse of her beauty mark before I make my way up to her face.

Her cheeks are flushed and her eyes are a bright, sparkly green, while her long dark hair fans around her on the sheets below.

Fucking gorgeous.

I settle myself at her folds but don't push in yet. Her hips buck and she whines, hardening me further as I grab her face, squishing her lips together.

"Beg me, Amelia," I rasp. "Beg for my cock."

Her eyes widen. I didn't think I was actually capable of surprising her this way, but it seems I am. Still, the heady look in her eyes only spurs me on more.

"Please," she whispers, but her eyebrows hitch the tiniest bit—telling me she can take more—and my smile darkens.

I'm gone. Lost to a lust-filled gas, breathing the dirty oxygen, letting it pollute my lungs.

"Use your words, baby. Be a good little slut and tell me what you want."

I'm fucking gone.

She takes the moment to tackle me to the mattress. She snatches the phone from my hand and holds it over me while sinking down, slowly pushing me into her as her hand comes to the base of my throat and a deep moan rattles in my chest.

Holy fuck.

"*You're* the slut, Roberts. And I'm going to give you what you need." She starts to slowly grind on my length and my hips thrust into her harder. With each thrust, the words I said hit me harder and harder.

"Whatever I want."

"Beg me."

"Slut."

I cringe as it barrels through me, but I still can't stop chasing the release her warmth is promising. "Amelia—I—" I choke out. "I'm sorry . . ."

She slows herself, dropping the phone as she cradles my chin in her palms. "Hey—did I use the word?" Her hips are still moving, but it's slower. Somehow it seems more about being connected right now than chasing our orgasms. I shake my head. "Exactly," she says, picking the phone back up and placing it on the pillow by the headboard.

"Now give me a show, Roberts. Don't make me ask you again."

The words fuel me and a growl rips from my throat. Keeping myself inside her, my arms circle her waist and I lift her up before pinning her back to the bed. I pull out just to slam back into her and she cries out.

So warm, tight, sweet.

Her legs wrap around my back as her hips meet mine, thrust for thrust.

I mercilessly pound into her, lowering my elbows to her sides to deepen my thrusts. "Fuck, baby, fuck," I grind out. "That's it."

She whimpers and my fingers thread through hers as our eyes lock, noses graze. Three more pumps have me spilling into her, shuddering my release as her walls tighten around me in her own climax, prolonging mine.

I collapse on top of her and our heartbeats pulse against each other's, sweat mixing, breaths tangling. She runs a hand through my hair, petting my head and I press my face into her chest.

I don't move. I stay inside her as her legs tighten around my back.

chapter thirty-one
amelia

Beatrice wants to murder Luke. I can see it in her eyes. The kids are on spring break this week and Annie had a last minute appointment not far from my apartment, so she asked if she could drop him off for a bit. But there's not really much for him to do here—other than terrorize my cat.

I would have packed up and moved us back to his house, but I've really got to finish up some school work. Spending every day with Luke and every night with Dean these past few days has made it tough to stay on top of it.

Luke keeps bopping Beatrice's head and her wide eyes, backward ears and slightly puffed demeanor force me to tell him, "Hey, kid. When a cat looks like *that*..." My eyes move to Beatrice. "It means they're about to attack."

His eyes get a mischievous glint, like my statement was a dare instead of a warning. I breathe a laugh. "How about some popcorn and a movie while I finish up my homework?"

"Homework?! Aren't you a grown up?" he asks.

I shake my head. "No, I'm just an old kid," I tease, as I walk to the kitchen.

Luke plops onto the chair in the living room. "Can I watch a movie with explosions?"

I snort a laugh. "Sure. Pick anything you want under 'Kids.' You know how to spell 'kids,' right?"

I toss the popcorn in the microwave as he mutters, "Duh, Miss Melia," and another small laugh escapes me.

"So how's it going at school? Still sharing snacks with your little pumpkin friend?" I lean my head through the archway from the kitchen and wiggle my eyebrows at him.

His mouth flattens. "No . . ." He squirms a bit as he picks up the remote and my eyebrows pinch.

I mosey over to the chair and give his head a rub. "Why not?" He starts to click through the titles on the screen, ignoring my nosy question when I push a little more "What? Did she switch to apples or something?"

He squints up at me, blinking—either unamused or unimpressed with my dumb joke, so I shrug, standing by as he clicks through a few more movies before he sighs. "She traded lunch with Carson."

Carson . . . that name sounds familiar . . .

Ah. He's the little shit that Luke punched in the back of the head.

I hum. "Well . . . that doesn't mean anything. Maybe he had a really good lunch that day."

Luke's lips tilt down with a shrug and it tugs at something in my chest. Something that is vastly undervalued is the very *real* emotions of kids. It's easy for adults to shrug off their feelings or not take them too seriously because the source of the distress is *seemingly* something small.

But it doesn't really matter why—they're still feeling it. And Luke isn't like other kids. When I was his teacher, he would never whine about not getting a sticker for good behavior—and the turd never *did* get one because . . . well, he's a turd.

But his sadness is subtle. Especially for a kid. He might go to great lengths to get attention, but he doesn't like to let people know he's hurting.

"Hey," I say, crouching down in front of the chair. "Did you know that you're my *best* friend?"

His eyebrows hitch but he just as quickly shrugs it off. "Nuh uh—you're a grown up."

"I thought we'd already established that I was just a really old kid?" I smirk, ducking my head to meet his eyes before I inch my mouth up my cheeks, slowly. Luke fights his own smile until he can't anymore and I scrunch my nose at him.

Gotcha.

I chuckle and Luke's eyebrow cocks. "Do best friends have superpowers?"

My lips twist. "Kind of . . . they *do* make you stronger."

"Like the Hulk?"

Goddamn. This kid. I can't.

Breathing another laugh, I tell him, "It's not really something you *see.* They make you stronger because they make you better *inside.*" I pat my chest and Luke stares blankly back at me.

I'm losing him.

"Look. What's pumpkin girl's name?" I ask.

"Jenna," he mutters with a slight blush as his eyes pull down.

I don't comment on the rosy cheeks but my mouth pinches. "Well, can't Jenna be friends with you *and* Carson?"

Carson sounds like a dick, but I'm playing the part of responsible Amelia right now. He seems to think I'm a grown up, after all.

Luke slinks farther into the chair before he says, "Carson *hates* me."

"Whoa, dude. That's a strong word. And your mom told me you've been really good lately. No more fights."

His lips quirk before he shakes his head. "You said smart boys fight with their brains."

An itchiness creeps up my throat, so I clear it before I say, "That's right."

His mouth finally turns up into a genuine smile. "I guess we *are* best friends. You made me better."

Holy shit. I'm going to cry.

Thankfully, I manage to swallow it as I tell him to start the movie. I go to the kitchen and work to compose myself, pouring some popcorn into a bowl, when I suddenly hear a knock at the door and my eyebrows pinch.

Maybe Annie forgot something . . .

I hand Luke the bowl but chuckle when I see he's already engrossed in the movie as I walk to the door. Twisting the deadbolt, I prepare myself for another shocked look from Annie as she watches me man-handle my door open, but when I yank it back, a large figure pummels through, pushing me into the wall just inside the entryway.

A hand locks around the back of my neck and suddenly there are lips on mine.

I'm still roughly pressed into the closet door, the knob digging into my back, as a revolted squeak tightens my throat. The sound is muffled by the mouth invading mine, but my eyes finally focus.

Tim.

I dig my nails into his hands, still gripping my jaw, as he jerks his face back.

"Oh, I've missed this," he murmurs roughly and then grabs the back of my hair. All that makes its way from my mouth is a pitiful squeak before his mouth covers mine again. I bite down hard on his lip and shove him as hard as I can until he stumbles back into the door.

"Oh, so we're playing that way?" He wipes his bloody lip, starting toward me again.

One of my hands shoots out in front of me, warding him off as I quickly peek around the wall, releasing a heavy breath when I see Luke still watching the movie.

Thank God.

"Oh, shit," Tim mutters, but there's a hint of amusement to his tone that burns through my veins.

"Yeah. Shit," I spit back at him through my teeth in a harsh whisper.

He drops his chin and shakes his head before pouting back at me. "You've been ignoring me . . . "

I don't even know how to respond. My brain feels like it's caught in a wind tunnel, swirling violently and beating against the walls of my skull as my eyes narrow at him.

"Miss Melia?" I distantly hear Luke's small voice filter through my ears.

Fuck.

My throat tightens, but I try as best I can to steady my voice as I say, "Everything's fine, bud," over my shoulder, keeping my eyes on Tim. "I've gotta step outside real quick, okay?"

I don't hear Luke answer me, so I peek around the corner.

My body jumps, startled, when I see him standing just outside the entryway.

"Who are you?" he asks, chin tilted up at Tim.

The air catches in my throat. "H-He's my neighbor," I stutter, trying to steady my heartbeat. "Go back and watch the movie. I'm gonna talk to him out in the hall real quick. But I'll be right back, okay?"

"You're the guy from the park!" Luke chirps.

My heart stops.

The *park?!*

My temples start to pulse and a cold sweat breaks on my forehead. I immediately position myself between them, but Tim peers over my shoulder. "Listen to the pretty lady and go watch the movie."

My back is still to Luke while I silently seethe at Tim. I resist the urge to tell him to *not* talk to him in the interest of not scaring Luke but . . . *I don't want him fucking talking to him.*

After a steadying breath, I hesitantly turn around, willing myself to stay calm as I crouch down to Luke's level. "Hey, bud, if you give me three minutes, we can toss blueberries to Beatrice and watch her chase them."

He takes a beat, then asks, "Can we blow up the blueberries?"

"Um . . . no." I'm alarmed at this new curiosity with explosives, but right now, I just need to get Tim out of here. "But if you're good, I'll see about getting us some sparklers next time we hang, okay?"

Tim's looming presence behind me feels suffocating as Luke raises one more curious glance at him before shuffling back to the chair. When I see he's sitting back down, I shove Tim through the door and out into the hall. Keeping the door cracked, I turn sharply toward him, narrowing my eyes.

"What the *fuck?!*" I hiss.

He tosses up a defensive arm. "How was I supposed to know there'd be a kid here?"

My fists curl at my sides, a tightness striking my limbs, but I do my best to channel a heavy breath through my nose.

"The *park*, Tim?! What the fuck were you doing at the park?!"

He shrugs. "Like I said, you were ignoring me . . ."

"So you *followed me?!* Do you realize how insane that is?!"

His smirk indicates that he *doesn't*, as he uses his thumb to wipe the small bit of blood still on his lip. Something about his gray-blue eyes feel like I'm staring into the dead of winter and an icy chill runs down my spine.

When he doesn't say anything, I finally huff out an overwhelmed breath. "Look. Whatever was going on with us? It's over."

He again looks amused, cocking an eyebrow. "Why?"

I grit my teeth in an effort to hold back my instinctive response: *"Because you're clearly a fucking psycho,"* and instead say, "It's just not gonna work. I'm busy, I—"

I'm cut off by him leaning into me and pulling my hips toward his. "Too busy for *this?*" he whispers, roughly. "A girl like you can't be going without it, so . . . what am I missing here?"

Jesus Christ. Is this really what I was into a few short months ago?

I nearly gag. Not just from his cockiness, or the fact that he indirectly just called me a whore—*but his smell.* He smells like patchouli—*earthy*—and not at all like the warm coffee smell I've become used to.

My stomach rolls and my urgency to get *him* out of here, and *myself* back inside with Luke starts to shake my limbs.

"You need to leave," I tell him, grabbing his hands, which are still locked on my waist, but he tightens his grip. "I'm not fucking around, Tim. Go."

I finally meet his eyes and my heart jumps when I remember them hovering over me, an inch from my face while he pinned me down to my bed. I take a deep breath and pull my neck back in an attempt to put some space between us, noticing a gash above his eyebrow. It's mostly covered by his shaggy blond hair, which is longer since the last time I saw him.

My heart pounds faster.

He still hasn't moved.

The longer he towers over me, the more constricted my lungs become. I've made it pretty fucking clear that I have no interest in whatever he came here for, and he's still here.

Still grabbing my waist.

A genuine panic is starting to race through me and it's only increasing when I realize that my resistance isn't deterring him. If anything, it appears to be egging him on and he pulls me closer until his lips hover over mine, again.

It's darkly familiar. Terrifying. Predatory.

"Do you know what I do to bad little sluts like you?"

The memory seizes my terror as he leans in the smallest bit and I flinch. When my eyes creep back open, a smug, satisfied smirk tilts on his cheek and I suddenly feel fire running through my veins.

Don't show your fear, Amelia.

I steel my spine, locking my eyes with his. I channel all the anger and intimidation I can muster and feed it through my glare as a low growl hums in my throat. "Get. Off."

The stare he gives me in return is even more unnerving. He looks like I just gave him some sort of salacious dare and the terror beats like a stampede through my chest. He lingers for a moment before he finally pulls away. The smallest bit of relief finds me, but he hooks his thumb under my jaw and my body stuns. It's like all of the adrenaline pulsing through me solidifies, cementing my fear.

"I'll be back. When you're less . . . busy," he says, a dark smile tilting on his lips.

I want to shove against him. I want to uppercut the sinister, snarly grin off his face. But my blood has run cold, freezing my limbs.

Why can't I fucking move?!

Finally, he releases my chin, whispering, "I'll see ya, Amelia," as he backs down the hallway and slowly saunters away. My body is tight and my teeth are clenched watching him disappear down the steps.

Standing, staring, I slowly feel the blood return to my extremities. I wiggle my fingers and release a heavy breath and then quickly push through the door, immediately locking the deadbolt. I stare at the door longer than necessary, his threat of returning still feeling like it's sitting just outside my door when it dawns on me . . .

Did he just call me Amelia?

chapter thirty-two

dean

Marnie opens the door, and I'm met with Ava's squeals and babbling.

"Baby!" I pull her into my arms and squeeze her tight. "How's the ear infection?" I ask Marnie.

She's not scowling, but her expression isn't exactly friendly. "The last two days have been tough but she's been okay today." Handing the bag to me she adds, "Just in time for you," but the words are dripping with disdain.

I love Ice Queen Marnie. She's the best.

I want to bring up the incident with her springing Shaun on me for pick up last weekend, but her mood already tells me it will just turn into an "argument." I hike the diaper bag over my shoulder and adjust Ava in my arms as she squishes my cheeks together.

"Okay, well . . . see ya," I say through my guppy lips. As I turn to leave, Marnie stops with an *"uhh"* noise that I already don't like the sound of. Turning back toward her, I see that she crosses her arms and then shuffles her feet before she peers back up at me.

I'm really trying to be patient but she's just standing there, chomping on her lip, so I finally ask, "What's up?"

She pulls a deep breath through her nose before her light blue eyes lock with mine. "We're . . . We're gonna go, Dean. To Michigan."

My eyes blink and my blood runs cold. She's not asking; she's not proposing another discussion. She's *telling* me.

And I fucking knew it.

I glance around for her bodyguard but I don't see him—not a windbreaker in sight—and my eyes narrow on my ex-wife. "The fuck you are."

Marnie's arms tighten as she scoffs. "Nice mouth, Dean. I bet she'll say *that* before she says 'Dad.'"

Wow.

I'd be impressed by her nasty little slight if I didn't already feel like I was about to snap. "Well, I hate to break it to you Marnie, but I *am* her dad. I've looked into it, and you can't take her without written consent from me, and I'm not signing shit!"

She shakes her head at me like I'm a petulant child and my temples start to pulse.

"I can, actually," she says. "It'll cost both of us way more money in court and lawyer fees, but all I need to do is file a motion for full custody and then I can do whatever I want."

My eyes bulge. *Full custody?!*

The surge of anger hits me hard. I clutch Ava like she's the paper weight to my sanity, seconds away from blowing off into the wind, but my eyes bore into Marnie. "So is *that* what you were doing last weekend? When you sent your little gopher to pick her up?"

You are holding your daughter. Keep control . . .

All she does is shrug and it *infuriates* me. This has been slowly eating away at me for months and it seems like she's playing a fucking game.

Deep breath. Keep control . . . keep . . .

My jaw clenches. "Can we talk about this inside?" I ask, tightly.

Her eyes falter just a bit but she shakes her head, straightening her posture before she says, "No, Dean. We can't. I'm willing to work with you on the visitations, but if you fight me on leaving, I'll file for full custody. There's nothing else to discuss."

Jesus fucking Christ.

The air feels thick, and the whooshing sound in my ears feels like it's flooding my brain. I suddenly feel Ava curling into my neck. Her sweet, honeysuckle smell and warmth only tighten my lungs and I choke on my inhale.

Oh my God.

This is happening. There's no escaping it. She'll win a custody battle for sure, and then I'll *never* see Ava.

I vaguely hear Marnie's voice, but the sound is garbled, muffled by the hurricane blowing through me. Everything starts to feel far away—*or maybe I feel far away.*

The slow, sinking feeling—the one I've tried desperately to never feel again—starts to pull me under and there's nothing that can stop it. *There's nothing that can . . .*

"Dean!" Marnie says sharply and I blink back at her. I can feel that the color has drained from my face, but it's confirmed when my eyes finally focus on her expression. "Jesus . . ." she mutters. "Let me get you some water."

I shake my head, blinking hard. "When?" My voice is hoarse and barely above a whisper.

"What?" she asks.

I hold Ava tighter, like that will somehow keep her here. My other hand is white-knuckling the railing as I ask her, again, "When are you going?"

She swallows hard and huffs out a breath. "Late June."

Two months . . .

My unfocused eyes float down to the pebbled concrete of the stoop. I've studied it countless times—back when I used to sit out here chain smoking—drinking myself into a state of numbed stupidity. I remember looking at the stones and wondering if it was random or if it was someone's job to strategically place them like that. The pattern seems arbitrary but clean, and I just . . . don't think anything *natural* actually happens that way.

It's never clean.

I've been working all year to strategically place my stones and it was all for nothing. Because a wrecking ball can come out of fucking nowhere and destroy it all.

Again.

"Dean?" Marnie says softly, her voice snapping my reality back into focus as she asks, "Are you sure you're okay?"

Definitely not okay.

I hold Ava tighter, pressing my lips to her brown curls as my limbs continue to shake. I try to breathe through it but . . . I can't.

I can't.

"Can you—Can I," I stutter, still not able to catch my breath, but I hand Ava back to Marnie and drop the bag on the stoop. Each word adds pressure to my lungs, but breathing through it seems impossible—it almost feels like there's *too much* air—and I'm one inhale away from popping them completely.

I find a way to say, "Can I come back and get her later? I just . . . I need—I need some time."

Nearly instantly, my panic turns. The despair shifts its light and becomes darker, harsher, and it beats in the back of my brain.

You never had control.

It was all a delusion.

And this *is your fucking wake up call.*

"Yeah, but Dean—" It's all I hear before I'm stalking down the street, leaving any idea of *"control"* on the pebbled stoop.

The first drag on my cigarette feels the exact same way it did a couple of months ago. It burns *and* soothes, clouding my unease as the smoke fills my lungs. There's a small buzz that I'm clinging to. Not just the buzz, but the time surrounding it.

A life that was easier.

I know my headspace is fucked. The fact that I bought a pack at all confirms I'm slipping. And the fact that I'm *aware* I'm slipping and did it anyway somehow makes it worse. My head shakes as I pound my feet down the pavement.

I just need something to bring me back.

And that something is in the beige brick building just a hundred feet in front of me.

My feet slow as I reach Amelia's building and stop just outside it, continuing my slip with nicotine when I hear the door pop open.

My hand digs through my pocket, pulling my phone out. I didn't tell Amelia I was coming. I wasn't entirely sure *where* I was going until I ended up here. As I click my screen to get to my message thread with her, I hear a guy clearing his throat.

"Hey, man. Mind if I bum one?" he asks.

My eyes flick up to see a man with moppy blond hair that hangs just above cloudy, blue eyes. He looks vaguely familiar but I have no idea where I might have seen him before. He's wearing a black and gray hoodie with wool-like fabric—*a drug rug*—an article of clothing I remember some baristas wearing during my delivery days with Red Line.

Maybe that's it.

I pull the pack out of my back pocket. Flipping it open, I offer him one and he takes it, asking, "Can I use your light?"

I suffocate my irritation with a grunt as I pull the lighter out of my back pocket. It seems a little off, though. Back when I was a smoker—*even when I ran out*—I usually had a lighter on me.

I should just give him the pack.

But I don't. I shove it back in my pocket and then refocus on my phone.

"Do you live in the building?" he asks.

Fucking hell. Why do I always get chatty moochers?

I'm distantly aware of how similar this all is to the night Otis caught me—the night I got into a brawl with the side of a building. My jaw clenches as I shake my head. I'm not in the mood to make small talk and with my control spiraling, the less interaction I have with people, the better.

He nods, puffing out a cloud of smoke before he adds, "That's good. I mean, it's a nice enough place but . . . kinda unsafe."

My eyes peer up. There's a veiled threat to the statement and I find myself asking, "What makes you say that?"

He shrugs, noting, "There's no gate, no security access," gesturing toward the door. He takes another drag and on his exhale, he says,

"Plus, my girl's door has been broken for months and the manager's never fixed it."

My muscles tighten, coughing as I push the smoke out of my lungs and gasp for a breath I can't seem to find. I finally swallow and my eyes harden as I stare back at him.

His girl.

Broken door . . .

The words spike my heart down to my feet as he brushes his shaggy blond hair from his forehead, shoving a hat over his head while he hauls another drag.

My eyes fixate on the hat. I recognize it.

A fist holding a carrot . . .

That day. That day at Villains—after the meeting. He's the guy who asked me how to get to the L . . .

His grayish-blue eyes meet mine for a second as his lips tilt in a smug grin before he says, "Thanks," lifting the cigarette before he starts off down the block.

What the fuck?

My eyes follow him, watching him get farther away as my knees start to shake. I lift the cigarette to my lips, but it's burnt down to the filter. Dropping it to the ground, I stomp it under my boot, grinding it into the sidewalk until it's completely dusted.

My eyes glance back up at the building I've come to know well, but the promising comfort it held five minutes ago is no longer there. Instead my fists are tightening at my sides. I have the urge to bum rush up there and snap her broken door off its hinges—crash it into the wall until it breaks and splinters, leaving nothing but rubble behind.

Fuck.

How am I back in this place?

Maybe I've been fighting fate this whole time. Not everyone ends up happy in this world. And I've never *been* "lucky" so maybe everything I've done this year was a pathetic attempt at tricking myself that I could rise from the ashes.

But I am *the ashes.*

I pull out my cigarettes and light another one. Another moment passes before my feet carry me away from the building. The farther and farther I get, the more I can feel the heat in my chest.

Time to burn.

When you've hit rock bottom more than once in your life, there's a numbness to it. Like most shitty things in life, the anticipation of hitting the floor is actually worse than once your cheek is on it, staring off into the oblivion.

Or maybe it's the second whiskey I'm throwing back. Either way, I feel less like I'm about to burst into flames and more like I've accepted my fate as a cactus and grown used to the desert sun.

I snort a humorless laugh as I sit on the bar stool. I'm fucking *drinking* right now but I can't even bring myself to care. All that matters at the moment is that I don't feel like I'm about to die.

Taking another sip, the whiskey burns down my throat, much like the cigarette, but when it sinks to my stomach and the heat spreads, my mind feels sedated enough to wander to what led me here in the first place.

Marnie is taking Ava away.

Ava's bright blue eyes pass before me and I shut mine tight, gulping another sip as my knee starts to bounce below the bar. When I open my eyes, there's only a small bit left in my glass so I knock it back just as I hear, "Helen?" behind me.

Fuck.

My chin lifts toward the ceiling before my eyes close with a deep inhale. I don't need to turn around to know it's Reggie. Obviously, I recognize his voice but he's also the only person in the world that calls me Helen.

A fact that annoys me even more now, as he slips onto the stool next to me. I lower my chin and my eyes slowly pull over to him, but he's missing his signature, devious smirk. It's replaced with something sincere—*worried, even*—and for some reason it irritates me more.

I look away, mindlessly tracing the top of my glass before he says, "What are you doing?" His voice low and laced with concern, chiseling my self-loathing into something real and tangible.

God. I just want to be alone. Why do people never just leave me the fuck alone?

"You're a smart guy, Reg. What does it look like I'm doing?" I shift in my seat, still feeling his eyes on me. Another moment passes before I lift my hand at the bartender, letting him know I'd like another.

"Fine," Reggie chirps. "We haven't had a drink together since our college days. Let's do it."

Goddammit. I can already feel the reverse psychology; the wily ways of his up-to-no-good antics. My jaw ticks as the bartender brings my drink over. I immediately take a sip, and it momentarily eases some of my tension the moment it hits my stomach.

Reggie orders a dry martini. *Of course he does.* I mean, the place has peanut shells on the floor, but whatever.

"Bougie bitch," I mutter under my breath.

He huffs. *"There's* the asshole I used to know."

A flutter of remorse passes through me. His presence alone is making it harder to escape, but I know I'm being a dick.

"Sorry . . . I'm . . ." I trail off, shaking my head. I go to take another sip but then put the glass back on the bar and close my eyes for a second. I hear the sound of the bartender putting Reggie's drink down next to me and my eyes reopen, peeking back at him as he takes a sip.

His shoulders do a small shimmy before he places the glass back down. "*Oof!* Say what you will about the ambiance, but I'd marry that man for his martinis." He glances at the bartender again, giving him a coy smile. "Makes me wonder what else he's good at," he says through his smirk and I actually *do* snort a laugh.

"So you're on the prowl tonight?" I mumble, but squint when I finally notice his sweatpants and a sheen of sweat lining his hairline.

"Extra night at boxing. Working on my summer bod," he says, taking another sip. "But I'm more interested in why *you're* here. This isn't even your neighborhood. And aren't you supposed to have Ava tonight?"

A sigh mixed with a groan rattles low in my throat. I push my fingers into the divots of the rocks glass, twisting it mindlessly on the bar. He's clearly not going anywhere and at least the longer I keep him here with me, the longer it takes for him to go run off to Evelyn and tell her.

I take another sip, but the bite from the liquor feels bitter, making my teeth clench as my lips pull tightly back. Another beat passes before I mumble, "Marnie's moving to Michigan."

My eyes hesitantly meet his, the charcoal color of his irises darken and he pauses mid sip, putting the glass back on the bar. "Shit . . ."

I nod, draining my glass, but there's no relief this time. It's one of the *many* fucked up things about alcohol. You keep drinking, hoping to find that initial buzz, but it's fleeting. It's as useless as trying to recreate sunrise at ten in the morning.

But it doesn't stop me from trying.

Reggie scoffs. "That is fucked, Dean. There's gotta be something you can do. I can't believe she would do that."

I shrug. "She wants to live with her boyfriend. He can't move *here*, so . . ." I pause, letting the thought sink in again before I add, "She said she'll go for full custody if I try to fight her on it."

Reggie's eyebrows hitch. "Jesus . . ." He shakes his head as the ghost of an impressed expression lifts his face. "Marnie's grown some balls since you guys split, huh?"

Under any other circumstance, I might laugh. But I'm too lost in it all right now. The alcohol has slowed me down, but it isn't working the way it used to. It isn't shutting everything off. Everything feels *very* real but somehow slower, like it's giving me time to *watch* everything slip through my fingers.

Reggie clears his throat. "Well, look. I know you're *Mr. Chicago* and everything but . . . couldn't you just move? To Michigan?"

I groan, reaching for another sip of my drink when I remember that it's empty. My hand tightens around the glass before releasing it again, scratching my jaw. "What the fuck am I gonna do in Michigan, Reg? My job is here . . . my parents, Otis . . ."

Amelia.

I don't say it out loud, though. It seems stupid to even entertain that thought right now.

Fuck. I'm buzzed.

"You could be her dad," Reggie offers simply. "And it's Michigan, not the moon. You can still visit your folks and Otis . . ." he trails off before he adds, "I bet Amelia would go with you if you asked her."

My eyebrows pinch and annoyance fills all the pieces of me that aren't already filled to capacity with distress. I only told Otis about how Amelia and I were *casually* seeing each other—but I should have known he would tell Evelyn, who of course told Reggie.

And so goes this decade-long game of whisper down the fucking alley.

But it's a ridiculous suggestion. We've barely crossed into a relationship and it might not even matter since she could be fucking someone else.

The thought doesn't quite sit right, but if I know anything—it's that my instincts are bullshit. I feel Reggie's awaiting expression in my peripherals and an involuntary scoff pushes from my throat.

"I'm not talking about this with you," I mumble. My hand barely raises off the bar to order another drink when Reggie roughly shoves it back down.

"Enough, Dean," he barks, and it surprises me so much that my neck juts back and my eyebrows slope. He grunts, rubbing his temples before he locks his eyes on mine. "*This* wasn't cute when we were kids, and it sure as hell isn't now."

His use of my real name feels like I just got *"middle named"* by my mom. Not to mention, in all the years I've known Reggie, I've never seen him look so . . . serious—*angry*—and I'm stunned silent.

He shakes his head, chomping his lip. "I hated you for what you did to Evie—*like, truly*—if you had told me eight years ago that we'd be sitting on a barstool together, I'd have thought you lost your goddamn mind." An annoyed groan rumbles in his throat as he massages his temples. "When are you gonna get it through that head of perfect hair that the only person who can actually fix anything in your life is *you*, dumbass?"

I'm still at a loss for words and the alcohol isn't helping, but I seem to have uncapped something in him because he continues, "Part of the reason I hated you so much was because I *knew* you were better than the things you were doing, but the things you did—you never *tried* to fix them. You took the easy way out and you're doing it *again*."

"Easy?!" I growl. "You think it was *easy?!*"

The word is triggering. I know because Evelyn said something similar to me last year at Christmas and I lost my shit that night too. She and Otis had just gotten together and when we confronted it, she had thrown back how *easy* it must have been for me to move to Denver and leave everything that happened behind.

But I didn't leave it all behind.

I brought it fucking with me.

It's still *with me.*

My mouth opens to shut Reggie down but he stops me. "No. Anything you're about to say to me right now is an excuse that I don't want to hear. No one denies that life has thrown you some curve balls, but welcome to being fucking human. Everyone's got *something.*"

I suck my lips into my mouth. I have to actively work to shove my defenses down and suffocate a rebuttal, but I swallow hard and stay silent.

"Why are you drinking tonight?" he asks, blankly.

I clear my throat, shifting in my seat. "I told you—"

"No," he interrupts. "Marnie's move is a symptom. What's the cause?"

I grunt again, irritated but trying not to be. Reggie's openly admitted to hating me in more recent years, but he's here—throwing me a lifeline. Still, I can't even begin to conjure up a response.

A long silence passes and I scratch the back of my jaw again, like maybe the friction will spark a good excuse.

But it doesn't.

I shrug. "I don't know, man. I was losing control. Everything just got to be . . . too much." My eyes peer up to him, expecting to see some sort of eye roll or frustrated glare, but it's absent. His expression seems . . . thoughtful, contemplative—honestly, it's freaking me out a bit.

"So you tried to regain control with an uncontrollable substance?" he says, some of his sass returning. He sighs, glancing down at his martini glass before he adds, "Life can be a lot of things, Helen, but one thing it will never be is easy. So stop expecting easy and just *accept* that it's hard. You're not *losing* control. You're willingly *giving* your power to your pain."

Well, I'll be damned.

Who knew that behind all of Reggie's clever quips and bizarre nicknames was the wisdom of fucking Gandalf?

It's a simple concept, really—one I may have even realized in some capacity a time or two. But for some reason, right now, with a guy I've known for a third of my life but never actually gotten to know— it resonates.

"Everyone's got something."

The notion churns in my mind, solidifying loose ideas.

Part of what makes despair so hopeless is the way our brain is able to convince us that we're the only ones who have ever felt this way— or the cruel way it's able to convince us that it will be this way forever.

It makes an "easy" button—like alcohol—all that much more appealing to people with addiction. People who seek to numb. People who struggle to admit that they're struggling.

People like me.

This year has been spent *resisting* my struggles.

I went to sober meetings, but I didn't participate.

I coparented, but I didn't communicate.

I took a shot with Amelia, but I bolted before I got any concrete answers. I told Otis we were casually seeing each other when it's become the furthest thing from casual.

I still kept my darkest haunting from her even after she'd told me hers.

I'm not recovering . . . I'm *rejecting.*

Running. Replacing. Resisting.

I started the habit back in college when life got too overwhelming. And when I ran out of stamina, I started to fill it with *this.*

Staring at my empty rocks glass, I feel a heaviness set in my limbs, like I'm filling with lead.

Dead weight.

This is all alcohol ever does. It's a placeholder for pain. It's an inability to cope. It's attempting to fill hollowness with something that ultimately empties me out completely.

Even with sobriety, I kept waiting for some divine moment of intervention. Something that clicked into place, but it's clear to me now that it was never going to happen. Because whether or not I realized it, I was still waiting for *something else* to shift the wind.

"It's always in our hands, Dean."

Just as Evelyn's words weave between my thoughts, I blink back to the bar.

I see Reggie take the final sip of his drink, tossing some cash on the counter. He wordlessly bends to pick up his gym bag when I finally speak up. "Hey, Reg?" He looks back up at me, less angry but still uneasy, and I swallow hard. "There's a meeting about ten minutes away." I clear my throat, my voice scratching as I ask, "You wanna go?"

He hauls his bag over his shoulder, pushing out a heavy exhale before a softer version of his signature smirk tilts on his cheek. "There better be some hotties at this thing, Helen."

chapter thirty-three
amelia

I've never been more convinced that sleep is where sanity is nurtured. Without it, we become crazed beings who think our hunches are pure, unadulterated fact.

Or maybe that's just me.

I kept my hearing aids on all night. It's wildly uncomfortable trying to sleep with them on, but I was too paranoid that Tim might come back. And when I couldn't sleep, I spiraled down the endless black hole of the internet, trying to figure out any possible way that he could have learned my real name, but I came back up completely empty. And then the crazy train in my mind convinced me that the reason I hadn't heard from Dean was because Tim was terrorizing him too, somehow.

And after he ignored my call this morning, I'm marching full speed ahead down his street.

See? Crazed.

I just can't shake the feeling that something is wrong. *Very wrong.*

Luckily, someone is leaving Dean's building as I reach the entrance and I trot up the steps. "Hey, can you hold the door?"

The woman holds it open for me and I mutter a thank you as I start the short walk up to his apartment. When I reach the front door, I'm slightly winded from the adrenaline, and embarrassingly, from the small incline I just climbed. But it's enough of a pause to give me a sobering moment.

How much crazy can this man take?

He's already seen so much of it. I've unloaded everything onto him and now I'm showing up here unannounced, uninvited, un-caffeinated . . . un-sane.

Go home, Amelia.

Pushing out a heavy exhale, I slowly turn to leave, just as I hear the door pulling open. An honest-to-God thought I have involves hurling myself over the banister and hanging from it until a good samaritan offers to help me down—that seems less embarrassing at the moment—but it's too late.

The door opens and I'm met with . . . Otis.

He startles a bit, obviously not expecting to see a crazy woman lurking outside his brother's apartment, but his eyes suddenly become nervous.

Fucking perfect.

Evelyn appears behind him suddenly and my stomach sinks even further. *God.* It would have been bad enough to have Dean catch me out here, but at least he's kind of used to me. I try to pull my mouth into a small smile but I think it mostly looks like a deer in headlights *trying* to smile.

"Hey," I sign, awkwardly.

"Amelia, hey," Evelyn signs, wiggling out from behind Otis. She sucks her lips into her mouth before giving a quick glance back inside.

The longer we stand here, the more I want to become part of the fucking floor. It's awkward, but there's also this heavy air, thickening the tension, and my heart starts to race.

"Is everything okay?" I sign.

Evelyn does the smallest peek over to Otis, whose mouth is slightly slack. A moment later, two other people are trying to scoot past them. They're older—a man and a woman. The woman has long, gray-streaked hair, pulled back by a colorful bandana and the man is tall with salt and pepper hair and dark brown eyes.

"Oh, hi," the woman says. "Are you a friend of Dean's?"

I'm too caught up in confusion to answer right away. My eyes finally blink, but before I can respond, Otis signs, "Mom, this is Amelia."

Mom?! Oh, fuck me.

I'm such an idiot. He couldn't see me last night because he was busy—probably with his daughter. And he didn't answer me this morning because his whole goddamn family was over.

Stupid, stupid, stupid!

"Oh, honey! It's so nice to meet you! I've heard so much about you. And holy crap, he wasn't kidding," she elbows the man—*his fucking dad*—and signs, "What a hottie!"

His dad shakes his head, rubbing the pads of his fingers over his forehead while Otis groans, "Jesus Christ, Mom!" his cheeks flushing, before he looks back over at me. "Sorry. She has no filter."

My brain cannot catch up to what's happening, but the smallest bit of warmth finds its way to my chest knowing Dean told his parents about me. I'll hold the memory close when he inevitably kicks me to the curb after showing up here like a lunatic.

"We have to get going," she signs. "But we'll be back soon. And we'd love to see you. Dean says you're quite the cook."

I blink, shaking my head.

Words, Amelia. Use your words.

"It was nice to meet you too, Mrs. Roberts," I sign, awkwardly. "Mr. Roberts."

You fucking goob. You're terrible at this.

His dad laughs and it sounds like Dean's, low and hoarse, as he signs, "I'm Paul, and the wild one is Gloria."

She elbows him again and I nod through a small, uneven chuckle before I finally see Dean in the doorway. The family reunion has spilled out into the hallway with me, but my eyes meet his with apology, and it's then that I see everything is *not fine.*

Shadowy, dark circles underline his brown eyes. They look destroyed and it seems to seep into everyone else's expressions too. They eventually say some quick goodbyes, lingering for a few seconds more before they make their way toward the stairs.

Once they're out of sight, I finally turn back to Dean, meeting his worn, coffee-colored eyes. But I stay put, keeping the couple of feet of distance between us. He doesn't exactly look happy to see me and I guess I can't blame him. He didn't invite me to this whole—*whatever this is*—for a reason, and I showed up anyway.

Because I'm an idiot.

Another few beats pass before I rock on my heels, signing, "So . . . your parents seem nice . . ." I give him a sheepish smile, but he looks so . . . *I don't even know* how to describe it. But I *feel* it. I feel the sadness in his heavy limbs, the despair in his tired eyes. I inch a little closer, signing, "Are you okay?"

He wipes his palm down his face, scrubbing it a couple times before he rubs the back of his neck and then signs, "What are you doing here, Amelia?"

My eyebrows pinch defensively, but I remind myself that he wasn't expecting to see me. That he has a life outside the little bubble we've created for ourselves.

But I don't have a good answer for him. *What* am *I doing here?*

I shrug lamely, as he continues to stand and stare at me. Another few seconds pass before he sighs, moving aside, silently inviting me into the apartment and I timidly shuffle past him.

My eyes curiously float around the living room before I turn back to him, signing, "Isn't Ava with you?"

He closes the door and then scratches the back of his head again, and it feels like it's grating beneath *my* skin, making the hairs on my arm stand on edge.

I walk closer, my hand moving hesitantly as I sign, "What's wrong?"

His chin dips, dropping a tousled, chestnut wave to his forehead before he peers back up to my eyes. He pulls in a deep inhale and finally shrugs. "I fucked up."

My eyebrows thread, not understanding. But it physically hurts to see him like this. I've never had to comfort someone before, but my instincts move me just a step closer. His demeanor is completely closed off right now, but I timidly reach for his cheek, holding it in my palm as my thumb brushes along the coarse bristles of his stubble.

This is bad.

Whatever is happening right now is *really* fucking bad; I can feel it like rolling thunder in my chest. I relax just a little bit when he leans his cheek into my palm, but my body stiffens again when the coffee smell I've come to expect is laced with something else. He smells like . . . stale smoke.

His dark eyes hold a weighted stare down at me. He shuts them and his eyebrows flinch as he shakes his head. When he opens his eyes again, they won't meet mine.

He pushes out a heavy exhale, signing, "I drank last night."

I swallow a gasp, feeling it sink to the deepest part of my stomach, dropping so intensely that it wobbles my weight. I steady myself before my eyes flutter back to him, but his shame is evident. He won't look at me.

Swallowing the lump in my throat, I croak, "Wh-What happened?"

It takes him a while. There's so much defeat and dejectment holding his limbs that his signing is slow, but he finally tells me that Marnie is going through with the move. That she's threatened a custody battle.

And my heart crumbles.

No.

My denial only lasts a second. It's all the time it *can* last because the devastation in Dean's expression solidifies the reality. That the decision is final.

Final and fucked.

I don't know Marnie very well, but I know she's a good mom. Dean has said as much himself. But I can't believe she's willingly putting this big, gaping hole in her daughter's life. Because whether or not Marnie realizes it, Ava *will* feel his absence. Maybe not right away, but she will. I'm sure of it.

He's her dad.

And a fucking great one, at that. He doesn't deserve this.

And he relapsed because of it . . .

My eyes watch his, and I get lost in the heaviness of his stare, feeling it in my own chest.

It's the craziest thing. I've had an opinion about drinking since before I can even remember. I thought it was disgusting—*weakness materialized*—because that's what I saw with my mother. But it looks completely different on him. I know how much his sobriety meant to him—*what* it meant to him. Staying sober meant he was moving forward. That he was becoming a better man for his daughter.

It's the first time I've been able to see the actual sickness in addiction and it's rattling.

I clear my throat, finally signing, "I wish you would have called me. Or . . . you should have just come over."

Dean releases an audible sigh as he scratches the back of his jaw, shaking his head, and the weight in my chest sinks.

I know I'm not exactly the model of stability but . . . I thought we were getting closer. I just wish he felt like he could lean on me. The way I've come to lean on him.

After another few seconds, he finally mumbles, "I did come over."

My eyebrows pinch.

"I ran into your friend downstairs," he signs.

I try to blink. *But I can't.*

I try to move. *But I'm stuck.*

My heart plummets.

Friend?

Dean starts to explain his short encounter with Tim, but the blood rushing through my ears starts to feel like a violent river pulling me under. My heart starts to race and I feel my stomach twist.

He *did* come to me.

Stupid.

He left because he thought I was with someone else.

Stupid.

And then he fucking drank.

Girl.

I choke on a sob as my eyes flood and spill down my cheeks. I couldn't stop the tears if I tried, and for once, I let them fall.

God. I really *do* have the ability to fuck up anything, even when I'm not trying.

"No, no, no," I cry, cradling my face into my hands.

My muscles tighten and my jaw clenches, but the emotion *pours* out of me. I suddenly feel Dean's hand moving between my shoulder blades, and it snaps my focus up to him.

"It's—That's . . ." I stutter and then take a deep breath, trying to compose myself enough to say a full sentence, but my throat feels swollen. My fists clench and I press my thumbnails into the crevice of my index fingers, trying to allow the pinching sensation to reel me in.

Stupid, stupid, stupid.

My hands tighten and my nails dig deeper. But Dean suddenly takes my hands, prying my fists open before he places his own hands in mine, and my heavy, soaken eyes drag up to his.

"Use mine, instead," he says quietly, with a rasp.

The offer sends a warm wave through me, and it strangely suffocates any embarrassment I have for getting caught doing this.

He already knew, I remind myself.

But I don't want to hurt *him.*

You've done enough damage already.

I shake my head, pushing out a shaky exhale before I frantically start to sign through everything.

And I mean everything.

I tell him about Tim forcing himself inside my apartment. I tell him about how he followed Luke and me to the park. I even tell him about the horrific cat and mouse game from a couple of months ago.

An icy current runs down my spine at the memory. "I thought my panic attack had somehow warped the game, but now . . ." I trail off, shaking my head. "I hadn't seen him since then, Dean. I swear." I sign desperately, keeping my chin down as the shame surrounds me.

Silence and stillness hang between us, thick and heavy, but when I finally brave a look at him, the expression on his face crackles through me. His fists tighten at his side, his jaw ticks and it kickstarts my heart.

Rage.

The feeling is so potent that it itches just beneath my skin and I swallow hard. Trepidation mingles with the stale oxygen filling the room and a cold sweat forms at the base of my neck.

I avert my eyes to the floor, and pull my legs closer to my chest as an urge to make myself as small as possible tightens and curls in my stomach. I jerk when his fist slams on the coffee table and a blinding flash tailspins my mind. It's hard and punishing, like the sound of my bedroom door swinging open and hitting the wall.

The anger becomes a living, breathing entity and it's glowering at me.

You did this.

It's your fault.

Stupid, stupid, girl.

The abrupt movement beside me makes me flinch, cowering back as my hands instinctively move in front of my face, whimpering pathetically. My eyes clamp shut while my body pushes deeper into the couch. I sink into the darkness of my closed eyelids and prepare for blunt impact.

But it never comes.

I'm breathing almost entirely through my nose as I hear, "Amelia," in a pained, hushed tone. The agonized timbre of Dean's voice cuts through me and immediately brings me back.

Back to his living room.

Back to the mortifying reality.

Oh my God.

Just when I thought I couldn't humiliate myself anymore—and now *this?!*

I'm so *fucked.*

His strong hands are suddenly rubbing my legs. "Amelia, baby, please look at me," he says, his voice breaking.

My eyes slowly creep open from the desperate plea, finding him kneeling on the floor in front of me. There's a devastated gleam in his eyes and my heart sinks deeper.

He's the one going through something. *I* should be trying to comfort *him . . .*

"I-I'm sorry," I finally say, breathlessly. Shaking my head as I try to regain some control but I think any sort of dignity went out the window long ago.

Dean shakes his head and pulls my hand to his chest. He simply holds my fist in his, tightly over his heart for a few, long beats, keeping his head down while he takes a series of practiced breaths. After another moment he says, "You have nothing to apologize for. *I'm* sorry, baby. I shouldn't have—I didn't . . ." He shakes his head again. "I just . . . reacted. I can't believe that son of a bitch—" He cuts himself off, grinding his teeth as his jaw pulses before he takes another deep breath.

I can see that he's trying to muscle through his anger. I know it's something he struggles with—that much was clear in what he told me at the park—but *my* reaction was involuntary, too.

My eyes peek back at him and a pained sigh pushes past his lips. "I would *never* hurt you, Amelia. I need you to know that. Not ever," he rasps, his voice cracking. It almost seems like he's fighting back tears. "Please don't be afraid of me."

His voice wavers and the urge to hold him overcomes me. I pull him into me so hard and so quickly, latching my arms around the back of his neck.

"I'm not," I whisper.

I'm not.

I know I'm safe with him, despite my body's response.

His rage *is* my fear, both born in darkness we can't control sometimes. *We match. Kind of.*

The longer we stay pressed together, the more aware I become of his racing heart against mine and it feels . . . *powerful.* Like they're pounding together to shatter the brokenness surrounding us.

I can't make sense of it, but maybe that's because I've never felt this way before.

He's everything I've spent my entire life avoiding wrapped up in one man. But what I'm realizing at this very moment is that all it takes is the smallest shift in the light to turn something triggering into . . . *a glimmer.*

Just the smallest change in angle or position to shift darkness into light—to find peace in something that once terrified you. To find beauty in something broken. I feel it in his arms right now and a current runs through me. It charges me—illuminating the dark, murky clouds of my mind.

My lightning.

He gently starts to pull back from me, and my gaze holds his warm, brown eyes.

"I love you," breathes through my lips involuntarily and his eyes widen.

Mine do too as he stays quiet, but his gaze flares, sending a buzz through my veins. My heart feels like it's thrashing against my rib cage the longer he doesn't say anything, but I can't seem to make any other words.

In an instant, his mouth crashes against mine. His soft, full lips move possessively before his tongue parts my lips and caresses the inside of my mouth, like he's trying to consume the words.

His movement slows and he pulls away from me, still holding each side of my face while keeping his gaze fixed with mine. He still hasn't said anything, so my heart is pounding fast and heavy in my chest, but his eyes have this deep, tender longing as he finally removes his hands.

My eyebrows thread as he lays his palm flat against his chest. His fingers tentatively curl into his palm, making an A handshape as he holds it to his heart before he taps his middle finger over the same spot twice.

"My Amelia."

My breath catches in my throat and tears threaten the corner of my eyes again, but I swallow hard, keeping my eyes on him.

A tired version of his dreamy smile returns as he signs, "I love you, too."

chapter thirty-four

dean

My stomach feels like it's levitating into my chest. It's a similar sensation to the first plunge on a rollercoaster. But instead of the relief of plummeting down the hill, I'm just over the top, staring down at everything, waiting to slide back or dive down headfirst.

Both thoughts are terrifying, honestly.

I'm at the community center, and the meeting wrapped up a few minutes ago.

I think it did, anyway—I'm not really sure how long I've been sitting here.

Amelia went with me to pick up Ava earlier and then offered to watch her so I could come here tonight. And while I'm eager to get home to the two of them, this is also the first moment I've had alone with everything that's happened in the last twenty-four hours and it feels slightly paralyzing.

"Hi," I suddenly hear a woman's voice and look toward her. She was the moderator at the meeting tonight. "I'm sorry, but I have to lock up."

I glance around the space and see it's completely empty.

Guess it's been more than a few minutes.

"Oh, yeah. Sorry," I mutter, standing.

"Do you have somewhere to go?"

Great. I guess I look as run down as I feel.

"Y-Yeah, sorry," I say again, quickly making my way out of the building and back to my truck.

After climbing in, I sit in the driver's seat for a second, still trying to settle everything stirring through me.

Relapse. Family ambush . . . Amelia.

"I love you."

The memory of her words filter through the whirlwind like a whistle in the breeze and it momentarily settles me, but then halts with a stark awareness.

I almost didn't say it back.

And not because I don't feel it. *I do.*

Honestly, I think I've known I love her for a while now, but it's just . . . *so fucking hard* to trust myself.

I've made so many mistakes and I . . . *I can't fuck this up.*

I cringe as a flash of Amelia wincing and hiding from me earlier swipes through my mind. The memory feels like it literally smacks me over the head and my hands tighten around the steering wheel.

She was terrified. *Of me.*

I breathe through the overwhelm, allowing my mind to drift through the rest of the memory. The horrified, regretful look that followed her fear was almost as gut-wrenching as the reaction itself.

Because even if for a brief moment she was afraid of *me,* I know it was an impulse.

She has *had to protect herself before.*

From her own fucking mother.

And *now,* that dickless shithead . . .

I grind my teeth together, the corners of my vision blurring as I think about him holding her down, her struggling. Following her. Barging into her apartment . . .

I clamp my eyes shut and press my fingers against my eyelids, trying to fight the blinding rage threatening to spill out if I keep letting my mind wander.

Because I *can't* react the way I have in the past. No matter how angry I get, no matter how strong the urge is, I *can't* let my anger run rampant.

Not with her.

She deserves someone that doesn't shy away from everything she's been through. And I *want* to be that person. I *want* to be someone who sees it all and holds it for her—someone she feels unwaveringly safe with.

Someone willing to bend so she doesn't have to break.

I push out another heavy exhale, tapping my thumbs on the steering wheel as I try to let the overwhelm settle into resolve.

In a couple short months, she's reawakened something in me I thought was dead.

She's worth trying to make this change.

She's worth everything.

I take another steadying breath, mindlessly staring out the windshield as a series of instances that have brought me to this street pass through me like a time-lapse.

The first time I went to a meeting, walking Evelyn to the L.

Getting my now null-and-void year chip with Otis.

Last night with Reggie.

The night I saw Amelia and convinced her to come back inside.

I've been on this street in triumph and turmoil and everything in between—and for some reason, it's stilling me right now. Like an old, reliable friend.

I snort. *Friends with a fucking street.*

My palm swipes down my face as my body sags into the seat, feeling the exhaustion weigh down my limbs as my eyelids suddenly become heavy. I glance along the street one more time, soaking in just a bit more of its comfort before I start the car, letting the rumble of the engine shake my remaining unease.

Whenever I start to get overwhelmed, I just have to make it back here.

And I can do that.

I slug my way up the steps to my apartment, feeling absolutely wiped.

I've never left Ava with anyone before, but Amelia is a natural. I assumed she'd be good with kids since she was a preschool teacher, but she's amazing with Ava. I love the way she talks to her. It's almost like she's having a conversation with a peer instead of a babbling baby.

I push through the door, and then close it behind me, locking it. As I turn to put my keys on the table by the door, I see Amelia asleep on the couch . . . with Ava conked out on her chest.

My heart is about to fucking burst.

As quietly as I can, I round the couch to get a better look. Amelia's head is propped slightly up on a pillow—against the arm of the couch. Her arm hugs around Ava's back while her cheek rests against the top of her hair. Ava lies flat along her torso, her mouth slightly parted with soft, little snores and my smile widens.

I pull out my phone and snap a quick picture. I stare at it a few moments more before a sharp inhale pulls my focus. Peeking back over at them, I see Amelia's eyes flutter open, rubbing Ava's back as she slowly wakes up.

Her eyes float up to me, a sleepy smile inching up her cheek as she signs, "Watching us sleep?"

"Taking pictures too," I sign, giving my phone a small wiggle.

She breathes a quiet laugh. "Creepy." She shifts a bit, trying to maneuver herself up, but then signs, "I didn't think this through."

I snort a laugh. Twenty pounds of dead weight is lying on her chest. I gently lift Ava off of her, and she doesn't even stir as I carry her to her room and put her in her crib. When I walk back out, I keep the door cracked and then turn on the baby monitor app on my phone.

Amelia's gathering some toys and a few books as I make my way back to the living room.

Like she belongs here.

A soft smile lifts. "She's *out,*" I sign. "Did you guys have fun?"

Amelia nods. "Oh yeah. We had a party. Milk shots, *The Very Hungry Caterpillar.* It was the social event of the season."

I sigh out another laugh before pulling her into me. My eyes lose themselves in hers for a second, completely and utterly entranced.

"She really is great," she signs.

All I can do is smile back down at her, feeling all my unease from earlier fall away the longer I hold her.

Life is so goddamn bizarre. I didn't even know her a couple of months ago, and now it feels like she was the missing piece to myself.

My Amelia.

I sign it to her again before pressing my lips to hers and she balls the fabric of my shirt in her hands, pulling me closer. We kiss for a few, long seconds before finally pulling apart.

"You're staying here tonight," I sign.

Her mouth tilts. "So bossy."

My thumb traces her bottom lip before I sign, "I happen to know that you like it when I'm bossy."

She chuckles through a nod. "Okay. But no funny business tonight, Roberts. Our collective bullshit is aging me terribly and I need my beauty sleep." She emphasizes it with an emphatic yawn.

Another small laugh escapes and I kiss her lightly, letting our lips solidify my ease.

"Our collective bullshit."

Maybe *that's* the difference with her. In all of my other relationships, I felt like the thing that muted their vibrance. But her love feels like it's the same shade as mine. Like we're enhancing our colors together.

She pulls away from me, giving me a playful warning look. "What'd I say? No funny business, fiend."

I smile. *"You're* the fiend, baby. I'm just here to serve."

She smirks. "Well, in that case . . ." She hoists herself around my waist and I wobble from the unexpected weight, before she signs. "Take me to bed and tuck me in. And if you're good, you can feel me up as we fall asleep."

Done.

The weight on the bed jerks and my eyes peel open.

I see some tapestries lining the wall, noticing the one Evelyn insisted on hanging in here. The one with the dream catcher on it.

My eyes squint before I feel the bed pulse again along with a small whimper.

Fuck.

She's having another nightmare.

She's been having them nearly every night since we came back from winter break and it's slowly crushing me to hear it night after night.

I've never actually thought about killing someone, but I want to find the son of the bitch that did this to her and tear every limb from his body. I want to chop his dick off and make him watch as I feed it through a fucking meat grinder.

It seems like a fair fate for a rapist.

A small grunt rumbles in my throat. Even if I had the ability to do such insane things, I have no idea who the guy is. All Evelyn could manage to tell me is that they knew each other.

Her cries become louder, her movement more violent.

Shit.

"Evie," I say quietly, trying to coax her into consciousness.

She starts to thrash, her whimpers turning into full-blown sobs.

I sit up, suddenly noticing some blood trickling from the corner of her mouth and my heart starts to race. I grab her shoulder and start to shake it.

"Evie, baby, wake up."

Her eyes stay shut as she roars, "Get off me!" panting wildly and pushing away from me. She scrambles to her feet and then stumbles out of the bed, but quickly falls to the floor.

I follow right behind her, putting my hand on her shoulder. "Baby . . ."

"Fuck you! Don't touch me!" she sobs, still unable to catch her breath and I pull my hand away quickly.

We got some sleeping pills, hoping they would help, but obviously they did fucking nothing to stop the nightmares. I think they were just making it harder for her to wake up.

Another brilliant idea from me . . .

I carefully walk around her crumpled body and sit on the floor just in front of her before her hazel eyes—bloodshot and broken—meet mine with a delirious glare full of pure hatred. "How could you?" she cries before her body folds over on the floor.

My heart stops.

She thinks . . . She thinks I'm him?

"What?" I hiss. The notion hits me like a sledgehammer. My heart fizzles out in my chest, leaving behind a cold, dark void.

Her body heaves while her fingers clutch and scrape against the floor like she's in physical pain and the sound slices through me.

She's so . . . broken. But she's not beyond repair. I know it. But I can't fucking fix it.

I want to help her so badly . . .

"I have a boyfriend," she mumbles, her forehead pressed to the floor. "Y-You ruined me."

Rip my fucking heart out.

I shake my head, "No, that's—" I stop myself as an idea suddenly wades to the surface.

She thinks I'm him.

The idea moves like tar through my veins, feeling the irreparable damage as it flows to my center and coats the walls of my chest.

But . . . maybe it will help her . . .

It only takes one more look at her, balled and devastated on the floor in front of me, and I swallow the bile rising up my throat.

"I-I'm sorry," I croak out, my voice breaking. "I'm so sorry I hurt you."

Jesus fucking Christ. I can barely breathe.

But her cries soften and the idea that his remorse may be giving her some relief pushes me to continue. "You didn't do anything wrong, and you're not ruined. Your boyfriend—" My voice cracks as I slice in half. "Your boyfriend still loves you."

I'm here. I'm right here. And I do love her. The internal reminder does nothing, though. Because right now, to her, I'm not her boyfriend. I'm her rapist. And it feels like a wrecking ball is tearing me down from the inside out.

Her cries shift to quiet whimpers. My chest tightens as she slowly pushes herself up off the floor. Her tear-filled eyes blink back at me rapidly, filling with recognition as a painful squeak escapes her. "Dean?"

I fade to black.

My chest caves in. My lungs constrict.

I drop my chin and . . . I fucking cry.

I sob, long and hard. The helplessness, the hopelessness—the minute I spent feeling like him—it swallows me in its undertow, sinking me to the bottom of the ocean floor until the air disappears completely. The wood pattern beneath me is just a blur behind my tears as my body convulses with guttural sobs.

"Dean?"

The voice jolts me.

It's familiar, but it's not Evelyn.

It's Amelia.

My chin lifts and I see her sitting in front of me.

I'm no longer in the apartment I shared with Evelyn, but in Amelia's bedroom.

Her hand reaches out and holds my cheek, brushing her thumb along my jaw.

"Why are you on the floor, baby?"

My eyes squint, unable to make sense of what's happening. But movement in the dark corner of the room catches my eye. It happens slowly, but still too quick for me to react fast enough.

A man emerges from the darkness. His eyes are menacing—chilling—and I try to move but I can't. The man almost seems like a shadow. The only thing I can make out are his stormy eyes as he grabs Amelia and pulls her away from me and then throws her on the bed.

No!

My body writhes, trying to move, but it feels like there are weights attached to every limb.

Why can't I move?!

"Dean!" she screams, and it echoes inside my skull.

The man grabs her by the throat, inching down toward her, growling, "He can't help you."

I jerk, mustering up any strength I can—I need to move but I can't.

Please, God, no. No, no, no, no!

chapter thirty-five

amelia

My eyes ping open, immediately panicking when I feel rustling movement beside me. I sit up and twist to see Dean writhing on the bed and my eyes squint. It's dark in here, but I can see his eyebrows are scrunched, the chords of his neck straining, and my hand instinctively moves to his cheek.

"Dean," I say quietly. Or at least I think I do. I don't have my hearing aids in so it's hard to be sure. When he doesn't wake up, I move my hand to smooth the hard line between his eyebrows and I hover my face closer to his. "Baby, you're having a nightmare."

He growls just before his eyes bulge open and he shoots up, roughly grabbing me, and I yelp. My heart jumps and his grip tightens, but I suck in as much air as I can through my nose and push it back out.

"Dean," I say again, though I can feel my voice crack.

"I would never hurt you, Amelia."

I take another steadying inhale. He's a mere inch away from my face. Small pockets of moonlight from the window allow me to see some moisture in his eyes and I push through my unease, latching my hands on his jaw, cupping his face. "It's okay," I tell him. "It was just a dream."

He blinks and awareness lands back in his eyes. It's like watching the wheels of a plane hit the ground. He comes back from wherever he was in an instant and releases my arms immediately.

He says something but I have no idea what. It's too dark to read his lips, but he shakes his head, scrubbing his hands down his face. Just as he notices the moisture on his palms, his chin suddenly jerks up and he stands quickly.

"Where are you going?" I sign, standing too.

He stops for just a second, simply signing, "Ava," and then starts toward the door again.

My hand gently takes his arm. "I'll get her. Go get some water."

He hesitates, but then his shoulders drop with a small nod and I head out the door and across the small hallway to Ava's room, trying to let my movement steady my heart, which is still rapidly fluttering in my chest.

You're safe. You're safe.

I repeat it over and over again as I push through Ava's door, finding her standing and reaching her arms out from her crib.

Her big, blue eyes are glistening with tears and a heavy exhale pushes through my lips. "Hi, pretty girl," I coo, picking her up and sitting in the chair next to her crib. I rest her against my chest, letting the weight from her small body soothe me as I rub her back and lean my head into hers. "It's okay," I breathe.

We gently rock. My palm comforts her as her weight comforts me. It doesn't take long for me to feel the heaviness in her limbs and the steadiness of her breath. I hold her for a few extra seconds before carefully placing her back in her crib.

I lightly brush her brown curls from her forehead, lingering a bit as my eyes sweep along her room. It occurs to me now that I've never been in here.

My body sinks mindlessly back into the chair, taking some ease in the soft glow of her nightlight as I glance around the walls.

To say Dean's apartment is scarcely decorated is an understatement. But Ava's room has the warmth of hominess. It's hard to tell with the lights out, but the walls definitely aren't the same off-white color as the rest of the apartment. I think they might be a pale yellow and the small dresser looks hand painted with little white flowers and vines all over it.

My eyes catch on something else—something on the table by the chair I'm sitting in. It's a small sheet of paper and I hesitantly pick it up to find "Ava Roberts" written a dozen or so times in different ways. Some of the signatures have jagged, angular lines, some are mixed with thick bold fonts and calligraphy-looking lettering.

They're really good.

I didn't know Dean had an artistic side. A soft smile pinches my cheek as I set the paper back down. Movement pulls my eyes toward the door and I suddenly see Dean slowly pushing it open. The distress in his eyes swells an ache through my chest, and I immediately feel bad for not going back to him right after Ava fell back asleep.

"Is she okay?" he signs, peeking over the crib.

"She's fine. Went back to sleep immediately." His shoulders sag, still looking over the crib before his heavy eyes timidly peek back over to me and I sign, "This room is . . ." I pause, glancing around again. "I like it."

The last thing I see is his chest inflating before he's suddenly bending and wrapping his strong arms around me, holding me so tight that it's hard to breathe. Lowering to his knees in front of the chair, he stays locked around my torso before I feel his body shuddering.

Oh, Dean . . .

I have no idea what his nightmare was about. I can't even be sure if this reaction is from the dream alone. The past two days have thrown a lot at him and I can feel it all pouring out on my lap.

Whatever this sadness is—whatever this pain is—it's unstoppable. I thought *I* was a pro at masking my pain, but I feel like an amateur compared to him.

The thread between us tightens with his grip around my waist. *His* tears begin to well in *my* eyes and I rub my hand along his back before folding my body over his like some sort of broken yin-yang.

But I swallow back my emotion, doing my best to whisper, "I've got your back, Roberts. I've got you."

I knew that sleep would be impossible after witnessing Dean's breakdown, but I eliminated the possibility when I put my aids on—just in case he wanted to talk.

It's not until the early morning sun starts to poke through the window above his bed that he finally tells me about his dream.

Well, a memory mixed with a nightmare—two realms twisting to completely shatter the beautiful, broken man beside me.

My chest tightens as I push my fingers through his hair and softly kiss his temple, breathing him in.

"That's . . . so awful, baby," I murmur against his hair, his arms tightly wrapping around my waist. He's been touching me, holding me, all night—like he's afraid to stop, like I'm tethering him to reality.

I feel my own eyes sting with tears when I think about the haunted, devastated look in his eyes just a moment ago while he told me about the minute he spent assuming the role of Evelyn's assailant. Even if it was only for a minute, it's clear that that minute has found a way to weave its way through years of pain.

"You're a good man, Dean," I whisper, still holding him. "I don't think many people could do that."

An unconvinced huff brushes my neck as his arms tighten around me. "It didn't help," he says hoarsely. "I don't even think she remembers . . . I mean, I know she remembers that night—but she was still too out of it to remember what I said . . ."

I pull back slightly just so I can look at him. I can see the defeat, the unworthiness still sitting in his stare and I wish so badly that I could make him see. It doesn't matter if she doesn't remember. Truthfully, even if she did, I'm not sure the apology would have necessarily helped her cope with the assault.

"You still did it. You fell on the sword for her and . . . it's beautiful. So, so sad—but beautiful."

A long, drawn out sigh escapes his lips. I see my words try to wiggle their way through his doubt, but they fall when his eyes drift down as he shakes his head. "All it did was set a giant fucking mess in motion."

My eyebrows pinch, confused, before it registers that he's referring to his infidelity and the blunt force of realization hits me.

I've known since that night at the park that there was more to the story. I never could have imagined *this* was the missing piece, but it feels like a mosaic finally falling into place. And it's not that it excuses his actions, but I can certainly understand how things spun out of control.

"We can be bigger than our mistakes, Dean. You *are* bigger than this mistake."

He sits up and rubs his palm down his face, seemingly trying to scrub the emotion from his expression while releasing a heavy sigh.

I inch closer to him, resting my hand on his thigh. "Have you ever talked to anyone about this? Like a therapist?"

His eyebrows thread. "No. Why would I? Nothing happened to me."

Oh, my poor, sweet man. Welcome to trauma school.

I blanch. "Yes it did. You may not have been violated but you sure as hell went through something. Something you're still carrying."

As shocking as it is to hear he thinks he has no grounds for his distress, I can't say it doesn't make sense. It's a trauma response in and of itself. But until this moment, I myself haven't given much thought to the long term damage someone might experience as the partner to a sexual assault victim. Justifiably so, my thoughts have always fallen with whomever was assaulted. But it's clear that this whole thing has a stronger hold on him than even he may realize.

Still, I don't push it. I can see the exhaustion in his eyes, his sagging posture, and it reminds me of how tired I am too. We both got shitty sleep last night and now we've accidentally pulled an all-nighter.

Soft baby whines filter through Dean's phone and both of our bodies sag. Dean sighs again, picking the phone up to confirm what we both already know. He starts to move but I hold his leg.

"I'll get her," I tell him. "Try to get some sleep."

He shakes his head. "You're exhausted too."

I am. But I'm pretty sure I got more sleep than he did. Plus, I had a nap with Ava before he got home. And if this is the only thing I can do for him right now, I'm happy to do it.

A lazy smirk tilts on my cheek, signing, "I told you, Roberts, I got your back." I start to stand but he pulls me back to the bed, holding me tightly to him, again, burying his face in my hair and breathing deep.

He doesn't say anything and neither do I. He just holds me a moment longer, a silent thank you passing between his inhales, appreciation sifting through his fingers as he pulls them through my hair before he lets me go.

"Whew, girl! That uppercut!" Reggie signs.

I'm panting, bent at the waist as he extends his glove-wrapped hand toward me and I bump it.

I went hard on the boxing bag tonight. *Really hard.* I nearly blacked out, and now my vision is spotty. It kind of freaked me out. I found myself imagining Tim on the receiving end of every one of my hits and I don't really want to get comfortable with *that* visualization.

But it did feel good.

Despite the sweat dripping down my back, a chill runs down my spine as I plop on the bench while Evelyn and Reggie continue some spat they started before class. But I'm still lost in my thoughts as I start to unwrap my hands.

I've always tried to avoid anger. I have a genuine fear of the emotion itself. The unpredictability, the violence that can accompany it. But the truth is: I *am* angry. I'm fucking furious that Tim found a way to re-instill fear in my life when I've barely recovered from my last haunting.

After I went back to my apartment a few days ago, I only made it about an hour before the unease became too much. I packed up Beatrice and hauled us over to Dean's place.

And if I didn't know he loved me before, I definitely do now.

Let's just say that when a man smiles and kisses you after you show up with a yowling cat and a bag of litter, chances are he's someone special.

Evelyn's small, low wave snaps me back to now, as she signs, "Smoothie?"

I nod, pushing off the bench and dragging my heavy limbs toward my cubby to grab my phone, a slow smile pulling at my lips from my new lock screen.

It's a picture of Dean. After he fell asleep last night, I decided to take the lipstick he loves so much and draw a small heart over his chest with it.

Reggie peeks over my shoulder. "God, he really is delicious. A pain in the ass, but oof!"

I breathe a laugh before sliding my phone into the pocket of my leggings and walking toward the juice bar.

I understand Reggie's frustration with Dean. I mean, he's a loyal king to Evelyn and I really do admire the quality. But Dean told me about how Reggie is the one who stopped his relapse from escalating so . . . I have hope that maybe they'll move past everything one day.

After we've all ordered, we settle into seats at the small table.

"So quiet tonight, Amelia," Reggie signs.

I chuckle, nervously. "I'm always quiet."

He nods considerately as Evelyn timidly signs, "How's Dean doing?"

I swallow, signing, "Good," as some awkwardness tightens the already dull ache in my muscles.

It all feels a bit strange—knowing what I know about Evelyn but not having heard it from her. It's something Dean has since confessed that he struggles with too. He said it was part of the reason he never talked about it with anyone.

And it's honorable that he respects the fact that it's her business to tell, but I'm glad he's trusted me with it. There's this small bit of warmth in knowing that I'm the only person that gets to know certain things about him. He's the only person *I've* told about my mom, and it makes me feel like we have our own vault, full of things we only share with each other.

Like treasure.

Sad treasure, but it's *ours.*

I blink, realizing I'm being *quiet* again, so I change the subject by signing, "So, you ready for the wedding? Just over a month, right?"

Evelyn nods. "I'm just glad we decided on something small. I can't imagine trying to organize anything more elaborate. It'd be too much."

Reggie claps. "Amen! I love you, baby girl, but you make breakfast complicated."

She scoffs. "Says the guy who turned down brunch last weekend because the orange juice wasn't 'freshly squeezed.'"

I breathe a laugh. "Oh, I've got to side with Reggie on that one. No pulp, no dice."

Evelyn lifts her chin to the ceiling, shaking her head. "You made two of them?" she signs upward, making Reggie and I laugh. When she pulls her face back to the table she glances over at me. "You'll be there, right? We didn't do formal invitations or anything since it's just a few of us, but I hope you'll come."

I hadn't assumed I was invited, but I nod. I'd love to go. I've never been to a wedding before.

My alert light on my phone blinks and I peek down at the screen seeing a message from Dean.

Dean: I'm stopping by Villains after the meeting.
Should be home by 8.

I tug my lip between my teeth, tapping out a quick response. Things have been so heavy this past week so I planned a little fun for tonight and now it seems I have more time than I thought.

"Ope. She's doing the FMC lip bite. Shit's about to go down," Reggie says, emphatically.

I burst out laughing and so does Evelyn.

"Jesus Christ, Reg," she laughs.

He narrows his eyes at her. "Don't even get me started on *you*, Miss Getting-Married-In-The-Library-Where-You-Gave-Your-Man-A-Rub-Down."

Evelyn gapes at him, but the corners of her mouth pull up.

Damn! Go Evelyn!

I resist the urge to give her a high-five, but even if I hadn't, she quips back at Reggie, "Those who bone in coat closets cannot throw hangers."

"Actually, we can," he signs. "The closet is full of them. And if you spent any time in one, you're entitled to throw whatever you want in there."

Evelyn breathes a laugh through a nod, tossing up surrendering hands. "Touché."

I laugh too. I really do love being around them. They're intrinsically warm and somehow it feels like I've known them so much longer than I actually have.

Even so . . . I've got man plans.

"On that note . . ." I sign. "I've got to head out." I stand up, taking another sip on my smoothie and Reggie whistles.

"Cheers to slurping," he signs, raising his cup.

I breathe another laugh, responding in jest.

Yeah. I really fucking like them.

I lean over the slow cooker, breathing in the smell of Wally's meatball recipe that's been cooking all day. My eyes drift through the cut out in the wall and see Beatrice. She's made herself right at home at Dean's place, essentially claiming one of his flannels as her own.

He made the mistake of leaving it on the couch *one* time and now she's obsessed with it. Currently, she's curled up in it on the couch like a little purr-ito and I snort a small laugh.

Just as I give the meatballs a stir, I hear the door unlatch and Dean walks through. After he drops his keys on the table, he takes notice of Beatrice, his mouth quirking at the corner before his eyes find mine like a magnet in the kitchen and in an instant his jaw drops.

Just the reaction I was hoping for . . .

I'm dressed in nothing but a black lace bra and my apron, tied snuggly around my waist. I showered after the gym so my hair is still a little damp and my natural curls are billowing over my shoulders. But the cherry on top is the red lipstick.

His eyes darken and he slowly stalks toward me. I can feel him stirring through his stare, making goosebumps ripple down my arms and as he reaches the archway in the kitchen. His hungry eyes rake over my body and then linger on my lips as one of his chestnut waves falls to his forehead.

God. He is *so fucking* sexy. I'm ogling *him* and *he's* completely clothed.

"I'm cooking," I sign.

Duh, Amelia.

His lips pull up in the dreamy way that makes my knees shake as he signs, "Well, don't stop on my account."

I'm essentially done, but there's this playful glint in his eyes that makes me turn toward the stove where I've made some extra sauce, putting the back of my outfit on display.

Or lack thereof.

His quiet groan from behind tells me he appreciates the black thong I put on under the apron. My lips pull up as I reach for the oregano and a moment later, I feel him against my back. His hand runs along my ass cheek, murmuring, "I'm fucking obsessed with this beauty mark, by the way."

His words halt my movement. My excitement swirls at his hard body pressed against mine before he whispers, "Keep going, baby," and I suddenly feel his finger pulling along the thin material between my ass.

I breathe deep, sprinkling the oregano into the sauce and then stirring it.

"Good girl," he says, low and gravelly, my toes curling. "Spread your legs."

He's right. I fucking love it when he's bossy.

I do as I'm told, widening my stance just a bit as he slowly snakes one arm around my waist, pulling me so that my back is flush with his front and I feel his erection press into my lower back. His other hand moves to the apex of my thighs, cupping me over the thin material of the thong, rubbing me with a slow and torturous cadence.

My head falls back against his shoulder and I moan, feeling his lips graze the soft spot right below my ear before he flicks it with his tongue. "Keep stirring, Amelia," he says quietly, never ceasing his movement between my legs.

I whine, but he simply keeps rubbing and I reluctantly stir the sauce, turning down the burner so that it's barely heating it anymore.

It was basically done already—but who am I to deny a hungry man some naughty fun.

The ultimate Chef's Kiss challenge.

He moves my thong to the side, slipping his finger inside me, groaning into my neck, "So fucking wet."

I whimper, still trying to stir, but the slow, deep rhythm of his finger is hypnotizing me and my hips start to grind against his hand.

He chuckles darkly. "My beautiful, needy girl."

I nod shamelessly, as a breathless, "More," escapes. "Please give me more."

A low noise rumbles in his throat. "What's the word, baby?"

Fucking yes.

"Lightning."

I love that it's our word.

I should have used safe words in the past, but I never did. Not until him. And ironically, he's the one person I know I'd never need to use it with.

But the word is so much more than that.

It's the crackling feeling in my chest that only he gives me. It's the unexpected strike of us finding each other. It's the promise of more.

He moves me to the side of the stove, twisting my body so that I'm facing him as his rough, calloused hands cradle my face, kissing me with so much force that my knees buckle. He moves one of his hands to my lower back, anchoring me, and with the added support, I lose myself in his mouth.

My tongue licks the seam of his lips and he opens for me as we catch each other's sounds. When he finally pulls away, his eyes are dark and devious, floating down to my breasts with an appreciative lift of his eyebrows.

His fingers dance along the cup of the bra. "I didn't even know you had one of these."

I swallow. "Just a couple. But I can get more."

His eyes pull back up to mine as he unhooks the bra seamlessly, pulling it down my shoulders. "You're perfect either way." Dropping it to the ground, his lips inch up the side of his cheek. "Let's give it a taste, hmm?"

My eyebrows pinch, but then I notice his fingers dip into the saucepan. He brings his sauce-covered fingers back to my breast and I yelp as he spreads it around my nipples.

It's hot, *really hot*, but he quickly sucks it off, flicking his tongue over the peaking bud before he blows on it.

Oh God.

It feels divine—the mixed sensation. And it's made even better by the low *"mmm"* sounds he's making. He does it to the other nipple and I start to pant, raking my fingers through his hair as he teases my breasts, sucking on one while massaging the other and my head falls back, knocking into one of the cabinets.

"Please," I pant.

I feel him smile over my skin, groaning again. "I love it when you beg, baby."

I'm already wild with need, but an idea sparks. I push us back to the other counter so that I'm in front of him, lowering to my knees as his mystified eyes meet mine.

My eyes widen, purposely trying to look innocent while I rub the bulge over his jeans with my palm. "Can I please have it?"

He inhales sharply, his eyes squinting before he catches onto the game. He runs his knuckles down my cheek. "You thirsty, beautiful?"

Just to appear even *more* desperate, I rub my face along his length, over his pants, kissing his crotch—even going as far as to lick it over the denim fabric, whimpering, "Yes, please," as I run my lips over the long, hard outline in his jeans.

His head drops back. "Holy fuck, Amelia," he grumbles, petting my hair and I smile at the desperation in his voice.

I want him *lost* in this moment. I want to let everything that's happening around us fade into blackness while we tap into the light we give each other.

I'm amping it up, but the desperation *is* real.

I need him. I need this.

I moan against him, running my hands up his legs. "I'll be good. I swear. Please."

He grabs my chin, leaning down to take my lips with his before he pulls away, still hovering his mouth over mine. "You *are* good, baby."

I smile. *He just can't help himself.*

Don't get me wrong, he can throw down in the dirty talk department, but he never denies me praise. He knows what *I* need and he never lets it fall to the shadows of his own desire.

I swallow, whispering, "I love you, Dean."

In an instant, he pulls me up off the floor, crashing his mouth against mine as he devours my lips again, kissing me with every bit of himself and I feel it buzz through my veins. Our tongues tangle and he lifts under my ass, urging me to wrap my legs around him before he pulls away from my mouth, but his lips still press against mine as he says, "I love you, too."

He carries me over to the stove, turning the burner off completely before walking us toward the bedroom. "And since you asked so nicely, I'm going to give you what you want."

chapter thirty-six
dean

I drop us to the bed, kissing her again. She keeps her legs wrapped around my back but releases her arms, balling the fabric of my shirt and urgently pulling it up and over my head as a growl rumbles in my throat.

I've been ready to explode since the moment I walked in and saw her dressed like a fucking fantasy. But I can see that she's trying to prolong—give us some escape.

It's the root of our connection. And though I think we're both trying to evolve past it, I also think the past few days have earned us a small, salacious getaway.

I flip her over so that she's on her stomach and slowly untie the apron before she lifts her hips so that I can slide it out from under her.

Jesus. She looks so fucking perfect.

Her ass in the air with the thong fit snugly between her cheeks.

It gives me an idea. It's not exactly what she asked for, but watching her grovel at my dick before makes me want to work her up even more. I walk to the dresser getting the green tie she wore the night she tied me up. I move in front of her on the bed, urging her to sit up and she obliges, immediately eyeing the tie in my hand.

"Hold your hair up," I sign.

She smirks, collecting her dark, curly hair in her hands as I quickly knot the tie around her neck, letting the material fall and hang between her breasts. She sits back on her heels and all I can do is sit and stare at her for a second.

A goddamn vision.

After another second of letting my eyes enjoy her, I take the tie in my hand, wrapping the end of it around my fist and giving it a small tug. Her hands fall out in front of her, catching herself before a devious smile pulls her lips up. "A leash, huh?"

I smirk back. "Take the thong off, beautiful."

I loosen my grip on the tie to make sure she can keep her balance. After she slides the thong off her ankles and kicks it to the side, I start to lie back on the bed, using the tie to pull her with me. When she starts to work on my jeans, I pull her a little harder, making her move closer to my face.

She crawls farther up my body and I rasp, "That's a good girl," before I use my other hand to position her legs so that she's straddling me. I shift down so that my face is right in front of her heat. My free hand winds around her, slipping a finger inside her from behind and she gasps, grabbing the headboard as her eyes peer down at me. "You're gonna ride my face, baby. But keep those eyes on me the whole time. Got it?"

I continue to pump my finger in and out of her slowly. She's so close that my mouth is watering and I swear I see the tiniest blush spread across her cheeks as she nods, making me lose my goddamn mind.

I keep one hand fisting the tie, giving her no slack as I pull her closer to my mouth. The second I lick her, she moans deep, shutting her eyes for a second before she remembers the rules and looks down at me between her legs.

An animal unleashes.

My mouth devours her. Licking and sucking, nibbling over her bundle of nerves like it's a fucking delicacy.

And it is.

I'm groaning into her, keeping my grip tight on the tie so that she can't pull away.

She looks fucking incredible. Her dark hair cascades around her face like a curtain while her green eyes shine desperately down at me. Her plush, velvety red lips twist and drop from arousal.

"Ahh—" she whimpers, chuckling breathlessly as she keeps her eyes on me. "This is a good look for you, Roberts."

A muffled *"Mmf"* sound is the only response I can give, pushing my tongue deeper into her as she rocks against my face.

I'd fucking live here if I could.

With one hand tightly holding the tie, I slide the other one to her ass, rubbing it with my palm. She gives me the smallest dip of her chin, a silent plea in her eyes. With that, I wind my hand back and smack her ass and her thighs clench around my face.

It isn't long before I feel her tightening, and she cries out, "Oh, God . . . Dean . . ."

I pull my neck back slightly, growling, "Fuck yes, baby," licking her furiously before I grind out, "Say my name while you come on my face."

The room is a symphony of her desperate whimpers and my hungry groans, and after one more slap to her ass, she comes. *Hard.*

She whisper chants my name as her fingers rake through my hair, holding me to her as she convulses and rocks against my tongue through her climax. I keep licking her through it until her hips slow and her muscles loosen.

I press a kiss to her core, and she shudders through a breathy laugh before I slowly release the tie and she rolls off of me, lying on her back while she continues to pant. I lean over her, brushing some hair from her face.

Her eyes meet mine and she grabs my chin, pulling me to her mouth and kisses me. It's passionate but slow and her tongue meets mine, tasting herself on my tongue as they tangle. She pulls away a moment later, murmuring, "If you don't fuck me *right now,* you get no meatballs."

I snort a laugh but quickly start to unbutton my pants. I'm dying to bury myself inside her.

And I really do want some meatballs.

After I've earned my meatballs, we lie tangled together under the sheets. I nestle my face in her hair, breathing her in while her fingers trace invisible patterns on my chest.

The untamed air in the room has cleared and it's almost as if I can feel the clouds parting, returning us to reality. I think Amelia feels it too. I can see it in her eyes as she lifts her chin and rests it on my chest.

God, she is so beautiful.
Beautiful and mine.

It still amazes me that we're together this way.

I must have a dopey-looking smile on my face because she chuckles, signing, "You're staring, Roberts."

"You're pretty, James." I sign.

She rolls her eyes but her lips inch up at the corner, still lightly stained and smudged with lipstick. They keep their amusement for just a second before falling. Her finger patterns on my chest stop as she starts to poke her thumb with each of her fingernails.

I gently take her hand, bringing it to my face and she smiles timidly, lightly running her nails along the coarse hair on my jaw.

"What's going on in that pretty head?" I sign.

She smirks, saying, "You're using your power for evil," as she breathes a laugh. She loses herself in her movement against my face for another moment before she wraps the sheet around herself and sits up. Her bottom lip tugs between her teeth, hesitating before she signs, "Have you given any more thought to therapy?"

Yep. There's reality.

I sit up too, leaning against the headboard. My eyes drift down with a sigh before pulling back up to her, nodding. "I'm considering it."

"That's good," she signs, smiling softly. "I really don't want you to feel like I'm pressuring you. You just . . . you have a lot going on. You've *been* through a lot. It might help having someone other than a fellow basket case to talk it out with."

My eyebrows pinch. I hate that she doesn't see what I see. That she doesn't know how strong she is. "You're the strongest person I've ever met, Amelia. I'm lucky to have you."

A small huff pushes through her nose. "Right. Who showed up here a few days ago with their tail between their legs because they were scared to stay at their apartment?"

I feel the heated bubble of anger start in my chest at the reminder of him, but it's quickly interrupted with her shrug. "But whatever," she signs. "That's not the point. I just think you've spent a long time believing your pain doesn't matter. And it does. It matters to me."

Any bit of anger evaporates. In the small bit of time I've known her, she's managed to dig straight to the center of me, uncover my biggest fear and bury it with four words.

"It matters to me."

Truthfully, I probably should have sought out therapy a long time ago. Maybe it would have helped with the anger, my struggles with control—drinking—but I never did. It was always so hard to justify something like this when I'd seen so many people go through worse shit and deal with it on their own. And to be honest, I just didn't care enough about myself to do it.

But here's this woman. This strong, incredible woman who's been through some of the worst horrors a person can go through and she's sitting here telling me that she sees my struggles and deems them worthy.

She deems me *worthy.*

The concept takes my breath away as she stares back at me, cautiously.

"Sorry. That's my whole spiel. And I know I'm a mess, so take from it what you will. But honestly, you could probably use a therapist just from having to deal with all of *my* shit," she signs with a nervous chuckle.

Enough.

"Stop saying that," I sign, locking my eyes with hers. "I'm not *dealing* with you. I'm *in love* with you. Whatever—*whoever*—made you believe that you weren't worth *everything*, only did it because *they* felt worthless." I swallow the lump in my throat, knowing exactly who made her feel that way. My thumb gently runs along her bottom lip before I press my forehead to hers. We stay like that for a few long beats before I quietly say, "*She* was the mess, baby. Not you. You're . . . magic."

She breathes deep and I can feel her muscles tense as she rubs the back of my hand with the pads of her fingers. She presses her lips to mine, tenderly, humming against my mouth. "If I'm magic, then you're the wizard. Harnessing and wielding my power," she laughs, softly.

I know she's joking, but . . . that actually feels appropriate. I *am* harnessing her strength. Knowing what she's survived and seeing her persevere is the greatest example of resilience I've ever witnessed.

It fills me with something that's only flickered inside since the night I ended up on that floor with Evelyn. I think part of the reason I drank the way I did was an attempt to drown the flicker out completely. Because to have it at all, and still feel stuck, somehow made everything even more painful.

It's hope.

For the first time in nearly a decade, I don't feel consumed by my bullshit. It's still there, of course, but it's more of an awareness rather than something that's swallowing me.

And that's because of her.

I kiss her again, but it's not out of lust or desire. It's my deeply intense gratitude. That somehow, among the mess—the wreckage of life—that I walked into that bar a couple of months ago and found her.

My safe place to land.

My breath is heavy and I can already feel sweat dripping down my back as I round the corner of the sidewalk, jogging to "The Phoenix" by Fall Out Boy.

Apparently, my hiatus from being a *runner* hasn't shaken my preference for listening to angsty music while I exercise. But it's helping me keep a good pace. And honestly, I had to do *something* to burn off my frustration from this morning.

I went to the cops about Tim, despite knowing it was a long shot—distantly hoping there might be *something* they could do to help, but it was a wash.

I don't even know the guy's last name.

But even if I did—even as I explained what happened to the officer—I knew it would lead to nothing.

There's no evidence, no record of any incident. And without a full name, they weren't even able to run a background check.

I groan, quickening my pace a bit as I let the cool breeze from the lake fill my lungs, trying to breathe in some calmness.

An old version of myself would have already gone to his stupid fucking garden and dangled his ass over the roof until he was pleading with me not to drop him and paint the sidewalk with his body.

But I know any sort of confrontation would likely only end up with *me* behind bars.

And that *can't* happen. It would sign my fate with Marnie filing for full custody. And for as little as I can do for Amelia now, I'd be completely useless from a jail cell.

As the helpless feeling starts to crowd my mind, I find myself running faster despite my protesting lungs.

I run like I'm running after *him.*

I even picture it—chasing him down and beating him to a bloody pulp for ever touching her—for scaring her.

My feet pound against the sidewalk, but they're still only moving at half my heart rate. It's racing so fast, that my breath catches in my throat and I stop abruptly, holding my weight on my thighs as I try to suck in some deep breaths.

Jesus Christ. Am I having a heart attack?!

Pulling my ear buds out, I blink down at the sidewalk through the green spots in my vision, still trying to get my breathing under control.

Too much too soon.

I continue to breathe. I probably look ridiculous right now, but I can't even worry about the onlookers watching me gasp for air.

One thing at a time, I remind myself.

I can't fix everything. Not all at once, at least.

I have no chance at holding onto sobriety if I try to take on more than I can handle.

Thankfully, Amelia's told me that Tim's been radio silent since their last encounter. And while I hate that he's made her feel unsafe again, there's a little peace in the fact that she's staying with me.

My lungs finally expand a little more and I straighten back up, taking my first full breath as I start to walk back toward my apartment.

One thing at a time, I remind myself again.

Today, that thing is my first therapy session. And I hope the therapist has a therapist.

chapter thirty-seven
dean

I wipe the sweat from my forehead before I drag the sander across the top corner of Amelia's door. I stealthily stole her apartment key off her key ring last night, and after my meeting for work downtown this morning, I came over here with pure determination to do something—*literally anything*—that might make her feel just the tiniest bit more safe.

If I can fix it, my plan is to have us stay here instead.

I know she misses her apartment. She had a tough night and mentioned that she wished she had her big, purple blanket. It was three in the morning and I nearly drove over here to get it for her, but then she panicked, convincing herself that Tim would somehow be here, waiting.

I suffocated the impulse to come over here anyway, *hoping* that motherfucker was dumb enough to come back here just so I could toss his ass out the window.

But . . . I'm evolving.

Or trying to, at least.

My grinding teeth beg to differ as I brush the excess dust from the top of the door. Climbing back down the ladder, I step inside the apartment, opening and closing the door a few times, but it's still sticking a bit. My eyes squint up, noticing a jagged edge on the molding at the top of the frame. It's in a tricky spot, so I bend down to my toolbox and grab some sandpaper before I climb back up the ladder and manually sand it down.

My phone suddenly buzzes from my pocket and I pull it out, seeing a video message from Marnie. As soon as I click play, I see Ava sinking her hands into some cake and then bringing her fists to her mouth, mostly smooshing the frosting against her lips.

Just as a small chuckle escapes me, she throws some cake bits in the air like confetti and yells, "Da-da!" making my mouth go slack and my eyes immediately mist. I rewind and play it no fewer than five times.

She said it. She said it before "fuck." I huff a small laugh, but there's no humor behind it.

I try to remind myself that missing her *say* it isn't a big deal—that the fact that she said it at all is a far bigger deal. And I get her for her actual birthday on Saturday, so I'm sure that's not easy for Marnie. But I huff again at the reminder that plenty of her future birthdays will likely be in Michigan.

I watch the video one more time before I text a "Thanks" to Marnie and then slip the phone back in my pocket and continue with my task.

I truly don't know what to do about the move. It was a hot topic at my therapy session with Dr. Leeves—who I was relieved to find out *does* in fact have his own therapist. But he encouraged me to redirect my perspective. That I need to stop searching for an "appealing" choice inside of a situation that I hate because I'll never find it—and I'll likely drive myself insane.

And I don't know if he hypnotized me or if he's some distant, descendant of Yoda, but it fucking resonated. I just need to figure out an arrangement that I can live with—something that won't completely derail me and make that expectation clear.

Easier said than done.

My eyes squint, seeing I've smoothed out the jagged edges on the molding, so I hop down off the ladder, and move back inside the apartment, closing the door again. When it seamlessly clicks shut, I dip my chin with a victorious sigh.

One thing at a time.

I pull my phone back out of my pocket and text Amelia.

Me: Meet me at your place after class.

A couple hours later, I've retrieved Beatrice and we're sitting on the big coral chair when I hear Amelia push through her door and immediately tumble into the wall on the other side of the entryway.

"What the—" she gasps.

"You okay?" I ask over my shoulder, already smiling. Beatrice stares up at me, blinking sleepily, and I give her a small scratch behind her ear as Amelia walks into the living room.

She stands in front of me, baffled. "So. The door's different."

I nod, smirking playfully as I sign, "Yeah, you know, it *did* seem different."

Her eyes pull down to Beatrice, who is giving us her best Rockette leg as she grooms herself, before Amelia looks back at me, a slow smile inching up her cheeks. "You fixed my door . . ."

God, she looks cute right now. Her hair is up in a ponytail with some loose pieces framing her face. And since it's finally a little warmer outside, she's swapped out her black bomber jacket for a form fitting hunter green zip-up hoodie.

But that smile is what's getting me.

"I want to show you something else," I sign, standing up and pulling her back toward the door.

"Does it involve you in a toolbelt? Because *that* sounds fun."

"No," I chuckle. "But noted."

I lead her back into the hall, positioning her right outside the entryway before I show her my other project from this morning.

Her eyebrows pinch down at the light switch just beside her door. She flicks it, and I direct my eyes inside the apartment, urging her to look. When she does, she sees that I've hung some twinkly lights along the perimeter of the living room, and they're hooked up to this switch plate.

She gasps and immediately sucks her lips into her mouth.

I had to call my dad for some help with it. He hooked one up to Otis's room—not with twinkly lights—but the overhead light in his bedroom. It'll just be a convenient way for her to know if someone's at the door without having to wear her hearing aids at home.

And she looks so damn good under twinkly lights.

Her eyes well, shaking her head. "I can't . . ." she starts, but a tear slips out of the corner of her eye before she says, "I can't believe you did this for me."

I swipe the tear with my thumb before pulling her into me. "I'll do anything for you, baby," I whisper against her hair. Her body shakes a bit as I hold her and I can tell she's crying. I try not to make a big deal of it because she's already told me she hates to cry, but it kills me to hear it.

I rub her back and keep kissing the top of her head before she pulls back and stares up at me.

"I can't believe you're mine," she says, her eyes still watery, beautifully green and full of awe.

And I feel it too. I've hated myself for a long time, but when she looks at me like this, it feels like she's looking at the person I used to be. The person I wanted to be.

Maybe the person I can be.

But I'm certain that every version of me is hers.

A few hours later, Amelia's fluttering around her kitchen, making dinner, while I try to not watch her like a creep and instead work on my therapy homework.

I have to think of words to describe myself and provide a visual aid, which kind of feels like one of those preschool projects where you have to spell out "Mommy" and then come up with a word that starts with each of the letters.

Ugh.

But I'd be lying if I said the excuse to draw again wasn't filling me up a bit. I used to do it all the time, but I stopped that night I made an enemy with a brick wall. At first I couldn't draw because my hand was so fucked up, but even after it healed, the urge to do so just . . . faded away like the rest of me.

My phone buzzed from my nightstand but I quickly buttoned it.

My girlfriend had been calling me incessantly, but I had no interest in talking to her. Not after I caught her sending sketchy texts to some other guy.

High school, melodrama bullshit.

Otis saw me ignore the call and signed, "Did you have a fight with Haley?"

I quickly shook my head. I didn't want to talk about it.

No, I was in the business of avoiding. And that avoidance was provided by my brother. We had decided to try and see if we could create a comic book in one weekend and it was the perfect distraction.

He was sitting at my desk, coming up with the story, and I was on my bed, sketching the illustrations.

"I think we should do an antihero," he signed.

My eyebrows pinched, signing, "Mr. Noble? You want a morally gray hero?"

He chuckled, shrugging. "Not morally gray per se. But they're more interesting, more human. Don't you think?"

I nodded, shrugging. "I guess even most villains believe they're the good guys."

Otis sucked his lips into his mouth, tilting his head considerately before he turned back toward the desk.

I lightly kicked the chair he was sitting in to get his attention back, signing, "Let's make him deaf, but telepathic."

His eyebrows hitched with a nod. "Yeah, it'll lend itself to the loner quality too." He scribbled some notes down, but I felt my chest tighten, knowing the "loner" comment was all too true for my brother. Being deaf could be really isolating. Otis handled it well, but being "different" wasn't easy.

He turned back to me and signed, "Should he have a sidekick?"

I nodded and my eyes absentmindedly glanced around the room, thinking. I caught a glimpse of my Cubs jersey peeking out of my closet and signed, "How about a bear cub?"

Otis laughed, signing, "Cub-Cub."

I cracked up and started sketching out Cub-Cub. We went back and forth like that for hours before we finally landed on the name, Signed, Retribution.

Our antihero, Retribution, was a cigar smoking, motorcycle driving, vigilante on the outskirts of society that specifically sought out the bullies of the world with the help of his trusty sidekick, Cub-Cub.

It was so late, but we were both riding the high of this goofy-ass project when Otis yawned, signing, "We need a love interest."

I rubbed my palm down my face, exhausted. But sketched something out quickly right before I passed out.

"B! Off the counter!" Amelia's scolding of Beatrice brings me back to now, but I smile as the memory lingers.

Green eyes. I gave Vera, the love interest of *Signed, Retribution* green eyes.

Amelia walks into the living room, signing, "I think she was less of a brat at your place," before she sits on the arm of the chair, running a lazy hand through my hair. I lean into her touch just as she gasps, "Oh my God, you *drew* this?!"

It startles me and I actually feel my cheeks heat a little bit. But I nod as she picks up the paper and looks at it, the emerald orbs of her eyes sparkling as they scan the drawing.

I squirm, signing, "I'm rusty, but . . . I used to draw. And I needed something for my therapy assignment."

She stares at it a second longer before her eyes peek back up to me and she fans herself with the paper. "Damn, Roberts. You really are a damaged girl's wet dream."

I grab her arm, twisting her down so that I'm cradling her on my lap, kissing her hard until it feels like I'm floating. Once our lips stop she looks at the sketch again, leaning her head on my shoulder.

It's a jasmine flower, with a spilled liquor bottle pouring out from the pistil and behind the flower I lightly drew the Chicago skyline with some lightning behind the clouds.

Amelia is looking at it in awe and it swells my confidence. She shakes her head, blowing an impressed whistle through her lips before she signs, "I'm pretty sure Dr. G gave me a similar assignment once and I drew a stick figure with a book in the rain."

I chuckle before kissing her again, breathing in her playful mood and letting it pump through my veins. I can tell that she's happy to be back at her place. And while fixing her door certainly didn't eliminate Tim's threat, I hope she feels at least slightly vindicated by coming home, reclaiming her space.

When our lips finally pull away from each other she picks up my hand, looking at it like she's appraising it. "So much talent in this hand," she muses, kissing each of my fingers before she glances over at me and gently bites on my index finger.

Every purr comes with a bite.

My dick immediately twitches and I surprise her by hooking the finger behind her bottom teeth and pulling her face closer to mine, my voice a gravely whisper as I say, "Don't be a brat," but a smirk tilts up my cheek, silently requesting she *does* keep up the attitude.

The corners of her mouth pinch before she cradles my hand and sucks on my finger, slowly pulling it out of her mouth before pressing another kiss to the pad. The timer to the oven goes off and she slowly stands, signing, "My punishment will have to wait until after dinner."

I swat her ass, unable to resist and she giggles before scurrying back into the kitchen.

chapter thirty-eight

amelia

S tupid, stupid, girl."

The voice is so vivid that I gasp, quickly twisting around to make sure she isn't right behind me, but there's no one there.

Where the fuck is she?

Stopping here was a mistake.

And if stopping here was a mistake, then I wasn't sure what the word was for someone who essentially broke into the seemingly empty home of her estranged, abusive mother.

I'm pretty sure that word is "unwell."

But seriously—what was I thinking?

It's been eight years since I've seen her. And I have a new apartment—a new life—waiting for me in Chicago.

Still, I shake my head, releasing a heavy breath as I continue to creep down the hallway.

As I make it to my old bedroom, I stare at the door for a few seconds.

I never gave it a proper goodbye. It was my small sliver of peace when I lived here and a soft swell of emotion passes through my chest as I look at the old, beaten up door.

I hesitantly push it open. Assuming it made some kind of noise, I peek around to see if she's lurking around anywhere.

Still nothing.

My eyes quickly sweep the room, widening when I realize . . . it looks exactly the same. My purple comforter is still on the bed. The tattered drapes to the single window are still pushed open. My desk even still has some school books on it—the ones I had dumped out of my backpack the night I ran away.

My eyebrows pinch. What the hell?

I can't believe she hasn't found something else to do with the room, but I guess that would require some kind of effort to upkeep the house. My eyes catch on a small glint bouncing off the window from the bit of sun shining in. I move closer, peeking over the side of the bed and see an assortment of glass liquor bottles on the floor.

She was drinking in here?

My mind searches for some kind of explanation. It doesn't make any fucking sense.

But my breath hitches when I see the light catch on the nightstand.

My eyes squint. Is that . . .?

I inch closer and confirm that it's the necklace Alex had given me for my birthday.

I thought I had lost it in the accident.

My hands move the new one around my neck, holding it tight as I press my thumb against the pointy bolt. I walk over to the nightstand and pick up the old one, letting the delicate, broken chain sift through my fingers. The small lightning bolt is tarnished and chipped, but it's definitely the same one and it only furthers my confusion.

How did she find it?

Why did she keep it?

Emotion creeps up my tightening throat as I hold the necklace in my palm, glancing around the room again.

I'm at a complete loss as to why it all looks exactly the same as it did eight years ago—like I still live here. My fist tightens around the necklace, ready to stick it in my pocket because . . . she doesn't deserve to have it.

But my eyes fall to the bottles on the floor again.

Something flickers in my chest. I feel my eyes mist as my mind tries to fight the feeling, but still, it stays.

I blink away the moisture and swallow the emotion down, but my shaky hand puts the necklace back on the nightstand, releasing a heavy sigh.

Whatever that flicker was, I strangely find myself wanting to leave some of it for her, too.

I wake to wet eyes, sprawled along Dean's lap on the big armchair in my living room.

"Hey," he says, quietly. "Are you okay?" Leaning over, he wipes the wetness from my cheeks and I sniff through a nod.

After my face is dry, he leans back in the chair, keeping a watchful eye on me as he hugs my legs on his lap.

"Just a weird dream, " I sign. "It was from the day I moved out here. I stopped by my mom's house on the way."

I watch his Adam's apple bob as he nods tightly. He doesn't say anything. He just waits. It's what he always does when something about my mother comes up, like a dutiful soldier.

I sigh, finally signing, "It was just strange. Usually dreams involving her are the terrorizing kind, but that day I actually had . . . some hope. Like maybe we'd figure things out somehow. I think deep down, that day might have been the reason I kept going to see her all these years."

He lifts his hand to tuck some hair behind my ear, wiggling the lobe between his fingers.

It's our new thing. When one of us is talking about something difficult and the other one doesn't have anything but something cliché or unhelpful to say, we give each other something affectionate. Something to let the other know that we're here.

He sighs. "Maybe the house is just fresh on your mind?"

I shrug. I guess it makes sense. Dean sat with me while I spoke with a lawyer a couple days ago about my mom's estate. Apparently, it's a duty you're allowed to just flat out reject. Her belongings and the house essentially get turned over to the state. And with the support from Dean and Dr. G—that's what I did.

"I guess it's just weird," I sign. "I always thought that one day there'd be some big, dramatic reveal. Some deep dark secret that made her such a monster—*something* that made it all click into place."

I peek up at Dean and his warm brown eyes study me as he breathes deep. Another moment passes before he shrugs, signing, "It could have been anything, baby. It could have been nothing. But it doesn't really matter. I kind of think the darkest things in life tend to stay in the dark. They never make it to the light and we're honestly probably better off."

My smile pulls up my cheeks as wonderment fills my eyes.

One thing's for sure—I'll never know the *reason* for why I deserve him, but . . . I can guarantee that I'd do it over and fucking over again if I had to.

Still, I can't help but tease. I release a groan, rolling my neck back before I sign, "Were you written by a woman or something?"

He chuckles, shaking his head. "Pretty sure she fucked up if that's the case."

My mouth tilts. "Ah, so you're a philosopher, then . . ."

He laughs again, signing, "Yeah. D. Fart's School of Thought," then proceeds to make a fart sound with his mouth and I crack up, curling with laughter.

We lose ourselves to a small laughing fit and just as it settles, my eyebrow cocks as I wiggle myself out from beneath him, straddling his lap on the chair as I say, "Which one of the philosophers said: 'What lies behind you . . .'" I move my hand behind me, walking my fingers up the inside of his thigh. "'And what lies in front of you . . .'" My other hand rubs his dick over his pants in front of me and he groans, grabbing my waist.

He wastes no time sinking his hand into my leggings, immediately holding his palm over my heat as he pushes his finger into me, rasping, "'Pales in comparison to what lies inside you.'"

A surprised whimper squeaks past my lips and I suddenly give zero fucks about what philosopher we're quoting.

He pumps his finger in and out of me slowly, while his other hand hooks around the back of my neck, pulling my lips to his. His hand picks up its pace between my legs as he grunts against my lips. "I have to leave for the meeting in five minutes."

Challenge accepted.

Dean offered to buy me my weight in queso dip at the Mexican place around the corner from the meeting, so I decided to go with him.

Because, cheese.

But truth be told, he knows I'm still struggling with being alone at my apartment.

Just as the meeting starts, a young woman walks up front, looking nervous. She's petite and her frame is frail. She looks to be younger—maybe early twenties—and her short, curly blond hair only hangs to her chin, while her wide hazel eyes look bloodshot and worn.

She takes a steadying breath before she says, "I'm Sarah."

"Hi, Sarah," everyone says, in unison.

"I—um . . . I haven't been here in a while. I relapsed, recently. I had been clean for three years but . . ." She shakes her head, trailing off while my hand finds Dean's on his lap. I notice him pull in a deep breath as Sarah finally adds, "I was sexually assaulted about a month ago." She clears her throat, shifting her weight and I feel Dean's hand tense up in mine. "He was my boss. I had been seeing him for about six months on and off. But we both live at this co-op in Lincoln Park and he runs the garden on the roof of the building."

Oh my God. Tim.

My spine tightens, along with my grip on Dean's hand. He squeezes mine back and I can feel his eyes peek over to me, but I keep mine on Sarah.

"But when I showed up for work this morning, he wasn't there. A coworker told me he was arrested. Apparently, he had been caught breaking into another woman's apartment."

I blanch as the sound in the room starts to feel far away.

Another woman?

Distantly, I know I *should* feel relieved—but *three* women have been harassed—terrorized—*assaulted* by this man?! And those are just the ones we know about.

He wasn't just a creep, he was a fucking *predator.*

I was hooking up with him for months and I had no idea I was willingly inviting a dangerous man into my home.

I *let* him fucking *hunt me.*

I can feel the start of my panic all the way in my toes. My fingers fidget in Dean's hand while my free hand scratches the top of my bouncing knee, over my leggings.

The urge to flee the building is strong, but Sarah is still up there—doing something incredibly brave—and I know I can't leave, which only makes my heart beat faster and my teeth clench as I struggle to catch my breath.

My body jerks as Dean's hand moves to the back of my neck, but I settle slightly as he starts to gently rub it. The movement is enough to pull my eyes over to him,

His eyes meet mine and a silent reminder passes through his gaze as he holds my hand tight.

I'm here.

My eyes pick up on his chest, watching as it slowly rises. I feel his fingers, still twined with mine on his lap, lightly pressing one-by-one between my knuckles. When he reaches my pinky, he pauses his movement between my knuckles and then releases a visible exhale, resuming the finger presses.

My breath stutters in my chest, my eyes squinting, but he does it again and I start to mimic the movement.

Inhale. One, two, three, four, five.

Exhale. One, two, three, four, five.

I can't be sure how long we do it, but the small movement of our fingers and the practiced breath slowly allows the sound of the room start to filter back in, the breaths come easier and my jaw releases. I wiggle out the remaining tension as I stare deep into Dean's coffee-colored eyes and a warmth finds me as he pulls my hand up to his mouth, kissing it before he gives me a small lopsided smile.

I'm here, Amelia.

I attempt to give him a small smile and a silent message of my own.

I love you.

We walk quietly back in the direction of Dean's apartment. Both of our appetites were shot after everything we learned at the meeting, so we've decided to save queso for another night. The late-April temperatures make for a pleasant walk, but a heaviness hangs around us.

Instinctively, I try to lighten the mood by signing, "So, that was some quick thinking back there, Roberts. Did Dr. Leeve's give you that technique?"

His downward gaze tells me he didn't see my hands. I stop on the sidewalk, touching his arm to get his attention and he slowly blinks back over to me.

"Sorry, what?" he signs.

My lips lift. "What's going on in that pretty head?" I sign, using his own words back at him.

He chuckles, but his smile doesn't reach his eyes.

I move into him, brushing my hand through his wavy brown hair, silently inviting me to tell him what he's thinking.

He holds me back for a moment, his gaze moving from one of my eyes to the other, seemingly searching, before he puffs out an exhale. It takes him another few beats before he finally pulls back and continues walking and I follow.

We take another few steps, silence hanging, when I finally see his hands move.

"I just . . . I can't believe how *big* of a problem this is," he signs, his mouth flattening to a tight line. My eyebrows pinch, confused, but then he continues, "How is it possible that there are *so many* fucked up people out there? Attacking women—*raping* women. It just . . . happens too fucking much . . . it could have happened to *you*—" his signing cuts off and his jaw sets. I see the muscles in his neck stiffen and I slip my hand through his, weaving our fingers together as I hold his bicep.

"It didn't," I say quietly, pressing my lips to his shoulder.

His throat bobs through a nod. With our hands now occupied holding and anchoring each other, he quietly rasps, "I know. It's just—hard to fucking swallow. And it scares me for Ava as she gets older . . . she'll be so far away . . ." he trails off, shaking his head.

My chest tightens. I want to give him some comfort, but I'm not sure there is anything I can tell him that will help.

I shrug. "Whether you're down the road or in a different state, it won't *stop* bad things from happening, Dean. We both know that they can just . . . happen." He pulls in a deep inhale, clearly trying to push through some anger and I rub my hand up and down his arm. "I think the best thing you can—*the only thing you can do*—is be honest with her. When she's old enough, you should have an honest conversation with her about what happened with Evelyn."

"Oh, I don't think I can do that," he says, shaking his head.

I stop walking again, which forces him to stop too. I step in front of him, locking my eyes with his. "Yes. You can." He stares back at me, worry and doubt still etching his features and I clear my throat. "You should of course talk to Evelyn about it first, and you don't need to dive into all of the ugly details. But knowing her dad was directly affected by something like this—*her aunt*—I can promise you, it will hold more weight. It will make her *more* aware. And more than anything, the silent message you'll be giving her is that you understand that this is a problem and she can talk to you about it."

His eyes slowly soften along with the worried line between his brows. He leans into me, pressing his lips to mine, they move appreciatively as his hand cradles my face. When we pull apart, he smiles, brushing his thumb along my cheek.

"It's like you worked with kids or something," he jokes, pressing a quick peck to my lips before starting to walk again.

I breathe a laugh. "Well, *that* and I was a troubled kid, which means I know how to fix everyone except myself."

"That's because there's nothing wrong with you, baby," he says, pulling my hand up and pressing his lips to the back of it. "You're magic, remember?" I huff a laugh before he adds, "Maybe I'll just have you talk to her."

Warmth I've never felt before spreads like a heat wave through every one of my limbs. I feel my eyes mist and tilt my chin up in an attempt to not turn into a puddle on the sidewalk.

I still think this kind of conversation would be better coming from him, but it feels like fireworks in my chest to know that he'd trust me with such an important talk with his daughter.

But the bigger thing—the unshakable, uncaged thing soaring through me right now is that he wholeheartedly believes I'll be a part of Ava's future.

His future.

And I am so fucking happy.

chapter thirty-nine

dean

I'*m in trouble.*

My dick is rock solid in my mother's kitchen and there isn't a damn thing I can do about it.

Amelia's standing at the stove stirring . . . something. Her hair is pulled back into an untamed ponytail, revealing her slender neck as her green tank top hangs delicately off her shoulders and I can't stop watching her.

Evelyn stole my baby upon arrival and the only other distraction I have is my dad talking to Otis and me about how the neighbor's lawn is a "disgrace."

I wonder: at what stage of "old" do people start judging each other for their lawn care?

Nevertheless, these are my options.

My mom is standing by Amelia "helping" with food prep—from what I can see, she's just telling her about a restaurant in the city that arranges your food in dirty, suggestive ways.

How she knows this, I don't want to know.

But Amelia doesn't seem bothered. Her smile is beaming and it's fully captivated me.

It was a tough ride up here. I know she hates driving, but it's Ava's birthday. And after I invited her to come up to my parents' house for the party, she was determined to power through it. About halfway through the drive and multiple bouts of panic, I pulled over and suggested she move to the backseat with Ava. It seemed to help a little bit, but I wasn't sure if she'd be able to shake it off.

Dad's low wave catches my attention and I reluctantly pull my focus back to the table.

"Do you want to go?" he signs.

I have no earthly idea what they've been talking about so I shake my head. "I should go check on Ava."

Otis chuckles. "I think Evelyn took her out back. Something about the blow-up pool."

Great.

Luckily, I always throw some extra clothes in her diaper bag since either she or myself tend to spill things. Dad and Otis leave and my eyes fall back to Amelia, my mom beside her, signing animatedly.

I discreetly tuck myself into the waistline of my pants, hoping not to mortify myself as I stand and walk over to them.

"Have you read *Untamed* by Glennon Doyle?" Mom signs to Amelia. She shakes her head and an excited groan escapes my mom. "You need to. Every woman should."

Amelia laughs through a nod, signing, "I'll have to check it out."

"Oh! You can borrow mine," she signs, practically giddy as she flits away toward the study.

Amelia's emerald eyes pull up to mine, her smile in place, and I have to fight the urge to not pull her into me. It will do me no favors with my current predicament.

"What are you making?" I sign.

"Pasta salad. I'll have to give it an ice bath to cool it down quickly, though."

I breathe a laugh. "Yeah, my dad and Otis are the 'planners' of the family," I sign. "Ironically they're both the 'eaters,' too, but neither one of them can cook so meals tend to be last minute and gone quickly."

She laughs, giving the noodles another stir before she signs, "It's okay. I'm up for the challenge." She puts the spoon down, glancing around the kitchen, her expression soft. "This house is nice."

My eyes drift around the kitchen, taking in the modest size. My eyes fall to the cabinet below the sink—the one that still hangs slightly off its hinges from when Otis and I decided to try and recreate a Mario Kart course in the house with our scooters.

It went as well as it sounds.

All in all, the house is nothing to brag about, but there's a warmth in her eyes that tells me she's not necessarily enamored with the *aesthetic.* I pull her into my chest—*boner be damned*—I can't *not* hold her. I press my lips to the top of her head, murmuring, "My Amelia."

Her arms tighten around my torso, burying her face in my chest as we stand, holding each other for a few beats before I pull back, signing, "I heard something about a blow-up pool so I was going to go check on Ava—but I can stay here if you want?"

She shakes her head. "No, go be with your baby. She'll only turn one, once," she signs through a chuckle. "Plus, you've distracted me enough. I've got to figure out how to spice up noodles, tuna, and mayonnaise."

I snort a laugh. *Sounds about right.*

With a parting peck, I open the back door to the screened in patio, immediately spotting Evelyn sitting beside an inflatable pool while Ava sits inside, splashing wildly.

I sigh, pushing through the screen door and Evelyn's lips pull back in faux apology as she raises her hands defensively. "She asked for it," she signs.

I chuckle, still walking toward them, signing, "Oh yeah?"

She shrugs. "Maybe she was saying 'poop' . . . "

My eyebrows lift and she laughs. "Just kidding," she signs, then looks back at Ava, scrunching her nose as she says, "Your dad is such a baby."

"Da-da!" Ava squeals, her crooked grin beaming up at me.

My heart squeezes as I smile back at her, plopping down on the ground next to the pool, across from Evelyn. We both watch Ava while she lives her best life—playing bongos on the surface of the water.

A few seconds pass before Evelyn clears her throat. "So . . . things seem to be going well with you and a certain classmate of mine." Her lips tilt as she looks over at me and I breathe a laugh, dipping my chin in a nod as her smile softens. "I'm really happy for you, Dean. She's awesome."

I smile back my agreement with a contented hum.

This moment feels a bit surreal—sitting in my parents' backyard with Evelyn, an easy air surrounding us as my daughter plays and giggles between us.

Evelyn peeks back at me, still smiling. "I told you."

My eyebrows pinch. "What exactly did you tell me?"

"That we were gonna be okay."

It takes me a second to place what she's talking about, but then I remember it's what she said to me at the end of our conversation after my accident. The one we had just before my first sober meeting where we spilled the past all over my kitchen table.

The conversation wrecked me, but . . . I do think there's something about *true* healing that demands honesty. And it's something I think I appreciate differently because of how many years I spent lying.

Lying to her, my brother, Marnie—*myself.*

But when I think about it, *that* conversation with her was the crack. The gradual chipping of the painted lies I'd spent years layering over the truth.

I blink, refocusing my eyes back to Evelyn, her stare curious from across the pool.

Shrugging, I tell her, "I mean . . . I don't know about 'okay.' My ex-wife is about to move to Michigan with my daughter and I have no choice but sit here and take it. Every visitation schedule she comes up with just . . . doesn't feel right."

Evelyn's eyes fall to Ava and then drift back to me. "Maybe that's because you know *visits* aren't enough," she says quietly.

I snort a humorless laugh. "Astute, Evie. Remind me to call you when she starts dating."

I wait for her comeback but my eyes squint back at her when I notice a soft smile tilting on her cheek. The expression confuses me until I realize . . .

I called her Evie.

Somewhere along the last year, the nickname had stopped and it just naturally resurfaced.

We silently appreciate the return before she breathes deep and says, "Listen. I don't envy this problem—and I'm not saying it isn't hard, but . . ." She shrugs, then adds, "Sometimes we make the hard things more difficult by rejecting an answer that's right in front of us."

A bristliness twitches through my limbs and I scratch the back of my jaw. "So, what? I'm supposed to drop my entire life and move to Michigan because *Marnie* made an impulsive decision?"

"No. I think you should do whatever you think is right for *her*," she says, her eyes pulling down to Ava and then back up to me. "And something tells me you know that the right thing to do is be wherever she is, but you're fighting it because you feel like it's unfair—and honestly, it is. But being stubborn about it isn't hurting *Marnie*. The only ones who have anything to lose from a long distance relationship are you and Ava."

In that moment, Ava's soaking wet body pummels into me with Evelyn's words, leaving the front of my shirt drenched as she giggles against me. "Da-da!"

Despite the water seeping through my shirt, my arms tighten around her. I press my mouth to her wet curls and breathe her in. It feels like I'm trying to memorize the exact size of her small body in my arms. My mind fights the notion of how quickly the size will change—how much *she'll* change between our time apart.

She slumps into me, letting me cradle her and my heart melts.

I've made *so many* bad decisions—shitty choices that turned me into a sunken, regurgitated version of myself. And Evelyn's right. I think most of them have come from *not* doing something I *knew* I should do and I just . . . didn't want to.

Or I convinced myself that I couldn't.

My eyes pull back to Evelyn, and I'm reminded of how sometimes the hard path pays off. If she and I hadn't had that difficult conversation a year ago in my kitchen, we may not be having *this one* today.

Clearing my throat, I start to say, "I—uh," I trip over the words, shifting my weight. "I hope this doesn't make you uncomfortable but . . . I feel like I should tell you. I had a nightmare a couple of weeks ago and I . . . I ended up telling Amelia about what happened—back at school."

An audible inhale pulls through her nose, "Oh—um," she fumbles, clearly a little thrown, but she shakes her head. "No, it's . . . it's okay. I've uh—I've actually been trying to be more open about it too. And I think it's helping. I . . . even told my parents a few months ago."

My eyebrows hitch. "Wow. That's . . ." Words escape me. I'm shocked. She was so adamant about keeping it secret back then—*especially* from her parents. But I'm so fucking proud of her for telling them.

"It was really hard," she says. "I mean—it *sucked.* But . . . Otis helped me through it."

I nod and a lightness slowly finds its way to me—*fills me*—as I take her in. The pink color of her cheeks, her wavy chestnut hair, the sparkly, earthy shine to her eyes.

The moment almost feels like déjà vu—but instead of it feeling like a moment that's already happened, it feels like I'm watching a moment that was always meant to be snap into focus.

I've seen my brother help her in ways I never could, but unlike before, the realization isn't running with jealousy or resentment. Because all I can see is a girl I knew, finally settling into the woman she was always meant to be.

Evelyn's eyes squint back at me. "What?"

A resounding clarity thrums through my chest as I hold Ava tighter, peering down at her before I look back up at Evelyn. "I think we're gonna be okay, Evie."

Amelia, of course, found a way to spice up my Mom's weird tuna pasta recipe. And after we eat, I steal her away and lead her out to the backyard.

Her eyes immediately rise to the treehouse, widening as she takes it in with a small gasp.

"Wow," she signs.

"I know, right?" I sign back.

It was Otis and my ultimate bragging right growing up and it turns out, even as an adult, I can't help but beam at it with pride. It's in a big maple tree near the edge of my parents' property—just inside the fence—nestled between the thick branches we used to sit out and spy on the neighborhood. There's two windows—one that overlooks the woods behind the house and the other faces the neighbor's yard.

Poor One-Eyed Willy. I wonder if he still lives there.

I step to the side of the ladder, inviting Amelia to climb up first and a small smirk tilts on her cheek before she starts to step up. I follow behind her, giving her ass a rub as she hauls herself through the small doorway—*because, why not*—and she chuckles as she crawls in, brushing her hands together to knock away the dirt.

"Smooth, Roberts," she signs.

I shrug just before I pull myself in the house and watch as her eyes dance around the walls.

Some of my drawings are still up. There's a couple of maps and recreated comic book characters—but there's one of Retribution and Cub-Cub that catches my eye, lifting my smile.

Amelia's gaze falls to me, her mouth tilting deviously as she signs, "On a scale of one-to-man whore, how many girls did you bring up here?"

I snort a laugh, shaking my head. My neck cranes behind me to see if the sign is still here. When I see that it is, I turn back toward Amelia and point up to it.

NO GIRLS ALLOWED. EXCEPT MOM.

An amused huff pushes past her lips. "I have a feeling you were the kind of boy that broke the rules," she signs with a chuckle.

I shrug. She's not wrong but she *is* the first girl I've ever brought up here.

Her eyes again scan along the walls. After a few seconds of drinking in the space, her smile softens as she signs, "This is really cool, Dean. Your family. Your home . . ."

My heart aches with everything she's *not* saying. It's still so hard to even imagine the way she grew up. She told me just a few nights ago about how through all the moves and essentially getting lost in "the system" she didn't even have access to language until she went to live with Wally and Doris and they taught her ASL. They're also the ones that put her in therapy.

And *God.* I wish I had been able to meet them—thank them for seeing how fucking amazing she is and taking care of her. It couldn't have been easy—taking in a traumatized kid—but I'm so grateful that somehow they found each other.

I'm so grateful we *found each other.*

I blink back to her, seeing a curious smile on her lips as she signs, "So, did you bring me up here for devious reasons or just to show off your fort? Full disclosure: either one will get you laid." She pulls on my shirt, pressing my body with hers.

I laugh, bending down to kiss her. It's soft, tender, filled with an anxiety that's been buzzing through me for the last couple hours.

When we pull apart, our breaths mix between our lips. I try to use her air to help ease my nerves and then press my forehead against hers. I need to keep my hands on her, so instead of signing, I move my hands down and lace our fingers together.

"I had a dream about you . . . a couple nights after we met."

She pulls her head back, a curiously playful glint catching in her eyes.

"Not *that* kind of dream," I chuckle. "I was on the ground. I think I was in the same alley as that bar where I hit the wall but I couldn't move. Ava wandered past me and almost walked into the street but . . . you picked her up and brought her back to me."

I had no idea what the dream meant the morning after. But it's clear to me now.

She brought me *back.*

She smiles, but then her eyes falter. "It had a happy ending . . . why do you look so sad?"

A heavy sigh releases and I press my forehead to hers once again. *Another breath. Another heartbeat.*

I swallow hard and finally tell her, "I think I need to go to Michigan, baby." I feel her wince before she pulls her head back, and stares up at me.

She doesn't say anything but I can see her trying to fight the deep wound in her eyes. Her throat works to swallow with a timid nod, her eyes processing.

"I can't *be* her dad from here, Amelia. Visits, summers . . . borrowed time. I just know that when she leaves, it'll ruin me and . . . it's too risky. Being far away and not actually *being* in her life feels like I'll be signing my fate to relapse again. There's always the chance, but this is something I can already predict will be too much."

Her eyes are glistening, filling with heartbreak but there's also a glimmer of awe shining in them. I pull her into me again, burying my nose in her hair. The smell of jasmine intensifies as a breeze sweeps through the treehouse. My eyes pull up to see my mom's jasmine flowers in full bloom through the window.

Another breath. Another heartbeat.

"Please come with me," I whisper.

Her body bumps against mine and she slowly unlatches herself, pulling away to look back up at me. "You . . . you want me to come with you?"

Jesus. How can she not know that she's the other half of my world?

I know everything between us has happened fast and out of order, but I'm certain—I know *implicitly* that I've never felt this way before.

It's pure, raw connection. Unintended and unanticipated.

But when she remains quiet, my heart starts to pick up, worried that I've somehow read this all wrong. I'm just about to tell her to at least think about it, but she finally sighs.

"I don't know, Roberts . . . that's a long car ride. We might need to get a hotel every twenty minutes."

The stutter in my chest makes me gasp. But it sounds like she's saying . . .

"I'll fucking walk you there, Amelia. I'll do *anything* to keep you."

She studies my face as another smile pulls at her lips. "You really mean that, don't you?" I nod and she sighs, dropping her chin to the ground before it pulls back up to me. "Beatrice is going to hate the suburbs."

My breath catches, still unsure if she's saying what I think she is so I force a shrug. "She hates everything, right?"

Amelia breathes a laugh. "Except you," she muses, her hand moving to my cheek as her expression shifts to something of pure bliss. She kisses me, whispering, "Yes," over and over again on my lips.

It's slow motion and lightspeed. It's crashing and soaring.

It's everything.

Our tongues tangle, knotting us together as I lift her up and she curls her legs around my back. Stars dance behind my eyelids, losing myself in her, breathing in her sweet breath.

I've felt like the shell of myself for *so long.* I've been fumbling around in the dark for over a decade just trying to find *something.*

And she's it.

My light.

My illuminating warmth. My fire.

And she's coming with me.

chapter forty

amelia

I t's been a while since I've come back here, and I picked a nice
day for it.

The sun is out and there's a refreshing, steady breeze in the air.
The light wind carries a distant smell, something I can only classify as
serene, while I take the small pathway and make my way to them.

After a few minutes of leisurely walking, I make it to their headstone. Settling down on the soft grass, I stare at the modest, marble
plaque in the ground. An involuntary smile pulls at lips as my finger
absentmindedly traces the engraved letters of their names and I push
out a heavy exhale.

Doris and Wally Adler. Beloved wife, beloved husband.

Their respective dates of birth and death are on it too, but I stare
at their names for long minutes—so long that they become slightly
blurry. Suddenly, the name *Cecilia James* passes through my mind and
my smile falls.

What would her plaque even say?

Would anyone even visit her gravesite?

I can't help but wonder if she's buried somewhere . . . maybe cremated.

I think I'll always wonder about her—how could I not? She was terrible, but she still made her mark on me.

Many marks.

And while I'll never know why, meeting Dean and at least learning about the inner workings of how addiction can manifest has helped a bit. I used to think my mom was soulless. That she didn't care about anything. But I wonder now if maybe she actually felt too much and used the alcohol to numb whatever it was.

A chill runs down my spine before I shake my head, letting out a heavy sigh. I'm trying to release her memory out of me, but I know it'll always be there—along with all the unanswered questions and reasons for why she was the way she was.

It won't make a difference.

Life is unexplainable. This is fact. Good or bad, some things just happen.

Like how I finally got lucky and ended up with them . . .

"Hey, guys," I sign, the hint of a smile pulling at my lips. "I know, it's been a minute."

I can picture the admonishing face Wally always gave me when I stayed away too long . . .

"Amelia," he signed, pleasantly surprised. "You don't call, you don't write."

I gave him a sheepish smile as he moved aside to let me come into the house.

My eyes drifted around the small, comfortable living room. There was some peace to the fact that it always looked the same. The big comfortable chair where Wally read at night, the various blankets that Doris crocheted draped over different parts of the furniture, never far from reach.

"Is she awake?" I signed.

He shook his head. "Afraid not, kiddo. It was . . . it was a tough night."

I swallowed hard, feeling even worse about not coming out to see them for the past month. I was working a lot, but to be honest, it was becoming difficult to come here. Doris was in such bad shape and it was painful to see.

I could only imagine how hard it was for Wally.

I tried to lighten the mood. "What's on the menu tonight?"

He shrugged, signing, "I don't know. Our girl hasn't had much of an appetite so . . . I don't have anything planned."

My heart sank. Things really must have been bad if Wally wasn't cooking. And here I was, keeping my distance because it was hard to see it all.

Selfish brat.

My muscles tightened as a heavy exhale pushed through my lips. I wanted to help, but I had no idea how. I usually just made things worse. Another beat passed before I peeked back up at him. "How about I make some of your famous meatballs?" I signed. "They're her favorite, and they'll keep. They'll be ready for her when she gets hungry."

The familiar, warm crease at the corners of his blue eyes returned as a slow smile pulled up his cheeks. "Great idea, Chef."

I gave him a closed mouth smile with a quick nod and shrugged out of my coat. Passing through the dining room, I made my way into their kitchen and got to work, moving through the cabinets, fridge, and pantry with ease.

Everything was still stocked, which gave me the smallest bit of comfort. They didn't have any ground beef, but there were two packages of ground chicken that would work just fine.

After I collected all of the ingredients, I started to make the mixture, adding milk and breadcrumbs to the consistency I knew Doris preferred.

"Meatballs should have a little crunch, don't you think?" Wally signed as he sidled up next to me.

I breathed a laugh. Doris always said that, but Wally and I vehemently disagreed with her. Still, this batch was for her, and I'd be damned if we didn't make them just the way she liked. I finished the mixture while Wally started on the sauce.

His shoulders relaxed a bit as he poured the tomatoes into the pot and then he minced the garlic with finesse. He eyeballed all of the seasoning, simply sniffing over the pot and dabbing his finger on the mixing spoon to taste.

I loved that he taught me how to cook. He took something that was a means of survival to me and made it into something beautiful. They both showed me the closest thing to love I had ever felt and a sudden, strong urge began to run through my veins.

My fingers were still coated in the meatball mixture, but I quickly ran them under the sink before I walked over to him, timidly wrapping my arms around his torso in a side hug.

His body pulsed with a surprised inhale. Not only was I not a hugger, but it was a weird time to hug someone. Even so, he wrapped one of his arms around my shoulders and leaned his cheek on the top of my head while his other hand kept a steady stir on the pot.

My eyes uncharacteristically misted; it just felt . . . nice, warm. I never knew my biological father—I'm not sure my mother even knew who he was—but this felt like something a dad would do with his daughter. An old tradition to bring us both comfort during a rough time.

We stayed like that for a long minute as the smell of Wally's sauce started to permeate through the kitchen. I finally unlatched from him and went back to the task at hand, rolling out thirty or so meatballs. Wally poured his sauce into the slow cooker and I carefully placed the meatballs in, one by one.

After we finished, he went to the bedroom to check on Doris, and I sat on the couch in the living room. My hands still felt busy from cooking and my fingers were itching to grab one of my favorite Doris blankets.

It was the big purple one draped over the arm of the couch. She made it with alpaca yarn, so it was extremely warm, but the texture was light and spongy. The yarn itself had a natural crimp, giving the blanket a wavy look. I finally pulled it over to my lap and ran my hands over it, letting all the fine hairs from the yarn tickle my skin as I intermittently wiggled my fingers between the small holes in the weaving.

A second later, Wally came back out, smiling as he signed, "The lady is awake and she's asking for you. Something about The Real Housewives of Atlanta?"

I snorted a laugh. That *sounded like the Doris I knew and loved. I quickly hopped up, keeping the blanket tucked in my arms as I went to her bedroom.*

I smile at the memory. "Doris, I'm not sure if Wally ever told you, but he let me keep that blanket," I sign. "It's taken permanent residency on my living room chair."

I'll keep it forever. It's a reminder of the first place that felt like home.

I clear my throat. "My mom died a few months ago and it was . . ." I trail off, unsure of exactly how to explain it, but there's only one word that comes to mind. "*Hard.* It was harder than I thought it would be and . . . I wish you guys had been here."

They just had a way of making the hard things easier.

A smile tilts my cheek, signing, "But I met someone . . ."

I could nearly see Doris's eyes light up, leaning in with her chin on her fist signing, "Tell me more . . ."

"He's in recovery. And he's got a bit of an anger issue," I sign.

I see them again, exchanging glances, silently agreeing that the money they spent on therapy went to shit.

A small chuckle escapes at the thought adding, "He has a daughter, Ava. She just turned one. And I love her too. He asked me to move away with them . . . and I said yes."

Their smiles pass through me, spreading warmth.

"I think I found my gibbon," I sign, as my eyes lightly fill.

God, I am not about this crying life.

I don't know if I broke some kind of barrier or something, but lately I cry at fucking everything. Just this morning I cried because I dropped half my bagel on the floor, and then I cried more when Dean gave me the other half of his.

I sniff again, signing, "So I probably won't be back here much. But I'll be bringing the blanket, Doris, and Wally, the Cubs hat will be coming with me too. Not to mention Beatrice, who has grown into the evil cat I always knew she would be, by the way."

Another teary laugh escapes, noticing a soft patch of dirt just beside their headstone.

It gives me an idea and my fingers dig a small but relatively deep hole. Once I'm done, I brush my fingers together to shake off the excess dirt before I move my hands behind my neck. I unclasp my necklace, twisting the lightning bolt pendant in my fingers for an extra second before I place it in the hole. My fingers move slowly to cover it up, keeping my hand there for a few moments after it's covered.

I don't know what possesses me to do it. But wherever they are, I hope they can see.

I just want to leave a piece of me with them, since I feel like there will always be a piece of them with me. They're the heartbeat of everything good that's ever happened to me and . . . things are good.

"I'm good," I sign. "Thanks to you. I'm good."

chapter forty-one

dean

one month later

I'm in Amelia's kitchen, trying to finish the remainder of my coffee as my phone buzzes from the breakfast bar and I see that it's my mom. *Again.*

She's called me *four times* this morning and it's not even ten.

"Yes?" I answer, out of patience.

"Dean Margaret Roberts, do not take that tone with me."

I huff a laugh. "Why do I always get the girl names?"

She ignores my question. "I just wanted to remind you to bring that soap for Ava. We don't have any at our house."

Right. The soap. How tragic that would have been.

Today's Otis and Evelyn's wedding, and Ava is staying with my parents for a couple days. They took the news of moving pretty hard and asked if they could take her for a night or two before we leave for Michigan and it makes the most sense that it's tonight since they'll already be in Chicago.

"I'll grab it when I go pick up Ava," I tell her, taking my final sip of coffee, though I'm wondering if I should make another pot if this is the kind of "fun" today will bring.

"Okay. We'll see you in an hour or so?"

"I'm sure I'll talk to you before then," I say dryly and she hangs up on me.

I sigh while walking back to the bedroom. Pushing through the door, I see Amelia on the bed, petting a curled up Beatrice next to her and I can't help the smile from inching up my cheeks.

Beauty encapsulated.

She's not dressed for the wedding yet, but her long dark hair hangs over her shoulders, softly curled, and the green color of her eyes is even more vibrant from the dusting of bronze eyeshadow. And of course, the red lipstick is making her lips look all the more inviting. She peeks over at me and the corner of her mouth quirks up.

A softness blankets my chest. She looks . . . nervous.

I think the stress of the move is weighing on her a bit. The past month has been spent finding a community college where she can finish her interpreting degree, and last weekend we took a trip out to a little lakeside town to look at some houses up for rent.

The town is about twenty minutes away from where Marnie and Shaun will be, and Amelia fell in love with a small cottage by the river. The second I saw the covered back porch with twinkly lights, I knew it was as good as done. So there's no doubt in my mind that she wants to go—but I think packing up her apartment has been a bit overwhelming. And I've discovered that everything she owns has a sentimental attachment, so it's all coming with us.

Even a goldfish bowl. Sans goldfish.

Plus, she had to tell Luke she was moving yesterday and she spent the afternoon a weepy mess.

I move toward her at the foot of the bed, lowering my face to hers and kissing her rosy cheek. "You look beautiful, baby."

My palm cradles her jaw and I can feel some tension fall, but she swallows again before she says, "Thank you."

I was going to wait till later for this, but she seems like she could use a little pick-me-up. I crouch down in front of her, pushing some of her hair off her shoulder. "I got you something."

Her eyes smile before her mouth follows as she looks up at me, signing, "A present?"

Could she be any cuter?

The nearly giddy expression makes my chest ache as I nod. I walk over to the bag I packed up for today, pulling out the small box before walking back over and sitting down next to her on the bed. Beatrice is instantly annoyed by the extra dip in the mattress and stands up, shaking her tortoiseshell coat before she hops down and trots out of the room.

"She's just jealous," Amelia signs and I chuckle.

I hand her the box and she takes it carefully from my hands, just staring at it for a moment. In an attempt to give her some ease, I tuck her hair behind her ear, whispering, "There's something inside it, ya know."

She peeks up at me, fighting a smirk, before she glances back down at the box and slowly opens it.

She gasps and her eyes widen as she looks down at it with pure wonderment.

It's nothing extravagant. It's just a necklace. It's gold with a round pendant and in the middle there's a lightning bolt lightly etched on it.

I found a jeweler that was able to transfer my simple drawing onto the gold and I thought she'd like it. Her teary eyes tell me I was right, which almost makes me nervous to tell her, "Turn it over."

She flips the pendant over and sees the words I had the jeweler put on the back in my handwriting:

My Amelia

Her hand covers her mouth and she cries.

No, she *sobs*.

I pull her into me, kissing her hair. "It was supposed to cheer you up, not turn you into a puddle," I tease, rubbing her back.

She sniffs, breathing a small laugh as she shakes her head and looks back up at me, wiping her eyes. "I love it."

Her lips fall to mine as my thumb brushes her jaw. We lose ourselves in each other's mouths for a few moments, breathing one another in before I pull back.

"May I?" I take the box from her, pulling the necklace out.

She eagerly nods, pulling her hair off to the side and turning away from me. I hold the chain between my fingers and then fasten the clasp behind her neck, pressing a kiss to her nape after it's secured. Goosebumps domino down her neck before her shoulders expand with a deep breath.

Just as another second passes, she turns around and pounces on me. I chuckle against her lips as she essentially eats my face. Her tongue plunges through my mouth and tangles with mine, ebbing and flowing in the most consuming way.

Hers.

She pushes me back so that I'm lying flat on the mattress while she grinds herself on top of me, stirring a low rumble in my chest.

I guess we're going to be late.

But fuck it if I care. It's hard to care about anything when I've got a goddess looking to worship, rubbing herself on top of me.

As she pulls her tank top up and over her head, my hands instinctively roam up her torso and cup her breasts.

God. I'll never not *love her aversion to undergarments.*

My thumbs brush over her nipples and she whimpers as the skin peaks under my fingers. I move one hand up to the chain of the necklace, hooking my finger around it and gently tugging it to lower her face back to mine.

"So this is a collar, then?" she laughs.

My dick twitches at the idea, again surprising me that it seems like something I'd be totally into. But I think it's just her. She brought me back to life in so many ways but *this* was the first one. She reawakened *this* part of me first and I'll do anything and everything with her.

My smile widens, but I shake my head. "No, but we can get one of those if you want."

She tugs her lip between her teeth, giving a small suggestive shrug before I flip her so that she's beneath me and then my mouth is everywhere.

Lips, neck, chest.

I tug one of her nipples between my teeth, giving her a soft bite and she whimpers. My lips trail to the other one as she breathlessly says, "Oh, Dean . . . please."

I groan as I start to work on her pants, pulling them down slowly and then inching my way back up by kissing the inside of her leg. I spread her wider, like a fucking display as my eyes roam everywhere.

Smooth olive skin, her perfect pink nipples—her desperate green eyes.

It happens. The language that only we know passes between our eyes. She's looking for escape—from what I'm not sure—but *this* is how we get lost before we find whatever it is.

"What's the word?" I sign.

"Lightning."

In an instant, I flip her on her stomach, ordering her on her hands and knees and she obliges immediately, pressing her palms into the mattress as her back arches while her gorgeous breasts hang below.

I kiss the beauty mark on her ass and then give it a small bite, making her yelp before I move to her side. My eyes feast on her trembling body, aching with need as I move my hand between her legs, groaning when I find a pool of wetness between them.

"Fuck," I rasp, pushing my finger into her and watching her hips immediately start to move against my hand. "That's it, baby," I praise, as my other hand moves to her hair and pushes the fallen strands to her back, watching as her eyes lose themselves in my touch.

She whimpers and my dick jumps while her hips greedily grind. I add another finger and she gasps as I hook my free hand under her chin. "God, you look so sweet like this. On all fours and just fucking taking what you need." Just as she moans I stuff my thumb in her mouth and she sucks it feverishly. Our eyes are connected, snapped together in a passionate charge.

It's fucking amazing.

She's amazing.

My dick is so hard, it hurts—watching her hump shamelessly against my hand. My thumb thwarts her climbing moans as my fingers steadily pump between her legs.

"Do you want to come on my hand or on my cock, Amelia?"

She moans again as her eyes roll back. When she doesn't answer, I stop moving my hand and she whines.

"Be a good girl and use your words. What do you want?"

Her hips wiggle against my hand desperately as she whimpers, "Cock, please," but it's garbled by my thumb still filling her mouth. I can feel her walls tightening on my fingers so I pull them out along with my thumb. Yanking my pants and boxers down, I move behind her and settle on my knees. My lips press the base of her spine and kiss my way up until I meet her jaw.

"I love you," I whisper as her eyes meet mine.

There's something deep in her eyes right now. I can't quite decipher it behind the cloud of lust but I know it's there.

"I love you too, Roberts," she breathes. "Now fuck me, please."

A dark chuckle rattles in my throat.

Anything for my girl who begs.

Instantly, I slam into her, unapologetically moaning at her tight warmth clenching around me.

Holy fucking God. So good.

She almost came *immediately.* I can already feel the flutter of her walls pulsing and it spurs me on more. My fingers drag up her spine and then curl around her throat from behind, pulling her upright so that she's sitting on me while I pump into her, deep and hard, from below.

"God, fuck," I hiss, pulling myself out and then thrusting back in.

Foreheads pressed, eyes fused, lost in an ecstasy of our own making.

"Dean," she gasps, as her arm hooks behind my neck.

"That's it, baby. Let go," I grit between my teeth. Her green eyes shine with desperation right in front of mine. "Hold onto me and let go."

A cry rips from her throat and vibrates against my hand. The sound spills into my mouth as her walls shudder in waves around me and it's my undoing.

It only takes three more pumps before a deep, animalistic groan releases and my dick throbs and empties inside her, filling her with my climax and she rides it out with me, scraping her fingernails through the base of my scalp.

It's rough and smooth.
Flawed and perfect.
Mine and hers.

We managed to only be a half hour late. And even that didn't really matter because it took Otis and me all of ten minutes to get changed. I'm walking back into the library after my quick errand, holding the bag from Portillo's in my hand.

Pushing through the door to the small room the library gave us to get ready, I find Otis sitting on one of the brown leather chairs. "I've got the goods," I sign, clutching the Portillo's bag and raising it up.

"Fuck yeah!" he chants.

I toss the bag on the small table, signing, "Reggie caught me on my way in and gave strict instructions to change out of our shirts. Something about how you eat like you've lived underground for a decade," I chuckle.

Otis's eyes squint, appearing offended, but then he concedes with a nod. He peels off his shirt and drapes it over the back of the couch and then changes into the T-shirt he came here in and I do the same.

We settle into the chairs before I sign, "Where are Mom and Dad?"

Otis takes a bite of his hot dog. "Mom went to the girls' room and Dad went to check out the garden."

I nod before digging in myself. We eat in comfortable silence and I lose myself to a minute or so of nostalgia. Thinking about that day we came here—well, *snuck* out to the city for the day.

I'm going to miss Chicago. It holds so many memories and a lot of them—good and bad—are with my brother.

I take a break from shoveling food for a second, signing, "Hey, I've got something for you."

It seems as good of a moment as any to do this since we're alone. I wipe my hands on a napkin before I dig through my bag. Otis almost blows it and wipes his palms on his pants, but then grabs a handful of napkins on the table as I hold the gift out to him.

His eyebrows pinch as he takes it, his eyes immediately widening when he sees what it is.

"*Signed, Retribution*?!" he signs, shocked.

I smile, signing, "New and improved," as my eyes drift down to the comic.

I was able to dig out the old one when we were at our parents' house last month for Ava's birthday. I redid the illustrations so that Retribution looks like him and Vera looks like Evelyn. And Retribution is now a writer who met Vera at her coffee shop. I basically merged the comic with *their* story.

"Oh my God," Otis says. "Cub-Cub!" I laugh, nodding. He pages through it, his smile widening. "Dean, this is . . ." he trails off, shaking his head.

My chest warms and tightens at his reaction. I'm glad he loves it, but I'm also just . . . so fucking grateful we made it *here*. That we somehow recovered from all of the bullshit and I'm sitting here with him today.

That I'm not *pretending* to be happy for him.

I am so fucking happy for him.

He's the best guy I know and he deserves every bit of happiness he's found with her. That's always been true, but I genuinely *feel* it today.

He looks up at me, smiling, but there's a curious glint to his eyes. "You're drawing again?"

I nod. "It started with a therapy assignment. But then I just kind of . . . kept going."

Otis smirks, signing, "I'm sure a certain green-eyed girl has something to do with it, too," before he starts to look through the comic again.

I breathe a laugh, shrugging.

He's not wrong.

Love is a force to be fucking reckoned with. It *demands* all of you, and I think that's why we miss the mark sometimes. Sometimes we're not in a position to give all of ourselves, but we try anyway.

And I think that's what makes it all the more powerful when things fall into place. It's an action that can only be set in motion when we're truly ready for it, and when it does, we need to hold on tight and prepare to meet every part of ourselves at its center.

I've painfully unraveled myself back to my core because to be anything less than what Amelia deserves would be a failure I'm *unwilling* to fall to—and I think the same can be said about what my brother has with Evelyn.

Otis closes the comic and looks back up at me. "I'm really proud of you, Dean." He raises the comic appreciatively. "Thank you for this."

He stands up and I do too as he pulls me in for a hug. The moment our palms reach each other's back, I feel a snap. It's the quickest flash of shoves and high-fives, late night talks in the treehouse, laughing and tears—it's like all of the moments live on a retractable line and they just zipped back to us.

Suddenly, the door to the room opens and I pull back from Otis, seeing Reggie slink inside. He's smiling, but it's void of any mischief as he catches our embrace. Another beat passes and the deviance returns to his expression.

"Change the shirts, boys. It's almost showtime."

chapter forty-two
amelia

J esus, *feck*, love! You look breathtaking," Mary says, as she stares at Evelyn in her wedding dress. I've only known Mary since last night, but I'm pretty sure I'm obsessed with her. I guess she used to work with Evelyn at her coffee shop, but today she's the officiant at their wedding. And I'm not gonna lie . . . I would *love it* if she somehow dropped a "feck" during the ceremony.

She's right, though. Evelyn looks absolutely stunning. Her dress is a simple off-white gown with a light wildflower pattern woven into the bodice, while the skirt flows whimsically down her waist to the floor. Her long, wavy brown hair is billowing over her shoulders, partly tucked just behind her ear with a vintage comb adorned with some green Tahitian pearls.

We're using a small room just down the hall from the ceremony space, and I'm holding Ava on my lap while Mary and Evelyn's mom help Reggie put the finishing touches on Evelyn.

"Bride management," as Reggie says.

I lean my cheek into Ava. "Doesn't Aunt Evelyn look pretty?" I whisper, squeezing her a bit and she squeals.

I kept her with me since we're doing "girl time" in here, while the boys get ready down the hall. Plus, I need some Ava time. I've been in my head all morning and my stomach is in knots.

"Amelia!" Reggie calls, making me jerk.

I blink over at him and he raises a champagne flute toward me, offering me a glass, but I shake my head. My eyes float down at Ava who is tugging at the tulle material of her sage green dress. When she peeks back up at me, I rub my nose with hers, making her giggle, just as Mary plops down beside me, sighing as she continues to look over at Evelyn.

After another beat, she turns to face Ava and me, extending her hand out. Ava grabs onto her fingers as a soft smile inches up her cheeks. "Such a beauty."

I run my hand over Ava's curls, nodding. "Yes, she is. I see high-blood pressure for her dad in the future."

Mary huffs a laugh, taking a sip of her champagne. "Oh, I'm sure he'll be just fine." There's a slight edge to her voice and I imagine it's because she's not the biggest Dean fan. And don't get me wrong, even though I love the guy with all my heart, I *do* find it kind of hysterical that she used to give him a hard time.

She's loyal.

"You and Evelyn are close, huh?" It's dumb question. I mean, she's officiating their wedding, but I'm mostly asking to make conversation—keeping my mind occupied.

She nods. "Never had kids myself, but she might as well be mine. I grew up in Ireland—foster care—so I'm a big believer in the family we make for ourselves."

My eyebrows hitch, surprised. I swallow before I tell her, "I— uhh . . . I was a foster kid too."

Mary's eyebrow cocks over her ocean blue eyes. "Were ya now?"

I nod. "I never really had the 'found family' thing, though. I did *love* the people I lived with right before I moved out on my own." A small pang swells in my chest thinking about Doris and Wally.

God. I wish they were here.

Mary smiles, her eyes drifting down to Ava before they meet mine, again. "Call me crazy, love, but it seems like you *did* find a family."

I hug Ava tightly to me, breathing her in, letting the soft hint of honey and citrus fill my nose and I smile.

I think I found more.

A tilted smile pulls up my cheek as I glance over at Mary. "You're kind of wise, you know that?"

She chuckles with a nod. "Why do you think they're giving me the microphone today?"

Wow.

I can't believe this room exists in a library. It almost feels like we're outside. The ceiling is made of glass so the room is showered with natural light, and there's live greenery draped along the wall.

I've never been to a wedding before and obviously, I never gave much thought to a wedding of my own because I never expected to fall in love but . . . I think this is the way to do it. Just a small gathering in a pretty place.

My eyes are glued to Dean as he stands next to Otis, holding Ava. And I'm trying not to melt into a puddle on the floor. He looks *so damn good.* His wavy brown hair is perfectly tousled, but it's his dreamy ass smile peeking out from his copper-colored scruff that has my heart fluttering. Not to mention the way his brown vest fits him perfectly with the green tie that will live in infamy.

The ceremony is short and sweet and Mary, as expected, is quite the master of ceremonies. I'm pretty impressed with her signing too. She's admitted that she's not fluent, but she learned how to sign everything she's saying today and, to me, that shows just how much she loves the two of them.

"You both know I'm not much of a romantic," Mary says. "But watching the two of you finally find each other and hold on tight has been a gift. A gift I'll cherish forever. It's a beautiful love that existed long before this day and will continue past our time on Earth. It's a love made by the heart itself. Tá mo chroí istigh ionat." My eyebrows pinch—*no idea what that means*—but Mary quickly clarifies, "It's a Gaelic phrase that means, 'my heart is in you.'"

She chokes up a bit but quickly shakes her head and Evelyn smiles adoringly at her. She takes a deep breath before she says, "I'm honored to pronounce you husband and wife," and then gives a soft elbow nudge to Otis. "Kiss her and live happily ever after, love."

Evelyn and Otis kiss and my eyes float to Dean again, smiling brightly at them, spreading a warmth through me.

I feel so much right now. Mary's words from earlier are still coursing through me, becoming me. The only thing crazier than the idea of falling in love was the idea that I might have a family one day.

I never really had one and somehow I think that morphed into a belief that I wasn't *supposed* to have one. But when I really think about it, *that's* what I've longed for my entire life. It's at the core of my resentment for my mother—that among everything else she did to me, she denied me the chance to feel like I belong.

I think I had some semblance of it with Doris and Wally, but I was still too caught up in the belief that I didn't deserve it to fully fall into place with them.

Hell, I even think I tried to make it work with Beatrice.

But with Dean and Ava . . . I know I've found my place in this world.

Dean's eyes find mine as everyone starts to stand and I feel my eyes misting.

"I love you," he mouths.

My smile widens and my heart quickens as I sign, "Same, Roberts. Same."

This day has been . . . overwhelming to say the least, but I'm just trying to muscle my way through it. Ava has been a good distraction. She's currently playing with my face as I feel Dean come up behind us.

Ava's smiling wide at him and I hear him say, "My girls," as he leans over my shoulder and peppers kisses over Ava's face, spurring some giggles. I laugh too, just before I feel his cheek against mine, right next to my ear. "Dance with me."

Oof. That voice. He could narrate a maintenance manual and I'd listen to every word.

A chill runs down my spine before I hand Ava off to Dean's mom and follow him to the small dance floor.

"Just remember you love me," I warn. "Even when I'm breaking your toes."

He chuckles, "I can live without toes," moving one of his hands to my lower back while the other one holds mine between us, over his chest. I ineptly move my free hand to his shoulder, but then slide it a little higher so I can run my hand over his jaw, letting my fingernails sift through his stubble.

He gave me this. He saw something broken in me and he didn't ignore it—he didn't even try to fix it per se—he just replaced it with himself.

My eyes pool as his eyebrows pinch, pushing some hair from my forehead. "What's going on in that beautiful head?"

I blink and a tear falls, which he quickly swipes away. Among all the other things he's become, "tear catcher" has been something he's dutifully done a lot lately. I wanted to wait until after the wedding for this, but I just can't hold it in anymore.

"I-I'm pregnant."

Dean stops swaying us. His eyes widen down at me and my heart starts to pound wildly in my chest. His mouth actually drops but the corners pull up as he shakes his head. "How? I mean . . . I thought you were on the pill."

My knees are shaking as I nod. "Doctor says it's uncommon, but it happens. Something like—seven percent chance."

We're no longer dancing, just holding each other. I can feel him shaking a bit, but he's gripping my waist tight as his eyes lock with mine, his smile widening. "Seven percent . . ." he muses.

I breathe a nervous laugh. I'm relieved that he knows now—that he can swim in this anxiety pool with me.

Because I'm terrified.

Suddenly, his lips crash against mine. My tightened body melts into his touch as he cradles my cheeks and tenderly kisses me. My hands move to his and my thumbs brush the back of his hands as he continues to hold my face.

"You're gonna be the most amazing mom, baby," he murmurs between our lips and I cry into his mouth.

Fucking hormones.

I have a feeling we're making a scene, but I can't even be worried about it. I need him to keep touching me. I need his words.

"Y-You really think so?" I finally ask, still trying to get my weeping under control.

His eyes shift back and forth between mine before he takes my hand and quickly leads me out into the hall. It's darker out here, but at least it's a bit more private since I decided to just blurt the news out in the most public setting possible.

Dean sits me down in the chair near the door and then kneels in front of me before he signs, "I don't think. I know."

My chest tightens. But the fear is still rattling my limbs as he brings my hand to his lips and kisses it. Another few moments pass as he stares back at me before he murmurs, "*She* was the mess, Amelia. You're the magic."

I gasp through another sob before I fall into him, draping my arms around his neck while he holds me back. I didn't have to tell him the fear out loud. He just knew. He has this inexplicable way of knowing exactly what I need and he gives it to me, no questions asked.

"Seven percent," he whispers again against my hair. "That's not *uncommon*, that's . . . that *is* fucking magic."

Seven. The most powerful magical number.

Another small sob escapes at the thought, his words—it quite literally takes my breath away, but a new sense of ease finds me in his arms.

I was used to being a statistic, but they were all unfortunate ones. Ones that made me feel unlucky—doomed. And if this had happened with anyone else, it might have felt the same way.

But it's with him.

I'm carrying *our* baby.

A timid wave of calm rushes over me as he pulls back and then kisses me again.

When our lips finally pull apart, I stare back into his coffee-colored eyes and run my hand through his wavy, chestnut hair, feeling every *bit* of the magic staring back at me.

I've wondered how I was able to fall so hard and so fast for him. But I think that growing up feeling unloved and unwanted actually made it all the more obvious that he was something to hold on to. It's almost as if I had always been looking for him without even knowing it, and finding someone who sees and knows the messiest parts of your soul is the most comforting thing in the world because anything life throws at me has to get through him too.

My hand instinctively runs over my stomach as I keep my eyes locked with his.

And I'll never be alone again.

He pulls away from me, running his thumb along my bottom lip before a small chuckle escapes. "So I guess it's safe to say that we don't do things in order."

Something between a sigh and laugh pushes past my lips as he pulls me back into him, holding me tight.

He's right. I've been too caught up in my anxiety to think about it, but somehow it makes perfect sense that he knocked me up *before* we moved away together.

We *are* out of order.

We don't draw the map in life but we're expected to live on it, navigate it—reroute.

And the love between Dean and I *is* a reroute. I never expected to feel this way about someone—a man that is quite literally a combination of everything I've spent my whole life running from—but I think that's telling in and of itself.

We're bigger than one part of ourselves, one instance, one mistake. And I think it's easy to forget that sometimes, especially when we're in the thick of our despair. Our brains have a nasty way of convincing us that this is how it will always be—that we're doomed to be unhappy or in pain forever.

But we're not—not if we don't choose to lose ourselves in the darkness. Sometimes, something as simple as meeting a stranger one night—in a bar you never go to—in a bar he should never have been in, can change the trajectory of your whole existence. Small, unexpected and unplanned things can add and multiply and carry over into something bigger.

A seven percent chance.

Dean stands, and pulls me up with him, smiling down at me as he signs, "Let's go tell Ava."

Oh, God. The tears again.

She's a baby and obviously won't understand but . . . we're giving her a little brother or sister.

A family.

I work to swallow the emotion before I smirk. "I think I'll keep you, Roberts."

He smiles down at me in the dreamy way that makes my knees buckle. "You don't have a choice, James. I'm yours. Now, come on."

He pulls me back toward the room and I laugh, signing, "So bossy."

His expression turns softly deviant. "You like it when I'm bossy."

Leading me back through the room, I keep my eyes fused on him, smiling, beaming, with me on his arm.

My gibbon.

epilogue

amelia

four years later

The Chicago skyline comes into view and I twist toward the back seat. "All right, babes, we're approaching. What do we want?"

Ava and Alice squeal, "T. Swift!" in unison and I laugh.

It's become our tradition when we go on trips. The girls get to pick the music for the last leg of the journey and Dean slowly caves in on himself.

It's highly amusing.

His exasperated sigh from the driver's seat makes me giggle. "I'm sorry, Roberts. You got a problem?"

"Yeah, Daddy. You got a problem?" Ava says, mimicking *my* attitude.

Alice wiggles in her car seat, saying, "Prooooooblem," making the rest of us crack up, including Dean. I hit the play button on my phone and Taylor Swift's "Shake it Off" starts to play through the speakers as my little Swifties in the backseat start scream-singing.

Dean sighs, "I don't know why I try. I'm outnumbered."

"If it makes you feel any better, I think Beatrice is pissed too," I tell him, peeking to the back seat.

She is. She's sitting with slow-blinking eyes between the girl's car seats, her expression reminiscent of Scar in *The Lion King* when he claims to be "surrounded by idiots."

I breathe a laugh, looking back at Dean before I run my hand through his wavy brown hair, giving it an affectionate tug before leaning over and kissing his cheek. The poor guy *does* live in a "girl house" after all, and the three of us show him absolutely no mercy.

After we moved to Michigan a few years ago, we started a yearly tradition of coming back to Chicago for a couple of weeks in the summer to spend time with Evelyn and Otis. Needless to say, it's helped with my anxiety in the car. And the girls love their baby cousin, Oliver.

Evelyn and Otis were having a tough time getting pregnant, so a couple of years ago, they decided to go the adoption route and it made me love them even more. Dean and I are looking into it too, but it's a little more complicated since we're not actually married.

Marriage isn't something I'm opposed to, of course. We're obviously committed to each other. It's just not at the forefront of our minds. I was busy trying to finish up school and then Alice was born. We have Ava half the time too, and between work and two little ones, we're plenty busy.

"Are you gonna see Luke while we're here?"

I nod. "Annie's gonna bring him to the cookout tomorrow."

Dean nods, a small smirk pulling up his cheek and my eyebrows pinch. "What?"

He shrugs. "Nothing."

It most certainly is *not* nothing. This I know. But I get distracted by Ava yelling, "Me-me, why aren't you singing?!"

I laugh, feeling my chest tighten at her sweet little voice and the name she gave me a couple of years ago. I turn back toward her and say, "Daddy's not singing either," before peeking up at Dean.

See? No mercy.

His chest rises and falls with a heavy sigh before he drops his chin, turning up the music. And then he sings, loudly, obnoxiously, "Haters gonna hate hate hate!" And the girls lose their minds, as do I. We spend the remaining ten minutes in the car rocking out.

Family style.

This house is bursting at the seams with life right now. Otis was picked up by a traditional publisher, and his books are on best sellers' lists week after week, so they've upgraded from an apartment to a nice townhome by the lake.

The kids are all in the living room, chasing each other around and tackling Dean while Otis helps me in the kitchen, and I honestly have no idea where Evelyn is at the moment.

I'm gathering the ingredients to make macaroni and cheese as Otis scoops some buffalo chicken dip onto a cracker. I hand him the milk and cheese signing, "Hey, you're supposed to be helping, not snacking."

His eyebrows pinch, making an "ooo" shape with his mouth. "I only signed on to help so that I could snack."

I huff a laugh. "Start to melt the butter. Once it's melted, add two cups of milk. You need to stir it constantly so that it doesn't burn. Once it's lightly boiling, that's when you add the cheese."

He sighs. "I regret my decision."

I snort another laugh as I pour the noodles into the boiling water when I suddenly see Dean carrying Oliver and *God*, he is so stinkin' cute. He's got chocolate brown hair and light blue eyes, while his T-shirt rides up his pudgy little belly. Ava and Alice are hooked around each of Dean's legs and he says, "I'm gonna take the maniacs out back. Try to burn off some energy."

If the sight of him dripping with kids isn't the sexiest goddamn thing, I don't know what is. My lip tugs between my teeth and Otis quickly signs, "Tell you what. Amelia has a super easy job that doesn't at all sound like torture. I'll take the kids out back while you help her."

Dean and I are caught in our trance as Otis takes Oliver from his arms. He lightly shoves Dean's shoulder before he signs, "Do not have sex in my kitchen," pointing at him to emphasize his point.

"What's *that* sign, Uncle Otis?" Ava signs, mimicking the sign for "sex," still slightly latched to her dad's leg.

Great.

Otis drops his chin, giving me an apologetic glance before he switches the subject. "Come on girls, let's go set up the blow-up pool." The sign is quickly forgotten as they unhook themselves from Dean and Otis takes Alice's hand while Ava races out the back door.

I cross my arms over my chest, shaking my head. "You have no business looking like a fucking snack, Roberts. I'm trying to cook here."

He saunters over, a chestnut wave sweeping to his forehead while his gray T-shirt falls perfectly, outlining the cut lines of his biceps, as he pulls me into him.

I giggle. "Hey, fiend. You heard your brother. No sex in the kitchen."

"I was never one for rules," he rasps, his lips pressing the soft spot below my ear. I laugh again, but we're quickly interrupted by Evelyn walking into the kitchen, making an awkward "uhh" sound as she catches us.

"Sorry," she says quickly, then shifts. "Actually, no. This is my kitchen. Not sorry, and Dean—I need to show you . . . something."

My eyebrows pinch as Dean's chin drops defeatedly before he looks back over at her. "Is it a bug?"

She pulls her lips into her mouth, rocking on her heels. "It *might* be a bug."

I snort a laugh as Dean sighs, giving me a quick peck before following Evelyn down the hall.

"Me do it!" Oliver says to Evelyn as she tries to feed him.

"You know what? Have at it, kid." She hands him his T-shirt and lets him struggle through trying to dress himself, signing, "He did it once before and suddenly he's Mr. Independent."

I laugh. "Alice was the same way."

Evelyn got back to the house about an hour ago and we relieved Otis of kid duty so that he and Dean could go play video games for a bit before dinner.

"How's everything going with work?" she signs.

"Good. It's a process. There's no real policies in place as far as interpreting is concerned. So it's a lot of research and keeping an eye out for homes with kids that need an interpreter. But I love it."

Evelyn nods, signing, "It's so cool that you ended up helping in the foster system. You're gonna change so many lives."

Honestly, what she's doing is amazing in its own right, too. She's been working with a theater to help employ deaf artists, produce more deaf-friendly shows. She's building a team of interpreters so that hearing audiences can enjoy them, too.

The deaf community is a severely marginalized group, so anything people can do to be more inclusive is a step in the right direction.

Evelyn finally helps Oliver into his shirt. He wiggles in her arms as she gives him a kiss on the nose and then he hugs her tightly around the neck before he pulls back and signs, "Popsicle?"

She laughs, saying, "Ah, so you were buttering me up with that hug," then signs, "You can have a popsicle after dinner." She signs it slowly but he stares blinking at her. "After dinner," she signs, again.

He shoves out a pouty lip as Ava yells, "Oliver, come on! We need to save Alice!"

Alice is holding onto Ava's hands on the slide and Oliver clumsily runs toward them, making Evelyn and I laugh.

"They're so cute," she signs, just as Dean and Otis traipse back outside. "That was quick!" she signs to them.

Otis shrugs, leaning down to kiss Evelyn. "We didn't want to miss out on the fun out here."

Evelyn smirks as Otis takes the empty chair next to her, but Dean stays standing as he runs his fingers through my hair. "Take a walk with me?"

My eyebrows pinch, signing, "Uhh—Annie will be here any minute with Luke and I've gotta start getting the rest of dinner ready."

"It won't take long," Dean signs.

"Reggie will be here soon," Evelyn signs. "We can put him on kitchen duty till you get back."

My mouth pulls up. *Subtle, guys.*

I can't be exactly sure what Dean's little lakeside walk is about, but I have my suspicions. It's July seventh—the anniversary date we gave ourselves a few years back. It's the day we moved into our house in Michigan.

We walk silently for a few seconds as the refreshing breeze from the lake pulls around us. He slides his fingers through mine, holding my hand before he steps in front of me.

"You know why we're out here already, don't you?" he says.

I smirk, shrugging. "Are you about to kill me?"

He snorts a laugh, shaking his head. "I'm going to pretend you didn't just ask me about murder when I was about to make a grand, romantic gesture."

"Hey, they say Ted Bundy was quite charming," I sign back at him.

He deadpans. "Amelia, stop talking about serial killers. I'm trying to propose."

It doesn't matter that I was suspecting that's why he brought me out here. It still makes me gasp in surprise. The humor and silliness dissipates as he lowers himself down to one knee, keeping my hand in his. "Since the moment I met you, I was yours. And you, our girls, you're my everything. I hope that you'll do me the honor of being my wife too."

He barely gets the words out before I fall to my knees in front of him, kissing him madly—deeply. I kiss him until I can't feel my lips anymore. He finally pulls back. "So I guess that's a yes?"

I nod frantically with a laugh as a happy tear slides from the corner of my eye. He quickly brushes it away and then pulls the ring out of his pocket. It's a simple rose gold band with one single diamond in the center, surrounded by a couple of brown and green sapphires. It kind of looks like a jasmine flower.

And it's perfect.

Just like him.

He slides the ring over my finger and I stare down at it in awe, feeling every bit of beauty surround me.

This man has given me everything and more. He's taken every broken piece of me and stitched an existence I never could have imagined for myself. When we met five years ago, I wanted so badly to not be that sad, scared little girl anymore.

But I think she'll always be there. She's a part of me. We don't get to pick and choose the pieces of ourselves. But if we're lucky—like really, really fucking lucky—we can find someone that sees all of our pieces and loves us anyway. Someone that takes them and molds them into something beautiful, something *more*.

I *am* that sad, scared little girl. I *am* broken.

But I'm more than I was because of him.

And now I get to be Amelia Roberts. *The woman who lived.*

the end

detention

rockford, il, 2000

The boy's regular desk awaited him, beckoning him like a friend saving your seat at lunch.

He always found his way back to "prison," as he called it.

Today, it was because he sucker-punched some moron in the cafeteria for making fun of how his brother talked. He'd decided it was worth it. The kid had it coming and the boy had no tolerance for bullshit.

As he settled at his desk, he took out his small notebook, preparing to kill the hour drawing, when a girl he didn't recognize walked into the classroom.

It was a little unusual. While Lincoln Middle School was big, the detention crew typically included the same group of delinquents—all there to think about their wrongdoings, all the while knowing they'd be there again soon enough.

What a joke.

Still, he was a regular, and newcomers always seemed to stand out.

Especially her.

The boy thought she was really pretty. She had long, inky black hair, and eyes as green as a jade stone.

Her eyes flicked up to him, and he smiled just as she sat at the desk in front of him.

He spent the whole hour of detention trying to work up the courage to tap her on the shoulder and ask her name.

A couple of other kids whispered nearby, wondering who she was, but she seemed completely unbothered, as though she hadn't even heard them. It looked like she was reading a book, but he couldn't see which since he was behind her.

The hour ended.

He hoped next time he ended up here, she would be too.

He hoped next time, he'd say something to her.

But there was never a next time. The boy never saw the girl again.

Well . . . not until many years later, that is. And by the time they saw each other, neither one remembered that day in detention.

author's note

Dear Reader,

Phew! I'm glad we made it.

About halfway through writing *in our hands,* I knew I *had* to write Dean's story. What started as a very one-dimensional character in Evelyn and Otis's love story became someone I deeply empathized with and I just needed to give him a happily ever after.

Writing this book was a completely different experience for me than writing *in our hands.* Where I felt like *in our hands* essentially wrote itself, I truly felt like I had to *find* this story. And it was "fun" writing three drafts of it and then scrapping them because I *found* them wrong. (You can't see me, but my face is the "ugh" emoji.)

But it was worth it. One thing I constantly strive to do with my writing is finding authentic, real people and I think sometimes that just takes time.

I really loved exploring Amelia's use of her hearing aids. Her hearing loss and the use of ASL was a little different than *in our hands,* and I loved finding that part of her.

Unlike Otis, Amelia didn't grow up in a loving household where her family learned ASL. Until she went to live with Doris and Wally she lived silently, which is unfortunately something that happens often with both Deaf and hard of hearing children both in foster care *and* in regular homes. Access to language is so, so important. *But . . .* I *loved* that the use of sign language with Dean is what set Amelia's growth in motion.

I imagine some people will wonder why the issues with Amelia's mother aren't tied up in a nice little bow for us at the end. And I won't tell you I didn't initially try to come up with some gasp-inducing moment, but the truth is—nothing felt more real than *not* knowing. It's a genuine human experience—we don't always get the *why* behind the what, and honestly, some things are so heinous that the why is unimportant. I think the thing Amelia needed was the closure she found in Dean. He gave her a steadiness in everything that once terrified her.

This story was also a little bit about Dean getting his groove back—wink, wink.

But in all seriousness, the spice was actually a really important element in this book. I intentionally turned it up a notch because I think Dean had a healthy sexual appetite before he lost himself. And meeting Amelia, a sex-positive woman who owns her sexuality, was important to his "un-becoming."

I think he likely developed a sense of shame surrounding sex after Evelyn's assault and that's why we see so many moments where Dean is almost surprised by something that turns him on.

Dean and Amelia's relationship was born from the idea that sometimes we need to peel ourselves back to find what's truly there. That sometimes the magic exists when we shed expectations or meet the challenge to change. It's about giving into that little voice that knows you want more and being brave enough to finally go for it.

Never let the noise of thunder deter you from the strike of lightning, friends.

(Oh, and go learn ASL—thank me later!)

Sincerely, thank you for reading.

Love,

acknowledgments

Always, first and foremost is my husband, Drew.

This book was really hard on me and thusly, hard on him. He's my constant sounding board and my shoulder to cry on and I needed both in abundance through the writing process of *finding more.* I'm only able to write books because I have his steady hand on my back and I just cannot thank him enough. We're also in the middle of navigating the adoption process ourselves and he's graciously taken the wheel while I finished Dean and Amelia's story. Husband, thank you. I love you.

To the Bookstagram community, I cannot thank you enough for loving in our hands. I am endlessly grateful for your reviews, messages, and posts about my books and I truly could not do this without you guys. Thank you for taking a chance a new author.

To my family and friends for being understanding about my retreat to my writer's cave for the past six months. (My writer's cave is my living room with an abundance of snack foods and tissues.)

To my beta readers, J. M. Failde, Stacy Paradiso, and Alex Moyer. Your feedback and brainstorming allowed me to nuance these people and deepen the moments so much and I appreciate your willingness to read (and reread) the book until it was the exact story it was meant to be.

And as always, thank you to my ASL teachers. I've been slacking a bit on my classes—but I'm so grateful for your constant guidance in continuing to teach me this beautiful language that I love so deeply.

WANT TO LEARN ASL?

Good news! There are so many online resources and classes taught by Deaf teachers. I was ecstatic when readers asked if I had any recommendations to learn sign language—and I definitely do, so if you want to learn this beautiful language, please message me on Instagram @sincerely_lovelarissa and I can give you some recommendations!

resources

If you or anyone you know is a victim of rape or sexual assault, please reach out. You are not alone.
National Sexual Assault Hotline:
1-800-656-4673

If you or anyone you know struggles with PTSD, know that there are people who care and want to help. If you or a loved one is battling addiction, be gentle with yourself and talk to someone.
Substance Abuse and Mental Health Services Hotline:
1-800-662-4357

Children need adults to advocate for them.
If you see something, speak up.
The Childhelp National Child Abuse Hotline
1-800-4-A-CHILD
(1-800-422-4453)